ALSO BY

VALÉRIE PERRIN

*Fresh Water for Flowers*

# THREE

Valérie Perrin

# THREE

*Translated from the French*
*by Hildegarde Serle*

Europa
*editions*

Europa Editions
27 Union Square West, Suite 302
New York, NY 10003
www.europaeditions.com
info@europaeditons.com

This book is a work of fiction. Any references to historical events, real people, or real locales are used fictitiously.


First publication 2022 by Europa Editions

Translation by Hildegarde Serle
Original title: *Trois*


Library of Congress Cataloging in Publication Data is available
ISBN 978-1-60945-755-6

Perrin, Valérie
Three

Art direction by Emanuele Ragnisco
instagram.com/emanueleragnisco

Cover design by Ginevra Rapisardi



Prepress by Grafica Punto Print – Rome

Printed in Canada

For Nicola Sirkis and Yannick Perrin
In memory of Pascale Romiszvili

# 1

*4 December 2017*

This morning, Nina looked at me without seeing me. Her eyes slid away like the raindrops on my coat, just before she disappeared into a kennel.

It was raining cats and dogs.

I glimpsed her pale skin and dark hair under the hood of her oilskin. She was wearing rubber boots that were too big and holding a long hose. Just seeing her gave me what felt like an electric shock in my stomach, five hundred thousand volts at the very least.

I deposited thirty kilos of dry pet food. I do that every month, but never go into the shelter. I hear the dogs but don't see them. Apart from when one of the dog walkers passes by me.

Bags lined up, side by side, in front of the entrance gate. An employee, always the same one, a tall, ill-shaven guy, helps me carry my consolation prizes to just below the signs saying ABANDONING KILLS, and PLEASE CLOSE DOOR SECURELY BEHIND YOU.

Every year, at Christmas and just before the summer vacations, but never on the same day, I slip some cash through the shelter's mailbox. Anonymous money, with NINA BEAU written in black felt pen on the envelope. I don't want her to know that this money comes from me. I don't do it for the animals, I do it for her. I know very well that it will all go into the feeding bowls and the veterinary care, but I want it to go through her without leaving a trace. Just so she knows that, outside, there aren't only people who toss their kittens into the trash.

Thirty-one years ago, she looked at me without seeing me, like this morning. She was coming out of the men's restroom; she was ten years old. The women's was jammed, and already Nina didn't like waiting.

Her eyes slid over me and she fell into Étienne's arms.

We were at the Progrès, the bar and tobacco store belonging to Laurence Villard's parents. It was a Sunday afternoon. The place was closed, the shutters down. They had gone private for their daughter's birthday. I remember the upturned chairs on the tables, legs in the air, one on top of the other. A makeshift dance floor between a pinball machine and the bar. The torn gift wrap on the bar, beside packets of chips and Choco BN cookies, the yellow straws in paper cups full of Oasis fruit drink and lemonade.

The entire fifth-grade class was there. I knew no one. I'd just moved to La Comelle, a workers' housing development in the center of France of about twelve thousand souls.

Nina Beau. Étienne Beaulieu. Adrien Bobin.

I observed their triple reflection in the mirrors all along the bar.

They had old-fashioned names, those of ancestors. Most of us had names like Aurélien, Nadège or Mickaël.

Nina, Étienne, and Adrien had just entered that time of their childhood when they were inseparable. On that day, and on all the other days, they didn't see me.

Nina and Étienne danced to a-ha's "Take On Me" all afternoon. An EP single. A twenty-minute number. The kids in my class kept it spinning on the deck as if they had no other records.

Nina and Étienne danced like grown-ups. As if they'd done it all their life. That's what I thought to myself as I watched them.

Under the strobes, they looked like two seabirds spreading their wings on nights of high wind. With only a distant lighthouse illuminating both their wings and their grace.

Adrien remained sitting on the floor, back stuck to the wall, not very far from them. When Cyndi Lauper started singing "True Colors," he sprang up to invite Nina to slow dance with him.

Étienne brushed past me. I'll never forget his smell of vetiver and sugar.

*

I live alone in the heights of La Comelle, although it's not very high, the countryside is just a bit hilly. I left and then returned, because here I know the sounds of things, the neighbors, the days of sunshine, the two main streets, and the aisles of the supermarket where I do my weekly shop. For around ten years, the price per square meter has been derisory, they're almost giving away the plots of land. I bought a little house for peanuts, and restored it. Four rooms, and a garden with a linden tree that provides shade in summer and lime-blossom tea in winter.

Here, people leave. Except for Nina.

Étienne and Adrien left, came back for Christmas, left again.

I work at home, sometimes correcting or translating texts for publishing houses. And to maintain a social link with life around here, I replace the freelancer at the local newspaper in August and December. In summer, I cover the death notices, wedding anniversaries, and belote tournaments. In winter, same thing. With children's shows and Christmas markets on top.

The translating and correcting are both remnants of my former life.

Memories, the present, and our former lives all change their perfume. When one changes one's life, one changes perfume.

Childhood's is that of tar, inner tubes, and cotton candy, of classroom disinfectant, of chimney fires exhaled by houses on cold days, of chlorine in municipal pools, of sweat-soaked sports clothes when filing back, two by two, from the gym, of pink Malabar gum in the mouth, of the glue that forms strings on the fingers, of CaramBar chews stuck between the teeth, of a Christmas tree planted in the heart.

Adolescence has the smell of a first drag, of musky deodorant, of buttered bread dunked in hot chocolate, of whiskey-and-Coke and cellars turned into ballrooms, of the body that desires, of Eau Précieuse cleanser, of hair gel, of egg shampoo, of lipstick, of detergent wafting off jeans.

The lives that follow, the smell of the scarf forgotten by the first person to break one's heart.

And then there's the summer. Summer belongs to all memories. It's timeless. And its smell is the most persistent. That clings to clothes. That one searches for all one's life. The over-sweet fruit, the sea breeze, the doughnuts, the black coffee, the Ambre Solaire, the Caron face powder of grandmothers. Summer belongs to all ages. It has neither childhood, nor adolescence. Summer is an angel.

I'm a beanpole with a decent enough chassis. Bangs, shoulder-length dark brown hair. A few white hairs sprouting from the mop, which I cover up with brown mascara.

My name is Virginie. I'm the same age as them.

Today, out of the three, only Adrien still speaks to me.

Nina despises me.

As for Étienne, it's me who can longer stand him.

And yet, they've fascinated me since childhood. I've only ever become attached to those three.

And to Louise.

# 2

*5 July 1987*

It starts with a tummy ache after the sandwich and fries dunked in ketchup. Nina is sitting under a Miko-ice-cream parasol in front of the fries stall. There are a few colorful metal tables, and a terrace overlooking the three municipal pools. While licking the grains of salt off the pads of her fingers, Nina listens to Madonna's "La Isla Bonita" and dreamily watches a tanned blond guy dive from the five-meter board. She runs her fingers along the bottom of the empty container to catch the crumbs in the grooves of the plastic. Étienne is rocking back and forth on his chair while sipping a strawberry soda, and Adrien bites into an overripe peach, it drips over hands, mouth, thighs, juice everywhere.

Nina often watches Étienne and Adrien. She never does so on the sly. She directs her gaze onto one part of their bodies and holds it there. It makes Étienne feel uncomfortable, and he often says, "Stop looking at me like that." Adrien doesn't seem bothered, she's like that, Nina, no brakes.

Again, sharp pains in the tummy, then a warm liquid trickling between her thighs. Nina understands. Not already. Too young. Don't want. Eleven years old in a fortnight . . . She thought one got *it* in junior high. Between sixth grade and ninth grade. She starts in fifth grade in two months' time . . . *The shame, if the other girls know I've got my period, they'll think I've had to redo that grade.*

She stands up, wraps herself in a scratchy towel, small but enough to go around her hips. She's very slender. "A wire," Étienne is forever calling her to annoy her. She returns the Walkman to him without a word, heads for the girls' changing room. Usually, she goes into the boys' room so she can undress and dress faster.

Étienne and Adrien stayed on the terrace. Nina had shot off without saying a word to them. Those three never part without saying where they're going.

"What's up with her?" asks Etienne, straw in corner of mouth.

Adrien notices that the strawberry syrup has turned his tongue bright pink.

"Dunno," he whispers. "Her asthma, maybe."

That day, Nina doesn't return to the terrace. A brown stain on her swimsuit. She gets changed quickly, slides a ball of toilet paper inside her panties. Like a swelling between the thighs. She stops off at the Petite Coopérative to buy sanitary napkins with the change from the fries. A packet of ten. The cheapest.

When she arrives home, her dog Paola considers her with a strange look, wagging her tail. She lifts her nose and then turns her back to go rejoin Pierre Beau, Nina's grandfather, busy in the garden. He hadn't seen her come in. She locks herself in her bedroom upstairs.

It's really hot. Nina would like to be with Étienne and Adrien in the trough. That's the deepest pool: four meters. Three diving boards look down on it: from one meter, three meters, and five meters. The water in the trough is too deep ever to warm up. The daily challenge is to go down and touch its freezing-cold floor after jumping in.

That evening, Étienne phones Nina. Just then, Adrien also tries to call her, but the line is engaged.

"Why d'you leave without a word this afternoon?"

She hesitates to reply. Thinks of a lie. What's the point.

"I've got my period."

For Étienne, periods only happen to girls with breasts, pubic hair, to mothers, to married women. Not to Nina. Étienne collects stickers in *Panini* albums and still secretly sucks his thumb.

Nina is like him. He's seen all the Barbie dolls lined up in her bedroom.

After a long, doubtful silence, he asks:

"Have you told your grandfather?"

"No . . . The shame."

"What are you going to do?"

"What d'you want me to do?"

"Maybe it's not normal at your age."

"Apparently, it depends on the mother. If mine got hers at this age, it's normal. But I can't know."

"Does it hurt?"

"Yup. Kind of cramps. Cramps from a disgusting onion soup."

"I'm glad not to be a girl."

"Well you have to do military service."

"Maybe . . . but I'm still glad. Are you going to see the doctor?"

"Dunno."

"D'you want us to go with you?"

"Maybe. But you'd have to wait for me outside the office."

*

The three of them had met ten months earlier, in the yard of the École Pasteur, on the first day of fifth grade.

At that age everything's a shambles. It's the age when children don't resemble each other anymore. Tall and short. Puberty, no puberty. Some look like they're fourteen, others eight.

The two fifth-grade classes are gathered in the schoolyard. In front of around sixty pupils, the two teachers, Madame Bléton and Monsieur Py, call the register, side by side.

It's the morning when the whims of chance and the blows of fate are felt. When one learns to tell the difference.

Each child silently prays—even those who've never set foot in Sunday school—for it to be Madame Bléton who calls them. The schoolmaster has a very bad reputation. Generations of traumatized former pupils have told the younger kids all about it. A total bastard who doesn't hesitate to take a swipe or lift a child off the ground by the collar, or smash chairs against the wall when he blows his top. And every year, he picks a whipping boy, and never lets them go. Usually a weak student. "So best to work hard, or you're dead."

Madame Bléton, line to the right. Monsieur Py, line to the left. They call out the register in alphabetical order.

Discreet sighs of relief can be detected in the right-hand line. Something about how the head is held that seems to thank heaven, how the shoulders relax. And a look of the condemned among those who join the line to the left.

There's an oppressive silence at École Pasteur that morning. Only the voices of the two teachers ring out in the covered yard. In turn, the pupils whose surname begins with an A are called.

Adam, Éric, line to the right.

Antard, Sandrine, line to the left.

Antunès, Flavio, line to the right.

Aubagne, Julie, line to the left.

Then it's the Bs.

Beau, Nina, line to the left.

Beauclair, Nadège, line to the right.

Beaulieu, Étienne, line to the left.

Bisset, Aurélien, line to the right.

Bobin, Adrien, line to the left.

And that's how Nina Beau, Étienne Beaulieu, and Adrien Bobin are brought together on that third of September 1986. Since the two boys seem stunned, Nina grabs them by the hand and drags them over to the line in front of Monsieur Py. Étienne lets himself be led. Letting a girl hold your hand is mortifying, but he doesn't notice, he's received a double sentence: he's just lost his friend, Aurélien Bisset, and he's with Py. At the École Pasteur, from first to fourth grade, all the pupils see that final straight before junior high as an ordeal. "You've got Py, shucks, it's hell with him."

The three of them wait, side by side, for the register to be over.

Étienne is much taller than the other two. He has the fine features, blond hair, and fair skin of the ideal child in antique prints, and his swimming-pool-blue eyes strike all who meet him.

Adrien has dark brown hair, a riot of unruly tufts, is very slender, with milky skin, and so shy he seems to be hiding behind himself.

Nina has the grace of a doe. Black eyebrows and long lashes framing ebony eyes. After two months of summer, her skin is brown.

Behind his glasses, Monsieur Py surveys his future pupils, seems satisfied, smiles, and asks them to follow him into the classroom, where he positions himself in front of the blackboard.

Still that chilling silence. Each step, each gesture frozen stiff.

Each child picks their desk at random. Those who know each other stick together as a pair. Inconspicuously, Étienne nudges Adrien with his hip to position himself beside Nina. Adrien complies, positioning himself behind her. He looks at her, forgets the teacher. He loses himself in her two braids, her brown hair, dark at the roots and sun-bleached at the tips, her two elastic bands, her middle part, the pearly buttons on her red velvet dress, the down on her neck. Beauty from behind. She senses his eyes on her and turns furtively around to give him a mischievous smile. A smile that reassures him. He has a friend. A girl friend. He can go home and tell his mother: "I made friends with a girl." He hopes Nina lunches in the canteen, like him.

"You may be seated."

Monsieur Py introduces himself, writes his name on the board. The tension eases, and in the end, he seems quite nice, he almost smiles, explains things calmly. Maybe he's changed, don't they say grown-ups can improve over time?

The morning goes by quickly. Textbooks handed out, to be covered that very evening, not tomorrow.

"I detest procrastination . . ." Monsieur Py declares, while fumbling in his leather briefcase.

Baffled silence in the classroom.

"I see that you don't know the meaning of that word."

Monsieur Py stands up, rubs his name off the board, and writes instead: PROCRASTINATION: FROM THE VERB TO PROCRASTINATE, which he underlines three times.

"That is to say, put off until tomorrow what you can do today."

Next, he asks each pupil to stand up in turn, state clearly his or her surname and first name, and specify his or her weak point and strong point.

No one moves a muscle.

"Dear, oh dear, you're all half-asleep! We'll have to wake you up! Right, we'll start at random."

He points at Adrien's neighbor. A wan blond girl. She stands up.

"My name is Caroline Desseigne, my strong point is reading, my weak point is that I get dizzy . . ."

Caroline blushes a little and sits back down.

"Next! Your neighbor," shouts Py.

Adrien stands up. Forehead flushed. Hands clammy. A dread of speaking in front of others.

"My name is Adrien Bobin. My strong point is reading, too . . . My weak point . . . I'm scared of snakes."

Nina puts her hand up. The teacher encourages her with a nod.

"My name is Nina Beau. My strong point, that's drawing . . . My weak point, asthma."

It's Étienne's turn to stand up.

"You didn't put your hand up!" shrieks Py.

Silence.

"Fine, it's the first day, generally, on the first day, my foot doesn't yet itch, the vacation has worn it out. Sit back down. If you want to speak, you raise your hand. Next!"

Étienne quickly sits down, a cold sweat down his back. His hands are shaking.

It's midday, the bell rings in all the classrooms. No one dares move. Monsieur Py asks those pupils who haven't yet introduced themselves to complete the exercise. Étienne puts his hand up several times to speak, but the teacher ignores him until he finally sends them all off to lunch.

As soon as they've left the classroom, Étienne and Adrien wait for Nina outside the door. As if to reconvene their group. When she joins them, Étienne is fuming.

"Everyone introduced themselves except me," he moans.

"What's your name again?" asks Nina.

"Étienne Beaulieu. My strong point is sport, my weak point . . . dunno . . . I'm pretty good at everything."

"You've not got a single fault?" asks Nina.

"Don't think so."

"You're never scared of anything?" asks Adrien, astonished.

"No."

"Even in a forest, alone, at night?"

"Don't think so. Dunno. Have to try it."

They walk side by side, in a hurry, they're twenty minutes late for the canteen.

Nina in the middle, Adrien on her right, Étienne on her left.

Pupil: Bobin, Adrien, 25 rue John-Kennedy, 71200 La Comelle, born 20 April 1976, in Paris, French.

Father: Bobin, Sylvain, 7 rue de Rome, 75017 Paris, banker, born 6 August 1941, in Paris, French.

Mother: Simoni, Joséphine, 25 rue John-Kennedy, 71200 La Comelle, assistant day-care nurse, born 7 September 1952, in Clermont-Ferrand, French.

~~Other person legally responsible, address, profession, date of birth, nationality, home phone number, work phone number.~~

Person to contact in emergency: Joséphine Simoni, 85 67 90 03.

Pupil: Beaulieu, Etienne Jean Joseph, 7 rue du Bois-d'Agland, 71200 La Comelle, born 22 October 1976, in Paray-le-Monial, French.

Brother: Paul-Émile, 19 years old. Sister: Louise, 9 years old.

Father: Beaulieu, Marc, 7 rue du Bois-d'Agland, 71200 La Comelle, administrative civil servant in Autun, born 13 November 1941, in Paris, French.

Mother: Beaulieu, née Petit, Marie-Laure, 7 rue du Bois-d'Agland, 71200 La Comelle, legal civil servant in Mâcon, born 1 March 1958, in La Comelle, French.

~~Other person legally responsible, address, profession, date of birth, nationality, home phone number, work phone number.~~

Person to contact in emergency: Bernadette Rancœur (domestic employee), 85 30 52 11.

Pupil: Beau, Nina, 3 rue des Gagères, 71200 La Comelle, born 2 August 1976, in Colombes, French.

Father: unknown.

Mother: Beau, Marion, 3 rue Aubert, 93200 Saint-Denis, profession unknown, born 3 July 1958, in La Comelle, French.

~~Other~~ person legally responsible: Pierre Beau (grandfather), 3 rue des Gagères, 71200 La Comelle, post-office worker, widower, born 16 March 1938, French.

Person to contact in emergency: Pierre Beau, 85 29 87 68.

# 3

*5 December 2017*

I keep turning that news item over in my head without really believing it. Me, who's solitary . . . what was I thinking the day I applied to work at the newspaper? A challenge? Temporary insanity? I'm not interested in either tittle-tattle, or retirements, or any more *pétanque* tournaments. And here I am, on the front line. Being hit by a tsunami, full in the face.

A stroke of bad luck, no doubt.

The Forest Lake. A former sandpit to the south of La Comelle, on the road to Autun. Subterranean expanses of water, communicating with the river Saône, filled around a hundred hectares with water. We often swam in it as kids. We knew it was risky, we liked flirting with danger, but we never lingered too far from the banks all the same, as underwater landslides could produce lethal sudden water holes. Few of us ventured out to the middle. Some boys sometimes did, to show off. And there were plenty of legends concerning this lake. It was said that, at night, one could see the ghosts of those who'd drowned in it, that they swam up to the surface in their shrouds. All I've ever come across there is campers and empty beer cans.

Many of us never bathed with bare feet. Personally, when I was too hot, I went into the water without taking off my sneakers. It wasn't unusual to cut oneself on some glass or a scrap of iron. I preferred the municipal pool for swimming. But on summer evenings, we'd meet up there to listen to music and drink beside a campfire.

It's years since I've been there.

In order to repair a bank, it's been partly drained off for the first time in fifty years. The local council is carrying out a feasibility study with a view to creating a sandy beach with an open-air café and waterslides. An area that would be monitored by lifeguards. In the hope of curbing wild camping and reckless swimmers.

It was while draining the western part of the lake last week that a car was discovered. To reach the banks, one must walk along narrow, winding paths. Generally, those who come in cars use a makeshift car park between two fields some three hundred meters from the main access point.

They've just identified the wreck's license plate; it's a Twingo stolen on 17 August 1994 in La Comelle. So far, nothing abnormal: the thief or thieves would have wanted to get rid of it. But the police are intrigued because that's also the date that Clotilde Marais disappeared.

17 August 1994. When I heard the newspaper's editor say that date, my blood froze. I asked him if he couldn't send a staffer, a seasoned journalist, but everyone's on vacation, and I'm on duty and on the spot. "An investigation is underway, get yourself to the lake as fast as possible. We want a photo of the car, and the article, by this evening."

I hunt for my press card in the bottom of a drawer. Usually, I don't need it. To write a piece on the crowning of Miss Pétanque, I'm never asked for it.

I didn't like Clotilde Marais. I was probably jealous of her long, slender legs, which she'd wrap around Étienne's waist. There's this image that comes back to me. Her sitting on a wall, him standing, French kissing each other. She's in shorts, her legs gripping the small of his back. Her feet are bare, red varnished toenails, a perfect pedicure. Her golden Roman sandals lie on the pavement. The quintessence of femininity. I feel like pushing her off. Taking her place. Being her. Of course I didn't go near them. I scarpered without breathing.

Clotilde Marais vanished in the summer she was eighteen. When she disappeared, our whole town was perturbed. Why go off without leaving any explanation, not even a letter? At the same time, it didn't surprise me that much, she was a snooty and secretive girl, didn't have any friends, and often hung around on her own.

I feel like phoning Nina at the shelter to tell her about the wreck in the lake. But I'll never do so. Just a sudden impulse that I stifle immediately.

As for Étienne, I don't dare imagine how he's going to feel when he hears about it.

# 4

The school year of 1986–1987 was the only one in which the teacher, Antoine Py, changed his whipping boy midway.

From 1955 to 2001, at the start of every autumn term, he tried to predict who his whipping boy would be. A little game he relished. He geared up for it, mentally, while doing his crosswords at the Sables-d'Olonne resort he went to every year.

Would he be blond, brown-haired, a redhead? Lanky, because he'd been held back a year, or puny, a wimp? Someone he couldn't stand from the start. The minute he'd put his ass on one of the benches in his classroom, the minute he'd say the word "present," his voice grating like a fork scraping a plate.

Only boys, the weaker sex didn't interest him. And based on the student files he'd have read beforehand, analyzing them for hours.

How he loved deciphering the first names, surnames, family circumstances of his pupils! How he reveled in all that information! Just like watching, from outside, in the dark, what's going on inside a house with lit-up windows.

Professions of father and mother. Never would he choose a pupil whose parents were executives or civil servants. That's what saved Étienne, on that first day back at school in 1986. If Py hadn't read on his file that his parents were senior civil servants, he would have been thrashed all year. Standing up and speaking without asking permission, whatever next!

And never would he touch, close up or at a distance, an Abdel Kader, as he loved calling pupils of the Muslim faith, when in the company of a few hand-picked friends—other teachers from schools other than his, met on the café terraces of Sables-d'Olonne.

Antoine Py had no friends in La Comelle; he had a standing, and, due to his profession, maintained a certain distance.

Once he had made an initial selection by studying the professional status and nationality of the parents, three days sufficed for him to pick his target. The criteria never changed: the pupil seemed totally dumb, wore a moronic look, demonstrated a slowness to understand, had a nervous tic, a crumpled shirt, some fat around the belly, scuffed shoes, an unsteady gait. He could also lay into a boy who seemed too sure of himself, pretentious, smirking, eyes wandering, a little joker. Those he loved to shut right up.

He looked for the most imperceptible flaw and pounced on it.

He had always taught the fifth grade, the last before pupils went off to *collège*, or middle school, which he considered "the great trash can of state education." He felt as if he were shaping precious stones just for them to end up in a gutter. "Pissing into the wind," as he said to his wife in the evening, while downing his soup.

In September 1986, he homed in on Martin Delannoy, who had had to repeat his second grade. Some problem with dyslexia, the child was seeing a speech therapist. Py took malicious pleasure not in making him read texts out loud in front of the whole class: too simple, not perverse enough, and, above all, too risky, the objective being never to arouse the parents' suspicion, all the parents, because did his pupils jabber, describing life in class as they tucked into their ravioli. Instead, Py sent Martin Delannoy to the board to solve unsolvable math problems for entire mornings.

He felt such delight, barely concealed behind a false smile, observing the quaking of a pupil, the pallor of his skin, the sheen of the beads of sweat on his temples and forehead, his choked-back tears, until a tiny puddle splashed onto the wooden dais, a drop of translucent blood, of sorrow held back too long, and then it was rivers down cheeks, like a dam bursting. And then he, Py, would say, in an unctuous voice: "Go back to your seat, my boy, you'll stay behind during recess, and I'll explain it to you."

He rarely shouted, was creepily gentle. Then, without warning, because a pupil was chatting, because his wife had turned her back on him the previous night, because a driver had refused to give way that morning, he would dart over to the child and lift him off the ground by his collar. Bad grades, going off the subject, sniggering, chatting, not paying attention, yawning . . . in all those cases, the walls shook and the man's voice resonated to the very top of the tall chestnut trees out in the yard.

No parent complained because no pupil had ever improved his or her grades as much as they did in Monsieur Py's class. His name was spoken respectfully, and a parent would whisper: "He's with Monsieur Py," with a knowing smile and satisfaction.

At the end of the year, he was given numerous presents, which he received with moist eyes, tirelessly saying: "You know, I'm only doing my job."

His lessons were extremely precise and clear. Py could spend hours explaining something, until every single kid finally understood. Even if it meant repeating himself, and then repeating himself again. Even if it meant getting a lesson written out, and rewritten out, until it was absorbed, once and for all. Even if it meant giving a list of homework assignments as long as two arms that would take up entire evenings and Sundays.

He was a remarkable teacher, so he was allowed to treat himself to a whipping boy, to unwind. Even the school's headmaster, Monsieur Avril, closed his eyes on his rather unorthodox practices in light of his exceptional results.

So, the school year of 1986–1987 started off with the pupil Martin Delannoy, he was the whipping boy until that day in March when the class photographs were handed out just before recess. One envelope per child, with the price of the photo, and of individual portraits, on a calendar, a bookmark, or a greeting card, attached.

That morning, Adrien Bobin and Martin Delannoy had been kept back to finish writing up a lesson on plural adjectival agreement. Py went off to the staffroom to have a coffee. He returned to his classroom at around 11 A.M., a few minutes before lessons started again.

He pushed the door open silently. He loved creeping up behind a pupil to make him jump. He observed Martin Delannoy, nose in book, head to one side, tongue circling lips as he copied out his lesson. Py was about to chide him over the way he held his fountain pen when he was distracted by Adrien Bobin. The mop-haired little boy who never batted an eyelid. Who worked hard. The type of kid who, generally, was left in peace—but that morning, he had dawdled.

An icy sword pierced Py as his eyes fell on him. His sharp mind took a fraction of a second to compute. His silent rage, his perversion, shifted from the one boy to the other. As though one was seeing an electric arc travel from the pupil Delannoy, sitting on the left side of the room, to the pupil Bobin, on the far right.

Adrien looked up and saw only black in Py's eyes. From behind his glasses, a wild storm was sweeping over him. Menacing and deadly. The kind that kills. Adrien instantly understood. He lowered his eyes, returned to his work, but it was too late.

# 5

*6 December 2017*

I hear the church bells pealing in the distance. When they ring out in the middle of the afternoon, it means someone's being buried. An elderly person, no doubt. If it were a young person, thanks to my being on call for the newspaper, I'd know about it. Here, there are only old people left. Of the two schools, the Pasteur and the Danton, only one remains, and for how much longer? When a factory loses its workers, it's also their children one loses. Here, for twenty years, there have been too many redundancy schemes and early retirements. The Magellan factory, which manufactures parts for cars, went from three thousand salaried workers in 1980, to three hundred and forty in 2017. The final blow came in 2003, when the haulage company Damamme was sold, and then, a few years later, relocated.

It's raining on my linden tree.

I'm busy correcting a manuscript while waiting to know more about the car found at the bottom of the lake. It's been taken to Autun. The cops didn't let me get near it. I took a few photos of what remained of it when lifted out of the water. This morning, that story is just a tiny insert in the paper. But if one or more bodies are discovered inside the car, it will make the front page. I get the feeling that the police are walking on eggshells when it comes to us journalists. According to an inside source, it seems bones were found in the car. I can't stop thinking about Clotilde Marais.

Earlier, while tidying up, I recognized her in my fifth-grade class photo. In March 1987, she was just eleven years old. I didn't recall Clotilde being in our class. It was a shock to see her again as a child. For ages, her portrait was pinned up in stores. But since a witness, on the evening she disappeared, positively identified her at the railway station, everyone thought she'd left without leaving a forwarding address.

In that photo, there's also old Py in his gray overall, as well as the three Bs side by side. Beaulieu, Beau, Bobin. Me, in the second row, fourth from the left, diaphanous, transparent, nonexistent.

In that "Py year," Nina, Étienne, and Adrien would meet up in front of the École Pasteur ten minutes before the bell rang. They had no friends but themselves. They were almost stuck to each other, like puppies from the same litter. And yet they in no way resembled each other. Neither physically, nor in their attitudes.

Eleven, that's the age when most girls stay with the girls, and boys with the boys.

Nina was often tired because she went to bed late. Some said she helped her grandfather sort the post into streets and neighborhoods for delivery the following day. Which was wrong, the sorting was done in the morning at the post office. No doubt she was drawing late into the night. Her fingers were forever gray from the charcoal sticks. Much as she scrubbed, with brush and soap, the black dust stained her fingernails.

I loved the bags under her eyes. I envied her them. They made her look older. Made her look serious. I'd have liked to steal the signs of tiredness from her. I'd have liked to steal everything from her. Her little nose, her style, her deportment, her smile.

As a child, Nina resembled Audrey Hepburn. Later on, too. But a sadder version. Although Audrey always did have a flicker of melancholy deep in her eyes. With Nina, it was darker. As though she'd seen it all before, when still just a kid. No one knew who her father was, but they presumed he came originally from North Africa or southern Italy, because her mother, according to the gossip, was a redhead with green eyes, and Nina's eyes were so dark, one couldn't make out their pupils.

The three Bs walked to school. Étienne and Adrien saved skateboarding for evenings, Wednesday afternoons, and vacations.

Nina and her grandfather lived on a workers' housing development, in one of those brick houses, all identical, stuck to each other on a dozen or so roads, with a vegetable garden around the back. Each garden fed an entire family, and a few neighbors if the season was good.

Adrien and his mother, Joséphine, occupied a three-roomed apartment on the fourth, and final, story of a building from the sixties.

Étienne, his parents, and his little sister, Louise, resided in a beautiful house surrounded by hundred-year-old trees. The elder brother, Paul-Émile, had left to study in Dijon.

Nina was brought up by an old man.

Étienne was the son of an old man.

Adrien that of an absent father and a mother who'd been part of the May 1968 movements, smoked roll-ups, and listened to "Say It Ain't So, Joe," by Murray Head, while cleaning her dining-room windows.

Give or take two hundred meters, all three of them lived at an equal distance from the school.

They were united by the same ideal: leaving when they were grown up. Quitting this hole to go and live in a city full of traffic lights, noise, and frenzy, of escalators and store windows, with bright lights everywhere, even in the middle of the night. With crowds on the pavements, of strangers, of foreigners one can't gossip about.

They spent all their free time together, recesses and lunchtimes included. They laughed at the same things. Taking the telephone directory, turning to a random page, ringing a number, and making bookings in a disguised voice. Watching *Magnum* and *Fame*, with doors and shutters closed, while gobbling sweets. Playing Mastermind and battleships. Reading a Tintin book, or the *Almanach de l'étrange*, together, stretched out on Nina's bed. "Finished . . ." Adrien and Étienne would say in unison. Then, only once the two boys had spoken, would Nina turn the page.

They loved scaring themselves, telling each other stories, dropping stink bombs in the aisles of the supermarket, recording themselves for hours on the radio-cassette player, playing at being radio presenters and then listening back to each other and bursting into helpless laughter. Étienne was the leader, Nina the heart, and Adrien followed with never a complaint.

Their rituals were also governed by the rhythm of Nina's asthma attacks. All three of them were dependent on her capricious bronchial tubes. Some attacks could go on for hours, despite the Ventolin. During the most acute ones, Nina preferred to stay alone with her rickety breathing.

Adrien and Étienne would each go home separately. Adrien to read, or to think over what they'd spoken about. Étienne to go skateboarding, or to watch the end of *Récré A2* on the TV with Louise, his little sister.

Nina was their link. Without her, Adrien and Étienne didn't see each other. They were three, or nothing.

The two boys loved Nina because she never judged anyone, whereas in La Comelle, everyone sized up everyone. Gossip was inherited. It was passed on from generation to generation. Nina dragged around the reputation of her mother, she was just the "little bastard of a total loser." Adrien, owing to his shyness, interested no one apart from Nina, who found him intelligent and mysterious. His mother, Joséphine Simoni, was the new recruit at the municipal daycare center, a free spirit whose long skirts trailed on pavements. No father. This mother-son couple was labeled "hippie." As for Étienne, he was disdained by quite a few pupils for being a "son of bourgeois." In La Comelle, people didn't mix. The napkins stayed with the napkins, the dishtowels with the dishtowels. The workers were respected, less so the foremen. The sons of management were disapproved of, affluence and wealth almost suspicious.

The three always went to the movies together. Always sat in the front row. There, Adrien wasn't relegated to sitting behind, like in their classroom; he sat beside Nina. Her in the middle, him on her right, Étienne on her left.

The day they saw *Manon des sources*, Nina grabbed both of their hands just as Ugolin stitches Manon's ribbon on to his actual skin, and she kept them gripped in hers for a long while after Ugolin hanged himself.

*Manon des sources* remained Adrien's and Étienne's favorite film, whatever they might say. When asked "What's your favorite film?" they answered "*Le Retour du Jedi.*" But they were lying.

# 6

*7 December 2017*

Thursday, shopping day. I always hope to come across Nina, it never happens. I buy essentials at the supermarket, then go down to the market. Again, I hope to see her, check any cars I pass, no one. It's as if she lived in hiding.

Once I've bought my fruit and vegetables, I have a coffee on the heated terrace of the Bistrot de l'Église. I watch people go by, with their carts and baskets. Couples, single women, widowers.

I like the waitress. She doesn't recognize me. Her name's Sandrine Martin. We were in seventh grade together. In the same class as the three. After that, she left to do an apprenticeship. She had that quirk of always spitting on the ground. She was pretty. She still is. But cigarettes and a life of precarious jobs show in the furrows on her face and the corners of her mouth. In winter, her sweaters hide a faded blue mermaid on her forearm. A mermaid who's never lounged on the terraces of grand hotels.

Sometimes, I feel like saying to her: "It's me, Virginie." But what for? To say what to each other? "Got kids?—No. And you?—Yup, two.—How old?—Fifteen and Eighteen.—Been serving beer here long?—Why are you back? It's dead round here."

I prefer Sandrine not to recognize me. We exchange a smile. She hands me the daily paper. I tip her 30 centimes. I feel like leaving 50, but for a coffee at € 1.20, it would be too much. She would notice me.

"Bye."

Sometimes, there's a good side to not being recognized. It makes for tranquility.

On my way home, I take a detour past my old school. It's been closed to the public for a long time. Too much asbestos, too many drafts. It's been repeatedly vandalized. Some squatters threw stones at it and tried to set it on fire. A few windows are covered with cardboard. It's surrounded by tall weeds.

They've built a brand new one, the Collège Georges-Perec, just outside the town. It brings together pupils from several suburbs.

This morning, when I drove past my old school, which always makes me think of an ocean liner abandoned by its captain on a sea of mossy damaged concrete, I slowed down.

Usually, I drive past it without really looking, out of habit, the way I'd do a detour to skirt the Eiffel Tower in my previous life.

I slowed down and then parked on the verge. After all that time talking about it . . . The excavators have begun their work: the Collège du Vieux-Colombier is being razed to the ground. I stayed ten minutes to watch the past being demolished. The blue metal panels torn down, the partitions stripped at the speed of light, as if it were a stage set, and not a real place where, for several decades, children had been taught.

In a few days' time, there'll be nothing left.

I thought back to when, from the third-story study room, during breaks, I would watch pupils walking in the yard. I often watched them thinking: *In a hundred years, they'll all be dead.*

Never would I have imagined that the walls of my old school would perish before its pupils.

The decimation of workers at the Magellan factory, and the relocation of Transports Damamme, meant the death of entire neighborhoods. Only the two main streets try to maintain a certain dignity. The last heroes of this modern world, the "small storekeepers," as they're dubbed on the TV news, are joining forces to reinvigorate the pinhead-small town center.

Here, the weeds have gained ground. All that's left of everywhere that was lively when I was a child is cracked walls, closed shutters, faded and rusty signs, moss-covered pavements.

All that remains of where Adrien and Étienne used to skateboard is a wasteland.

# 7

From Monday 9 March 1987, the day when Py started detesting Adrien, the latter counted the days like a prisoner counts those keeping him from freedom. Not counting Saturday afternoons, Sundays, Wednesdays, and public holidays, to reach the summer vacation he'd have to hold out for sixty-one-and-a-half days.

Sixty-one-and-a-half days of entering the classroom with lead in his stomach and in his shoes. Sixty-one-and-a-half days of crossing out the day that's over, every evening, with a black felt pen, pressing hard on the tip to feel better. He crossed out the days on a fire-service calendar, featuring photos of firemen tackling road accidents, floods, or fires: Adrien's state of mind precisely now that he was being tormented by his teacher.

He was kept back at every recess, and in the evening after class. Py's excuse was a lesson not learnt, a text badly written, to be rewritten with bigger loops; he made him redraw a parallelepiped rectangle, revise prefixes, suffixes, orders of size, write out a hundred times: "I will not daydream in class."

Since 9 March 1987, Adrien no longer daydreamed. No longer looked at Nina's neck, her hair, her elastic bands, her dresses, her shoulders, her back.

Py was always leaning over his shoulder and sniffing him.

As soon as Adrien lowered his guard, Py sent him to the blackboard, the better to humiliate him in front of the whole class. In vain.

The shy are neither weak, nor cowardly. Torturers don't necessarily have the upper hand over them. Never did Adrien cry. He looked Py straight in the eye and did his utmost to answer his questions, however pernicious and incomprehensible they might be, while the pupil Martin Delannoy, the first whipping boy of the year, breathed easier. Still unable to believe this miracle: the onslaught had shifted to another camp.

In the evening, after Adrien's detention, Nina and Étienne would be waiting for him, like two lost souls, sitting on a pavement. They walked him home. Adrien ached all over, his muscles sore from cramp.

Nina was forever asking him:

"But why has he got it in for you?"

To which Adrien always answered:

"One day, I'll tell you."

"But what will you tell me?"

And Adrien would withdraw into his silence.

Étienne asked him if he'd like him to go and puncture old Py's tires, or put dog shit in his mailbox. "I know where he lives . . ." But Adrien said no. Py would suspect something, and it would be worse if he had it in for them.

Adrien cried in his sleep. When he woke up, his pillowcase was wet.

They no longer read the same book together in Nina's room, and the TV remained switched off. As if the heroes of their favorite shows had died.

"He's screwing up our Wednesdays . . ."

"He's screwing up our lives! It was good before."

"I saw him in town once, he looks gross, that's why he wears a smock in class, to hide his fat ass."

All three of them kept on repeating: "Roll on summer."

Movie outings had become rare—all three felt weighed down between classes—but when they did go, they sat in their usual places: Nina in the middle, Étienne on her left, Adrien on her right.

That's how they discovered, together, *Le Grand Chemin*, the film by Jean-Loup Hubert. That day, Adrien realized that one could detach oneself from daily life, oppressive as it might be, by immersing oneself in a work of art.

*

On 4 May 1987, Py noticed that some exercises for marking were missing from his briefcase. Without thinking, he swooped on Adrien and gave him a hiding in front of the other terrorized children, accusing him of having stolen the exercises during his detention. Nina and Étienne stood up together to intervene, but a look, just one look, from Adrien was enough to make them sit back down immediately.

Adrien's body couldn't withstand this latest onslaught and he fell ill. No one had ever beaten him before. His father had never touched him, even though his near indifference had left its mark on him, invisibly but indelibly. His mother was gentle, never would she have laid a hand on her son.

On the way home, Adrien made Étienne and Nina swear that they wouldn't say a word. His two friends raised their hands and swore.

When her son got home, Joséphine found him very pale. And preoccupied, almost absent. She tried to make him talk, but in vain. After supper, she phoned Nina to ask her if something had happened at school, but Nina said no, nothing special, same as usual.

During the night, Adrien started shaking, then developed a fever. The diagnosis was bronchitis, which turned into a nasty pneumonia. He was hospitalized for a few days. He was absent from school for three weeks. Nina and Étienne collected his lessons and duplicated notes and went round to his house every evening after class.

Joséphine, who now smoked on her small balcony, would warm up their afternoon snack, which they would eat around the Formica table.

Joséphine's hair still had hints of a particular fairness, now yellowing and white in places. A small head that could have evoked that of a rodent. And yet her features were fine, smooth. Her eyes conveyed gentleness and incredulity.

She hadn't started over, after being the mistress of Adrien's father. A man who blew hot and cold, was detached, and married to another woman he wouldn't leave. He had warned: "Never." When he'd learnt that Joséphine was pregnant, he hadn't reacted. Neither anger, nor bitterness, nor joy. The day he'd left without saying that he wouldn't be back, Joséphine was making an apple tart. Her hands were in the butter and flour when he'd handed something to her. She hadn't understood until reading an amount on a check. She'd left a greasy smudge on the signature.

Sylvain Bobin had only returned to recognize the child. Joséphine hadn't found the strength to tell him that wasn't necessary. She no longer loved him. And yet she had desired him, waited for him, wanted him. But that was before the deception, the nasty words, and the cowardly behavior. She would have let him come close to the cradle, but he'd remained at a distance.

Sometimes, he would reappear. Like some public-works inspector, or cop. He barely rang the doorbell before coming in. He would glance around the apartment, at the paintwork, the plumbing, Adrien's school report, leave yet another check on the table in the sitting room, and leave. No doubt with his conscience clear.

When Adrien was in hospital, Joséphine phoned him. It was the first time in eleven years. Sylvain Bobin was abroad; she left a message at his hotel. He called her back. Interference on the line. Over the phone, Joséphine reassured him. More of a scare than anything terrible. Adrien was already much better. A nasty bronchitis that had got worse.

Right now, Joséphine was watching the three, sipping from their steaming bowls with their little mouths. She liked Adrien's new friends. Especially Nina. Joséphine would have like to have a daughter like her. A little doll with dark eyes. Two stars set in an adorable little face. *And that haven't finished shining*, she thought.

After doing their homework, Nina was off, giving Adrien a hug, as was Étienne, saluting him and saying, as ever, like a litany, those words: "Roll on summer."

After his illness, on returning to school, Adrien continued to cross out the days separating him from his release. He had calculated that, by taking away the long weekend after Ascension Thursday, Whit Monday, Wednesdays, Saturday afternoons, and Sundays, there were only thirty-one-and-a-half days to go.

Adrien had read somewhere that the expression "*avoir le diable au corps*" could mean doing something superhuman. It seemed superhuman to him that for thirty-one-and-a-half days he would get up, drink hot milk, get dressed, set off on that path, enter the grounds of the École Pasteur, cross the yard, climb six steps, hang his jacket up, sit in his seat, smell the eau de cologne of evil incarnate dressed in that tight gray smock, and meet those eyes swimming behind his glasses.

It seemed superhuman to him not to have a father to defend him, hold his hand, tell him: "I'll protect you, my son, don't you worry."

The day he set foot back in the classroom, even the presence of Nina and Étienne didn't calm his racing heart. The urge to take a crap. Stomach knotted. Throat swollen.

That morning, Adrien became convinced that he'd caught Nina's asthma, so hard did he find breathing.

Straight away a smile, honey in the teacher's voice. No blackboard for hours, no detentions. Neither during recess, nor in the evening.

Py had got a fright. It was the first time a whipping boy fell ill. Usually, he sensed those things, and toned it down before things turned sour.

The weeks went by. Adrien got good grades for his homework, and encouragement from his teacher in red ink, in the margin, in the top right-hand corner: "Very good, very good work, a conscientious pupil."

One evening in June, Adrien remained in the classroom of his own initiative, while Py was working at his desk. The pupils had to produce electricity with a twelve-volt fan, sticking a magnet on each blade of the appliance and connecting it to a transformer with the aid of two dominoes. Adrien found the exercise fascinating and made a wooden frame that he carefully painted white, and to which he then connected three colored bulbs. Since he still hadn't finished at 6 P.M., Py, keen to leave, asked him to finish the task at home.

Adrien worked on it all weekend, varying the electrical power with the use of a switch, which impressed Nina.

"You're mega intelligent."

"It's not intelligence, it's physics."

"Same thing."

When Adrien, Nina, and Étienne arrived outside their classroom on the Monday morning, the headmaster, Monsieur Avril, looking serious, was waiting for all the pupils at the door. Avril made them file in and requested that they sit in their usual seats, get out their grammatical lexicon, and read the last lesson in silence.

Py was absent. He'd never once been absent during his entire career as a teacher.

The pupils were exchanging questioning glances, without breathing a word, when one of them finally dared to raise his hand:

"Where's Monsieur Py?"

"In my office," replied the headmaster.

A murmur of disappointment could be heard. The pupils had hoped to be sent home, go on their bikes, play board games, watch TV, even though there were no kids' programs on a Monday.

No, Py hadn't been abducted, he was neither sick, nor dead, there would be school today.

It was then that Avril looked around for Adrien, before saying:

"Adrien Bobin, would you please follow me?"

Upon hearing his name, he felt his stomach lurch. He stood up like an innocent man who's condemned without knowing what he's accused of, glanced anxiously at Nina and Étienne, and followed Avril with his head bowed.

Look at the tiles on the floor. Not laid straight. Try counting them to stop thinking about anything. One, two, three, four. An ominous feeling. Why was Py absent? Why had the headmaster summoned him? Him, and only him?

Yes, an ominous feeling.

When Avril and Adrien went into the office, a former study room now used for admin, with cabinets of school files, a telephone, and a typewriter, Py was there, seated, legs crossed. He wasn't wearing his gray overall. He was in sky-blue shirtsleeves and Terylene slacks. It was the first time Adrien was seeing his teacher in casual clothes.

Py didn't look up, didn't look at Adrien, even when he greeted him. He merely smiled at the headmaster as if Adrien didn't exist.

"Right, we're not going to beat about the bush, Monsieur Py informs me that you have stolen supplies."

Adrien didn't immediately understand. He looked at Py, whose eyes were still fixed on the headmaster sitting opposite him.

"You know that the supplies used in labs must remain on the premises . . . It's written in the rules of the school."

Adrien was incapable of uttering a word. He was being accused of theft, Py had cornered him, he'd won the fight. Adrien felt himself welling up. But no, Py wouldn't get his tears. He swallowed them immediately, like a bitter soup. Dug his fingers into the skin of his forearms. One detail helped him. Subtle at first. Then no longer a detail, but blatantly obvious. As Adrien gradually breathed, and his heart calmed down, he smelt it. At first faintly acrid, then increasingly persistent, forming ever increasing circles, until it could no longer go unnoticed in the room: a smell of sweat. Py stank. The stench of lying was oozing out of him.

Avril interrupted his thoughts:

"Do you have nothing to say in your defense, Bobin?"

His silence was accusatory. Silence is consent. He consented to be punished until the end of the school year. Lines to be written out every day and handed in to the headmaster.

He was accused of theft in front of the whole class and isolated, at a table at the back, against the cold radiator.

No warning or report was added to his school file because Adrien Bobin was a good pupil, and he had brought back his wooden frame that very morning. And it was only three bulbs, some electric wires, and other material of no monetary value. The punishment was on principle. The point had to be made.

When Joséphine Simoni heard what had happened, she wanted to meet with Avril and Py immediately, and take those false accusations right up to the commissioner of education.

Adrien didn't want that.

"Py's right, I stole the gear."

"Do you take me for an idiot? Why are you defending him?"

"Only nineteen days to go before the vacation."

"I'm going to call your father!"

"Haven't got a father! He doesn't give a damn about me! If you call him, I'll run away! I swear, I'll run away! And you'll never see me again!"

Joséphine gave in. She called no one. Neither Sylvain Bobin, nor the commissioner of education.

Joséphine took her son at his word: Adrien was capable of disappearing. She had always known it, sensed it. It was like an insidious threat. Her son dragged something serious around with him. Not remotely related to childhood. Adrien was never carefree. He was gentle but serious. No need to ask him to do his homework, brush his teeth, lay the table, help tidy the apartment, he did it all off his own bat. He often laughed, a crystal-clear laughter that Joséphine adored; he could give in to fun, especially when Nina and Étienne were there, watching a comedy or some other show on TV. But he always fell back on his feet. Those of an adult wearing size 4 shoes.

From that day on, Adrien was always wary of others, of their perversity.

He never trusted anyone ever again.

That school year had given him two friends and taken away his innocence.

# 8

*8 December 2017*

I must have picked up tonsillitis. Scarf around neck. Owing to silence, to living alone, my throat is delicate.

It isn't dry-food day. And yet I leave thirty kilos of it at the gate of the shelter.

As usual, I hear the dogs but don't see them.

As usual, the tall, ill-shaven guy comes to collect the food, muttering:

"Thanks from *them*."

"Is Nina around?" I ask.

The tall guy stops for a moment. As if put on "pause." Usually, apart from hello and goodbye, I say nothing. I have an instant change of heart, and, not giving him time to reply, head for my car. His eyes follow me. I wave vaguely in his direction. I don't know what came over me.

A mix of emotions, no doubt.

The Vieux-Colombier school demolished, that class photo turning up, the memory that returns so often in a dream, the one I had again last night where I see myself back there. At Nina's. It's the evening of the funeral. The horror, the shock, the slow movements. Étienne, his pallor, the shadows under his eyes, his breathing; and Nina who's off somewhere getting laid.

But what haunts me even more is that they've found a body inside the car from the Lac de la Forêt. The news is confirmed. The cops will be following procedures to identify it. I don't know why, but I'm not allowed to mention it in the newspaper for now.

And I'd so like to tell Nina about it.

*

Nina is sitting at her desk. Chewing the cap of her pen.

Horrid day. Two to the dog pound. Gun dogs. Unidentified. Crawling with parasites. Haven't had an adoption for two months. One of the volunteers has left. Luckily, amid all the crap, a glimmer of hope: someone's interested in old Bob. Four years he's been here. Sixteen seasons of concrete. The person has just phoned, she's coming by, at three this afternoon, to see him. She spotted his photo on the shelter's website. Bob appeals to her. The group photo Nina took of the mutts works almost as well as a dating site.

She smiles to herself. She should give it a go, sign up to tryaguy.com, just to see what happens. But even the thought of being alone with a stranger at the bookmaker's puts her off. And anyhow, there are no strangers in La Comelle. She already knows all the guys of her age. Paunchy married men with nicotine-stained teeth, drunkards, or withered once-sporty types. She has fun on her own. It does her good. Feels like lighting up inside. Got to smile when that's all one has, smile to keep going.

Christophe comes into the office, pours himself a tepid coffee and dunks a cookie in it.

"That woman who leaves dry food every month, this morning she was back. Asked me if you were around. Usually, she never says a word. Know who I mean?"

Nina looks up from her schedule. Her eyes glaze over. As though processing the information.

"Yes, I know exactly who you mean."

"Really?" asks Christophe, surprised.

"It's a ghost."

Nina slips her jacket on and heads for the infirmary, just beside the cattery. It's time for Orlan's injection, suspected coryza. Nip in the bud, before the rest catch it.

# 9

*July 1987*

"Adrien, d'you think I got my period because my mother's a whore?"

"Well, no, Mother Teresa got her periods at ten years old . . . like you."

"Mother Teresa?"

"Yes."

"You sure?"

"Yes. I read it in *Science et Vie* magazine."

Étienne and Adrien flank Nina as they make their way to the doctor's. They haven't seen each other since the previous day, at the swimming pool, when Nina had shot off without a word to them.

The boys are on their skateboards, Nina on foot. They roll at her pace.

Since the pool, the blood hasn't stopped flowing. She made an appointment with Dr. Lecoq without disguising her voice. A real appointment in her own name, Nina Beau. They know her well there. Due to her asthma, she has regular checkups. It's the first time she's seeing her family doctor on her own. Usually, her grandfather goes with her. The feeling she has of being disobedient makes her ill at ease.

"Did you tell your grandfather about it?" asks Étienne.

"No," replies Nina, annoyed.

"Can you go to the pool?"

"Well, no . . ."

"How long does it last?" asks Étienne, concerned.

"Not really sure . . . About six days . . . But you two must still go to the pool."

"We're not leaving you all alone!" exclaims Adrien, outraged.

Suddenly, Étienne is jubilant:

"We'll rent videos! The gardener and Madame Rancoeur are on vacation! We'll have the house all to ourselves!"

"What about your sister, won't we disturb her?" worries Nina.

"Never there."

When the three arrive outside the doctor's office, Nina asks the boys to wait for her a bit further along.

"You don't want us with you in the waiting room?"

"No. I'd rather go alone."

Nearby, there's the parking lot of the garden center. The two boys can skateboard there, in and out of the lines for the trucks.

They speed up, do some jumps. Étienne is much better at it, and more daring. Faster, too. It's like he's levitating on his board. The two of them seem like teacher and pupil, thinks Adrien. A pro and a beginner. Étienne has total control of his body. His agility and suppleness are innate, and he's grown again, now two heads taller than Adrien. On wheels, in water, on land, Étienne's movements are all balance and beauty. You should see him doing the crawl across the big pool.

It's a fact of life that Adrien has already taken on board: we're not born equal.

With grazes on his knees and arms, and aching wrists from trying to copy Étienne's moves, Adrien is taking a break, while retying one of his laces, when he senses someone's eyes on him, like a knife blade plunged into his back. Shocked to feel such extreme discomfort, he turns around, and turns to jelly. It's like a kick in the stomach. That winds him.

*He* is there. About three-hundred meters away. How long has he been watching Adrien? Had he followed him? In a fraction of a second, he spins around, quickly closes the door of his car, and heads inside the garden center.

It's like an impulse, like someone pushing him, like a violence he doesn't recognize, maybe it's the person he always seems to hide behind, that unbearable shyness, walls coming down. All the tears he kept inside to spite Py are coming out now, totally out of sync.

Adrien darts off, leaving his skateboard on a low wall, not hearing

Étienne asking him where he's going. He runs across the parking lot, opens the store's heavy door, gets hit in the face by it: his movements are too uncoordinated, his body no longer responding, his legs charged with electricity.

A first aisle, empty. Another one, also.

Adrien is looking for Py the way a hound tracks down a wild creature.

He bumps into an employee, who smiles at him.

"Hello, young man."

Adrien no longer hears a thing. His heartbeat pounds in his ears, a fish floundering in a net.

The smell of the classroom comes back to him, a mix of paper, glue, ammonia, chalk, and sweat.

Third aisle. He's there, sizing up different bags, calmly selecting seeds for his garden. Wearing the same fake smile he put on before leaving home, as he does every morning.

Adrien knows that smile very well. It still wakes him up every night.

Py doesn't have time to see Adrien lunging forward, the punch hits him square in the face. And yet it's a small, clenched fist, that of an eleven-year-old who's but knee-high to a grasshopper. But there's such rage in that hand, such tension and sorrow, that the punch has the force of a bullet fired at point-blank range.

His glasses shatter and cut him. Blood on nose. His vision blurs. Then a kick in the balls, staggeringly hard. Py sways, leans forward, doubles up, as Adrien hits and screams like a lunatic. An employee grabs hold of him, holds him back, he struggles like a demon.

Then another cry, dreadful and distraught, it's Nina:

"Adrien!"

Nina's face contorted with fear, tears welling, and, beside it, Étienne's, incredulous, mouth agape like some half-wit.

Heat rising in his body. Pins and needles invading his limbs. His legs give way. And then nothing. Blackout.

Adrien comes to in a storeroom smelling of plants, of damp soil. Two policemen and three garden-center employees are looking at him, he grasps the words "Monsieur Py won't lodge a complaint . . . the mother will pay for the glasses . . . superficial cuts . . . concern for the child . . . doctor's on his way . . . but whatever came over him?"

Nina is having a full-blown asthma attack, her breathing is rasping, sometimes shrill, like a broken whistle in her throat.

Étienne, skateboard under arm, is still staring at Adrien, as though he doesn't recognize his friend. A stranger lying beside sacks of compost. Adrien has injured his hand on Py's glasses.

Joséphine turns up, panic-stricken.

*Where's Py*? Adrien wonders, before blacking out again.

*

For several days, since they can't go to the pool anymore, they listen, nonstop and at full volume, to U2's album, *The Joshua Tree*. With the shutters closed, they dance and sing in the large living room at Étienne's house. Since they're in the dark, they completely let go. Their movements are disjointed. They revel in the darkness, laughing raucously like kindergarten kids.

"*With or without you . . .*"

These joyous afternoons heal them of Adrien's moment of madness. The days go by without them ever mentioning it. Adrien saw a doctor, who sought to understand, but the boy remained silent. He hasn't trusted the medical profession since he was six.

On the day Adrien beat up Py, Dr. Lecoq had reassured Nina. Getting her period at her age was entirely normal. Nothing to be alarmed about. Maybe one or two years earlier than other young girls, but nothing serious.

"Did you know my mother?" she asked her doctor.

"Yes, of course," he replied, moving his stethoscope around on her back.

"Did she get her period at ten years old?"

The doctor rummaged around in some drawers with runners. Pulled out a file in the name of Marion Beau, born 3 July 1958. He tried to decipher the notes he'd written inside it.

"Sorry, Nina, I don't know . . . I can't read my own writing."

The doctor recommended she have a blood test, mentioning

progesterone and other hormone levels, but she wasn't listening to him. She was staring at her mother's medical file, lying on the desk. Dates written in red pen, consultation dates. Like proof of her existence. Marion had come into this room, had lain down there, Lecoq had checked her blood pressure, measured her, weighed her, listened to her heart.

At home there were no photos of Marion. Pierre Beau had made every trace of his daughter disappear.

Nothing remained of her, except Nina.

Lecoq refused to take the check Nina handed him to pay for the consultation. She had stolen it from Pierre, the last one in his checkbook, so he wouldn't notice for as long as possible. Talking about her period to her grandfather was unthinkable.

Before she left his office, the doctor did ask her whether she had a boyfriend, to which, blushing, she answered no.

"If that occurs, you must come back and see me so I can prescribe you a contraceptive pill."

Had he said the same thing to her mother?

She emerged from the doctor's office in a trance. Imagining Marion's sore throats and fevers, her bicycle falls, her bruises, and tummy aches.

She looked for the boys in the garden-center parking lot, impatient to tell them all, like when one returns from a long journey.

Inside the store, she saw Étienne from the back, helpless, Py lying on the floor, and Adrien hitting out like a lunatic. Kicking, face contorted with rage, red as the redcurrants in the garden, hair plastered with sweat.

Nina felt terribly scared. Something like terror. They would take Adrien away from her, separate them. Like in the films that made her cry, when delinquents were locked up in hellish boarding schools. Adrien was going to abandon her just as her mother had, shortly after her birth.

She screamed his name.

Adrien stopped dead. Stupefied, he backed away, looked at his teacher lying on the floor, and blacked out. Nina's bronchial tubes went berserk. An attack of rare ferocity. People rushed over. Py got up without looking at anyone.

"With or without you . . ."

All three yell at the top of their voices. Dance with their eyes closed, despite the room being plunged in darkness. For a few days, the sitting-room's parquet has been their dance floor, they've eaten junk food, watched videos, sliding them into the player several times in a row when they like the film, and are mesmerized. Nina always sits between Étienne and Adrien. Sometimes, Étienne sucks his thumb on the sly.

They also decided to make music together. To form a group. Étienne has already dropped the piano, preferring the synthesizer and mike he's set up in part of the basement. Nina and Adrien will write the lyrics, while Étienne searches for tunes. They started by writing a few complex, convoluted, English phrases that make no sense. They mean to be original, still unaware that, frequently, the most beautiful songs are stunningly simple.

*

On 20 July, Étienne is off to Saint-Raphaël, on the Côte d'Azur, just like every year. It's the first time they're apart since they met. Apart from Adrien's stay at the hospital in Autun, during what they would later dub the "Py plague."

After Étienne's departure, Nina and Adrien are like two lost souls, splashing around all day in chlorinated water. Between dives, they spread out a towel on the yellowing lawn surrounding the pool, the part behind the security fences where one's allowed to eat and smoke, where teens French kiss before their incredulous ten- and eleven-year-olds' eyes. Nina and Adrien always settle under the same tree, and trace imaginary drawings in the sky that they make each other identify. They share a Walkman, taking turns with it. They change the cassette once the sponge headphones are over their ears. Adrien listens to Niagara, and Nina to Mylène Farmer.

"You ever kissed someone?" Nina asks Adrien.

"On the mouth?"

"Yes."

"With tongues?"

"Yes."

"Are you nuts, I'm eleven. And you?"

"Same."

"Anyhow, it looks gross."

One late afternoon, their eyes bloodshot from the swimming and the sun, Adrien accompanies Nina back home. They are greeted by her cats and her dog, Paola. Pierre Beau is having a nap. After doing his rounds, before going to the post office to hand in what he hasn't delivered, he always sneaks forty winks.

Nina asks Adrien to follow her into a windowless room at the end of the corridor.

"Don't worry, my grandpa's sleeping. I'm going to show you something, but you must swear, on my head, you won't tell anyone. Not even Étienne."

Adrien swears.

In this room, three small leather pouches sit on an old workbench. Nina opens one of them and turns it upside down. It's hot, there's no fresh air, just a vague smell of polish and dust. The contents spill out: dozens of letters, and postcards featuring the sea. Views that Nina can study for hours. And always the same words on the back: "Great weather, all's well, much love." Nina imagines that wherever there's the sea, all's well and the weather's always great.

"I take advantage of his nap to nick a few. Sometimes I . . . read them."

"Why?"

"Well, to read them."

"Your grandpa, does he know you do that?"

"Are you mad! He's never noticed. I put them straight back in their place. Want to have a go?"

Adrien fears he understands only too well.

"Have a go at what?"

Nina takes a pile of envelopes and picks some out. She chooses the handwritten ones—those enclosing bills or official letters don't interest her. She fans them out and presents them to Adrien.

"Close your eyes and pick a letter at random."

Adrien complies. He pulls one out as if it were a playing card in a magic trick. He feels Nina snatching it from his hands. When he reopens his eyes, she's already behind the door.

"We're going to my room!"

She switches on a small kettle on her bedside table, and a few moments later, waves the envelope over the steam from the boiling water, and then, quick as a flash, opens it. She hands the letter to Adrien.

"Go on, read it out loud."

Adrien feels as if he's at the center of the greatest scam of all time. He can already see himself in a reformatory. Where minors are locked up, and then beaten up by sorts worse than Py. He's a delinquent who not only laid into his old teacher, but also reads stolen correspondence. He feels his breathing and his heartbeat quickening. He grips the paper hard with his fingers so Nina doesn't notice that he's shaking like a leaf in the wind.

He sees handwriting that's fine, sprightly, in purple ink. He takes a deep breath before starting to read so his voice doesn't betray his fear.

"My dear children,

A little hello from the Alps, where the weather is really lovely.

The evenings are cool. And if, sadly, it does start to rain, we shiver. But being July, that's still rare.

My stay is going very well. The doctors want to keep me at the sanatorium for several more weeks. I hope to be back with you before school resumes. I hope you're behaving well with Daddy.

My dear Léo, are you reviewing your spelling often? My sweet Sybille, are you enjoying the outdoor center? Are the supervisors kind to you?

I'm missing you lots, my angels.

Tell Daddy I love him with all my heart, just as I love you, and that I'll be better very soon.

Mommy"

Adrien returns the letter to Nina, who's been hanging on his every word.

"My mother, she's never written to me . . ." she says.

"D'you know where she lives?"

"No."

"You've never seen her?"

"Yes, I have. She came back several times. To ask my grandfather for money, no doubt. The last time was in 1981. I was five."

"D'you remember it?"

"A bit. She smelt of patchouli."

"What's her name?"

"Marion."

"What work does she do?"

"Dunno . . ."

"Why d'you say she's a whore?"

Nina shrugs her shoulders.

"And d'you know who your father is?"

"No."

"And your grandpa, does he know?"

"No, don't think so. And you? Your father, what's he like?" asks Nina.

"He's married, in Paris."

"And d'you see him?"

"Sometimes. He stinks of chlorophyll. He's forever chewing that gross gum of his. I hate that smell. Sometimes, he comes to get me to take me to the restaurant. It's horrendous. I've got nothing to say to him. And neither has he to me. I wait for the pudding, asking him questions I've prepared in advance. So there aren't too many awkward silences."

"D'you think he's got other children?"

"Dunno."

"You might have a sister. Or brother."

"Maybe."

"He's never told you?"

"Never."

From the bottom of the stairs, Pierre Beau's deep voice booms up:

"Nina! What are you up to?"

It makes the children jump. Nina hides the envelope under her pillow.

Adrien, skateboard under arm, goes down to greet his friend's grandfather. Solemnly, the man says to him:

"You, I need a word with you."

Adrien suddenly feels very uncomfortable. He thinks Pierre Beau is going to lecture him over his violent altercation with Py. Adrien follows him to the kitchen with the look of a condemned man, maybe he's even going to ask him not to hang out with his granddaughter anymore, which would be unthinkable, intolerable, impossible.

Nina is Adrien's light. Like a sister, and the opposite of a sister because they chose each other. Nina is Adrien's certainty. Even if she does use the boys' washroom and read stolen letters.

Pierre Beau closes the door behind Adrien and looks intently at him for a few seconds. Nina doesn't resemble her grandfather. The old man's eyes are bluish gray. A bit like the color of the washing his mother often pulls out of the machine, cursing: "Oh, shit! The color's run again!" His skin is as weather-beaten as the leather jacket Steve McQueen's wearing on a poster in Adrien's room. Doing his rounds on a bike has tanned his skin. He furrows his brow as he observes him, looking serious. Adrien's mouth is dry. He could almost be on the dais in front of the blackboard, facing Py and his class.

"I've thought of a present for Nina's birthday, but I'd like your opinion. An easel and some tubes of paint . . . do you think she'd like that?"

Adrien struggles to reply. He so wasn't expecting those words that it takes him a while to take them in.

"Yes."

"You're sure?"

"Yes. I think so."

"You think so, or you're sure? Because she only does black. I thought it would be good for her to learn to do color, with paintbrushes."

# 10

*10 December 2017*

*We can't hold onto the foam*
*In the hollow of our hands*
*We know life wastes away*
*And there's nothing left*
*With one candle that's lit*
*You can still choose the path*
*Your path*
*Do you think it all comes down*
*To the salt between our fingers*
*When lighter than a feather*
*You can guide your own steps*
*Without sadness or bitterness*
*Going forward, go forward since everything goes.*

Yesterday, Johnny Hallyday's funeral.

Soeur Emmanuelle, Marie Trintignant, Nelson Mandela, Cabu, Wolinski.

What have Nina, Adrien, and Étienne done with all those years of silence?

The three haven't sung along to Stromae, haven't applauded Roger Federer, or watched *Le Fabuleux Destin d'Amélie Poulain*, or cried over Michael Jackson, Prince, Alain Bashung, David Bowie together.

"Have you seen the news? I've only just heard about it." All those things we no longer say to each other once we're beyond the door.

A man killing children in the yard of a school, a concert hall devastated. Terror. Those events that should make us dial a phone number, check on each other, wipe the slate clean.

The last time Nina, Adrien, and Étienne spoke was a long time ago.

And as for me, I'd like to tell them that tomorrow, all the region's journalists have been summoned by the public prosecutor of Mâcon regarding the case of the car in the lake.

I'd like to, I can't. That's an old song by Françoise Hardy.

*I want, I can't . . .*
*But if one day you think you love me*
*Don't wait a day, or a week . . .*

I should go to bed, but I keep turning things over in my mind while listening to music. Sometimes I stand up, I sing, imagining myself on the stage of a stadium, Wembley, for example.

*Completely crackers.*

Outside, it's been dark for a long while.

I'm alone in my home. How could it be otherwise? I asked for it.

## 11

*September 1987*

On the first day of sixth grade, they arrive together at the Collège du Vieux-Colombier.

The list of pupils divided into classes is pinned on a wooden board. They go up to it with fingers crossed. *Let's hope we're together.*

The verdict is pronounced: Nina Beau and Adrien Bobin are in 6A, Étienne Beaulieu in 6C.

Seeing only his name surrounded by unknown names, Étienne feels excluded. He feels like bursting into tears but holds them back.

Adrien is transfixed. He can't believe they've been separated. But at the same time, he can't help thinking, it means he'll get Nina back, all to himself. And for a whole year.

Nina quickly wipes away tears of rage and disappointment with the sleeve of her new jacket. The shame if she's seen crying like a baby at middle school. She orders her bronchial tubes to keep quiet. *No attack today, body, I forbid you, I forbid you, I forbid you.*

She's wearing a sweatshirt, stiff jeans, and sneakers that are too white, with her almost empty school bag on her back.

Étienne takes his sweater off. Too hot. He pushes back a stray lock of hair. Lowers his head. His profile is perfect. Nina could spend all her time drawing him. Even if he's only just leaving childhood behind and entering adolescence, there's a dichotomy between his face and body. The build of a tall, muscular sporty type, and a face with features that are almost girlish. The same contradiction is there between his ordinary clothes and the badge of punk-rock band Bérurier Noir he's pinned to his denim backpack.

Adrien remains silent. He observes the middle-schoolers. Loads more of them than in the elementary-school yard. And so much taller. There are some fourteen-year-olds who are at least one meter eighty. Adrien feels minuscule in this vast enclosure. In jeans, white sneakers, and a black leather bomber jacket his genitor found for him in Paris, he feels disguised. Adrien had cut out a picture of the singer from Depeche Mode and mailed it to him with a note: "I want the same bomber jacket as him for going back to school, thanks."

He looks at the school buildings with their many windows. Each building bearing the name of a poet: Prévert, Baudelaire, Verlaine, Hugo. He notices that there are no women. Is it because women *are* poems that they don't write any?

He turns around and looks at Nina. Yes, girls are silent poems.

All the other pupils go off to their classrooms.

They remain planted in front of the bulletin board, in a daze. As if someone is going to turn up and tell them there's been a mistake, that in the end they're back together.

"Right, well, I'm off," says Étienne, seeming detached. "Meet outside the cafeteria . . . You'll wait for me, hey."

Once he's turned his back on them, he bites hard on the inside of his cheek. *Shit list*. Mustn't cry in front of the others. He finds his class number, Hugo building, room 12, he's late, with blood in his mouth.

The class teacher, an ugly beanstalk. A bit crooked, scoliosis. Heavy-duty glasses. She will also be his English teacher. One who takes no nonsense, lays her cards on the table:

"I will be paid to teach here until I retire. If you want to work, great; if not, you can just sit at the back of the class, not my problem."

First exercise of the year: identify the best pupil. A solitary girl. It's obvious just from her mug that she's studious, and her shirt collar, her posture. Etienne locates her, sits beside her. He knows her by sight. Thinks they were together in first grade. She smiles at him. All girls smile at him. Yes, it's Edwige Thomassin. A brainbox. He can copy from her during tests. He'd have to deploy the same tactic for all subjects. Try to stick to Edwige at all times.

Étienne has always given his mother the impression that he works hard. When, in fact, he cheats. The Arsène Lupin, the gentleman thief, of the crib sheet. Last year, too easy to copy from Nina. The previous year, from Aurélien Bisset. Already in kindergarten, he just replicated his neighbor's drawings. It's not so much that he can't manage, he just lacks courage. It's on his skateboard and in front of his synthesizer that he has courage.

He gave up tennis. Claiming that his timetable at school was too full. "I've already got music . . ."

How often has Étienne's father flung at him: "Follow your brother's example." Competitiveness, being the best, winning the gold medal, working like a maniac, for Marc Beaulieu, it's an obsession.

His little sister Louise is on the same track as Paul-Émile, the eldest. Whereas he, the second sibling, a bit of a failure, lazy, scrapes by with average grades.

Scoliosis's name is Comello, she spells it out several times. Étienne imagines what Nina and Adrien are doing. What their class teacher looks like. Maybe not as ugly as his. They must be sitting next to each other. Must be together, anyhow. Unless they arrived late and all the desks were already taken. Which he hopes, pinching the palm of his hand. *God, if you exist, make sure Nina and Adrien aren't sitting next to each other. In that way, we'll each be properly separated, and when we meet up again, we'll all be equal.*

The hours drag on. The three bump into each other several times in the corridors before lunch. Étienne feels like a kid looking at his parents for the last time before leaving for summer camp. A lost child, without bearings, with no desire to talk to the others. Mustn't mix.

They meet up at the cafeteria at noon. Waits for each other in front of the trays, then follow each other, fill their plates in turn. Compare their timetables.

The days that follow are all the same.

After 5 P.M., life returns to normal. They go to Nina's or Adrien's. They listen to Depeche Mode's "Never Let Me Down Again," while drinking their hot chocolate. Then they settle at a table to work. Or pretend to. It's the solution they've found so as not to be separated after school. If they do their homework conscientiously, they'll be taken seriously. If they get good grades, they'll get to the baccalaureate together, and can be sure to opt for the same specialization. That way, at the lycée, come what may, they'll be on the same list.

Étienne waits for Adrien and Nina to finish their homework so he can copy it. He changes only a few words.

He reads comic strips, or *Rock & Folk* magazine, beside them. Whether at Adrien's, or Nina's, Étienne positions himself so he's facing the door in the room they're in, never turning his back on it. That way, if Joséphine or the mailman turn up, he can bury his head in a notebook or book.

Neither Nina nor Adrien criticizes him. It's as if they're paying dues for the injustice of not being with him in class. They let Étienne copy their work without a fuss. As if it were normal. Nina asks him just to read and understand what he's writing, "because you never know."

"You never know what?" Étienne asks.

"You never know," Nina replies, tirelessly. "I could die from my asthma and you'd find yourself not knowing a thing."

Sometimes, their classes take a bus together to visit some castle or abbey. Étienne arrives first to save three seats at the back. As he's taller than the rest, no one says a word. The journeys rarely last more than an hour, but no one's taking that hour away from him.

It's quite clear, Étienne is hating this year apart from them.

*

*9 June 1988*

The sixth-grade year ends in a few weeks.

They discover the Indochine album, *3*, on Étienne's turntable, when he's celebrating his twelfth birthday.

About thirty adolescents around the fine white-leather sofas that Marie-Laure Beaulieu has covered with bedsheets. A mix of sixth- and seventh-graders, who don't yet dare to dance. Girls with girls, boys with boys. A bit like when oil is poured into water, the droplets of oil gather.

Étienne handed out invitations to several classes because he heard his father saying to his mother that he was forever stuck to Adrien and Nina. "There's something unwholesome about their relationship."

What does "unwholesome" mean? Etienne consulted the Larousse dictionary, didn't quite understand the definition. And anyhow, he can't be bothered to read to the very end. Nothing bores him more absolutely than a dictionary. He invited a crowd of buddies so his father would shut up, with his "unwholesome."

Louise, his little sister, is sitting in a corner. She looks like him. Same clear skin, same blue eyes, nose, mouth. She's only just eleven. Before, Étienne thought that Marc didn't love him because he wasn't his father. That his mother must have sinned between the eldest and the youngest. But seeing how Louise looks like him, it's impossible. His mother surely can't have slept twice with another man.

*But three nights a week*
*It's my skin against her skin*
*And I'm with her . . .*

Nathan Robert has brought a bottle of whiskey under his coat and pours a glassful into each plastic cup. Most of them discover the taste of alcohol.

Nadège Soler, a girl from class 6B whom Nina likes because she smiles all the time, asks her: "Are you going out with Adrien or Étienne?"

"Going out where?"

"D'you French kiss them? D'you feel each other up? What's it like, doing that as a threesome?"

Nina is shocked by the question.

"Oh, no way. *We* don't do that."

Nadège seems not to believe Nina but couldn't care less about her answer. She's off to dance. A few others copy her by singing: *Such a shame . . .*

Nina, who has refused to drink Nathan's whiskey until now, pours herself a little before drowning it in cola. A first mouthful, unpleasant, lingering in her throat.

She's already tried some dregs of wine when clearing the table—disgusting. Alcohol really is gross.

She watches Étienne dancing. He moves well and is the best looking. All the girls watch him. Brazenly, or surreptitiously. Étienne seems absent. He doesn't look happy this year. Must be because they're separated.

Why do they like each other so much? Could she marry one of the two when they're grown up? No way. They pick their teeth side by side, don't close the bathroom door, aren't bothered if they bump into each other first thing in the morning, tend to their respective pimples and grazes, yell at each other "You stink, go brush your teeth," and "I hate what you're wearing," and "Get rid of that moustache, you look like the bearded lady." Their sayings and reflexes are those of an old couple, they're jealous if one of the three looks at someone else, but they never flirt. Nina is very conscious of being the link between Étienne and Adrien, but not a love interest. For neither of them. Étienne considers her as a sister, Adrien as a model, almost an ideal.

Nadège's words and the alcohol are making her head spin. "D'you French kiss them? D'you feel each other up? What's it like, doing that as a threesome?" She remembers the demos Étienne did for them with his fingers and tongue, for the day they'd have to know how to kiss someone they fancy. Because he'd already done it with Solène Faulq, a girl in 4D who'd been kept back for a year. And Adrien, as he watched him, asked: "The tongue, d'you think it should be turned clockwise, like the hands of a watch?"

Nina has thought about love since she was very young. And about physical love for a few months. Love like in the letters she still secretly opens. She thinks of the very last one she read, and reread. She knows the person it's addressed to, the name on the envelope. It's the mother of a girl in Étienne's class. Nina sees this woman every day, in her car at the school parking lot, listening to the radio while waiting for her daughter. When she opens the car window, Nina hears the music and sees the curls of smoke she blows out while gazing up at the sky.

*I'd like to undress you like last year. Strip you like last year, feel your hot cunt in my hand, make you come. But when I meet you, you cross to the other sidewalk. Why? Answer me. Tell me something. Give me a sign. Any sign.*

"Make you come." Nina keeps thinking about that. Her mother must come. That's all she must be doing. And she preferred *that* to her daughter.

Nina discovered pleasure alone in her bed. She went after a warmth. Like an itch. Rubbed her vagina against the sheet, and then, evening after evening, her head spun and her body arched. A feeling of exaltation coursing through her. Even better than the swimming-pool water.

She doesn't yet talk about physical love to Adrien and Étienne. Just about kisses exchanged with the tongue. She senses that, one day, they'll no longer be able to hang out together all the time. Soon they'll want to kiss older eighth-grade girls, to fondle them where she touches herself. She knows very well it's going to end up happening. And that they'll drop her.

For now, Étienne and Adrien are still young. Younger than her, even if they're the same age. That's how it is with girls, they're older from birth.

Nina can feel her breasts growing, when neither Adrien nor Étienne have a single hair on their chin and think mainly about making music and skateboarding.

Her breasts feel sore. For now, they don't show, and she wears baggy sweatshirts. She doesn't want the boys to notice that she's changing. Her smell, her pubic hairs, her desires, her thoughts, like a revolution going on under her skin. She doesn't like it. She'd like to return to childhood, to the little girl she was. To the sweetness of the hot milk she drank in the evening before falling asleep. How harsh it feels to grow up, to change, to have to adapt. Thank goodness she's got drawing. Reproducing the features of those she loves in charcoal lines on paper allows her to dismiss the fear of the unknown. When she's drawing, she no longer thinks about a thing, it's like a life-saving playground. Her mind takes flight, she has several lives. Each drawing she completes is one of them. Someone's face. A landscape. A profile. A smile. She's started to paint. It's tricky, the paintbrush. With charcoal, she's in contact with the paper. It's physical. With paint, she feels obliged to keep her distance. There's less precision. And she doesn't like color. She doesn't know how to handle red and blue.

Everyone's dancing to "3e sexe" by Indochine. Nina joins Étienne.

Breaths stinking of alcohol, bodies that move awkwardly, that don't yet know, the bodies of clumsy children who sing in unison:

*And we hold hands*
*And we hold hands*
*Girls in the masculine*
*Boys in the feminine . . .*

# 12

*10 December 2017*

Someone pushes the door open, Nina, nose in the account books, pays no attention. Thinks it's Christophe, or a volunteer, coming into the office to grab a coffee. Every morning, Nina makes a pot for everyone.

"Hi, I phoned you yesterday, I've come to see the dog . . . Bob."

A man on his own, that's rare. Usually, it's women or families with children who come on a first visit, the one preceding adoption.

Nina puts on a suitably nice smile. It's not every day they have a client.

She gets up to greet him. She has a firm handshake, as does he. That pleases Nina. The man is tall, which reminds her of Étienne. At sixteen, he already measured one meter eighty-two.

"Hi, Romain Grimaldi."

"Hi, Nina Beau, manager of the shelter."

Nina is disconcerted. It's the first time a potential adopter radiates a certain charm. He's not like the others, even if, over seventeen years at the shelter, she's quite certain she's seen, encountered, heard, experienced it all.

He's a bit like Adrien's friends. The ones she saw around him when he lived in Paris. The artistic and brilliant sort, or something like that. A certain elegance. Not a guy from around here.

As for herself, she knows she's no longer radiated anything at all for a long time, apart from a vague whiff of damp dog. Short hair, more practical. Makeup, unthinkable when the day starts with sweeping up the shit in the kennels. Her clothes, almost a uniform, with an army vibe: variations of khaki or murky brown, comfortable and hard-wearing. Rubber boots forever on her feet. Her hands, short nails. Manicures are for other women, other lives than hers.

She accompanies the visitor through the shelter, to Bob's kennel. A cold drizzle is falling on them.

Romain Grimaldi glances guiltily at the dogs barking behind the gates. Anyone from outside this place needs to be tough, it's a bit like humanity's dumping ground here. Anyone who works here sees it differently. The animals are safe, get plenty to eat and drink, plenty of petting, and are taken out every day. They're respected, and if sick, they're treated. They're spoken to as well. Like to buddies one's sharing hard times with. A bad summer camp. That one can't wait to be over to go back home.

"Do you have any pedigree dogs?" asks Romain Grimaldi.

Nina doesn't like this question. They're not in a pet shop. You don't come looking for pedigree or beauty. They live surrounded by mongrels. Blue eyes and white coats are few and far between.

"It's rural around here. The few pedigree dogs I've come across have been hunters, setters, spaniels, pointers, or fox terriers. But they remain the exception. If an animal can make money, people don't let go of it, they try to sell it. Or swap it. Did you see the photos of Bob on our website?"

"Yes."

"He's a good dog. Have you adopted before?"

"I've always adopted, in fact."

Nina likes his answer.

"Do you live around here?"

"I've just been transferred to La Comelle. I'm the new headmaster at the Collège Georges-Perec."

*The Collège* . . . Nina thinks of her own that's just been demolished. She thinks of it without sadness. For Nina, what's past is past.

"Do you have any other pets?"

"An old cat. Radium."

"How is he around dogs?"

"He's used to it, and he sleeps all the time anyhow, he's seventeen years old."

Nina opens Bob's kennel and asks Romain Grimaldi to wait for her outside. She never lets a stranger in. The dog goes up to her, wagging his tail. Bob is a small, black mongrel, probably a fox terrier-cocker spaniel cross.

"You've got a visitor, old boy," Nina whispers to him.

She bends down and strokes the animal. The coat is rough. Romain Grimaldi speaks to him from the door:

"Hello there, loving your little face . . ."

Bob doesn't look at him. Nina slips a collar and leash on him.

"We're going to walk to see how he behaves with you."

"Do you think he's going to like me?"

Nina smiles.

"Yes, I think so. Bob's shy. He never goes up to strangers spontaneously."

"He looks like the first dog I had, when I was little. He took my fancy on your website. How old is he?"

"According to the veterinarian, about eight years old."

"Any idea where he comes from?"

"Found in a nearby village. Four years he's been here, already."

"Why does no one want him?"

"Perhaps because he was waiting for you."

They walk side by side. Nina hands the leash to Romain Grimaldi. They're on some wasteland beside the shelter. Land that belongs to no one, like the dogs that are walked on it every day.

"Do you live alone?" asks Nina.

"Yes."

"In a house, or an apartment?"

"House. With a garden."

"Have you thought about how you'll organize your day for Bob?"

"I'm thinking of taking him with me to work."

"To the school?"

"Yes. That's why I don't want a puppy. During the day, he'll stay in my office. At lunchtime, I'll take him outdoors, and in the evening, we'll go home together."

"Are you allowed to have him there?"

"Yes, if he stays in my office. Before, I was head of an establishment in Marnes-la-Coquette, and I always brought my dog in with me."

"Why did you come to these parts?"

"For a change. What do I need to do to adopt Bob?"

"Fill in some forms. And you can come and collect him tomorrow."

"Is there something to be paid?"

"Since he's old, you give whatever you want."

"And if he wasn't old, how much would it cost me?"

"Four hundred euros for a dog, three hundred for a cat. Which includes vaccinations, sterilization, identification, and all the rest: meals, ancillary care . . ."

"I can't take him today?"

"I'm not allowed to give him to you before he's been checked in the veterinary hut."

Nina has got butterflies in her stomach. She observes Bob out of the corner of her eye. She gets that feeling every time she places one of them. He's finally getting away from here. That's the difference between her and her critters.

She will never leave again.

*

Nina is seven years old. It's a Sunday in June. On the radio, Jean-Jacques Goldman sings "*Au bout de mes rêves*." The sun's shining. The previous day, her grandfather said to her: "Tomorrow, I'm taking you somewhere, it's a surprise."

She's put on a pretty dress, new shoes. She's done two plaits, which she's attached with a daisy-shaped barrette.

They drive for a good hour in the blue Renault 5. Pierre Beau is looking conspiratorial. Where on earth might they be going? Nina wonders, sitting at the back—"You can sit in front when you're ten."

Nina spots the first billboard thirty kilometers from their destination: "SAP . . . Safari Amusement Park." She bounces with joy and says to her grandfather: "Grandpa, I've guessed where we're going!"

The closer they get, the more photos of animals and carousels she sees on giant colorful billboards. She wriggles around. She stamps her feet. Pierre Beau smiles, he's pulled it off.

Locally, everyone talks of the SAP as a paradise: carousels, a little train that goes right round the park, fries, and cotton candy. And animals that one never normally sees: hippos, big cats, elephants, wolves, monkeys, giraffes.

All around Nina, families, laughter, a few tears, childish tantrums. Holding a balloon, she watches the other people watching the animals. Nina often stands back. She views things and people in wide shot.

Nina's hand is in her grandfather's. That hand like an island. And yet she feels unwell. Headachy. Bloated. Tired legs. Is it because of the crowd? The heat? Is it the absence of parents? Of her parents? Those surrounding her, those of her age, are tucked between a father and mother.

She hears: "Mommy! Come and see!" and "Daddy! Look!" She has never said those words. Whether in pits, or behind glass screens or bars, she finds the animals all look alike. As if captivity homogenized them, gave them the same attitude, the same look in their eyes.

A black panther, carrying her little one in her mouth, paces back and forth in her cage, she's looking for a way out under the curious and fascinated gaze of the visitors. No corner to hide in. No privacy. Served up, subjugated, scrutinized.

Nina feels ashamed. What entertains the others horrifies her. She's too small to understand what this shame means. She just senses that she's not the same. That something's rumbling deep inside her.

She's relieved when she boards the little train that goes right round the park at two kilometers an hour. She dozes off against her grandfather's shoulder, exhausted by all she's felt since entering this place.

"Want to go see the wolves before we leave?" her grandfather asks her, taking her little hand back in his own, a great paw, warm and soft.

"No, I'm scared."

She's lying. Nina is never scared of animals of any kind.

She's relieved to be back in the R5, as her grandfather drives off. She's relieved to turn her back on that place.

"Did you like it?"

“Yes. Thanks, Grandpa.”
“What did you like best? The giraffes or the lions?”
“The train.”
“Why the train?”
“Because it’s free. It goes where it wants.”

# 13

*July 1988*

All three of them move up to seventh grade. They've chosen German as a second foreign language to be sure of being together. Their leitmotif: never to be separated again. Pupils opting for the language of Goethe are rare, apart from a few very studious ones. In seventh grade, most do remedial English or Spanish.

At first, Étienne's parents opposed it: "You're not at that level." But the three had anticipated and memorized the arguments to put forward if turned down: "German is the future. The class teacher says that, for etymology, it's the best. Statistically, all pupils who opt for German make good progress in their other subjects, it boosts motivation, German strengthens mental and physical endurance . . . And if I meet Claudia Schiffer, I want to speak to her in her mother tongue."

The three are at the swimming pool. The girls of their age look at Étienne. He shows off. A trick. He walks along the edge of the twenty-five-meter pool, with feigned concentration, climbs onto the No. 3 starting block, the one in the middle, stretches, propels himself into the water with a perfect dive, swims the length of the pool underwater, reemerges straight up the ladder, and goes back for another dive. His skin is the color of a *pain au chocolat*. His body is just as slender and muscular. He's already one meter sixty tall.

Nina floats on her back. She gazes at the sky. A few stray white sheep. She rounds them up in her mind, plays at being a sheepdog. It's hot. The sun prickles. She feels good.

Distractedly, Adrien hangs from the pool's edge, seems to be dreaming. Ducks underwater from time to time with eyes closed.

In a fortnight, Étienne will be leaving for Saint-Raphaël and they'll be back on their own again, Nina and him.

"Next year, I'll take you both with me," Étienne had said, eagerly. "My parents are almost O.K. with it. I just need to raise my average grade by two points."

When you're twelve years old, next year is an eternity. But Nina would like to see the sea. So she hopes that, after an eternity, she'll finally get to see it. She'll help Étienne to earn her dream.

"I'm starving!" says Etienne, getting out of the water.

The three of them head for the terrace, tuck their towels under their butts to avoid burning them on the metal seats of the chairs.

Étienne orders and pays for three cartons of fries, which they dunk in ketchup.

It's the quiet period. The morning swimmers, retirees, and other adults, have all gone home. The afternoon swimmers, children, start appearing at around 2:00 P.M. So all that's left is a few adolescents like them, lazily covering themselves in sun cream and exchanging sidelong glances. The girls laugh loudly on the plastic loungers, while the boys hurl themselves from the diving boards.

Their bodies have changed. They've shot up, filled out. When Étienne and Adrien discovered Nina's breasts under her bikini top, they stared wide-eyed.

"Does it hurt?" Adrien asked her.

"A bit," Nina replied, tersely.

Étienne didn't bat an eyelid. He's becoming a regular flirt. But it never lasts long. He goes out with girls for about two days. The first day, he seems to be in love, the second, not even remotely.

Nina became infatuated with a ninth-grade boy. A certain Gilles Besnard. A gangly guy who smokes cigarettes and goes clubbing. Nina thinks he looks like the actor Richard Anconina. No one else does. They've never spoken. Just exchanged looks when passing each other in the school corridors, or cafeteria. Next year she won't see him anymore, he'll be off to a vocational school. So she hangs around the streets of La Comelle in the hope of coming across him. She looks out for letters to him, and to his parents. Gilles Besnard never receives a thing. And his parents, just boring bills. She feels like a gold fossicker finding in those piles of letters only sand and never a nugget.

Étienne doesn't know that Nina opens some of the letters before her grandfather delivers them. Only Adrien knows. It's the secret that binds the two of them.

*

Once Étienne leaves for Saint-Raphaël, Nina and Adrien steal numerous letters, and discover the ordinary lives of La Comelle locals and their correspondents. They tell each other what the weather's like, and how their grandchildren are growing.

Before unsealing the envelopes, Nina breathes them in, closes her eyes, tries to guess their secret, and, after she's opened them, is often disappointed. Well, people clearly have no imagination, or are short on love.

When Étienne is back, they finish the summer all together, between the swimming pool, the music cellar, and Nina's room, where she sketches the two of them.

Étienne has grown even taller. The three of them are sitting side by side on the edge of the big pool, absentmindedly watching the swimmers go by, while sucking candies.

Nina has tied up her hair with an elastic band. Like every summer, her skin has tanned. Her eyes seemed to have darkened, too.

Adrien hates his complexion, which never tans, but reddens as if awfully shy.

"In Saint-Raphaël, I slept with a girl," Étienne says, out of the blue.

"Properly?" asks Nina.

"Properly . . . It made me feel weird. She's sixteen. She lay on top of me. She was hot. I mean, her skin was hot like when you have a fever. She was burning me, I closed my eyes, but I still slept with her."

"Was it good?"

"It was wet . . . and a bit stinky."

They laugh. A mix of embarrassment, curiosity, avidity. The questions come faster, intersect, overlap.

"Where d'you do it?" asks Adrien.

"In the pussy."

They giggle inanely.

"I mean where, in a bed, at yours?"

"Nope. On the beach, like everyone else."

"In front of everyone?" exclaims Nina.

"Nope. It was dark. No one around."

"Are you in love?"

"Nope."

"So why d'you do it?"

"Gotta do it sooner of later. Now, just like that, I'm not a virgin anymore."

"What's her name?"

"Cynthia."

"Sounds like an actress's name. Have you known her long?"

"Since I was small. I see her there every year."

"Is she in love with you?"

"Dunno."

All three of them are lost in thought again, Nina breaks the awkward silence:

"Well, I'm going do it when I'm in love . . ."

"Well, you're a girl. It's not the same," says Étienne.

"Why isn't it the same?" exclaims Adrien.

"Because girls are romantic. Especially Nina."

"Did she come?" asks Nina.

Étienne blushes. It's the first time they've talked about sex together. The first time Nina has asked such a bold, even blunt question.

"Don't really know . . . She was breathing heavily."

They burst out laughing at the same time. The laughter of children who no longer really want to be children.

But all the same, childhood was fun.

Caught between candies and the future. Between mischief and a breaking voice. Between bike spokes you make sing with bits of cardboard and dreams of endless motorbike rides.

# 14

*11 December 2017*

Nina parks in front of the shelter. She greets two volunteers waiting for her outside the gates, Joseph and Simone. Joseph is a retired workman, a ruddy-faced little fellow with a roll-up forever between his lips. Occasionally, he deigns to relight it. Simone lost her son in a car accident. If she didn't walk the dogs every day, she'd do herself in. The leashes she grips keep her upright. Abandoned animals are her white stick.

Since starting at the shelter, Nina has seen many volunteers pass through. They come and they go. A kind of eclectic procession. Bricklayers, nurses' aides, middle-class women, widowers, old people, slightly damaged young people. Solitary and somewhat oversensitive souls who put themselves back together by cleaning out the kennels, patching up the fencing, meeting people, having a chinwag over a hot coffee, repairing the shelter's corrugated-iron roofs. And then one day they're off, because they're feeling better, or moving house, or getting married. One day they announce that it's too hard, or too late, and they disappear as suddenly as they arrived.

This morning, Nina has an appointment with Romain Grimaldi. This morning, Bob is off.

At the shelter, whenever a cat or dog finds a home, everyone goes around silently celebrating. Adoption days are special. One eye cries for the animal you've inevitably grown attached to and won't see anymore, and the other eye smiles because its abandonment is over. It's job over with one. And it's thanks to these moments of relief, this living Tetris game, that you keep going.

Romain Grimaldi is waiting for Nina outside the door of the office. They go in together after shaking hands. *He still smells as nice.*

She loves what he radiates. It makes her think back to her husband, to their early days. It's all about the senses, she thinks.

"I've prepared the forms. In a month's time, Bob will officially be yours."

"He isn't mine today?"

"You have a month to change your mind."

"No reason to."

"You never know. Adopting an animal is like a marriage. One can want a divorce in the first year."

"Does it happen often?"

"No, not often, but occasionally a dog is brought back to me because it doesn't meet its owners' expectations."

Simone arrives in the office with Bob. She greets Romain, whispers, "He's a good dog, take care of him," hands him the leash, and leaves immediately.

Before, Simone couldn't care less about animals. She would never have harmed them, but she didn't notice them.

Two days before her son Éric's funeral, when she had to go into his studio to find some clothes to give to the mortician, she was met by an elderly dog that Éric had taken in without telling anyone. Simone remembered that this dog was her son's dream, a dream she'd refused him throughout his childhood. Simone and the animal stared at each other for a long while. Simone recognized her own pain in the eyes of the dog. It had understood that its master wouldn't be coming back. By consoling it Simone consoled herself. She took it in her arms, never to let it go. When the dog died, when the veterinarian said, "Nothing more can be done," Simone went to see Nina. "I need to walk the dogs." Nina took her on that very day. Nina knew Simone by sight. She knew about the death of Éric, who'd been at school with her, about Simone and the dog being inseparable after the funeral; she was a shadow walking a dog along La Comelle's every pavement, walking the dog the way one carries around sorrow. Nina understood her need to work there, one more wounded soul. It would be tricky to handle, the sickness, old age, death of some animals, but she had no choice. Hadn't the heart to say no. To send her back home. They'd make the best of it.

"I really admire what you do," Romain said to Nina, while signing the adoption papers.

"Same here. Can't be easy to manage a school."

"What's hardest to manage isn't the pupils, it's the parents."

Nina smiles. Romain writes out a check.

"You don't have to," Nina tells him.

"I know."

"Thanks, on their behalf."

Romain takes Bob with him. Heads for his car. Opens the passenger door and makes Bob jump onto the front seat.

"I'll keep you posted."

Nina takes a photo of Bob with her mobile phone.

A wave, and the car disappears. Nina remains rooted there for a few seconds, still smelling gasoline and damp dog.

Then she returns to her office, goes onto the shelter's website, posts the photo of Bob she's just taken, and writes: BOB ADOPTED, with a heart beside it.

# 15

*10 November 1989*

They're in eighth grade. First lesson of the day. Same setup as in Py's class. Nina sits beside Étienne, and Adrien, behind her, gazes at her nape. She's just had a haircut. Looks a bit like a boy, Adrien's not that keen. Nina has started putting kohl under her eyes, a clumsy line that brings out her dark eyes, Étienne says "it looks dirty." To which she retorts that he "sure ain't no rocker."

When Monsieur Schneider, their German teacher, enters the classroom, he seems totally electrified. Something has happened. Suddenly, everyone stops chatting to look at him. Usually, he's a reserved man whose head seems sunk between his shoulders, as if it's been hit so it gradually disappears inside an awkward, stiff body. An individual who speaks quietly and has bored pupils for more than twenty years. He's wearing a rucksack, as if he was off traveling and had come to bid farewell to his pupils before leaving them.

"*Eins, zwei, drei, die Mutter ist in der Küche . . .*"

Usually, no one stops chatting on seeing him enter his classroom. But this morning, something has changed. Nina even thinks the teacher has been drinking, so shiny are his eyes. His books tumble to the floor as he opens his bag. The entire class bursts into laughter. A small class: only fifteen pupils are learning German, seventh- and eighth-graders combined.

Monsieur Schneider steps up onto the dais, breathes in deeply, and announces solemnly:

"*Meine lieben Kinder, ich habe gute Nachrichten, eine Nachricht, die das Gesicht der Welt verändern wird: die Berliner Mauer ist gefallen.*"

No one reacts. No one seems to understand a single word of what he's saying. It's the first time he's addressing them in German outside of a lesson.

But what follows continues to leave the schoolchildren speechless and plunges them into a kind of waking dream. Monsieur Schneider pulls four bottles of champagne out of his rucksack, opens them one after the other while laughing and emitting strange little cries. A joyous madness has taken hold of him, which seems to disconcert the pupils, who hate the school's strict regime, but at the same time, find it reassuring. Their teacher places plastic cups on his desk and starts filling them, while shouting:

"*Lang lebe die Freiheit!*"

It's 9:10 A.M., and everyone starts drinking. The teacher elatedly clinks cups with each and every pupil.

It's all over for the wall of shame, he says, Germany is reunified, he can't quite believe it, it's historic, unbelievable, miraculous, and unexpected! The pupils end up understanding that it's the fall of the Berlin Wall that's put Monsieur Schneider into this trancelike state. Hurriedly, and sometimes with tears in his eyes, he tells them how many were killed attempting to cross the wall. Nina asks him if he has any family over there, and on which side. He replies, overcome, that his parents were in the East.

After knocking back two cups of champagne, both in a single gulp, Schneider enters the other classrooms without knocking, and invites all the teachers and their pupils to come and celebrate the news with him. By 10 A.M., on the third story of the Charles Baudelaire building, there are more than two hundred people listening or dancing to Nina Hagen's "African Reggae." Monsieur Schneider has slipped a cassette into the player he normally uses for grammar lessons. As soon as the song ends, he rewinds to hear it again.

Schneider dances and sways his hips, proclaiming:

"*Lang lebe die Freiheit!*"

He twirls his pupils around, one after the other, girls and boys alike.

Étienne finds school interesting for the first time. Thinks it should always be like this. That all the walls in the world should crumble.

Never would the pupils have imagined that their German teacher might listen to Nina Hagen, let alone have a drop of whimsy in his veins.

That morning, Adrien realizes the effect freedom has: a boundless joy that transforms bodies and faces.

That evening, in front of the TV news, sitting beside his mother, who's gripping a handkerchief in her fists and wiping her eyes when emotion gets the better of her, Adrien watches the images being broadcast worldwide: the tears of the Germans, the families reunited, the girls kissing the guards, the derisory hammer blows, the shards of wall falling, the crowds, the fragments of concrete being slipped into pockets, pieces to be kept as mementos.

Adrien asks himself questions about his own wall, the one separating him from himself, the one he's been hiding behind ever since he could breathe—how big is it?

# 16

*11 December 2017*

Gone. All that will remain are a few pictures in archives and class photos in cupboards.

The Collège du Vieux-Colombier is no more. A wasteland. All the rubble cleared away. Exit Prévert, Baudelaire, Verlaine, and Hugo. The town hall has already had billboards put up showing that residential buildings for the over-fifties will be built instead. That one can contact a certain agency to reserve one of the high-rise apartments to be ready in 2020.

I wonder what Nina thought, on seeing that it had been razed to the ground. She passes it every day to get to the shelter, there's no other route. No doubt she felt nothing, she's always hated nostalgia.

I never see her while I'm doing my shopping, but I sometimes pass her in the car. She drives a Citroën combi van, with the letters ADPA (for the *Association de Défense et de Protection des Animaux*) on both sides. She seems tiny behind that big steering wheel. Always lost in her thoughts, as if the pedestrians and drivers she passes didn't really exist.

Does she know that I've come back to live here? Does she see my articles in the local paper? Does she even read it?

This evening, the Vieux-Colombier wasteland resembles the lake when I went there to take some photos last week. You don't know anymore whether it's land you're staring at, or water. Nothing moves anymore. Frozen into oblivion. The figures of the trees, shivering and naked, seemingly still standing out of pique, ghostly. A sinister drizzle, a freezing cold night in the headlights of my car. As if dawn had decided never to break again. A picket line.

I'm returning from the press conference in Mâcon. The state

prosecutor confirmed to us that bones had been discovered inside the Twingo that the police divers pulled out of the so-called "Lac de la Forêt." The vehicle was identified thanks to the license plate. It had been stolen from Monsieur and Madame Guillaume Desnos on 17 August 1994, in the early afternoon, from outside their home in the municipality of La Comelle. It seems almost certain that the wreck had been underwater since that date, for twenty-three years.

At this stage of the investigation, the identification of the body will be lengthy and complex, owing to the condition of the bones. They will undergo DNA analysis, for comparison with the DNA of the families of people who disappeared at that time in the area.

The Twingo full of silt was buried seven meters deep. The diving squad is continuing its investigations using sonar in the zone the vehicle was retrieved from, to detect any items potentially belonging to the victim.

If it's Clotilde Marais, will we uncover her secret? The secret that only the three think they know.

I remember us skimming pebbles across the lake on summer evenings. As adolescents, we smoked grass there. We drank anything straight from the bottle, whatever we could lay our hands on, stolen from a cupboard, a father's vermouth, a grandmother's brandy, a brother's whiskey. Étienne would bring along his cassette player. He used to make compilation tapes, mixing every kind of music. Behind us, our bikes, lying flat on the ground, waited for us to finish our antics before taking us back home.

# 17

*20 April 1990*

On the ground floor, their eighth-grade class is celebrating Adrien's fourteenth birthday. For the occasion, Étienne's parents have lent them the large sitting room in their house.

Nina is alone in the Beaulieus' bathroom, having closed the door behind her. When leaving the toilet, she was drawn to the perfume bottles and the sunlight filtering through a window, casting radiant reflections on the floor.

Music blaring all around, walls vibrating.

Nina listens and whispers the words of "Lullaby" along with Robert Smith. She sniffs the body creams, the bubble bath placed on the edge of the generous tub, the multicolored soaps. She opens a first cupboard, discovers several makeup bags, tweezers, and medicines stored in racks. Nina likes rummaging, searching, discovering the other side of the picture. In her eyes, cupboards conceal as many secrets as the letters she steals.

She jumps. She thought there was someone behind her, but it's only her reflection in a cheval mirror. She observes her shapeless form, she's slouching, she straightens up, holds her tummy in, long arms, small body, runs her fingers through her short hair that's greasy within hours, peers at her dark skin, her blackheads, her unlovely teen's face. She looks like a boy, and she doesn't like it. But if she had long hair, she'd look like a girl she didn't like either. She smiles at herself without really smiling, to see her braces. Why is one so ugly at thirteen? What *is* this mug? She hopes it'll sort itself out. Or else she's for the scrap heap.

She turns away from her reflection and continues with her explorations. At the Beaulieus', the huge family bathroom seems to be Marie-Laure's domain.

Nina contemplates the many perfume bottles. Some seem to have been empty for a long time. As if they'd belonged to other women.

She has an idea.

She goes back downstairs and heads to the kitchen, where the door is closed. Nina opens it and comes face-to-face with Marie-Laure and Joséphine. Étienne's and Adrien's mothers are sitting at the table and chatting over a cup of tea. Nina finds them so different from each other, never would she have imagined coming across them in the same room.

"Why aren't you with all the others?" Joséphine asks, with surprise. "Is something missing from the table?"

"No . . ." Nina replies.

*Someone's missing from this kitchen, my mother*, she thinks.

Marion should be with them, nibbling cookies while waiting for their kids' party to be over.

Nina looks at Marie-Laure, who smiles kindly at her.

"So, Nina, we're taking you with us to Saint-Raphaël this summer? Étienne mentions it to me every day."

"Adrien, too," adds Joséphine. "He talks to me of nothing else."

*The sea is close*, thinks Nina. *The sea is close*. This thought makes her smile. Étienne raised his average grades thanks to her and Adrien. They're on the verge of a one-way ticket to happiness.

"Yes, that would be nice," she replies. "But . . . I was wondering . . . Did you know my mother, Marion Beau?"

Marie-Laure doesn't hesitate a second before replying:

"Yes. I was with her at elementary school. We must have done second and third grade together. And one or two classes at middle school."

Nina considers Marie-Laure for a few moments. Her words resonate. Why didn't she think of it before?

"What was she like?" she finally asks.

"Marion was funny . . . kind . . . chatty, too."

"Do I look like her?"

"Not like how I remember her. She was blond, almost ginger. And she had green eyes, I believe. You don't have any photos of your mother?"

"No. Not one."

Nina gets impatient. She'd like to ask a thousand questions, but her mind is racing.

"What was she like otherwise?"

"Very kind. She changed a lot when your grandmother died. She put up a wall of silence."

"Shall I leave you two to chat about it?" asks Joséphine.

"No, it's fine," says Nina, more curtly than she'd meant to. "Thanks, I'll get back to the others."

She turns and leaves the kitchen. She feels tears welling in her eyes. She wishes she wasn't so sensitive. But as soon as her bronchial tubes go crazy, or her mother is merely mentioned, she can't cope. She loses her bearings. *Perd père. Perd mère.* She'd written lyrics from that: "*Perd père, perd mère, pervers, un père impair, par terre.*" Totally moronic, that song.

Marion put up a wall of silence when Odile died, Marie-Laure Beaulieu said. If only Nina could bring up the subject with her grandfather. But she doesn't dare, she senses that it's too painful.

Nina finds Adrien sitting on a chair, looking vacant. The others are dancing to "Charlotte Sometimes." Adrien returns to earth when he senses Nina's presence near him. He recognizes her vanilla perfume, an essence she's been spraying over herself for a few months. He focuses his eyes on her. He has to shout to be heard:

"What's up? You been crying?"

"Étienne's mother . . . she knew mine."

"Here, everyone seems to know everyone."

"Where were you, then, before coming to La Comelle?" Nina asks him.

"Clermont-Ferrand."

"Why d'you come here? You've never told me."

Adrien shrugs his shoulders.

"Because I knew you lived here."

Nina smiles.

"D'you think that, sometimes, life gives back so as to be forgiven for having taken away too much?"

". . ."

"For example, my mother, she left me. Even cats, when their kittens are taken from them, they cry."

"Maybe your mother cried when she left you."

"Don't think so. Or she'd have come back to get me. But you, you're here. It's as if life's given me back part of what it took from me when I was little. D'you understand?"

"I understand," Adrien replies.

He often tightens his throat to keep his tears down. Like the underground river he saw in the Labeil cave, on vacation in the Larzac with his mother. Water that doesn't rise to the surface.

"You'll never leave me?"

"Never."

"Swear to me?"

"Swear to you."

"You'll always be there for me?"

"Always."

Étienne finds them. He doesn't like seeing them together for too long without knowing what they're saying to each other.

"What are you up to? Coming for a dance?"

Nina follows him. Adrien stays seated. He's pleased, loves watching them.

He feels a kind of draft behind him. It's his mother.

"Everything O.K., darling? Having fun?"

"Yes."

"You're not dancing?"

"God's sake, Mom."

When Adrien turns around, Joséphine is already gone. He thinks again of Nina's question: why did he come to live in La Comelle? One morning, Joséphine had announced to him that she was changing day-care center. That she'd be looking after other children, somewhere else. That they were leaving, moving a hundred-and-fifty kilometers away, to Saône-et-Loire. And he couldn't have cared less. In Clermont, he had no friends.

Until the day he met Nina and Étienne, Adrien felt like ink that didn't print. An empty cartridge. He'd always had the feeling he'd been born colorless, totally transparent. Until Nina and Étienne, one could press all the buttons, but the paper remained blank. Nina and Étienne gave him back his five senses. His breath, too. And certainly hope. That's why he's so attached to them.

The lights go out, the music is switched off. Joséphine and Marie-Laure announce to him in unison that his present is in the cellar. A synthesizer. The same one as Étienne so they can play music together. Marie-Laure adds that he can come over whenever he likes. As usual, in other words.

A synthesizer. He's overcome with emotion. He was dreaming of one.

Everyone starts singing "Happy Birthday to You."

The cake, fourteen sparkler-candles. Nina shouts to him to make a wish. Adrien closes his eyes. His wish, it's always the same one.

# 18

*11 December 2017*

The car has been at the bottom of the lake for twenty-three years now. Étienne reads and rereads the article on his computer screen.

Relieved. He could almost smile, despite how tragic the situation is.

*I'm not mad.*

17 August 1994. A stolen car. A body found inside it. If it's Clotilde, what was she doing there? Did someone come to find her there that evening? But who?

*No, impossible, it's just a coincidence, a mere concomitance.*

Why is this memory resurfacing after so many years? Does it have any meaning? A few days before he returns to his parents' house for Christmas?

Why didn't his colleague in La Comelle tell him about it? Do Adrien and Nina know about it?

*Obviously.*

Such a long time that he hasn't seen them.

Sometimes, he finds himself dialing the number of the shelter and then hanging up before anyone answers. Sometimes, too, he phones during the night, just to hear Nina's voice on the answering machine: "Our offices are open Monday to Friday, from nine to twelve and two to six. Saturday from nine to twelve. In case of an emergency, contact the local police on . . ."

Her deep, distinctive voice. "The voice of a smoker who's never smoked," as Adrien so rightly put it.

He misses his friends.

Or then, is it his youth that he can feel slipping away? That he'd like to hold onto?

The last time he saw Nina was over there, in 2003. Since then, they've not spoken anymore.

They'd sworn they'd be friends forever. All three had made a blood pact in sixth grade, had each pricked a fingertip and then mingled the drops of blood. "To eternal friendship." A kids' thing.

He picks up his guitar and strums a few chords. His wife and son are in bed. He likes this late hour, this solitude, when the town sleeps. Music from his headphones. Cleansing himself of the day. Looking up concerts on YouTube. Watching videos on Facebook. He could send a "friend request" to Nina. "Hi, how are you doing?" He'd just have to go to her profile and click on "add."

But every time he does, he changes his mind. What's he scared of?

If she replied to his "Hi, how are you doing?" what would he say to her? It's all too much.

A searing pain in his back makes him grimace. He takes a strong anti-inflammatory. Prescription only. *Handy having a doctor in the family*, he thinks.

He returns to his computer and types the keywords, "Lac de la Forêt, La Comelle, car found."

# 19

*21 April 1990*

Nina is alone in her room. Thinking about yesterday, Adrien's birthday, his synthesizer, Marie-Laure's words: "Marion was funny, kind, chatty, too . . . blond, almost ginger, green eyes. After your grandmother died, she put up a wall of silence."

Nina hears someone pushing open the gate outside her house. She recognizes Étienne's heavy step, the sound of the wheels as he puts his skateboard down on the steps. And if Paola doesn't bark, it's because she knows the person entering her territory.

Nina drags herself away from her thoughts, stashes the contents of an envelope under her pillow. What had intrigued her, when rummaging in her grandfather's bag, was the name and address being composed of letters cut out from a newspaper. Like in that old Clouzot film, *Le Corbeau*.

Nina had swiftly slipped the envelope into her pocket while Pierre Beau's back was turned. And then had read and reread these words:

> JEAN-LUC, YOU, THE IDIOT, THE CUKOLD, SHAME OF THE UPPER DISTRIC, YOUR GONNA DIE, ITS YER LAST YEAR, EVRYONE WILL THINK ITS AN AXIDENT NO ONE WILL KNOW NUTHING CEPT YOU, YOU KNOW WHAT YOU DONE AN WHY YOUR GONNA PAY AND THEY'LL SURE SCREW YER WIDOW.

Such hatred shocked her. For the first time, she decided to burn the letter. Not put it back with the rest of the mail.

Or should she go to the police? No, she'd be arrested, and her grandfather sacked from the Postal Service. And what if they found his fingerprints on it and accused him? But what if she destroyed it, and these nasty words weren't just empty threats? And if something did happen to the addressee? Jean-Luc Morand. Who is Jean-Luc Morand, 12 Place Charles-de-Gaulle in La Comelle?

Before deciding, she goes downstairs to welcome Étienne. He wants to be a cop, she thinks as she opens the door to him. What if she asked for his advice?

Étienne looks weird. He kisses her, asks if she's well, he's got something for her. And so Nina forgets the anonymous letter.

"But before I show you, you must get your Ventolin," he tells her, solemnly.

"Why?"

"Because I know you."

"But . . ."

"Obey," he orders her.

Rolling her eyes, Nina goes back up to her room to get her inhaler. Sometimes she wants to kill Étienne, he annoys her so much. Now she won't show him the letter, he's too much of a control freak.

She finds him in the kitchen. Filling a glass with water from the tap. He's put his backpack on the table.

Étienne is changing day by day. Of the three, he's growing up the quickest. A faint moustache is starting to appear on his upper lip. He finds it unsightly and shaves it off every morning. He has no acne, unlike Adrien. And if an unfortunate red blotch, the merest imperfection, appears on his face, he zaps it with creams and lotions of every kind. Étienne spends his time looking at himself in the mirror. His voice has started to break. He looks like he's seventeen, when he has yet to blow out his fourteen candles.

Nina has a quick puff of Ventolin in front of him.

He takes an envelope containing three photos out of his bag.

"My mother gave me this for you. They're photos of your mother that she found."

Nina looks at a black-and-white class photo. Girls in school smocks. The one in the middle holds a slate reading: "École Danton 1966–1967." Nina stares at it, wide-eyed. There are lots of girls. Before searching for her mother among them, Nina looks at the two other photos. They seem more recent. Almost identical. A group of seven middle-schoolers posing side by side and smiling. On the back it says: "Abbaye de Cluny 1973." You can tell it's windy, they're all holding back their hair, and squinting because of the sun.

"My mother told me it was a school trip they'd been on."

Étienne points out two people.

"Mine's there, yours here, right beside her."

Nina looks closely at the young woman of fifteen. A ghost with light eyes. Marion Beau is smiling, her teeth seem to protrude slightly, her hair is tied back in a ponytail. She's wearing a short skirt, a sweater, and white socks. Nina also looks at Marie-Laure, right beside her. Same face as today, even with the chubby cheeks.

"Are you sure that's Marion?" whispers Nina.

"Yes. The girl in the white socks."

"I don't look like her."

"Not remotely . . ."

"But then who do I look like?"

"Well . . . your father . . . no doubt. You can keep the photos. A gift from my mother."

"Not interested. She abandoned me."

Étienne feels uncomfortable. Sometimes, he finds Nina's reactions strange. She's too unpredictable. She's the one who asked Marie-Laure if she knew Marion, and now she doesn't want to know anymore. Girls sure are complicated.

"What you doing today?" he asks, to change the subject.

"Dunno. I'll study a bit. Adrien's expecting us at his place at four, to watch a movie. Will you stay with me in the meantime?"

"No, I'll see you at his."

Étienne is relieved to be off. He doesn't shut the door. A draft through the house. The three photos, left on the kitchen table, fall to the floor.

Nina closes the door behind him, picks them up, and goes to her room.

*

The following day is washing day. Pierre Beau is only working in the afternoon. He collects the bed linen in his room, opens the window, gets some fresh air on his bare mattress. Then he moves on to Nina's room. He usually knocks before entering, but she's at school.

A heap of clothes on the floor. A muddle of clean and dirty. Two cats sleeping on it. Seeing him arrive, one of them stretches lazily. Empty hot-chocolate cups. Piles of textbooks and notebooks. Hundreds of pages of sketches, on the floor, in portfolios, some hanging above the desk. Mainly of animals and his granddaughter's two friends. She draws so well. Maybe one day she'll be famous, and her works will be fought over around the world.

In the meantime, her mess must be tidied up. Pierre Beau sighs. Not easy, raising a young girl on your own. He thinks of Odile, his wife. If she was still of this world, none of this chaos would exist. Nothing would have been the same with her around.

On the walls, posters pinned side by side, Indochine, The Cure, Depeche Mode. Odile liked only Joe Dassin. Pierre was even a bit jealous of that. After his wife's death, he didn't throw the LPs away. He could have given them away, but he found the thought of someone else listening to them unbearable. Five years after Odile, it was Joe Dassin who died. Pierre thought: *He's going to meet her up there. This time I've really lost her. I can't compete.*

*And if you didn't exist,*
*Tell me why I'd exist . . .*

At least Dassin was always well-groomed and smartly dressed. In white suits. Not like the guys Nina exhibits in her room. With their hair sticking straight up and their lanky looks. Men wearing make-up, we really have seen it all. Strange times.

One morning, Odile's parents had moved into the house opposite his family's. To speak to her, Pierre had found no better excuse than to steal her bike one Thursday afternoon, and then return it to her the following Saturday. Three days during which he hid it. "Hello, I believe this is yours, I found it in the upper district, against a fence." Odile had pretended to believe him. They'd got married at seventeen.

And then Marion had been born. But no other children. Pierre would have liked three: a girl, a boy, a girl. Odile had stopped at the first girl.

Pierre Beau clambers over Nina's clutter, removes the duvet cover, sheets, and pillowcase. Three envelopes fall to the floor. Including one letter.

> JEAN-LUC, YOU, THE IDIOT, THE CUKOLD, SHAME OF THE UPPER DISTRIC, YOUR GONNA DIE, ITS YER LAST YEAR, EVRYONE WILL THINK ITS AN AXIDENT NO ONE WILL KNOW NUTHING CEPT YOU, YOU KNOW WHAT YOU DONE AN WHY YOUR GONNA PAY AND THEY'LL SURE SCREW YER WIDOW.

Pierre Beau reads the names on the envelopes. A few seconds to realize that Nina's opening the mail. He'd suspected as much. Didn't want to admit it to himself. One day, he'd thought Nina had a strange look about her as she hovered around his delivery bag. The look of someone guilty. The same look as when she sneaked a kitten home and hid it so he wouldn't notice a thing. Until the day she said: "*Please*, grandpa, we're keeping it, it's been living here for ages and ages anyhow."

He panics. Like lightning in his eyes. He's brought straight back to his daughter, Marion. His punishment. She was the same. Something like misfortune running in their veins. The mother has contaminated the daughter. The mother and the daughter. An affliction.

Anger makes him shake. He leaves the sheets and envelopes on the floor, goes out without closing the door behind him.

He wouldn't be able to say what he sees on the journey, apart from red. A desire to kill. All he's done for her. Working, staying alive, for her. Getting up, washing, having breakfast, going to work, getting back, preparing supper, for her. Tightening his belt, for her. Just for her. So she never lacked a thing. He can see her as a baby. The feeding bottles, the Gallia milk for the first three months and after, the teething, her vaccinations, her first steps. Buying her dresses, not knowing the right size, her shoes. Every morning she's there, and he can't quite believe that she's there. That she's growing up. That he's bringing her up, and she's bringing herself up.

Nina opens the mail. Behind his back. A betrayal. Has it gone on for long? If someone finds out, he'll lose his job. He'll be sacked for gross misconduct. He's not allowed to take mail home with him. He'll be judged. Certainly convicted. A suspended sentence, or maybe actual prison, and what will become of her? Who'll look after her? What will people say? They'll lodge complaints. Opening others' mail, that's serious. Nina will be sent to a foster home. Pierre's worst nightmare ever since she was born. *If I die, where will she go? It won't be her mother coming to collect her.*

He'll say it was him opening the mail. He'll say that Nina is innocent. That it's got nothing to do with her. That he alone is responsible. A scatterbrain.

He parks in front of the school. It's midday. Clusters of kids are starting to emerge. Nina lunches in the cafeteria. He enters the building, barges into some pupils, he looks like a madman, uncontrollable twitches making him blink. First, he sees Adrien, then Étienne. Then her. The three inseparables are chatting together in another group of pupils. A circle of three surrounded by around fifteen others.

Nina's wearing a sweatshirt. She hasn't put on her woolen jacket. He's forever asking her to cover up well, due to her asthma, but she just does what she wants. She's there, throat bare in April, when they say "ne'er cast a clout til May be out." What good are sayings if you don't apply them? Odile's favorite was: "A bird in the hand's worth two in the bush." Adrien mutters to Nina that *he*'s there because she looks up in his direction, stares at him, vaguely smiles, as if to say: "What are you doing here? Did I forget something at home?"

Seeing the rage in his eyes, ravaging his whole face, seeing his clenched, whitened fists, Nina immediately understands—the letters—and within seconds, changes color. He slaps her in the face once, and then a second time. A dull sound. That resonates. The silence spreads like wildfire out to the yard. The pupils are all shocked. They don't cry out, seem paralyzed, not understanding what's going on. An adult hitting a pupil inside the school . . .

It's the first time Pierre Beau has struck Nina. Just a kick up the backside at six because she'd daubed blue acrylic paint on all the vegetables in the garden.

He grabs her by the collar, lifts her off the ground while shaking her, and says, in a tone at once beseeching and chilling:

"But do you have any idea? Do you have any idea what you've done?"

He could kill her on the spot. Tear her apart. It's the silence around him that brings him back down to earth. Back to his senses.

*And me, what am I doing right now*?

He puts his granddaughter back down, slowly. As if his movements were slowed down by his own stupor. Nina, a marionette, cheeks red. The imprint of the fingers of the man who raised her. Tears in eyes. Like reflections, feverish. Pierre Beau realizes that the rest of the pupils are all looking at him. A supervisor, about twenty years old, approaches them, saying: "What's going on here?"

"I'm sorry," Nina barely whispers to her grandfather.

Distraught, Pierre Beau turns tail, almost like a thief. When he's back in his car, he clings to the steering wheel and starts sobbing. Nervous convulsions. He imagines that Odile is watching him from where she is, with Joe Dassin not that far from her. He imagines that she will never forgive him for what he's just done to their granddaughter.

"But you must admit, she really asked for it!"

Odile doesn't reply. She's in a huff. Joe Dassin's sure to take advantage of the situation, the bastard.

# 20

*12 December 2017*

Twenty-seven years later, I can see every detail of that morning in April again. That moment suspended in time. Us, looking at Pierre Beau, petrified. The two slaps, the grandfather's violence on the school premises, swooping down on Nina, incomprehension, between dream and reality. The speed of it all, too. It lasts less than a minute. Her dark little head, as if she'd come apart. She's wearing a black sweatshirt with gray butterflies on it. Butterflies like wilted flowers. She says sorry to her grandfather. I can still hear her, that sorry she whispers. She doesn't defend herself, doesn't seem angry with him. Everyone wonders what she's done. And then there are those who saw, and those who saw nothing. Later, after the "event," back home, they will imagine, suppose, extrapolate:

"She must have slept with someone. She's like her mother. The old man found out and couldn't tolerate it. Which one's she sleeping with? Beaulieu or Bobin? Both at the same time? She's pregnant. Pregnant at fourteen. Yes, that's it. A bun in the oven. What a shame."

After Pierre Beau's departure, at first there's just one question in the schoolyard, like a rumor being relayed: "Who's that old man?" Then the answer bursts out: "Her grandfather."

Embarrassed faces, twitches, forced laughter. "What've you got this afternoon?—An hour of study. The sports teacher's sick. And you?—English. Two hours of math with a test . . ." A few pupils, girls, ask Nina if she's O.K. They keep a certain distance from her. As if there was a safety zone to respect, a barrier separating Nina from the others, as if Étienne Beaulieu and Adrien Bobin had priority access, and lodged in every mind, behind every gesture, look, comment, were the words: "Hands off."

After, I remember that Adrien dragged Nina off to the infirmary, and Étienne just stood in the middle of the yard in a total daze, before going off with his sister to the cafeteria. That day, the grandfather's two slaps blew up the trio.

Nina blamed her mother. She told Adrien that she'd spent the previous day scratching out her mother's eyes on three photos Étienne had brought her. And because of that, she'd forgotten all the rest. And it was that rest her grandfather had found under her pillowcase. That thing that only Adrien knew about, the stolen letters. The secret they shared.

Her mother would always bring her bad luck. Best to drop her. Stop looking for photos, proof of her existence. Best to stop trying to understand what she was like and why she'd left Nina, like a bag of dirty laundry, at her father's. The only person who'd wanted her, and whom she was now letting down.

I'm just preparing the Christmas envelope for Nina's shelter. I slide the euros inside. Write: "Nina Beau, private and confidential" in capital letters, to avoid her recognizing my handwriting. As if she could possibly imagine it was me.

Through an association of ideas, I think back to the anonymous letter that betrayed her. The origin of the drama. I don't think Nina ever knew what Pierre Beau ended up doing with it. Whether he'd thrown it away, or delivered it. The only thing I do know today is that the addressee of that foul letter, Jean-Luc Morand, is still alive, and his so-called widow is, too. They compete in all the belote tournaments.

I always wait for nightfall to go up to the shelter, like a thief, and slide this unusual Christmas gift into the mailbox. Like those cowardly people who prefer to abandon their dogs, tied to a railing, during the night rather than face up to others' scrutiny in the light of day.

That's three times now I've been to the shelter since the beginning of this month. That's never happened before. My envelope is lying on the passenger seat.

In winter, I never go out after nine. I have my own habits now. Very little ones. Because habits are often little. My work, my TV series, my programs, social media sites, my meals, a pile of novels beside my bed.

In my headlights, plastic Santa Clauses hanging on houses, fir wreaths on doors, strings of flashing lights around windows, a "Merry Christmas" sign dangling from a storefront, about to fall.

A Christmas without snow. Here, it arrives later. Around mid-January.

I drive along the wasteland where, only a month ago, the Collège du Vieux-Colombier was growing old, rotting away alone. Abandoned by everyone. Even by those subjects that were popular, music, drawing, handicrafts.

This evening, it's as if it has gone under.

Fog, slow down, a patch of black ice. I take the small road leading to the shelter. Two or three scattered houses. Red and green lights on one of them, in the distance.

Christmas. In about ten days' time, Étienne will be turning up at his parents' to celebrate. Like every year. Like an obedient child returning home punctually. It's the only time in the year that he can be seen, once again, striding across the streets of La Comelle to buy his cigarettes at the tobacconist's. His big car parked in front of the church. Where he used to meet Nina and Adrien, on his skateboard, to go to the swimming pool.

Does he think about them? Does he think about *that*. Will he be bothered by the police if the body found in the car is Clotilde?

On the two occasions I saw him again, I ground to a halt. I parked my old bones in a corner and waited for the feeling to pass. To pass like an icy draft, a sudden heavy downpour, or sunburn.

Étienne Beaulieu paralyzes my movements, robs me of words.

Last year, I almost brushed against him going into the church. I wasn't expecting to see him. Although I know the only chance of coming across him is between 23 and 26 December. It was 6:20 P.M. In La Comelle, midnight mass is celebrated at 6:30 P.M. Wrapped in a long coat, I was walking up to the entrance, where a few stragglers were chatting outside, when I recognized his silhouette, his way of moving. He was barely a meter away from me. Alone. Squeezed into a thick, fur-lined bomber jacket. Head covered by a hood. My skin was on high alert, gooseflesh. *It's him.* He didn't see me, I glimpsed his mouth, a cigarette, his hand, a drag. Tall. Very tall. I always forget his height. I turned around, saw him from the back, walking toward the town center. What's left of it, at least.

I was left shaking afterwards, for a long time. A very long time. That evening, I took some photos of the baby Jesus for the paper, they were out of focus. I kept revisiting Étienne passing so close to me, dissecting every fraction of a second of that moment.

The shelter's car park is empty. Not a sound. The dogs must be sleeping. I leave the engine running and headlights on while I nip out. The mailbox is rusty. The flap creaks as I slip the envelope inside. A shiver runs through me. I'm half-terrified. As if I had something to feel guilty about.

"Is that you?"

I jump. Freeze.

"Is that you?" she asks again.

As if it was perfectly natural. Like a couple, married for twenty years, greeting each other at the end of the day: "Is that you? Did you have a good day? Relax, I've poured you a drink.—Are the kids home? Did your mother phone? What's in the freezer?"

Nina's silhouette appears, like a ghost, behind the wire mesh-covered door. Then her face in my headlights. Her pallor. Fine drizzle in her hair, spangles, frost.

"Yes, it's me."

# 21

*April 1990*

Back home from the school, Pierre Beau, still shaking, re-seals the stolen envelopes, puts them back among the other letters to be delivered, washes the sheets, remakes the beds, and never speaks of it again. Not even to Nina. That evening, when she gets in, racked with shame, wanting to disappear, bury herself alive, he serves her two *croque-monsieurs* with a green salad, telling her to eat up while it's still hot. Nina still bears the trace of his fingers on both cheeks. She daren't say she's not hungry, she swallows her tears and her salad without a word. Then she goes up to her room, sees her tidy bed, the fresh linen. Automatically, she looks for the anonymous letter under her pillow: gone. She opens the top drawer of her desk, takes out the envelope containing the three photos of her mother, half-opens the window, sets fire to the envelope with a lighter Étienne left behind, throws it onto the flat roof while repeating these words several times: "It's your fault, filthy whore."

The previous day, she'd strained her eyes trying to decipher her mother's face and body on the three photos. *What was she thinking about? Was she in love? Which of the other girls were her friends? Étienne's mother? Can friendship be passed down several generations? Did she confide in anyone? Did she already know my father? Do I have her eyes? Her nose? Her smile? What was her voice like? What's happened to the clothes she was wearing that day?*

She watches the envelope turning to ash in the gutter.

A few days later, she finds a letter addressed to her on the kitchen table. Going by the postmark, it was sent the previous day from La Comelle. She recognizes the handwriting on the envelope, that way of forming letters.

She goes up to her room to open it.

"*Mon petit*,

This letter you won't need to steal from my bag. This letter belongs to you. Reading other people's mail is a very serious matter, but I ask for your forgiveness. I should never have hit you. I was afraid. The fear of an old man who worries too much. What you did doesn't justify my hitting you in front of all your friends. I should never have touched you, you who are so small. You, defenseless. You, the apple of my eye. I'm ashamed. And I'll always feel ashamed of this uncalled-for and unacceptable action. I hope you will forgive me.

Your grandfather who loves you"

Pierre's shaky, childish handwriting touches Nina, profoundly. She sends him a postcard, in an envelope, in return. On the front, a lovely engraving of "The Blue Bird," in memory of the fairy tale her grandfather read her every evening when she was little.

"Grandpa,

I received your letter, and it's I who ask for your forgiveness.

I was looking for love letters. And just knowing that there might be some in your bag, it made me go a bit crazy. But I'll try never to do it again.

Sorry again, Grandpa.

*Ton petit*"

# 22

*15 July 1990*

Nina is going to celebrate her fourteenth birthday at the seaside, in Saint-Raphaël. She's packed her suitcase. Pierre Beau gave her Odile's. "You can keep it." A suitcase she'd always seen stored on top of the wardrobe in her grandfather's bedroom. Brown, made of imitation leather and cardboard, old-fashioned.

She phoned Adrien:

"What's your suitcase like?"

"A kind of hippie bag belonging to my mother. With pink flowers, like something out of Woodstock."

"My case is a hundred years old. It stinks of mothballs."

"D'you want to swap?"

"I can't. It's my grandmother's. If Grandpa found out, it would upset him."

Pierre Beau gave her ten 100-franc bills. It's the first time she has so much pocket money in her little coin purse. He has also prepared a crate of vegetables to take on vacation. Nina feels ashamed of turning up with tomatoes and green beans, but she hadn't dared say so to her grandfather. She can see he's doing what he can, that he, too, would have liked to take her to the seaside.

Nina is lying on her bed, eyes wide open. It's three in the morning. She's listening to the beating of her heart. In an hour, her grandfather will knock on her door, and she'll be ready. Then he'll drop her off at the Beaulieus'. She'll get into the back of the Renault Espace, along with Adrien, Étienne, and Louise.

And at the end of the journey, there will be the sea. Like in the film, *Le Grand Bleu*, that they've seen three times. "A film by us," Adrien had joked.

She must have gotten up, opened her suitcase, checked its contents, and reclosed it twenty times. She feels bad about leaving Paola and her cats at home, but then, it is to go and see the sea. She's been waiting to do that for years. It's like having an appointment with a dream.

What's she going to do for a whole hour? No way can she sleep.

In the neighboring room, Pierre Beau isn't sleeping, either. He's thinking about Odile's suitcase. He never could bring himself to throw it away. The last time he'd opened it was when he'd returned from the hospital. There hadn't even been time for Odile's belongings to be unpacked. She'd been carried off in a matter of days.

They had arrived too late.

If he could turn back the clock . . .

They had bought that suitcase in 1956, at the Grand Bazar store in Autun. Odile wanted an indoor drying rack, for rainy days. And when she'd seen the suitcase at a reduced price, she'd said to Pierre: "Shall we buy it? It will be for our holidays."

They had never set off on holiday. Until the day when Odile set off, but alone.

On summer Sundays, Pierre and Odile would bathe in the rivers, and in the Lac de la Forêt, dance at hops and local celebrations. Sometimes they went to the Lac des Settons to ride on a pedalo and picnic under the trees, but never had they gone beyond the Morvan region.

Once, they had fallen asleep in the same sleeping bag, squashed like sardines in a tin.

Tonight, Pierre Beau hears Odile's laughter, as her eyes were counting the stars.

It's the first time Nina is going to be away from home. Since the day Marion left her there, she's never been away. An emptiness he's preparing himself for. In his mind, he runs through the days to come. Days off without any rest, like every year during July. He'll work in the garden, walk Paola, repaint the rivets, do the spring cleaning in summer. He'll keep his hands occupied.

He's rather ashamed that he's never taken his granddaughter to the seaside. It's not that expensive to rent an apartment through the workers' council. It's not a question of money, but of changing one's habits, leaving behind La Comelle's roads, driving for a long time, going far away, toward the unknown, getting lost, figuring out road maps, discovering new faces, putting on swimming trunks.

He tries to remember the last time he wore swimming trunks. At least thirty years ago.

Finally, it's time to set off. Everyone says their goodbyes beside the Renault Espace. Nina watches Joséphine hugging her son tight. Her grandfather kisses her half-heartedly, awkwardly. But that's not what matters. What matters is the love. Nina has a lump in her throat, it's the first time she's leaving him. He whispers in her ear: "Sure you've got your Ventolin?"

Everyone takes their places, fastens their seatbelts. Marc Beaulieu behind the wheel, Marie-Laure in the passenger seat—she'll drive occasionally if he wants a rest. The children and crates of vegetables at the back. Goodbyes are said with a wave. Pierre Beau and Joséphine Simoni side by side on the pavement in the dark.

Nina thinks that, in life, there are those who stay and those who leave. And then there are those who abandon.

# 23

*12 December 2017*

"I suspected those envelopes of money were you . . ." Nina says to me.

I feel as if I've been caught out. Almost guilty. I get back in my car, switch off the engine, and the headlights, return to her.

She turns the key to open the gate.

"You knew I'd moved back?"

"Yes," she replies.

Nina pours some coffee into an "I Love La Comelle" mug for me.

In her office, three weak neon lights.

Posters about sterilization.

The portrait of a cat with a missing eye: "We all have a chance of being adopted here."

Photos of dogs and cats pinned to a board. They each have a name. Diego, Rosa, Blanquette, Nougat . . . I wonder if it's Nina who names them.

At the school library, there was a dictionary of names. Nina would circle some in pencil. Those she'd give to her children later.

I can feel her looking hard at me. I don't dare look up at her. I stare at her hands. As a teenager, she'd put red polish on her fingernails, they'd end up chipped. I loathed it. That slovenliness.

I feel like standing up and hugging her. But after what I did to her the last time I saw her, how could I dare?

I'm already lucky that she asked me in and offered me a mug of her dishwater.

After a long silence, I say: "What are you doing at the shelter at this hour? It's late."

"I was waiting for you. Well, I think I was," she replies.

*

*15 July 1990*

Saint-Raphaël.

"We're here . . ." They said these words in turn. Each in a different way. Marie-Laure, happy. Marc, relieved. Louise, shyly. Étienne, for Nina.

Nina's heart is beating erratically, happiness putting it out of synch, her eyes scour the landscape, searching for the blue.

Inside the car, a smell of chips. Empty packets. Hours on the road behind you. A stop for gas and a coffee near Valence. Tired legs, aching muscles.

They half-open the windows. In the distance, a blue line. The sea, as if the sky had sat on the ground. It reminds Adrien of an Alain Souchon song.

*You'll see that one fine morning, tired,*
*I'll go and sit down on the pavement next door . . .*

Étienne whispers:

"Nina, look, there's your sea."

Adrien puts his hand on Nina's shoulder and gives it a little squeeze. As if to say to her: "At last, it's there."

"Kids, while we go and collect the keys to the house, you can wait for us on the beach," says Marie-Laure.

Louise wants to stay in the car with her parents. She'd rather leave the others alone. The three together: a wall, an insuperable barrier.

Adrien, Étienne, and Nina jump out of the car. Blinding light. It's midday, it's very hot. Towels and kids' games on the sand. The sea lies before them, vast, never-ending, sparkling, alive. *The sea is water that's shivering*, thinks Nina. *It's water that breathes in and breathes out*. Its color is like nothing she's ever seen before. It's less beautiful on postcards and TV than in reality. It's powerful, paradoxical, at once spellbinding and unsettling, exactly how Nina imagines freedom to be. *La Chèvre de Monsieur Seguin*. The worst story. The most grotesque she's ever read, and yet that she rereads often. When her grandfather was donating stuff to charity last year, she'd retrieved her *Contes pour Enfants Sages* from the bags.

Her grandfather. She wishes he was here. That he could see what she's seeing. Breathe in what she's breathing in, the wind carrying the sunlight, the sweetness, and the musk.

Étienne hoists Nina up onto his right shoulder and strides quickly across the sand, avoiding the towels. Nina laughs loudly, lets out little yelps. Adrien follows them, casting panicky glances all around him—parasols and bare breasts. It's the first time he's seeing the exposed breasts of women sunbathing. He's already seen some in films and magazines, but never in real life. Whereas Nina is discovering the sea for the first time, for him, it's breasts. A faint, anticipatory smile plays on his lips.

Étienne takes off his sneakers and then Nina's, while she struggles, crying: "No! Stop it!"

Étienne goes into the sea, with Nina still on his shoulder, walks a few meters and then throws her, fully dressed, into the water. It stings, it's cool, it's salty. Adrien goes into the water without taking any clothes off, either. The three of them swim in their clothes laughing, splash each other. They're overexcited. Étienne screams: "I'm the king of the world!" He hoists Nina back on his shoulders so she can dive in, headfirst.

Étienne hasn't been like this for a long time. As if he were letting go. As if he wasn't controlling anything anymore: his appearance, his style, his clothes, his hair, his skin, his good grades.

They remain like this for a long while, all three of them, gradually calming down. Letting the slowness enter their every pore, licking the water, spitting it right out again. Their clothes like rubber rings of fabric, wet butterfly wings. They float on their backs, their skin drinking in the motion of their own bodies. They hold hands. Form a star, their very first. A unique star that's landed on the water.

From time to time, Nina sings "Tes Yeux Noirs," mixing up the words on purpose.

*Come here, come with me, don't leave again without me . . .*

*Go on, come here, stay here, don't leave again without me . . .*
*And we'll see each other every day once we're back . . .*
*And your dark eyes are shining*
*Where d'you go when you leave, to nowhere . . .*
*And you take your clothes, you put them on . . .*

Swimming in the sky.

*

Out of politeness, I finish the disgusting coffee Nina served me. *Cat piss*, I think to myself while looking at a photo of a sheepdog, Banjo, seven years old.

"I saw your name in the *Journal de Saône-et-Loire*," she says to me.

"I temp there when the correspondent is on vacation, like right now. Did you read about the Lac de la Forêt?"

"The car, yes . . . Do you think it's *her*? That she was down there for all these years?"

"They don't know yet. They found a skeleton."

"How dreadful."

"The only thing linking Clotilde to that stolen car is the date."

"17 August 1994 . . . the day of the funeral," mutters Nina.

There follows a long silence. I know she's thinking about Étienne. Like me. But doesn't say his name.

"You don't want a cat by any chance?" she asks me.

"By any chance?"

Nina leans over, lifts a blanket: a tiny black kitten is sleeping in a shoebox, a man's shoe, size 43.

While I can, I look at Nina's hands, her fine, slender fingers, her fingernails cut short. I pretend to look at the kitten when in fact I'm breathing her in. I'm trying to find her vanished vanilla smell. I want to close my eyes; I want to spend what's left of my life close to her. Sometimes, nostalgia is a curse, a poison.

"It's just been found beside some trash cans. You don't want to take it with you? Black cats, I find them hard to home. That old superstition about bad luck . . ."

"Alright."

"You'll take good care of it?"

"Yes."

"Better than of me?"

". . ."

"And Étienne?" she questions me. "Have you seen him again?"

"No."

She returns to her thoughts. Removes an imaginary speck of dust from her sweater, and finally asks:

"And Adrien? Is he well?"

"I think he's well."

She looks me straight in the eye. She hasn't changed. Still direct, open, straight to the point.

"I miss him," she says.

As though she regretted what she'd just said, she shoves the shoebox into my arms. The kitten opens one eye, then closes it. I bury my nose in its fur. A smell of straw.

"It has been weaned. I'll give you some pouches of food. For the first few days, keep it indoors. It's winter, anyhow, so it has no business being outdoors. I'll also give you a tray and a bag of litter. Never forget to leave a bowl of fresh water out for it."

"How did you know that I was coming this evening?"

"At the end of the year, you always come by between 15 and 20 December, no? Thanks for the money."

"You really knew it was me?"

"Who else?"

She puts on a coat.

"Could you give me a lift home? Christophe has gone to see the veterinarian in the shelter's car. I'm exhausted, I'd like to go home."

"Christophe, is he your husband?"

"No, he's an employee. The tall, bearded guy you give the dried food to."

"You also know that the dried food is me?"

"Yes."

"O.K. I'll take you home."

She sits in the passenger seat. I switch on the ignition and the song

"La Vie est Belle," by Indochine, booms out. I switch off the radio, she says:

"Leave it on, please, I love that song."

"You still like them?"

"Of course."

*We'll go and do life, succeed at least at that*
*We'll go and do the night, as far as you can . . .*
*Life is beautiful and cruel at once, like us sometimes*
*Me, I was born to be only with you . . .*

Nina hums along while focusing on the road as if she were driving.

"What are you going to call it?" she finally asks.

"Who?"

"Your cat."

"Is it a girl or a boy?"

"A male, I think. It's too young for me to be sure."

"Nicola. With no 's.' Like Indochine's Nicola Sirkis."

Nina smiles for the first time.

# 24

*22 September 1991*

They're fifteen years old. They've just started high school, have chosen their courses together.

The look on the guidance counselor's face when all three of them walk into her office together.

Étienne is doing option A1, literature and math, Adrien A2, literature and modern languages, and Nina A3, literature and fine arts. They have several subjects in common, share the same teachers and classrooms.

None of them does a thing without the other two. Decisions are made together. Which trousers, which dress, which music, which T-shirt, which party, which film, which book, at whose place.

Nina and Étienne often squabble. She says that Étienne thinks he's her big brother, orders her about: "Don't do your hair like that," "Speak less loudly," "No, you're really being too stupid now," "Come on, stop showing off." He seems to be forever contradicting her just to annoy her.

Adrien calms thing down, never raises his voice. Feels closer to Nina than to Étienne. He relishes those rare, privileged moments when it's just the two of them in Nina's room. Just to listen to her talking, explaining how she feels, help her tidy her things, pose for her to draw him for the umpteenth time.

"Don't move."

When she hands him the portrait she's done of him, Adrien never recognizes himself.

Of the three, Étienne is the most rebellious, Adrien the touchiest, Nina the most sensitive.

The distance Nina feared would grow between them when they

got older isn't there. She hadn't had to find herself a best girl friend. Even when Étienne wonders out loud what size his penis will be: "Will it be long or wide, or both?" "How long does it keep growing?" "D'you think it stops when you're twenty?" "D'you think it's hereditary? That I'll have the same one as my father and brother?"

Such questions don't make her feel uncomfortable. They broach the subjects that a brother and sister never would. It's as if, for Étienne, Nina is neutral territory, genderless.

"I'm your Switzerland," she often tells him.

In addition to their unshakeable friendship, they're bound together by the tunes and lyrics of the songs they spend hours composing. United by a plan for the future that nothing and no one can prevent: leaving after the baccalauréat. They'll rent an apartment. Share the bills. Do casual work, and wind up on the stage at L'Olympia.

Adrien secretly dreams of recognition, he wants his compositions to be lauded to shut his father up, and never have to smell his chlorophyll breath ever again. Étienne dreams of what accompanies fame: the gilded existence, the easy life. Nina hopes to sing, draw, and fall passionately in love. She says it loud and clear:

"For me, it will be the love of my life, or nothing."

She wants to marry and have three children. Two girls and a boy. She's already chosen their names: Nolwenn, Anna, and Geoffroy. She'll draw them, and sing for both them and her husband.

"First you'll have to *find* yourself a husband," Étienne often taunts her.

Despite their flirtations elsewhere, their puberty, their hormones leading them toward other desires, other bodies, they never tire of sharing their anxieties, their chewing gum, and their opinions.

"Me, I'm left-wing," states Nina. "I'm for sharing."

"Me, too," agrees Étienne, just to go against his father.

"Same here," murmurs Adrien, who worships François Mitterrand because his favorite novel is *Belle du Seigneur*.

*

Like every year, the funfair has arrived on the square outside the church. La Comelle disguises itself for one weekend only. In the streets, smells of marshmallow and burning.

Since early afternoon, Étienne has been at the shooting range. Adrien and Nina are squashed together on the Waltzer, humming along to the hits booming from the loudspeakers, "*Bouge de là*," "*Auteuil Neuilly Passy*," "Black and White," "*À nos actes manqués*."

With her hair flying in the wind, Nina checks out the older boys. Those of her age don't appeal to her.

She has completely forgotten that Gilles Besnard she was infatuated with two years ago. One evening he kissed her outside the school gym, and she hated his tongue shoved into her mouth, his smoky saliva. They parted with sore lips, muttering: "Bye, see you tomorrow."

Nina phoned Adrien in a panic: "What on earth do I say to him if I come across him? It's nerve-racking." Adrien told her that she just needed to say hi normally, with a peck on the cheek. And that was it.

With Adrien, everything is simple, calm, clear. Apart from that day when he smashed Py's glasses, Adrien is a river whose currents and whirlpools can't be seen.

From time to time, Étienne comes over and squeezes in between Nina and Adrien to do a circuit on the Waltzer with them. Then goes back to shooting. When he wins a prize, he asks Nina to choose between a polar bear and a glitter pen. He tries to win the big stuff—hi-fi system, TV, video recorder—even though he already has all that at home. Girls come and hang around him. Stuck beside him for hours watching him take aim. Sometimes, he deigns to leave with one of them, often the prettiest, the most made-up, the one with breasts and no acne. He's too scared it might be catching. He does a circuit on the bumper cars with the chosen one, kisses her, then goes back to shoot more balloons.

On Saturdays, they've got into the habit of sleeping together. The boys each have a camp bed in Nina's room. Pierre Beau doesn't disapprove, he considers Adrien and Étienne part of the family. But he does prefer them to sleep at his rather than letting Nina stay at theirs.

Sweet little Nina has changed. Pierre barely recognizes his granddaughter. It was better when she sneaked animals into the house.

Now, she makes lots of noise. Slams doors, turn her stereo right up so the walls shake, screams that he doesn't understand her, bursts into tears at the slightest problem, rolls her eyes whenever he makes a remark about her, spends hours in the bathroom, forgets to wipe off the traces of her henna hair dye on the basin, locks herself into her room, covers herself in makeup like a stolen van, shrieks in outrage as soon as a pimple appears on one of her cheeks.

She becomes sweet again when asking him permission to go to a friend's birthday party.

"We're all sleeping over there. The parents'll be there . . . Please, Grandpa . . . please . . . I got 17 in my nat-sci test."

"What kind of subject is 'nat-sci'?" he risks asking her.

She rolls her eyes.

"Well, natural sciences, of course," she tells him, as if he were senile.

Pierre knows that that subject doesn't feature in her course track, but lets it go.

Pierre had better not say no to her, or Nina turns into a tyrant. So he gives in. He hands out yeses like gold stars to have peace. And she's good at school, so she'll do alright in life.

When one of her classmates is celebrating a birthday, everyone turns up with a sleeping bag and stays the night. The parents are there, but not in the same room. They knock on doors before going in. The windows stay open to allow the wreaths of cigarette smoke to clear away.

No more afternoon snacks and bottles of Oasis. They yearn for sensations, and try whatever is forbidden them: alcohol, cigarettes, cannabis, shisha.

As an asthmatic, Nina is the only one who doesn't touch all that. She's always less stoned than everyone else. Even when drunk, it's she who holds back girls' hair when they're vomiting, watches out for the wandering hands of guys trying to take advantage of them, doesn't hesitate to kick their asses. Everyone knows it and has accepted her. "If you invite Étienne, Nina and Adrien will be there.

If you invite Nina, Étienne and Adrien will be there, too." Adrien is rarely invited. But since he's no trouble, he's tolerated. He's too taciturn to interest fifteen-year-olds, apart from certain more mature girls who appreciate his company and his silences. And he also reads, writes songs, plays the synthesizer, and drinks tea. Certain girls adore musicians who read and drink tea.

# 25

*12 December 2017*

Nina lowers the sun visor, has a quick look in the mirror, and puts it back up. On her knees is the shoebox, in which the kitten, Nicola, still seems to be sleeping.

What am I going to do with it when it wakes up? Am I capable of looking after it? I'm aware that I've never had a dog or cat of my own. Not even a snail.

"Do you think I've changed?" she asks me.

"No."

"Surely a bit."

"No. Not even a bit."

"I'm forty-one, for goodness' sake!"

"It's not age that makes people change."

"Oh really, what is it then?"

"Don't know. Their life perhaps."

"Well, in that case . . . at least I've given a little!"

"Yes, but *he* didn't take everything from you. The proof, you haven't changed, I swear. You're the same Nina Beau."

"No, I'm not the same."

"Where do you live," I ask.

"You know very well."

"How would I know?"

"You think I don't see you driving past mine from time to time? Looking to see if I'm home . . ."

" . . . "

She says nothing more. Focuses again on the road. In three minutes, she'll be getting out. I drive slowly. I'd like to play the breaking-down trick on her, but we're just five-hundred meters from her house. I should have made at least one wrong turn.

"Shall I switch the music back on?"

"No, thanks," she replies, sadly.

I park outside her place. When she gets out, she murmurs:

"Thanks for the ride."

"Will we see each other again?" I ask.

She has a quick look at the kitten.

"Bye-bye, Nicola. Be good."

She slams the car door. Turns tail. The silhouette of an adolescent. From the back, she could be fifteen. I have tears in my eyes. She opens the gate to her house. Disappears into the night.

She hadn't answered me.

*

Nina goes inside. Closes the door behind her. Listens to the car's engine fading, escaping. Throws off her shoes, a tiny stone under one heel. Exhaustion. Aching muscles. Cats around her legs, six in all, old ones, lame ones, one-eyed ones. She harbors those who've had the hardest knocks, the least likely to be chosen.

"Hello, old soldiers!"

She coughs, must have caught cold. Or maybe it's her asthma. After all the years she's had it, she can tell the difference between an impending attack, and the start of a nasty cold. She goes to the kitchen, sings to the cats while feeding them:

*Life is beautiful and cruel at once, like us sometimes*
*Me, I was born to be only with you . . .*
*Your blood and mine, we'll become just one*
*And we'll be invincible, succeed at least at that . . .*

She warms up some of yesterday's soup in the microwave. Two *biscottes* and some cheese spread. She vacuums quickly to get rid of the cat hairs, half-opens the windows for five minutes.

She turns up the heat in her bedroom, where it's cold because of the cat-door, through which the cats are endlessly toing and froing between the house and the garden.

She takes a seriously hot shower, gets into bed, three cats on it already. Switches on her computer, checks first her own Facebook page, then the shelter's. She's received a message on the former. A message from Romain Grimaldi, giving her news of Bob, with a photo of the dog asleep on the sofa beside a plump cat.

> Hello Madame Beau, all's well. I knew Bob would be my dog as soon as I saw his photo on the shelter website; we're never apart. My old Radium has adopted him, too. Hope you're well, see you soon.
>
> Romain G.

Without thinking, Nina types on her keyboard:

What are you doing this evening?

She can see he's online, and he replies immediately:

Nothing in particular, it's 9:00 P.M., I've had supper. Bob and Radium have, too. Why?

Would you like to meet up?

Now?

Yes, now.

To talk about Bob?

No. Where do you live?

7, Rue Rosa-Muller.

I'm on my way.

O.K. . . .

She gets up. Goes into the bathroom. Puts some salve onto her chapped lips. Pulls on her favorite jeans, the ones she hasn't worn for ages, and her only decent sweater, black, that she wears for big occasions, so never, aside from the mayor's New Year address. She runs her hand through her hair. Don't think. Above all, don't think. She doesn't have her car. Rue Rosa-Muller is right beside the church. A ten-minute walk from her house.

She walks quickly, with half of her face warmed by her breath, cocooned by the collar of her coat. Keep warm, don't think. Striding along these pavements she knows by heart. Past fences, houses, gardens, sheds, garages, store windows that she could recite like a poem. Walking toward the church, like when she'd meet Adrien and Étienne there to go to the pool. Her adult footsteps in her child's footsteps. Frost in her hair. How many years has it been since she last walked toward someone?

## 26

*February 1993*

To get to the high school, ten kilometers outside La Comelle, they take the bus at 7:00 A.M., arriving at around 7:35, having picked up pupils living in isolated spots along the way, those waiting at the edge of the road like the condemned. They're rounded up in the silence of morning sleepiness, all that can be heard is the bus's double doors opening and closing. The adolescents are still half-asleep. They went to bed late, listened to *Lovin' Fun* on the radio, the Doc and Difool answering questions—identification, flirting, acne, fear, phobias, G spot, shame, condoms, lubricant, sodomy—with their ears pressed to their transistors, trying to detect each time whether they know the girl or boy daring to ask their existential question live on air, or talk about their love life and sexuality. "My girlfriend doesn't get wet, it's hopeless."

For a small half-hour, in the yard, under the awnings, the pupils chat, smoke, finish homework against a wall to avoid a detention. Crosses are marked on calendars, differentiating between days of lessons and days of vacation. They ask each other questions on the topic of the next test. They talk about AIDS, global hunger, where to rip their jeans, grunge music, the Israel-Palestine conflict, the TV series *Beverly Hills, 90210*. The girls want to look like Madonna or Mylène Farmer, and they read poetry by Verlaine; the boys want to look like Kurt Cobain or Bono, and they admire the tennis player Jim Courier and the footballer Youri Djorkaeff on the TV.

Classes start at 8:00 A.M.

Even though they're in eleventh grade, the three always do their homework together. Étienne is still loath to do any work. Dawdles a bit, glances at Adrien's and Nina's notes, often merely copies. A math tutor comes to his house on Sunday afternoons, to help him catch up in the many areas he's behind. He doesn't dare snap at his parents: "For god's sake, not on Sunday."

His father always views him with disappointment, or indifference, he can't really tell. Étienne can clearly see how Marc Beaulieu looks at his older brother, smiles at him, and always gazes fondly at Louise. But as for him, nothing. Indifference. If he deigns to look at Étienne, it's always forced.

At around 7:30 P.M., while Pierre Beau is busy preparing supper in the kitchen, Adrien and Étienne go home.

Adrien returns to his mother, they pick at food on the coffee table in the sitting room, in front of the eight o'clock news. Adrien feels more at ease, not having to eat in silence, just him and Joséphine. Despite the sound of bombs going off, the terrible images of civil wars and other conflicts, these TV suppers remind him that every evening can seem like fun, a picnic between four walls.

Étienne always drags his feet going home. Darkness falling at five o'clock makes him terribly anxious. If he could, he'd drink alcohol every evening to ease the tight knot in his stomach at this time. A whiskey-and-Coke calms him down, makes him laugh at everything, it's like he's flying, like all his organs were pumped with helium.

When he gets home, Étienne finds Louise there. He's not interested in her, barely greets her. He goes down to the cellar to play his synthesizer. Then, sitting at the counter in the kitchen, he has supper prepared by Madame Rancoeur, who keeps an eye on them before going home.

Once he's eaten, Étienne goes back down to play on his keyboard or his games console. When his parents come home at around nine o'clock, he goes back upstairs, exchanges a few words with Marie-Laure—"Good day at school? Were you nice to your sister? Did you eat enough? Time for your shower?"—and then he goes up to his room, watches TV, or flicks through porn mags he nicked from under a pile of sheets in his brother's cupboard. Old issues with well-thumbed pages, but in which the girls always seem to be twenty years old. He masturbates and falls into a deep sleep.

On this morning of February 1993, the high-schoolers don't catch the usual bus. They all talk and laugh loudly. They've left their sleepiness back at home. Along with their textbooks and notebooks. They're off to celebrate Shrove Tuesday. All pupils and teachers from the region will be gathering in Chalon-sur-Saône to parade in the streets. On everyone's lap there's a bag containing a sandwich and a bottle of water.

Boys dressed as girls, in wigs and heels, giggle as they lift up their skirts, revealing their long hairy legs. Others, dressed as a Bioman, Darth Vader, or Spider-Man, watch the landscape go by while discussing last night's TV. Étienne is dressed as an American footballer, his helmet hindering him from flirting with a girl from the grade above. She's sitting on him. Perched on his left thigh. She's gesticulating, talking too loudly, touching his hands, leaning over him. Nina, dressed as a fairy, is dying to whack her head a couple of times with her magic wand.

"She really gets on my nerves, that girl. I'd sure like to mess up her blow-dry," she mutters, with irritation, to Adrien.

He's been gloomy since getting on the bus, he tells her she's just jealous.

"Garbage. I'm used to seeing Étienne with tarts, that one just gets on my wick. And anyhow, what's up with you? You've been sulking all morning."

"Nothing," replies Adrien. "Nothing at all."

"Well, it doesn't seem like it. Is it your cowboy costume that's getting you down?"

Adrien shrugs his shoulders: what nonsense. Three of Étienne Daho's songs keep going round in his mind. "Il ne dira pas," "Mythomane," and "Cowboy."

*Cowboy, return to your horse and gun*
*The car park's full, so turn the page of your picture book . . .*

Louise is at the front of the bus with her classmates. The young ones, in ninth grade, always sit at the front.

*There are always people smaller than you*, thinks Adrien. Those put in the front row in group photos.

Louise is dressed as Columbine. Three black tears drawn on her cheek. From time to time, she turns around to watch her brother, Nina, and Adrien. Several times her eyes meet Adrien's, and he doesn't look down. He faintly smiles.

Saint-Raphaël, their furtive memories combine.

Adrien feels like screaming. He remains calm. Digs his fingernails into his hands. Nina's in a huff with him. He sees that there are tears in her eyes. Her adorable little face looks upset. Adrien takes a deep breath, nudges her with his elbow, Nina turns to him, looks glum. Adrien shows her the fake revolver he's attached to his belt, draws it, aims at the girl sitting on Étienne.

"Want me to bump her off?"

Nina bursts out laughing.

# 27

*12 December 2017*

I daren't take Nicola out of his box, I'm scared of breaking him. He purrs in his sleep. The litter's there, its tray still wrapped in a Label Nature paper bag. I placed everything in the middle of the room. I observe the kitten the way one observes a stupid mistake. The list of those stupid mistakes started a very long time ago. The goldfish brought home from the fair, playing hooky, cheating, shoplifting, driving after drinking, letting off firecrackers during a heat wave in a parched garden, forgetting the bath tap's running, the marriage proposal, the wrong answer, the wrong person, knowing that but going ahead anyway, making promises one won't keep, missing trains, signing up for store cards, canceling at the last moment what one's been waiting forever for, going out into the cold with bare arms, looking down to avoid greeting someone because it's neither the day nor the moment and regretting it forever, signing a bill of sale at the notary's, committing, pulling out, disgusting alcohol, ghastly evenings, the notorious one glass too many, the miserable mornings-after, getting into a car with a stranger, the patterned sweater bought as a change from black and never worn, the latest book by the writer you never manage to finish—"But this time I'll love it"—going to sale days, scraping together, rummaging, gossiping, criticizing, sniggering, the impossibly tight trousers you'll wear when you've lost weight, all that stuff in the cupboards of our lives, but that make up our lives.

And being ashamed of Nina when I was twenty-four years old. Bumping into her in Paris, in the foyer of a theater, and behaving badly. She comes up to me, hugs me. I tense up. She whispers a happy, timid good evening to me. A "Good evening. You see, I came, I'm proud of you."

"Oh, hi."

Yes, really, merely replying to her: "Oh, hi."

Shame on me. I'm young. Well-dressed. My name is on the bill for the play she's come to see. I think I'm something that I'm not. That no one ever is. Never take yourself for what you aren't.

I hear her uncouth accent. And that's all I hear. Yet Nina has never had any accent. I want to talk to those who know how to talk, who use those lovely words. Not to the denizens of La Comelle, as if they stank of a childhood I disown, my provincial origins.

Nina blanches, smiles, stiff in her outfit that looks new to me, she's dressed up for the occasion. She wanted to surprise me.

She stays, doesn't leave, doesn't turn her back on me, finds her seat in the auditorium, clutching her ticket, a ticket she has bought.

She hadn't received an invitation.

She's in the rows at the back. At the end, I see her applauding vigorously.

I make sure I disappear into the dressing rooms. I picture her waiting for me on the pavement, for a while. In vain. Going home alone. Finding mitigating circumstances for me.

Shame and regrets don't attenuate over the years.

# 28

*12 December 2017*

Romain Grimaldi opens the door to her. He sees only her dark eyes. Bright pools.

Nina says good evening and throws her coat onto a chair. Along with the coldness she's ridding herself of. Putting far away from herself. She blows into her hands. On the sofa, Bob lifts his muzzle, recognizes her, comes over to welcome her.

"Hello, old boy."

"Would you like something to drink?" Romain asks her.

She turns to him, looks straight at him. Approaches. He smiles at her, awkwardly.

She says: "My body has been dead for years. Skin that's no longer touched, it dies. A body that's never looked at, it's in permanent winter. Layers of cold accumulate. Never-ending snow. There are no other seasons anymore. No more desire. No more hope of return. It's frozen in the past, stuck somewhere. I don't know where. It's afraid. I'm afraid. My body has no present anymore. I'd like to make love. I'd like to know if it's forgotten everything. If it still knows anything. I like you. And me, do you like me?"

He answers yes.

A yes that also questions. A wary yes. That's scared of her, of her candor. Music that spells danger.

"I'd like something strong to drink."

"Me too."

Romain goes into the kitchen. Nina hears him opening cupboards, taking glasses out. Her heart is beating like when she discovered the sea. She takes time to look around the sitting room. Lamps, books, a coffee table, the TV on mute, a documentary on

India, the Ganges, women in saris. Don't think. Trust yourself, for once.

He returns, holding two glasses, a brown liquid, bourbon. They down it in one go while holding each other's gaze. He's wearing jeans and a black sweater, like her. Twins that a mother's dressed the same.

He opens his mouth to speak, to say something, they kiss on a shared impulse. Neither makes the first move, they make it together. Despite the shaking, some awkward swaying, they know how to find each other, touch each other. They rediscover soft gestures, slowness, and swift hands. Feeling their way. He pulls off his sweater, his T-shirt. She likes the smell of his skin, that's the first step. Once you like the smell of the other, associate it with something familiar, of the same sensory strain, all the rest follows. He kisses well.

She'd not been mistaken in going for him. Sensitivity and sensuality.

His tongue against hers. She truly thought that would never happen to her again. Someone else.

She can't quite grasp it. She's almost in a state of hypnosis, of unreality. She runs her hands through his thick hair, right now she'd like to make him melt into her, all of him. His evening stubble pricks her cheeks, her chin, her mouth. She, in turn, pulls off her clothes. He tastes her skin, a sweet cocktail of vacations.

He says: "We'll be more comfortable in my bedroom." She responds: "Switch off the light."

He asks if she's sure that's what she wants, darkness. Yes, she's sure.

He smiles. They smile.

He pours them another drink before going upstairs. Last one for the road. All that way to go. The stairs. Barefoot on the carpet. They're disheveled and burning hot. They perspire against each other. And groan. A prelude. *What's more delightful than the preliminaries*, thinks Nina. Adolescence perpetuated. It's even better than promises. Than a word one's going to keep. They hold each other, cling to each other, meet each other, hurry, they have time. The whole night before them. It belongs to them. Rich in the moment. Hands full.

## 29

*May 1994*

"I'm pregnant."

They're naked in Étienne's bedroom. He removes his condom with his fingertips. Clotilde lies near him, legs tucked up. He looks at her mouth. A rodent. He's always thought that, that her mouth's ugly, too thin, too small. And then she wears lipstick, as if to accentuate her defect. White teeth, all straight, but protruding slightly. Blue eyes she shadows with mauve. Her best feature. Everyone looks at her eyes. Girls and boys. A small, straight nose, fine. White skin. Like milk. He loves her breasts, her pale pink nipples, her firm tummy. Her slender, sporty-girl's body. Not that tall. Barely taller than Nina. He compares all of his conquests with Nina. Never with Louise, she's his sister. A little sister can't be compared. Nina is something other than a sister, something indefinable. A childhood friend. That's what he says when he introduces her: "My childhood friend." It saves him having to explain anything, like "She's not my girlfriend, we're forever together but not an item." "My best friend" is how he describes Adrien. Even if that's not what he thinks. Adrien, too, is something other. Before, the two of them never did anything without Nina being there. Since he was fourteen, Adrien has been coming to Étienne's on his own to play the synthesizer, and games on the Sega. The console is plugged into a TV twenty-four hours a day, beside their keyboards. They sit on an old sofa, select *Cosmic Carnage* or *Sonic*, and play for hours on end. When Nina turns up, Étienne reluctantly lends her his joystick. But she soon loses patience, which annoys the two boys.

He takes a drag on a joint. Closes his eyes. Only opens them when Clotilde mutters:

"I don't know how I've fucked up with my Pill."

He pauses a while, covers his penis with the sheet. As though suddenly modest, or wanting to end their proximity, their intimacy. Étienne thinks of his father. What will he say if he finds out? The insults will come thick and fast. He'll be able to speak his mind. Until now, he's shut up because Marie-Laure won't tolerate Étienne being compared with Paul-Émile. But if Marc discovers that his brat has got a girl pregnant, he'll feel justified in spouting hurtful words.

"Oh shit . . . That's shit," groans Étienne.

"I know," says Clotilde.

"You sure?"

"Yes."

"Seen a doctor?"

"Not yet."

"Must do that fast."

"I know."

"We're doing our bac in a month's time."

Every Wednesday afternoon, Clotilde and Étienne have sex at his house. They lock themselves in, take their time, limber up, experiment. Two novices of seventeen who explore, seek, and discover pleasure. For fun, nothing else. As for love, Étienne will see about that later. When he pictures his future, he sees himself living with Nina and Adrien in Paris.

It's the first time he's stayed so long with a girl, five months, and the first time he's had sex with one.

He doesn't yet fully grasp what Clotilde has just told him. "The other side of the coin," his father would say. The joint is spacing him out a bit. A dual impulse. Running away and being proud. He'd got her pregnant. Something akin to virility would almost make him puff out his chest. And a rising anxiety: being a father at seventeen, a nightmare. A nightmare that would mean staying in La Comelle. Being like his parents. Leaving the house early, coming home late. Forgetting your dreams. That kid would take his place in the pool, on his skateboard, in nightclubs, and would play on the synthesizer and the Sega instead of him, while he'd be slaving away to feed it. No way.

As for Nina, that's all she thinks about. Getting married, having children and a house. Disturbing. Étienne doesn't believe her when she sees herself living this phony life, he tells himself that she'll grow out of it, and the three of them will live on freedom and fresh water. That they'd surely do gigs all over the place, and maybe even some world tours.

Étienne gets dressed. He must meet up with Adrien and Nina, at hers, to revise. They cram for hours using index cards, and keep testing each other. Without them, Étienne would never have got into tenth grade, not to mention eleventh grade. He still can't believe he's in his final year, and he reaps some of the benefits: his parents leave him free to come and go as long as his results are good. If he wants to go to Paris next year, he'll have to pursue his studies. Any studies. Never will his parents let him go off to "make music." After thinking about it, and watching the detective series *Navarro* and *Commissaire Moulin*, he thinks he'd like to be a cop. Cop and musician, that's classy. And he has an advantage over the others, his high level in sport.

He watches Clotilde slipping on her dress. Pregnant. As surreal as when Nina had her period at ten years old. A thing that just doesn't exist in his world.

"I'll give you a lift," he tells her.

They come across Louise, sitting on the sofa, engrossed in a book. Say a brief "Hi, see you later." Étienne wonders how one can read a novel when one isn't forced to, purely for pleasure. Adrien and Louise lend each other their books. Étienne senses something's going on between his sister and Adrien, but carries on as if their relationship didn't exist, when it's blatantly obvious. Doesn't want to know.

He hands Clotilde her helmet, starts up his motorbike, speeds through the streets of La Comelle. She clings onto him. He feels like braking suddenly so she falls backwards, lets go of him, ceases to exist. He is horrified by his thoughts. And almost relieved when he drops her off outside her house. Before leaving her, he asks her to go and see a doctor as quickly as possible. He finds this story hard to believe. How could their sexual games have resulted in pregnancy? She says she takes the Pill and they use condoms. It's true that those things sometimes slip or split, but that must have happened once or twice, no more than that.

"Are you going back to *them*?"

There's an implied reproach in the question: "Take a break from your two buddies. You're forever stuck together."

"Yup. All three of us are revising."

Étienne literally escapes to Nina's, opens the door, goes upstairs. They haven't knocked for years when arriving at each other's places. They feel at home. The adults are used to it. When they were little, the parents told themselves it would pass, it was a childhood phase, one changed, especially at middle school, one made other friends. But since they're at high school now and still *around*, they just put up with it. It's natural. They're like children in the same family. Who grow up together. Who sleep at home, share meals and days off. A very strong bond. Joséphine totally adores Étienne and Nina, always strokes their hair, kisses them affectionately, knows their favorite dishes, makes them especially for them. Pierre has grown attached to Adrien and Étienne as though to the children of a brother or sister he'd never had. Marie-Laure and Marc always include the two others in any suppers, and if Nina or Adrien don't come round for a while, don't keep in touch, something is missing. They've all used the familiar *tu* with each other for years. Each family has watched the children of the other two families changing in appearance and outlook. Metamorphosing.

Étienne climbs the stairs two at a time, pushes open the bedroom door. Nina and Adrien are already sitting cross-legged on the floor. They're asking each other questions in English. Étienne says a general hello and stretches out on the bed. He's not into sitting on the floor.

"What's up with you?" Nina asks him. "You're white as a sheet. Like me when I've just watched *The Exorcist*."

Étienne doesn't feel like talking about it. He feels rather ashamed. Étienne and Nina aren't in the habit of hiding things from each other, they talk openly about anything and everything. Adrien listens to them, but remains quiet, secretive. Rarely intervenes in their conversations. Unlike the other two, Adrien only talks about how much he detests his father, what he's reading, his lyrics, but never about sexuality or love. When it's just the two of them, Nina keeps on at him:

"And you? Who do you love? D'you prefer girls or boys? Is it true you're in love with Louise? Have you already kissed her? Have you slept together?" To which Adrien always replies: "I love you." And then Nina gets annoyed: "You're a pain in the ass never answering. You just duck the question. Whereas I tell you everything."

On Saturday nights, they go to Club 4, a nightclub about thirty kilometers from La Comelle. Their parents take it in turns to drive them there, and then come and collect them in the car park at four in the morning.

They get ready together, choose their outfits carefully, eat early, sneak in a few drinks. They perfume themselves and brush their teeth side by side. Sometimes, Adrien and Nina swap T-shirts—Étienne, much taller than them, can't join in. Nina puts on a little makeup and the boys watch. "Not too much, or it'll look tacky," Étienne is forever telling her.

They consult magazines, do their hair like rock stars, sharing the pot of gel. Étienne pushes his blond hair over to one side, he's obsessed with looking like Kurt Cobain, who's just died. Adrien dries his dark, curly hair with his head down, he dreams of having David Bowie's charisma. Nina styles her short bob to look like the young Debbie Harry. She's forever changing hair color. Tries all kinds of haircuts.

When they get ready at Étienne's, Louise joins them in the bathroom, which smells of perfume, hairspray, cigarette smoke, vodka, and shampoo. She'd like to go to Club 4 with them, stamps her feet, begs a little, but her parents refuse:

"You're only sixteen."

"Nearly seventeen! And Adrien is already eighteen! He can watch over me."

"Forget it."

*

*12 December 2017*

Club 4. I remember that, in my senior year, I loved it. There I'd find the groovers from my class and a few others from round about.

Club 4 was pretty select, not anyone could get in. Tots, soaks, and scruffs were barred.

We'd arrive at around eleven, have our first drink with our entry ticket, which allowed us two free drinks. Then one of us always had a bottle on them and topped us up from under their coat. The manager knew it, but turned a blind eye. Attractive youngsters in her establishment, they brought in the punters.

At Club 4, a mixed bunch rubbed shoulders: schoolkids, mature types, gays, serious clubbers, married couples, transvestites. For a provincial nightclub, it was pretty trendy. Some people even came from Paris. I remember there was a back room that we never set foot in, but we knew that people were screwing behind the red curtain covering the entrance.

Looking back, I find it insane that we were allowed into this borderline-depraved place, when most of us weren't yet eighteen, and it was our own parents who dropped us off there as if it were a "normal" nightclub. They can't have known that inside, nothing was remotely normal.

Our big thrill was sniffing poppers, openly on sale at the bar. All evening we'd pass around the little bottles and then look at ourselves in the mirrors: our perceptions were distorted, blurred, we'd lose our balance, we'd laugh, we felt like we were doing something forbidden.

The music was excellent, the DJ a buzzy artist who mixed techno trance most of the time. It gave us wings, set our hearts racing. We danced tightly packed together, drunk with sensations we were all discovering at the same time. We played at being grown-ups, uninhibited and free, when we were still just kids who kissed on the mouth and had barely started to explore our sexuality.

At one in the morning, the DJ cut the electronic music, and transvestites who were squeezed into sequined dresses took over the dance floor to impersonate American divas—Gloria Gaynor ("I Will Survive"), Donna Summer ("I Feel Love"), Eruption ("One Way Ticket").

After the show, there was always a game of Kiss in the Ring.

Nina never picked Étienne from the circle when she'd just been kissed in the center. Too dangerous. Too complicated. Flirting together would mean putting their friendship at risk. And anyhow, they knew each other too intimately. Only strangers seemed desirable, intriguing to them. They were like those old couples who no longer really look at each other.

Adrien never joined in, he stayed sitting at the bar, watching Nina and Étienne from a distance, with a smile. How many girls and boys held the scarf out to Étienne? He was the most lusted after, endlessly in the center of the circle. He had a whale of a time, French-kissing the girls and, if he was drunk, even giving the boys a peck on the lips. In his senior year, Étienne was going out with Clotilde Marais, even more reason to flirt with other girls during the game. The only time she'd allow it. Although she sometimes sulked if the kiss went on forever. Or took her revenge by, in turn, picking another boy. Which Étienne couldn't stand either. Cheated on in front of the others, he'd rather die.

Nina still hadn't "done it," as they said, and that's all she thought about. It was her obsession. She wanted to do it with a guy she was in love with. Especially the first time. She was crazy about one Alexandre, with whom she must have, at the most, exchanged a: "Hi, you well?—Fine, and you?—Have fun." Words that had left her trembling, ecstatic, and faint. He always turned up at Club 4 at around two in the morning. When she made him out in the half-light, saw the figure he cut, the clothes he was wearing, she'd leave the dance floor. Nina and he hovered around each other, made sure they were never far from each other, but he had a girlfriend who stuck to him like a leech. Even when he went to the restroom, she posted herself outside the door like a bouncer. Guessing that Nina would sneak inside to avoid the line at the girls' restroom. Just once did they come face to face. Alexandre had pressed and kissed Nina against the wall, a sensual kiss that had left her reeling. When she'd reopened her eyes, he'd already gone.

Nina sensed Alexandre's eyes on her, they smiled at each other, hoped for each other, occasionally brushed against each other's hand or shoulder, but the leech was watching. They'd been a couple since they were fourteen. Like kids old before their time, as good as married because they'd been together for so long. "He doesn't love her anymore but daren't leave her," a mutual female friend had led Nina to believe.

Nina loved telling herself this tale of impossible love. That if Alexandre were free, they would love each other.

Alexandre was twenty-one, studied law in Dijon, and lived with the leech. Deep down, Nina dreamt of that: an apartment, a red sofa, a fitted kitchen, and a ready-to-assemble prince charming. She repeated to anyone who'd listen that, after school, she'd be off to Paris with Étienne and Adrien to live the life. But in her heart of hearts, she kept wavering: one day she'd be dreaming of a love story handed to her on a plate with children and assembly instructions, and the next of total freedom, with lovers, as many lovers as countries she'd visit, singing and dancing through her artist's life.

While her dreams might go from one camp to the other, one thing was sure: no one would ever separate her from Adrien and Étienne.

# 30

*12 December 2017*

D'you do that with all the men who adopt a dog at your shelter?"

Nina smiles.

"How old are you?" he asks.

"In dog or woman years?

"What is it, again, one has to multiply by for dogs?"

"Depends on the size of the dog. I must be about a hundred-and-eighteen, and you?"

"The same."

"I'll be off," she says.

"You can stay."

"I haven't slept in the same bed as someone for an eternity."

"An eternity's a long time."

"And you?"

"What about me?"

"How long since you shared a bed with someone?"

"I'm pretty sure it's an eternity, too."

"You're not married?"

"Divorced. And you?"

"Same."

"That's already two things we have in common . . ."

"D'you have kids?"

"No. And you?"

"Neither."

"I don't know what one calls a man and a woman who haven't had children."

"Brat-free? Or strays, contrarians, hermits, no-diapers, nodescendants, lucky, egotists, barren, hand-less, tummy-less, rapture-less, nuisance-less, heir-less, carefree, life-annuities, eternal teens, kids forever, footprint-less, joyless, layette-less, buggy-less, life-after-life-less, 'and not a soul at your funeral' . . ."

Nina bursts out laughing.

"You're damn beautiful when you laugh," he says.

"I'm still sloshed. Your bourbon knocked me out."

"You only laugh when you're sloshed?"

Nina gets up and starts getting dressed.

"A man can have kids up to his eighties. Chaplin, I think he was a father very late. For you, all is not lost."

"I'm alright, then. And for you? Is all lost?"

"Seems like it."

"Shall I give you a lift?"

"No, I'll walk home."

"Will we see each other again?"

"Yes, if you come to adopt another dog."

Romain smiles.

"I'm not your type anymore?"

Nina doesn't respond. She's already turned her back on him and is on her way downstairs to find her jeans and sweater, dropped somewhere in the sitting room. The leftovers of love. The TV's still on, different program, black-and-white images, Hitler, the crowds, swastikas. Bob hasn't budged from the sofa, he looks at Nina with his beautiful sad eyes.

"Hello, old boy."

She puts on her coat. Doesn't go back up to say goodbye to Romain. She'll send him a message. Simple words: "Thank you for bringing me back to life." Or just: "Thank you." Or: "Thanks and goodbye."

She closes the door very gently behind her. Once she's in the street, she thinks back to the question: "I'm not your type anymore?" *No*, thinks Nina, *you're too eloquent, I don't trust those who are too eloquent.*

She shivers. She doesn't regret coming. Love's never forgotten.

# 31

*15 December 2017*

I find Nicola at the bottom of a cardboard box in my storeroom. After an hour of searching everywhere for him. I could cry. I feared he'd escaped when I opened the front door this morning. I gently catch hold of him and hug him tight.

"What are you doing here?"

He starts up his purring machine. I love his warmth and his smell. Just a few days since he and his shoebox arrived at my house, and it's already too late realistically to envisage any separation. Place him in a family more suitable than me? Not being a family myself? This little ball, this heart that beats, laps up, runs, dozes, meows, looks for me, would already recognize me among others. Here am I, the owner of a life. Responsible. I who didn't want anything, here I am with everything.

He was lying on my diplomas. I blow some hairs off them before closing up the box. I haven't taken them out once since I moved into this house. What for? To frame them? To hang them on the walls to impress the few souls who'll enter my home? These trophies, piled one on top of the other, are no longer of any use to me. Just a paper mattress for my kitten.

Their names on the list.

Nina Beau: Pass with merit. Étienne Beaulieu: Pass. Adrien Bobin: Pass with distinction.

They were holding their breath. Waiting to be sure that their names were there before celebrating. All three of them scream at the same time. Even Adrien, usually so reserved, always having to repeat himself because he speaks so quietly, lets out a Tarzan-like yelp. Nina sobs in her grandfather's arms.

"I got it, Grandpa, I got it."

Pierre Beau can't hold his own tears back, he looks up at the sky, thanking Odile.

*To life, to love*
*To our nights, to our days,*
*To the eternal recurrence of luck . . .*

Étienne, drunk with gratitude, goes from Nina's arms to Adrien's, whispering:

"Thank you, my friends, thank you."

It's the first time he's hugged Adrien. Then he meets his father's gaze, a gaze that speaks volumes, and falls into the arms of his mother, who murmurs:

"Congratulations, son, bravo, you see, when you want to."

Marc Beaulieu says nothing, remains aloof. Étienne merely passed. There's always one who's mediocre, academically, among siblings.

Joséphine cries hot tears as she hugs Adrien tightly. Their hug lasts a long time. She's succeeded in raising him all on her own, what will his father say when he discovers his son graduated with distinction? What will he think, he who always regarded them as his two youthful indiscretions?

Adrien, Nina, and Étienne break away from the circle to mingle with their other classmates, share their elation. Joséphine, beaming, suggests they all have an impromptu aperitif at her place. Everyone gladly agrees.

"We need to recover from all this excitement together, with *our three children*, and any others who want to come, we'll stretch the walls."

I'm like Louise, my precious friend, we observe others discreetly, without being noticed. Louise has just passed her pre-baccalauréat in French, getting 17 in the oral and 19 for the written exam. She's in eleventh grade. She wants to be a doctor and knows that nothing will stop her. That's what I like most about her, her determination.

Among the throng of pupils, Clotilde finds Étienne, throws her arms around his neck. He kisses her back, hugs her. He doesn't dare leave her, since the abortion. He accompanied her to the hospital, waited for her, brought her home. The weight of guilt. He's waiting for July, a month of vacation, he'll break up with her on his return. In the autumn, she'll be going to university in Dijon, when he'll be moving to Paris. He'll make Clotilde a distant memory. She whispers "I love you" in his ear, which chills him, he responds, tersely, "Me too."

It's six o'clock, we're at Joséphine's, who has opened all the windows in the apartment to let the July sun in. Around twenty people in the small apartment. She has poured large bags of peanuts into salad bowls and placed port, Martini, whiskey, and pastis on the coffee table.

"Help yourselves! If there isn't enough ice, get more from the fridge."

The smokers take turns to go onto the tiny balcony. Fearing it may collapse, they go out two by two.

There's much talk of future plans. They merge into the alcohol. Other towns, somewhere else. Dijon, Chalon-sur-Saône, Autun, Paris, Lyon. Most of the school-leavers are going on to university. Adrien, Nina, and Étienne have put in a request for student accommodation in Paris. The flat of their dreams will have to wait. Étienne is unlikely to get a student room, but Marie-Laure has promised: "I'll rent you one not far from Nina and Adrien," who will both get grants, and do their best to find casual work on the side. The three kids from La Comelle map out their futures: Adrien will do the preparatory course to try to get into the École Normal Supérieure, Étienne will do the entrance exams for a police academy, Nina will study art at the École des Beaux-Arts. They say yes to everything, but their shared dream underlies it all, their unspoken quest: making music. Playing in bars. In the streets. In the metro. Recording an album.

That evening, I'm near Louise and I make the most of this joy, savoring it along with Joséphine's port, as I watch her coming and going, like a bird hopping from one thing to the next, and preparing to fly off. I'll never forget Pierre Beau's look of pride and determination as he gazes at his granddaughter, or Marie-Laure's look as, ignoring her husband's scowl, she downs one Martini after another. The smiles of all the parents, our collective relief: it's over, we've got our diplomas under our belts.

All the glasses rise more than a dozen times, the toast always the same: "Here's to our children!"

I also notice that one can be in paradise in a flimsy apartment of forty-five square meters at most, fourth story with no elevator, charmless apart from the life inside it. The joy that can't be bought from a realtor's plan is right here. That evening, I revel in our youth, our hopes, our parents who believe in us, in the good fortune of having grown up together in this provincial town that overprotected us.

And me? What will I become? What will my choices be? What will I make of them?

After that aperitif at Joséphine's, the youngsters agree to meet up, from ten onwards, at one of the banks of the Lac de la Forêt. Bring as many bottles as possible, that's the watchword.

We all gather around a huge bonfire. About a hundred of us. Some pupils from the year below join us, including Louise. We drink beer and whiskey, sing and dance together. Étienne has brought his cassette player and two speakers. The others have brought along cassettes of Nirvana, Bruce Springsteen, NTM, La Mano Negra, IAM. Together, we all sing along to the KOD song hundreds of times:

*Each to their route, each to their path*
*Each to their dream, each to their destiny . . .*

At eleven o'clock, we're nearly all in the lake in our underwear. Some boys are skinny-dipping. Some girls have stayed around the fire. They didn't want to undress in front of the others. Louise and Clotilde are among them.

When the last group finally decides to go home, it's already daylight.

# 32

*Friday 15 July 1994*

Pierre Beau drops Nina off outside the reception of Transports Damamme. He hadn't wanted her to apply for a summer job at the Post Office. Even though employees' children are given priority. He never wants to see her touching mail, directly or indirectly, ever again. He's unaware that she still rummages, steals, opens certain envelopes, delights in the words inside others. It's stronger than she is, like some latent defect.

"Have a good day, and work hard, *mon petit*."

He had always called her that, "*mon petit*." As a child, she had asked him: "Grandpa, why do you call me *mon petit*, when I'm a girl?" He had explained: "*Le coeur* is masculine. And you are *mon petit coeur*."

"See you this evening, Grandpa."

Nina presents herself at reception:

"Good morning, I'm Nina Beau, I'm starting today."

It's Étienne's mother who helped her get this job. Marie-Laure wrote a CV for her and delivered it personally to the head of human resources, who is a friend of hers. Nina is escorted to the office she's going to be working in for a month-and-a-half, she's replacing Mademoiselle Dalem during her August vacation, she'll be trained up in a couple of weeks, she'll see, it's nothing complicated: receiving faxes, sending them, filing invoices alphabetically in the archives down in the basement, typing a few letters.

"Are you proficient in Word?"

"Yes."

"You don't make too many spelling mistakes?"

"No."

At that precise moment, Étienne is in the back of the family car beside Louise. He's relieved to have left La Comelle this morning. He can't stand the sight of Clotilde anymore. She hinted that she might come to see him in Saint-Raphaël, he swiftly responded that he wouldn't be there. That this year, he and his family were setting off to sail around Corsica.

Not true. No big deal. He's had it up to here with that girl. It's crazy how you can love someone, love everything about them even, their smell, body, saliva, voice, and then suddenly loathe all of it. Like the B side of a record when you've listened to the A side continuously. Music one no longer recognizes. Being unable to bear even just her presence anymore. A leech, a ball-and-chain, a weight too heavy to carry. "Do you love me? Do you swear? Will we stay together forever?"

*No. I won't stay*, he thinks.

Étienne observes his sister, she seems lost in her thoughts. She tried to read one of her books, but reading in the car makes her feel sick.

"Are you in love with Adrien?" he asks her, quietly so his parents don't hear.

She stares at him for a few seconds, flabbergasted.

"That's the first time you've asked a question about me. Normally, you only speak to me to borrow something off me, or to ask me to lie to cover up for you."

Étienne is hurt by Louise's comment.

"You really are just a pain."

He turns his head, pretends to look at the landscape.

"Yes. I'm in love with him. It shows, doesn't it?"

He studies her, suspiciously.

"I knew it. Have you slept together?" he asks, more aggressively than he'd meant.

Louise shrugs her shoulders and blushes. She immediately clams up. Étienne already knows she won't say another word before they reach Saint-Raphaël.

Adrien looks at himself in the bathroom mirror. He thinks to himself that, in the end, he'll be less ugly than expected. He looks increasingly like his mother. More amiable, more bearable. High cheekbones, fine nose, lips thicker than he'd hoped, straight white teeth. Since getting a bac with distinction, his eyes have changed, as if victory had set his hazel eyes alight. He's still slim, almost thin, apparently that changes as you get older. In any case, everything will change with age. He's unlikely to exceed one meter seventy-five in height. He hates his milky skin, like a garment he'd like to discard. He'd sell his soul to the devil to have Etienne's, with its bronzed tone. He examines his pale face, the shadows around his eyes. Thinks that, with the summer, he'll tan. He'll look better when he arrives in Paris.

He starts his vacation job today, like Nina. Minimum wage to dispense gasoline and collect the deposits on gas cylinders outside a supermarket. Two months separate him from Paris. In the meantime, he can do any old job to earn his living.

*

*Sunday 31 July 1994*

Nina and Adrien have been working now for fifteen days.

*Just a month to go until Paris . . .*

Lying side by side on the same king-size towel, they've covered themselves in sun oil to speed up their tan. Adrien suggested going to the Lac de la Forêt, but Nina prefers the municipal pool. It's the blue of her childhood. That blue and that whiff of chlorine she likes to get back on her skin every summer.

"It stinks of bleach. You really are weird," Adrien tells her.

"Me, weird? You can talk," she hits back.

She likes the shrieks of the children, their bodies splashing into the water when they hurl themselves from the diving boards. Nina has still got the taste of chocolate ice-cream on her tongue. Adrien has dozed off. She listens to his breathing. Every evening, from a phone box, they call Étienne to talk about their day, just to hear each other's voices, chat about this and that, tell him about their jobs. Nina asks him how the sea is. "It's lovely," Étienne always replies. He has asked them not to tell anyone that they're talking, that he's reachable, especially not Clotilde. "Sure, promise. Anyhow, we never see her, apparently she's working at the Harbor Pizzeria."

Adrien dispenses gasoline and diesel oil. "Have to take care not to confuse them." He takes payments, cleans windshields, listens to the radio in the small sales kiosk while waiting for the next client. "It's O.K., the days go by fast."

For Nina, it's the same story. She likes her work, she's a secretary, feels like she's playing a part in an American soap. And best of all, something new has happened: Emmanuel Damamme has turned her life upside down. The boss's son, twenty-seven, tall, dark, and handsome, stares at her all the time. Whenever she looks up, he's looking at her. They don't dare to talk to each other. Just exchange a few words. He has no need to be in her office, no excuse to ask her anything at all. Emmanuel has a personal assistant. She needs to lure him somewhere, but where? Getting him to come to Club 4 one Saturday would be a miracle. They must talk before her contract ends. Before she leaves for Paris.

Gazing at the wind in the leaves of a tree that's on the lawn beside the small pool, Nina thinks of a ruse to lure Emmanuel *over there*. After a glass or two, it will be easier to talk to each other than at the office. She has no idea where she might bump into him in La Comelle. He has a car, seems to live with his parents in a very fine property with several buildings, a tennis court, and a swimming pool. No chance of bumping into him at these municipal baths. She knows he studied in Lyon before returning here to take up the reins.

The first time she saw him, she almost fainted. She could feel herself blushing. He said a "hello" to her that she'd never forget. She adored his voice, its deep, sensual tone. She responded by stammering like a silly goose. Although she's not sure that geese stammer. She laughs out loud. Adrien wakes up, opens his eyes.

"Laughing on your own?"

"Yes, I'm thinking of Emmanuel."

"Again?"

"Yes. You know very well that when I'm in love, that's all I think about."

"And what about Alexandre?"

"Not interested."

"I thought he was the man of your dreams . . ."

"How can we get Emmanuel to come to Club 4 next Saturday?" Nina interrupts him.

"Slip an invitation onto his desk."

"Impossible."

"Onto his windshield?"

"Unthinkable."

"Who's his favorite singer?"

"Dunno . . . Why?"

"Find out and then make him believe that he or she is singing at Club 4 next Saturday."

"Crazy. Why would he believe that?"

"A private concert. It wouldn't be the first time. Famous singers have played there before."

"What if his favorite singer is dead. What do we do then?"

They burst out laughing simultaneously.

"Where does he park, your Emmanuel?"

"What?"

"Where does he park when he's at work?"

"Well, in the Damamme car park."

"Go and see if there are any cassettes lying around on the dashboard of his car. Then you'll know what he listens to."

"The shame of it, can you see me lurking around his car?"

"I'll do it. No one knows who I am."

"You?"

"Yes, me. What time does he arrive in the morning?"

*

*Saturday 6 August 1994*

Emmanuel Damamme enters Club 4. As soon as Nina spots him, she goes over to him, pretending to look sorry.

"The concert's cancelled. Étienne Daho's got bronchitis, he can't come."

She can see the amusement in his eyes. No disappointment. She realizes that he'd never fallen for the far-fetched story she'd told him:

"On Saturday evening, Étienne Daho is coming to sing at Club 4, it's a surprise for the regulars, a private concert. He's great friends with the owners. Do you like Étienne Daho?"

Emmanuel had smiled before answering:

"I imagine it's already booked out."

"No, it's a surprise. A Saturday evening like any other . . . There's no shortage of tickets."

"If it's a surprise, how come you know about it, then?"

"I have my informers."

And now, Emmanuel is here, right up close to her. More relaxed than at the office, freer. His eyes are shining. *He's never been so handsome and desirable*, thinks Nina.

"Can I get you a drink?" he asks.

"Yes."

They smile at each other, make for the bar. Shout to speak to each other. Nina thinks to herself that everything's going even better than in her dreams.

From the dance floor, Adrien watches them. He's never seen Nina behaving like that, being so entirely engrossed in someone. Nothing and no one seem able to distract her. Adrien sees Emmanuel for the first time. The thing about him is that he doesn't look like the others. Those surrounding him in this club. Or even the inhabitants of La Comelle. He's got the class of an English dandy. Like he's stepped out of *The Avengers*. Adrien immediately senses the danger. *That one*, his inner voice tells him, *he could steal Nina from you*. Adrien regrets Étienne being away. If he were here this evening, it would all be different. Étienne would go over to her, would take her by the hand and say: "Come, let's dance." Or: "Come, we three are going home to take in a movie." Or then, bluntly: "Come, this guy's ten years older than you, he's too old to take your virginity."

Together, the two of them are stronger. Can reason with Nina. Calm her passions. Of the two, it's Étienne who always brings her back down to earth.

Right now, she seems to be levitating.

"Do you come here often?" Emmanuel asks her.

"Every Saturday," Nina replies.

"I used to hang out here before leaving for Lyon. A depraved place for a young girl."

Nina bursts into laughter. Emmanuel observes her, she has something of Audrey Hepburn that he far from dislikes. Nina is wearing a black cotton dress that hugs her figure. A bob frames her face, bangs cover her forehead, her mouth is sensual, her eyes very dark. *A superb racial mix*, he thinks. She had immediately caught his eye. There's something delicate about her. The granddaughter of a mailman, someone had found out for him. A friend of the Beaulieus, whom Emmanuel vaguely knows.

"Where are you from originally?"

"From an unknown father and a depressive mother," she says, ironically.

"Interesting."

"In September, I'm off to live in Paris," she tells him.

"Paris?"

"With my two best friends, they're like my brothers, we're a band. We're going to record an album."

"What kind of music?"

"Electronic. We've got two synthesizers and I do the vocals."

"You sing?"

"Yes. It feels strange, you saying '*vous*' to me, makes me feel like your grandmother."

"O.K., let's say '*tu*.' So . . . you sing?"

"Yes."

"Could you sing me something, here, now?"

*And you, tell me you love me*
*Even if it's a lie*
*Since I know you lie*
*Life's so sad*
*Tell me you love me*
*Every day's the same*
*I need a love song . . .*

"Very good. I missed Daho, but I got to hear Lio."

"I've never made love, have you?"

"Is that the title of a song?" he asks, ironically.

She smiles, the alcohol is giving her confidence. They move closer together. She feels his mouth against her ear, his voice, his perfume. The brush against each other, it's electric. She could marry him right now. Without a second thought. She could disown her father and mother. Which is convenient as she doesn't know them.

They're stuck to the bar. They're jostled, they don't notice a thing. Emmanuel starts to run his index finger along the top of her hand.

"I have done it before."

"What?"

"Made love."

Nina drinks a few sips to give herself courage.

"Could you teach me? I'd like to do it before leaving for Paris."

"We could come to some arrangement."

# 33

*22 December 2017*

Nina has gone into the little boutique, in the town center, for the first time to buy herself three blouses, a white sweater, two pairs of trousers, and a dress.

*A dress and a white sweater . . . but what am I going to do with them?*

For ten days now, she's spent all her evenings with Romain Grimaldi. After work, she goes home to have a quick bite to eat, take a shower, and change her outfit. Then she walks to Rue Rosa-Muller. She leaves him after loving him, with the excuse that her cats are waiting for her at home.

She's just blown 300 euros on things she'll never wear. So that's how stupid a woman can be? *Go easy on yourself*, a voice whispers to her. *Let it go, and don't get into a state.*

Nina is in the infirmary. She's observing three kittens sleeping under an infrared lamp. The mother's whereabouts aren't known, and they haven't been weaned. A few schoolkids are taking it in turn to feed them. Teenagers love giving their time to the shelter to look after the baby animals.

Today is the anniversary of the death of Eric, Simone's son. Couldn't a better word be invented for *that*? "Anniversary" sounds like a celebration. Nina could ask Romain, seeing as he managed to come up with so many terms for those without children.

Nina watches Simone through the infirmary window. Attaching a long leash to the dogs' harnesses and taking them out for a walk one after the other, while standing so straight. Simone has the deportment of a prima ballerina. Wrapped in a fleece jacket, and with an Hermès scarf on her head, she looks like some grand lady who's lost her way among the cement huts. A queen of England in the favelas. This morning, all she said to Nina, as she looked for her gloves in her handbag, was: "It's three years ago today." And then added: "I'll come in on 25 December, you can take a day off for once."

It's only 8:30 A.M., and Simone has already taken out Rosy, a kind of Pyrenean mountain dog, and Boulet, a beautiful big black griffon, whom Nina had renamed "ball-and-chain" because on two separate occasions he'd made his own way back to the shelter after being adopted. At a year's interval, having left with his new family, he'd escaped, found his way back, and sat quietly outside the gates, waiting for opening time so he could return to his kennel. Nina settled him down at the entrance, close to her office, in the biggest kennel of all, and she opens the door for him every morning on arrival, so he can wander around freely. He's no longer offered for adoption, he'll live out his days here. Nina almost took him home, into her house, but really her home is here. It's here that she spends most of her time.

A cold morning. A wintery light, a steel-blue sky. Nina goes into the cattery, where there's plenty of stretching, yawning, patient waiting. Waiting for arms, an apartment, a house, a balcony, a garden, basically, a view. A routine somewhere other than here. An old bachelor or a large family, rich or poor, no matter, what counts is the attention and affection. During the open days, people look at them, stroke them, prefer some to others. So, while they wait, they snooze in the padded baskets given by donors.

Nina pulls on some latex gloves, changes the litter trays, cleans the floor areas with detergent, talks to the cats, who sleepily observe her through half-closed eyes. The youngest ones play, chasing each other, climbing, and sharpening their claws on the cat trees. The old ones spit if there's too much of a ruckus.

"Yesterday evening I made love."

Their yellow, blue, or green eyes stare at her with interest. As if she were telling a story to children.

"Don't look at me like that, I am a woman, after all. Not just your cleaning lady. Remember the tall guy who adopted Bob? It's him. Yes, it's true, I didn't look very far afield, and you must think me pretty pathetic, but anyhow, one makes the most of what one's got. As you well know."

Simone finds her inside the cattery.

"Talking to yourself?"

"No, I'm talking to the cats about sex."

"I could tell them a few things, too . . . vestiges of the past."

Simone goes to stroke them, takes them in her arms. There are more than fifty of them at the moment. Soon, Nina won't be able to accept any more. She'll have to send them to other shelters. Previously, the cattery would be overflowing with kittens in spring, now it's all year round. A disaster. Most were given or sold to any old person, ended up in a trash can among the potato peelings, or in the street, eyelids stuck together, scrawny, and infested with parasites.

Nina would like to launch a sterilization campaign with the assistance of the mayor.

*Life really doesn't make sense. They produce plenty of little ones, I can't produce any, and Simone did produce one and he died . . .* thinks Nina.

"You O.K.?" she asks Simone.

"I'm O.K. I'd like it to be tomorrow. Since Éric passed, I always want it to be tomorrow. The present weighs me down . . . I don't know what to do with it."

"There are plenty of us in today, you could go home if you feel tired."

"No way, no way . . . Right, I'll get back to it."

Nina goes into the kennel area. It's all about the look in the eyes. Nina knows which animal suits which person. As soon as someone comes into the shelter asking to see the "white pussycats," it's not unusual for them to leave with a tawny tomcat. Each one has its personality, its way of life, its peculiarities.

If someone falls in love with a dog, and that dog ignores them, Nina doesn't let the adoption happen. It would be destined to fail, resulting in a speedy return. Nina doesn't seek to offload them at any price, she wants to build up a real rapport between individual and animal. In her seventeen years at the shelter, she has sometimes been wrong, but that happens in any job. Nothing's worse than those who return the animals: "It's not working, it's scared of everything, keeps groaning," "It's aggressive, seems not to like us," "I'd rather have had a cat than a dog," "I'm getting divorced and my wife doesn't want it," "It smells, it's molting, it's ugly, it farts," "It costs me too much."

*

Nina is walking across the shelter when her attention is drawn to a familiar silhouette, swaying from one foot to the other. A teenager standing outside the entrance to the offices. She takes out her Ventolin and has a quick puff. It's getting cold, a kind of drizzle, the sky has covered over in minutes, a shiver runs through her. The resemblance is striking. It feels like a punch to her stomach, the closer she gets. He seems to be alone. Instinctively, Nina glances over to the car park to see whether an adult is waiting for him in a car. He smiles at her when she reaches him. It's *his* smile. Nina blanches, her throat is dry and tight. She immediately thinks it may be some bad news. She's scared to speak first.

"Good morning, *madame*," he says, cheerily.

"Good morning."

"I'd like to give my grandmother a cat for Christmas."

Same voice. The eyes are slightly different. Rounder, but identical in color. The nose a double. The mouth similar. Nina's legs feel like jelly. She wants both to run away and to give him a big hug. Run far away and caress him. Hold his face and breathe him in. Put her hand through his hair.

"Your grandmother, does she know you want to give her this present?" she asks, her voice quavering.

"No, it's a surprise."

"Do you think it will be a nice surprise?"

"Yup. Since hers died, she's been sad. She says she doesn't want another one . . . but I don't believe her."

"Where does she live?"

"La Comelle."

"How old is she?"

"I'm not really sure, around sixty . . . something like that."

Nina can't resist asking this question:

"And you? How old are you?"

"Fourteen."

"What's your name?"

"Valentin."

Nina stares at him. There can be no doubt at all. It's a flashback of unbelievable intensity.

"Valentin . . . Beaulieu?" she dares to ask.

The teenager stares back at her. As though caught with his hand in a bag.

"How d'you know?"

"You look like your father."

The kid widens his eyes, feigning surprise, badly.

"D'you know him?"

"We were at school together."

"Was it with you he used to do his music?"

Second punch in the stomach, she takes out her Ventolin again, another quick puff.

"What's that thing?" asks Valentin, indicating the inhaler she's clutching in her hand.

"Treatment for my asthma."

"Does it hurt?"

*Less than seeing you*, thinks Nina.

"No. On the contrary, it gives me relief."

"Does it cost a lot to take one of your cats?"

"Depends on the age of the cat."

"How long do they live?"

"Between fifteen and twenty years. Want to see them?"

Valentin smiles.

"Yes."

"Do you have pets?"

"My mother doesn't want any . . . I'd really love a German shepherd."

*My mother* . . . Which woman did Étienne end up getting pregnant?

"I had a German shepherd when I was little . . . She was called Paola."

"Lucky you . . ."

Valentin follows Nina. He seems extremely disturbed by the presence of the dogs in their kennels. They bark as they pass, sniff at them, whimper, groan. Valentin spots one on its own, in a separate part of the shelter, whose eyes are as gloomy as the weather. Valentin points at it.

"Why's that one over there? Looks like he's being punished."

"He arrived yesterday. If he hasn't been claimed by his owners in three weeks' time, he'll join the others. For now, I'm obliged to leave him in quarantine."

"But why?"

"It's the law."

"That's sad," he says.

"We take good care of them, don't you worry."

They go into the infirmary, and along the corridors leading to the cattery. Through a window, Valentin spots three kittens in a cage with an infrared lamp shining down on them. He stops.

"They're too cute."

"Yes," say Nina, "that's their great misfortune."

"Why?"

"Because everyone wants cats when they're little, but when they grow bigger, they no longer interest that many people."

"Does it make you angry?"

"Yes. But I'm not here to judge humans, my role is just to protect animals."

Inside the cattery, all is calm.

"I present to you all our pussycats."

Valentin goes over to stroke them.

"It's less sad here, it doesn't feel the same as with the dogs," he murmurs.

Nina lets some time go by. She observes him. She finally asks the question she's dying to ask:

"Does your father know you're here?"

"No, no one knows. I came on my own."

Valentin seems to know exactly what he wants.

"How's Louise?" Nina asks.

"Auntie? She's well."

*Auntie*. Nina thinks to herself that she's neither mother nor auntie. Nina thinks to herself that's she's nothing. She thinks of Romain's words that had made her laugh: "And not a soul at your funeral."

Feeling weak at the knees, she goes to sit on a bench. The "strokers' bench." Every week, middle-school pupils, mainly girls, volunteer to come and cuddle the cats. It's the same girls who feed the kittens. Nina calms down, breathes slowly, while Valentin carries on looking around, with a dozen cats rubbing up against his legs.

"How did you find our address?" Nina finally asks.

"Granny's got your calendar in her kitchen."

One of Simone's ideas. The team take photos of the animals needing adoption, and create calendars with the aid of some software. They're sold every Christmas in the stores of La Comelle, to garner donations. *Marie-Laure Beaulieu buys it . . . Doesn't surprise me, she's so generous. She's one of the things I'm most ashamed about*, thinks Nina. *She tucked me in, protected me, supported me, loved me, and I've never been back to see her, not even just to see how she's doing.*

"How on earth can I choose? They're all so cool," Valentin murmurs, at a loss.

"I have an idea . . . On Christmas Eve, you can slip an envelope addressed to your grandmother under the Christmas tree, with, inside it, a voucher for a cat from the shelter, then she can come and choose one herself."

Valentin's face lights up.

"Come, we'll organize it together in my office."

"Do we have to go past the dogs again to reach your office?"

"Yes."

Valentin grimaces.

"There's no other way?"

"You can just close your eyes, I'll hold your hand. And you can use *tu* with me."

"O.K."

Nina pulls off her gloves. She wishes this walk across the shelter would last forever. That young hand in hers, already larger than hers, but so soft. These fingers gripping hers remind her of Étienne's and

Adrien's fingers. They connect her right back to her adolescence, those carefree times. Like a socket into which you slide two pins. A lamp in winter. Sunburn. With eyes closed, Valentin lets himself be guided. As if he were walking on a high wire and had vertigo. His perfect profile, just like his father's. It's raining now. Melted snow in his hair.

They go into Nina's office, let go of each other's hands.

Nina is alone once again.

She opens one of the drawers, takes out the shelter's stamp and two stickers. She starts to make a kind of Christmas gift voucher using a piece of squared paper from a notebook. She's never done this before. Will never do it again. The animals can't be exchanged for a coupon, but it's an exceptional circumstance.

"What was my father like when he was small?"

"He was never small. I've always known him as huge."

Valentin's eyes sparkle, the same joyous bubbles as in Étienne's eyes. A long silence falls between them while Nina draws a cat in ballpoint pen. It's not an awkward silence, but already the kind of silence shared by those who know each other well. Who don't feel obliged to fill in the gaps.

"You're really good at drawing."

"Thanks. I'll give you a lift home," says Nina, handing the voucher to Valentin.

"I can walk home."

"It's snowing."

He pulls a 20-euro note out of his pocket.

"How much do I owe you for the cat?"

"Just this once, nothing at all."

"I want to make a donation."

"I'm not allowed to take money from a minor."

"Why?"

"It's the law."

"The law's stupid. It's like that dog in the pound, it's stupid. You can just say it was my father who gave you this note."

Nina takes the 20-euro note, slips it into a money box, and hands the boy some stickers for the shelter in exchange.

"Here, I'm allowed to sell you these. You can stick them wherever seems good to you."

They stand up at the same time. Valentin follows her. He, too, observes Nina surreptitiously. He doesn't look at her normally. Not like your average adopter. This story about a cat for his grandmother, she doesn't believe it anymore. It's doubtless a pretext he came up with. She turns around, looks Valentin straight in the eye.

"You didn't come here by chance, did you?"

Valentin pretends not to understand what she's trying to say to him. He looks away.

"Is it me you wanted to see?" she insists.

Valentin's face changes. His features tighten.

"Yes . . . It's because . . . my father's going to die."

# 34

*Friday 12 August 1994*

*Three more weeks and Nina will be off to Paris*, thinks Pierre Beau as he pedals up a hill. *It's good, she'll have a lovely life, I've pulled it off, in the end, I didn't do too badly at all, she's a sweet kid. And she won't be all alone, with Étienne and Adrien there I've nothing to worry about . . .*

He stops to slide an envelope under Madame Brulier's door, a charming lady who lives at No. 15 in Rue John-Kennedy. Her shutters are closed, she's on vacation. Like every year, before leaving, she'd asked the mailman not to put anything into her mailbox.

Pierre Beau knows the roads of La Comelle by heart. He's been up and down them on his bike for thirty-six years. One delivery bag in front, two behind, one on his back and the satchel containing money on his stomach, secured by a leather strap from left shoulder to right hip. He's changed bicycle and uniform at least ten times since he first began. He's lost count.

He started in 1958, the year he was twenty. These dark streets, sunny lanes, dead ends, shady squares, he's known them in all weathers. Thirty-six years of rounds on his bike, that makes a hundred-and-forty-four seasons, a hundred-and-ninety thousand kilometers, seven dog bites, three falls, one of which landed him with a broken shoulder. Two months of sick leave in 1971. On average, five hundred mailboxes a day. From the kepi to the cap, from De Gaulle to Chirac, via Giscard and Mitterrand. He used to be overtaken by 4CVs and haulage vehicles, today it's Twingos and Safranes. He's done the same round since he joined the Post Office. The awkward bends, the hills, the former one-way streets, the new one-way streets, the traffic lights, the rights of way, the humps, the stop signs no one respects, the roads where the wrong sort live, the mongrels that hate him, threaten him, the nice dogs, the scared dogs. Just like their owners. Those who move house, leave without giving a forwarding address, the *poste restante* types. Those who have died, who offer him a cup of coffee, a glass of white wine he pretends to knock back, an orange juice, a cookie. Those who won't open the door to him when he has certified mail to be signed, who live on the sixth story with no elevator; the mailboxes with no name, which overflow, in which kids have peed, the doormats, the window ledges, the notes taped to the door: "Mailman, if I'm not in, leave parcel with neighbors on right." The folk waiting for good news, the young girls who kiss him, the fathers who dread getting a water bill that's too steep, who insult him, yes, him, because they've received a tax reminder in the mail. The adorable grannies for whom he changes light bulbs, runs errands, fills in tax returns, collects medicines from the chemist. Their only contact is him, their mailman, the only person they see all day, when they don't have physiotherapy or a friend's funeral to go to.

He has always started work at 5:00 A.M., after the vans have been unloaded, the mail spread out on the sorting tables, first a general sort, then by neighborhoods, and finally divided into streets, *his* streets. Before setting off, there's the certified mail and money orders to collect. Ever since becoming a mailman, he's started his day with millions of francs on him. Until last March, it was Pierre Beau who paid out the allowances, welfare, pensions, child benefits to those who lived on his round. For thirty-six years, he's sometimes pedaled with ten million francs in his satchel to pay out up to fifty money orders a day. For five months now, his satchel has been empty, they've invented automatic payments direct to folks' bank accounts. As for him, he doesn't understand that much about computers. Apparently, it's progress. Now, people send each other faxes and tap away on Minitel. If it carries on, they'll be sending letters through their wretched computers and mailmen won't be needed at all anymore. His colleagues even claim there'll be no more military service, no more letters from soldiers to young girls, and people will walk around with their phones in their pockets. No more floral writing paper or fountain pens will be sold. All that will remain is the tunes of songs with no lyrics. The death of words written by hand.

He has always finished his round at about 3:45 P.M. He's always been back home between 4:00 and 5:00 P.M., to have lunch and grab a nap. Even during his wife's time. A dark, deep sleep, without dreams. Tired muscles. At first, he pedaled fast. Today, he can feel the years in his legs and his breathing. He cycles increasingly slowly, and it infuriates him.

He has always gone back to the post office at around 5:15 P.M. Before March 1994, he'd return any money he hadn't delivered, and adjust the accounts. Now, he only returns the certified mail, to be redelivered, if possible, the following morning. The rest of the mail he sometimes keeps at home, to simplify the sorting. Everything is recorded and must stay at the Post Office, but his other colleagues do the same thing. It's known, but not spoken about. The boss closes his eyes. That's why Pierre went crazy when he discovered that Nina was stealing letters. An unforgivable professional mistake when he'd never put a foot wrong. Apart from with Odile, when she'd fallen ill.

This evening, Pierre Beau is on vacation. It's the first time in his life he's taking it after 15 August. And all because of *Juste Prix*, the TV game show presented by Philippe Risoli.

Bertrand Delattre, Pierre's colleague and friend, had taken part in the game at the end of last year. There were fifteen of them from La Comelle who had travelled to Paris in a minibus. When Bertrand returned from his trip, he was all mysterious, saying to Pierre, with a strange look: "Watch the program a week from Monday and two weeks from Sunday, I leave you the surprise. Could we swap our summer leave this year?"

On the Monday, Pierre interrupted his round at lunchtime to watch his colleague on TV. Pierre had never seen this program. Didn't even know such a program existed.

His friend Bertrand was randomly picked out of four participants, then walked down a staircase to applause from the audience, among whom Pierre recognized a few people from La Comelle. Bertrand took his place behind a lectern. When Philippe Risoli, the presenter, asked him where he was from, Bertrand replied: "From La Comelle, in Saône-et-Loire." And behind him, everyone had cheered, as if coming from there was something special. As if they'd won the soccer World Cup.

"And what do you do in Saône-et-Loire, Bertrand?" asked Philippe Risoli.

"I'm a mailman."

And there again, everyone applauded and cheered. As if all mailmen had walked on the Moon.

Next, it was the selected prize, and a pretty girl stroked "a ceramic lamp perfectly balanced on its round tripod, complete with matching lampshade." The four participants each took turns to suggest a price. It was a Sandrine from Dordogne who won by saying the price of the lamp was 2,615 francs.

Never had Pierre seen a more stupid game.

A Gilles Lopez, from the Ardèche, then made his entrance.

"And what do you do in life?"

"Farmer."

Cheers from the audience. So, it wasn't only mailmen who were marveled at, farmers were, too.

Next, the price of "an array of accessories for elegant ladies" had to be guessed at. It was the farmer who joined Philippe Risoli and won an engagement ring set with thirty-two diamonds in a row. The lucky winner looked rather put out because he was already married. So Philippe Risoli found the solution, suggesting he just "give it to some gorgeous creature."

When he heard that, Pierre started laughing on his own, in front of the TV, and Paola gave him a puzzled look.

Finally, it was Bertrand who guessed the right price for "a striking sofa in a crimson cover for cozy evenings in." As he was joining the presenter on set, he almost fell over, bringing tears to Pierre's eyes. One eye was crying with sympathy, the other with dismay.

Before Bertrand played, Philippe Risoli made an announcement: "If you, too, dream of taking part in *Juste Prix*, just fill in the form inside *Télé Z* magazine every Monday."

And then it was back to serious matters, to the "suite of garden furniture coated in solid tinted resin."

Bertrand answered everything correctly.

Pierre had to lower the volume of the TV, so deafening was the victory jangle. General hysteria, the audience clapping wildly, it was as if they'd been drugged, or plied with drink. Maybe both.

Bertrand looked embarrassed at winning all that money, he remained stoic, kept his emotions in check, which seemed to disappoint the audience.

"Are you usually lucky?"

Bertrand replied:

"Well, no, not really."

"How did you find yourself taking part in the show?"

"It's my wife who filled in and sent the form . . ."

The presenter looked straight to camera and said:

"On Minitel, 3615 code TF1 . . ."

At the end of the show, three participants turned an enormous wheel and it was Bertrand who won a place in the finale. The losers left with a talking Philippe Risoli badge and a basket of gifts.

"See you again tomorrow at 12:20!"

Closing theme music.

Pierre Beau got back on his bike to finish his round. He thought back on the entire show between mailboxes. It was Monday, he'd have to wait until the following Sunday to know whether Bertrand would win the "showcase," in other words, the final prize, which was "enormous, gigantic, amazing," so the little grannies he delivered to told him.

Pierre heard nothing from Bertrand before the following Sunday, as if he were hiding. The program had been recorded several months before being broadcast, and his participation had been kept quiet as a state secret.

Then the big day arrived. Pierre watched the finale with Nina, Étienne, and Adrien. The children couldn't stop laughing at this appalling game.

They screamed out prices, suggesting any old thing. And Nina finally said: "How uptight does Bertrand look!"

Pierre wondered whether there was a "right price" for life. And whether the lives of some people were the same price as the lives of others. The lives of people one didn't know. The life of his wife, who had passed away so young. And that of his daughter, Marion. Where was she?

For him, the most precious life was Nina's. It was worth all the others combined.

Bertrand guessed the right price for a "ceramic pedestal with matching lamp," at 5,290 francs, and for a "700-watt microwave oven with grill, turbo-grill, and automatic defrosting for seven food types," at 3,490 francs.

But how did his friend know all this? Pierre wondered. He'd known him for thirty years and never knew this about him. This knowledge of the price of things.

And then Bertrand ended up in the finale with another candidate. One Martine, retired, from Cagnes-sur-Mer.

When the girls in skimpy outfits presented the showcase, Bertrand's jaw dropped: a bedroom suite, a bathroom with furniture and whirlpool bath, a halogen lamp, a rattan table with beveled-glass top, armchairs, a transparent vase "evoking the clearest ocean," a car, a motorbike, a fridge, a vacation in Tunisia, an electric model train.

They had to guess the price of all these prizes combined. Whoever's price was the closest to the correct price would win.

The two finalists each wrote down a figure on a slip of paper. Philippe Risoli read their answers out loud:

"For Bertrand, the showcase presented this week totals a round 134,000 francs, for Martine, 220,000 francs. The right price of this showcase is . . . 163,459 francs! Bertrand is the winner!"

Nina screamed: "Wow, grandpa! Your buddy's actually won!"

They were running a little late, the presenter said. A voiceover announced the following week's showcase, with a new audience and new participants. Cue closing theme music.

Pierre couldn't believe it. His friend had won all that and had told him nothing. He'd just mentioned swapping their summer leave. But where had he put that bathroom, that car, and that motorbike? His apartment was tiny, and he didn't even have a garage. His old Renault 4 slept outdoors.

"I sold them," Bertrand told him when he asked him the question. He'd only kept the vacation in Tunisia, and given the money from his winnings to his two remaining children. Bertrand had had three, the youngest had died at a year old.

And that's how Pierre Beau came to change the dates of his vacation for the first time in his life, because of *Juste Prix*.

If he wasn't so tired, it would make him smile. And one has to look on the bright side of things: in three weeks' time, he'd be able to accompany Nina to Paris and stay a few days with her there.

Back in 1981, on 6 May, a woman had opened the door to him to receive a parcel, and she was stark naked. He'd almost had a heart attack from the shock of it. That's exactly how he feels when a Transports Damamme lorry refuses to give him right of way and smashes headlong into him.

# 35

*22 December 2017*

Marie-Laure Beaulieu is in the kitchen. The previous evening, her three children arrived. The only time of year everyone gets together. A five-day hiatus. They never visit at the same time otherwise, but they'd never miss a family Christmas.

She's preparing two free-range chickens for lunch. She always stuffs their rear end with garlic, salt, and thyme. Never fat, only spices she marinates the day before in a few drops of olive oil. She's going to do grilled potatoes for Valentin and Étienne, who are mad about them, green beans with fried onions for Louise, and a zucchini gratin for Paul-Émile.

She draws back the curtain and sees the car from the shelter stopping outside the house. She thinks Nina has finally come to see Étienne. But Valentin gets out on the passenger side and Nina immediately drives off. Marie-Laure doesn't get the chance to go out and make her stay, ask her to come in, offer her a coffee. Look at her, hear her, touch her. Years, now, that she hasn't seen her. Sometimes she crosses paths with her, always at the wheel of that car. Never on a pavement. Marie-Laure knows that Nina has been working at the shelter for years, she could go up there to talk to her. Or she could go to her house. But she doesn't dare. It still upsets her, even after all this time, that Nina and Étienne don't speak anymore.

"What were you doing with Nina Beau, dear?" Marie-Laure asks her grandson as he comes into the kitchen.

"Hi, Gran. D'you know her?"

"She was like my own daughter. A long time ago."

"She's coming over this evening."

". . ."

"I invited her to have an aperitif here, with us, at six. First she wants to go home to have a wash and smell nice . . . That's what she told me."

Marie-Laure looks at Valentin, dumbfounded. How does he knows her? And, more to the point, how had he managed to get her to come to their house?

"I'm going up to see if Dad's awake!" Valentin announces, before disappearing up the stairs.

Marie-Laure switches on the oven to preheat it, 180 degrees, and pulls out a chair to sit herself down. There's a faraway look in her eyes, an absence of the present.

It was 12 August 1994. She will never forget that date. In every life there are some befores and afters.

She was back from the beach. At the end of every afternoon, she always set off alone, leaving Marc and the children behind. She loved having this time to herself. The empty house, readjusting to the darkness again, the shutters closed to stop the sun getting in, the cold tiles underfoot, the warmth from the walls, the chirping of cicadas, the refreshing shower, the cream one covers the body in, getting back to that novel in a deck chair in the shade, before preparing supper while sipping a rosé on the rocks. The taste of paradise.

The house phone rang, she answered it after about ten rings, thinking it wasn't for her but for the owners, who rented this place out in the summer. It was too early to be Adrien and Nina, the only ones to know this number. They rang every evening at around nine. At the end of the line, Marie-Laure heard someone choking, panting, crying, sniffing. She didn't immediately recognize Adrien's voice, didn't understand his words, finally did understand them, wanted to slam the phone down on him, to go backwards, return to the beach, take her clothes off, look at the sea, kill the sky. All she managed to get out was:

"Does Nina know?"

"No, not yet, well, don't think so, she's at work."

"Where's your mother, Adrien, where's Joséphine?"

"Away for the day, I'm all alone, what do I do?"

Marie-Laure had forgotten the time. After four weeks in Saint-Raphaël, she couldn't even remember where all the watches had been put. *There's no clock in this vacation house.* That's what she thought. *There's no calendar, either.*

"Adrien what time is it?"

"Four twenty-five."

She did a quick calculation: after telling Marc and the kids, packing everything up and setting off, they wouldn't get to La Comelle before two, three in the morning.

"Adrien, what day is it?"

"Friday."

"Right, that means that tomorrow, neither Nina nor you are working."

"I am. Nina isn't."

"Right . . . Doesn't matter. Listen to me carefully. Are you listening to me?"

"Yes."

"You're going to dry your eyes, and go and meet her as she leaves work, you find any excuse and you take her far away, very far away. For the time it takes for us to get back. She mustn't return to her house. Make her believe you've got two free days ahead of you . . . Make something up."

"But she'll see I've been crying! I'll never pull it off!"

"Yes!" Marie-Laure almost shouted. "You will manage to! You'll do it for Nina!"

She heard Adrien's sobs down the line. *He's only eighteen, I'm asking the impossible of him.* She thought of the Damammes, maybe she should contact them, call them to warn them. But Nina barely knew them. Yes, but they would find a way to take her somewhere until she herself got back to La Comelle to handle the "sequel." She thought of Marion. Saw her again in the schoolyard. Heard her laughter. They were so young, so carefree. Why had she decided to lose touch with everyone? Why did one lose touch? Her father had just died. How to let her know? How could she have abandoned Nina? Why? Mustn't pass judgment . . .

Adrien's voice brought Marie-Laure out of her torpor:

"I'll manage," he whispered, and hung up.

*

At the same time, Nina, sitting behind a desk, was filing old invoices, from 1993, by month, and then alphabetically. She'd reached March. She wondered what she was doing in March 1993. She was still in fourth grade. She wouldn't have liked to go back to that time. Going through the bac again, no thanks. She didn't know that, a few hours later, she'd give anything to go through it again, every year, even, if only she had the slightest chance of going back to around March 1993.

It was lovely outside. She was bored in this office. Thought of September, in Paris, as liberation. She thought of it as she did of the sea, a vista of possibilities, an infinity, an *untranquility*. Discovering, drawing, singing, composing, meeting people, and returning every evening to Étienne and Adrien. All three of them living, together, soon.

She'd been going out with Emmanuel Damamme for six days. Each day he'd been waiting for her in the evening after work. They had supper at his place. Nina had never seen anything like it, a meal for two waiting for them, on the kitchen table. Ready to be warmed up. Like at a restaurant, with several starters, two different mains, and a dessert. So that was how it was, having staff, not shopping anymore, not Hoovering, not washing one's clothes. Everything was done for Emmanuel, down to making his bed. He lived on his parents' property, in an isolated and independent house. The previous day, he'd left to join friends for a few days in Saint-Tropez. He'd phoned her an hour ago, at the office, with laughter in his voice, to know if she was working hard. He'd said to her: "Miss you." She'd replied: "You too."

She couldn't get over it, her appeal to this boy from a good family, when she saw herself as a girl from a bad family, because of her "whore of a mother." She always felt like some abandoned dog that a decent guy had finally given a home to.

That Saturday at Club 4, the night when Daho was supposedly appearing, Emmanuel had made her drink. They'd stayed at the bar, stuck to each other. Nina had forgotten about Adrien on the dance floor, had forgotten everything. She was like someone else, a girl whose life she'd borrowed just long enough to be happy. Emmanuel had kissed her. His tongue against hers, quite a promise. Nina didn't know kisses like Emmanuel's even existed. This guy was undeniably sensual. Nina felt like her feet weren't touching the ground anymore, like she was offering herself up, he could have done anything with her. Like when life becomes so much bigger than one imagined it to be. He had caressed her, his hands on her dress. After three gins, he'd dared to move further down, lightly touching her privates through the fabric, with increasing urgency. She'd groaned, a desire that spread across her skin, armies of ants, an invasion of exquisite tingles. But she didn't feel like doing the same to him. When she'd barely brushed against his erect penis, it had terrified her. Like something violent.

Finally, he'd murmured: "We're going to have to go." He'd taken her hand, led her to his convertible, and said: "As it's your first time, I'm not going to fuck you in the car. We'll go back to mine."

"To fuck you." These words had shocked her. Brought her back down to earth. Sobered her up. As if someone had shoved her. She'd felt scared. Would it hurt her? Would she bleed? Would she know what to do? She hadn't thought things would move so fast, between Emmanuel entering Club 4 and their first kiss. Barely an hour. And now they were leaving together. She hadn't had time to alert Adrien. It was Joséphine who was coming to collect them at closing time: "See you in the car park at four, as usual." Nina had hoped to go home with Emmanuel, she'd told Adrien the previous day, laughing, praying, jumping on her bed, and now, she wasn't laughing anymore. She was scared. All that remained were prayers. *Dear God, I don't know where you're hiding, but make it go well.*

What would Joséphine think when she'd see no Nina with Adrien in the car park?

She couldn't quite believe she was sitting in this car, the one that made her heart race as soon as she glimpsed it around a street corner. A red Renault Alpine A610. A sports car, a rich person's car, a grown-up's car. And her still just a child. Cinderella in Damammeland.

Club 4 and La Comelle were thirty kilometers apart. Nina Beau and Emmanuel Damamme a world apart. A billion light years. So, was that what being "beautiful as the day" meant? An expression she was forever hearing around her. Being able to attract a man who looked like prince charming?

Thirty kilometers during which Emmanuel told her to choose the music.

"Look in the glove box, and above the dashboard."

Dozens of cassettes, including two Etienne Daho albums, *Pop Satori* and *Pour Nos Vies Martiennes*. She felt like laughing as she pushed in an Oasis cassette. Liam Gallagher's voice. Emmanuel lowered the volume.

"Tell me more about you, Nina."

She felt useless, stupid, tiny, uneducated. Shyness took over.

"I'd rather it was you telling me about you," she heard herself replying.

"How about we don't talk?"

He took Nina's hand and placed it over his prick. He stroked himself with her fingers, gently, barely pressing on his jeans. Not like a lout. He was gentle, but terribly determined. Again, Nina hated this feeling of violence. After so long dreaming of this, the dream was taking a strange turn. She longed to arrive at his place. To down even more drinks. Fill herself with that alcohol that's so good at making us think the sun's shining even on rainy days. They went through a gate. Nina saw a kind of manor house in the distance, surrounded by trees, glimpsed a swimming pool in front. Everything was plunged in darkness.

"Will you be able to take me home after?" she almost implored.

He smiled and replied: "If there is an after," then, sensing Nina's discomfort, he reassured her:

"Everything's going to be just fine, I promise you."

He drove on for about two hundred meters and then parked in front of a stone house, a smaller one. Ivy raced up the walls. The wooden shutters were open and looked as if they always had been. The front door wasn't locked. Inside, it smelt of candles. Inside, it was even more beautiful than Étienne's house. It looked antique and precious. Nina had never seen so many paintings on walls.

Emmanuel poured her a drink, a gin and tonic, lots of gin for her and for him, they clinked glasses. Before going up to the bathroom, he told her: "Settle in, chill out, choose the music," indicating a hi-fi system.

He felt like gobbling her up, fucking her, felt himself going crazy, but seeing her fearful face, he had to hold back.

*Control yourself*, he told himself in front of the bathroom mirror.

This girl really did it for him. With a sexual intensity he'd not yet experienced. None of the girls he'd slept with had had that effect on him. And yet she was awkward, young. Very young. He must go gently. He'd found it hard to believe that she'd never gotten laid, she went out a lot, there was something lively, sassy about her. At the office, he'd watched her, she was confident around the others. He'd thought that she must be lying, like with that Étienne Daho story. That she took him for an idiot. But since they'd left Club 4, with her defeated look, her weak smiles, tense gestures, shaky voice, she'd lost ten years. He'd seen the little girl, not the young woman anymore. He'd realized that she was a virgin.

He found her downstairs, leaning against a kitchen unit, nose in her already empty glass. He took her in his arms, said to her: "Come over here." They lay down on the sofa, fully dressed. He caressed her. First, he must reassure her, he sensed her relaxing. Next, make her want it again, like at the club, earlier. They must share it, or it was pointless. She must be part of it, so that, whatever happened, it would be a nice memory for her. Emmanuel was no thug. His image was very important to him. He wanted to please, in every way.

When Nina saw him coming downstairs from the bathroom, she thought how handsome he was, very handsome. His hair was tousled, his desire for her glowed from his eyes, like burning embers. She sensed it, saw it, breathed it. The way he looked at her, with an animal desire. That's what terrified her. She knew she wouldn't be leaving this house as the same person. That he would take her virginity. She thought of Adrien and Étienne, what would they say if they saw her here, in this house, with *him*? Étienne would definitely make fun of her, couldn't handle her being touched, so would hide behind his sniggering and sarcasm. As for Adrien, he would smile at her with that enigmatic smile that, since childhood, she'd never managed to decipher. She missed them intensely, she chased them from her mind, as one chases away a dung fly.

Emmanuel had taken her hand and said, "Come over here," the gentleness flowing between them, he led her to the sofa, lay on his back, with her lying on him, light as a feather. His hands on her body had lifted her dress, touched her bra, unfastened it. She let him go on, he already knew many things that she didn't. Caresses that made her groan, brought warmth and pleasure to her tummy that radiated down to her vagina without him touching it. Just poking his tongue in her ear or nibbling it where the skin was most sensitive. Parts of her body that Emmanuel was awakening and revealing to her.

One night, when Étienne and Adrien had fallen asleep right beside her and she was zapping, she'd seen a porn film. She'd checked that the boys were sound asleep, and held onto the remote control, ready to switch channels if one of them opened their eyes. She'd have rather died than get caught. She'd lowered the sound and watched those gaping, wet vaginas. Disgusting and fascinating at the same time. The actors didn't caress each other. There was no love. It was mechanical. Sausage meat. An abattoir. The cold store at a butcher's.

The following day, she'd said to the boys:

"Last night I saw a porn film on TV. It shocked me."

Étienne had said to her:

"Shut up, I don't want to know anything about your sex life."

"But you tell me all about your girlfriends' tits!"

"It's not the same for me."

"And why's that?"

"You're a girl."

And Adrien had smiled, shyly.

Emmanuel had caressed her for a long time, looking at her every now and then, asking her if she was O.K. His face was red, he was sweating, he'd lost his cockiness, he looked like a lunatic. She'd answered yes.

That's all she'd been able to say, yes.

He got up to switch off the light. He did it for her. It didn't bother him. He lay her on her back, took off her dress with a sure hand, and her bra, now dangling on her tummy. He stripped off himself, releasing his smell, a mix of cologne and sweat, and they found themselves naked, one against the other, and she found him heavy. He went down on her, licked her. For Nina, a mix of happiness and unhappiness at being exposed like this to the tongue of a stranger, his fingers inside as though searching her. Desire and repulsion were hand in hand, pleasure and disgust entwined. He came back up to her, face against face, his mouth smelling of moist vagina, and she felt like running away, being a seven-year-old child once more, being no taller than the white fence outside her grandfather's house. He parted her legs, entered her without force, it hurt her, she stopped breathing, while he went back and forth inside her body, breathing very hard. He clenched his fists, tensed up, whispered, "I want you too much," and it was over. He wasn't moving anymore. His breath on her neck. He removed his condom with his fingertips. Murmured in her ear that they were going to start again, take their time.

*So that's what makes the world go round and people write songs. I must rework those lyrics*, thought Nina.

*

Adrien kept seeing the scene again and again. He was filling up a white Renault 5, license plate 69, when the fire engine, sirens wailing, passed the service station. He paid no attention. Eyes riveted on the numbers scrolling on the pump's screen, he was keen to finish and get back to the kiosk to finish a novel he was gripped by.

The fire engine stopped three hundred meters away without cutting its sirens. Adrien automatically looked over, could make out a gathering, passersby running. The owner of the Renault said: "I've just driven past it, it's dreadful, someone said it's a mailman who's been knocked down." Adrien instantly knew it was Pierre. He knew his rounds, his streets, that the lower part of La Comelle was his patch.

Adrien had had supper at the Beaus' the previous day because Emmanuel had gone off to Saint-Tropez. Since she'd slept with him, Nina hadn't left his side. She even stopped calling Étienne in the evening. Adrien had questioned her: "So? What's the score? D'you love him?" But Nina had remained evasive, only coming out with this weird expression: "Nothing to break a duck's three feet over." Adrien had found these words so unexpected, so incongruous, that he'd had a fit of the giggles. And Nina had joined in, without saying a word more.

While the three of them were having supper in the garden, Pierre had complained of aching muscles, with a smile. "I'm no spring chicken anymore."

Adrien stopped squeezing the nozzle, the numbers froze, and, leaving the tank open, he raced toward the flashing lights. Those three hundred meters seemed endless. Like in those nightmares when you run without moving forward, when you try to scream but not a sound comes out. He finally saw the man lying on the ground, his lifeless legs. Pools of blood, splashes of vermillion. Adrien thought: *What will become of Nina*? The lorry hadn't been damaged, not a scratch on the paintwork, as if the driver had parked in the middle of the road just to pop into a store. He was standing there, pale, distraught, unscathed, repeating: "I didn't see him, I didn't see him." One of Pierre's bicycle wheels stuck out from under the engine. As if the lorry had swallowed the bike and then spat out what it didn't want. The upper part of Pierre's body, including his face, was hidden under a blanket. Like in films when victims have just been murdered. Adrien had noticed a delivery bag left on a bench, just beyond. What was it doing there? It had been battered, too, crushed. He grabbed it without thinking, went into a telephone box. At his home, the phone rang and rang, then he remembered, his mother had gone to Lyon for the day. He felt totally alone, looked out, saw the firemen taking Pierre's body away on a stretcher. He rummaged in his pockets, found the scrap of paper Nina had scribbled the phone number of the Beaulieus' vacation house on.

And Marie-Laure, finally, answered.

Once he hung up, Adrien ran like a lunatic. He went back to his kiosk, took 2,000 francs from the till. It was madness, he needed this job to go to Paris, move in, eat. He was going to lose everything, but now he was acting purely on instinct, his reason had departed with

Pierre Beau on the stretcher. He must take Nina far away, very far from here, until the Beaulieus got back from Saint-Raphaël.

Be quick, very quick. Before anyone tells Nina.

He walked straight into Damamme, past security, his face red as a poppy. At reception, a fat woman with white hair and black-framed specs, looked at him, flabbergasted. She knew this kid by sight, recalled he was Nina Beau's friend, maybe even her boyfriend, the young didn't bother anymore, they just waltzed straight into the building during office hours.

"I have to see Nina!"

"Good day. She's working," the woman replied, drily.

"I have to take her far away."

"Excuse me?"

"Does she know?"

The woman stared at him as if he was crazy or drugged. Right then, the police station had phoned to inform Ms. Black-framed specs that one of the company's drivers had just knocked over a man on Place de Gaulle. A fatal accident. Monsieur Damamme senior needed to come to the station urgently, the cause of the accident, and who was responsible, hadn't yet been established.

Meanwhile, Adrien was opening every door he came to. Offices, printer rooms, storerooms. He hid the mailbag on a top shelf, behind some boxes, Nina mustn't see it.

Adrien finally found Nina sitting behind a desk. When she saw him, she gave him a quizzical look without saying a word. Adrien knew how to put her off the scent, hadn't he always been doing that?

"It's Friday, we're young, in a month we're off, Nina, off to Paris. Before that, I feel like doing something crazy, we've got the weekend, I'll take you anywhere you want to go, right now. I've told your grandfather. He knows you're with me, he said fine, it even made him laugh. Come on, we're off."

She smiled. At that moment, and because of that smile, Adrien pinched himself hard on the inside of his arm so as not to crack. She was his sister, his favored one, the girl he loved most in the whole world. It was at this instant, in this gray room with its view of nothing but walls, that he knew, knew for certain. Nina was going to suffer, and it was unbearable, but for now, he was giving her her last two days of being carefree. Her last two days of childhood. She had time enough to discover the truth, to become an adult from one day to the next.

To avoid going back through reception, he opened the window behind her and climbed through it, saying to her:

"Follow me."

"But I haven't finished my day's work!"

"Who cares, you're sleeping with the boss."

"You're silly . . ."

She slipped a jacket on, took her bag. They took the small streets to get to the station. Mustn't bump into anyone. They got to Mâcon on the 5:10 P.M. regional express. In Mâcon, Nina picked Marseilles on the departures board. Adrien bought two tickets with the stolen money.

"But where's all that cash from?"

"From my father, a reward for my distinction . . . So, let's make the most of it!"

At 11:00 P.M., they were drawing into Saint-Charles station. From a phone box, Adrien called his mother while Nina was buying two chocolate-and-banana panini. Joséphine had heard about Pierre Beau, everyone was worried sick, Emmanuel Damamme was searching everywhere for Nina, the manager of the service station had called Joséphine, furious, about to report Adrien to the police, she'd returned the stolen money to him, end of story, and explained about Nina's grandfather. Adrien asked his mother to go to the Beaus' house to look after Paola and the cats—"The door's always open, but just in case, there's a key under the big red pot beside the doormat"—they'd both be back on Sunday, he'd take Nina straight from the station to Étienne's, where they should all wait for them, late afternoon, to break the news to her all together. He'd already hung up when Joséphine asked: "But where are you?"

Adrien bought the train tickets for Sunday, and then they caught a bus that went down to the sea, stopped at a small inlet called the Plage du Prophète. The air was mellow, some youngsters had lit a campfire, Adrien and Nina joined them. They chatted, drank beers, ate pizzas, danced to "Sous le Soleil de Bodega," Nina seemed happy, she looked at Adrien the way one looks at a beloved. The sand was cold, he asked Nina if she fancied sleeping under the stars, she replied: "Yes, wonderful." At two in the morning, they settled against a small beach cabin, stretched out in each other's arms. Adrien whispered to her: "I love you, Nina, I'll always love you." She replied: "I know." Adrien didn't sleep a wink all night. Thinking about Pierre's death, the repercussions, the sadness. How could life take such drastic turns?

Nina was woken by the daylight, they stripped off, plunged into the Mediterranean, it was still cool, but the sky was a pure, promising blue. In front of them, the Frioul islands radiated a white, almost lunar, light. They lingered a long time in the water, which was calm as a lake that morning, as if waves were but a myth.

Making the most of every second, they spent the day on that packed beach, it was the middle of August, after all. Nina loved the Marseilles accent. She listened to the people talking around her, the way one listens to the words of a song.

In the afternoon, while she was resting, Adrien bought some soap, toothpaste, a toothbrush, two bottles of water, tomatoes, a watermelon, and some savory biscuits. They wore the same clothes for two days, jeans, T-shirts, and their jackets, which they put on at night. During the day, they were in their underwear. Nina didn't want to leave that beach. There was a public shower outside the cabins, and at the end of the day they had a wash and dried themselves in the sun, sitting on a rock and watching the sailboats and the last swimmers. Nina said: "This is the most beautiful day of my life, if only Étienne and Grandpa were here to see it."

# 36

*22 December 2017*

She rings the bell. Étienne opens the door. An awkwardness, a long silence, face to face, eye to eye. They haven't seen each other for fourteen years. But it all collapses like a soufflé just out of the oven. In the end, it doesn't matter that much. It's not as important anymore. It's not because you loved each other before that you have to love each other now. Time has passed. It seems it takes everything with it, the proof being that she's not trembling.

He's wearing carpet slippers, doubtless borrowed from his father. He knew she was coming, he could have made an effort, got changed. Nina is sure he's done it on purpose. Showing himself at his worst.

He has thickened, has the features of a mature man, the beginnings of a coarse beard, darker hair, his beauty is somewhat diminished, a bird of passage, then, when Nina thought it would never leave him. That it was inscribed in his genes. Beauty becomes what one does with it. All that's left now is a look that says he's given up on it all, that all we call life, joy, desire. No more hope, few laughs, immense weariness. A man who is bored. Finally, he half-smiles at her, sardonically. That he hasn't lost.

"I thought you wouldn't come."

His voice, deeper, drawling. Where has his confidence gone? He lays his big hand on Nina's shoulder and kisses her on the cheek. Just one kiss. He has drunk. She smells it on his breath.

"I promised Valentin," whispers Nina.

"So, you've seen, he's great, my kid . . . You're expected, your aperitif awaits, come in."

The corridor she'd known so well, its smell, still the same. A synthetic rose scent. The stairs leading up, the furniture that hasn't moved, the phone table where the family kept the directories, none of them anymore, usurped by the internet. The shoe cupboard she'd so often chucked her sneakers into before going up, barefoot, two steps at a time, to find Étienne in his room. The kitchen on the left, the door's open. A new kitchen like everyone's got, with a central island, a white dresser, a sky-blue driftwood finish. In the corridor, the same wallpaper. What seemed so stylish when she was young suddenly looks outdated. As if the house had aged badly, like Étienne. Not that special after all.

Valentin turns up, in his socks, clutching a mobile phone.

"I requested you as a friend on Facebook, did you see? Are you on Instagram and Snapchat?"

"No," she replied, with a forced smile.

Inside this house, Valentin looks even more like his father at the same age. It's his presence that unnerves her, not Étienne's. What she's feeling right now is that *her* Étienne has gone. That all that's left of him is dead skin. That all the cells in his body have regenerated, leaving behind this stranger leading her to another room. Too much water has flowed under the bridge. What does he like to eat now? At what time? What's become of his habits? Which is his favorite band? And his favorite film? What are his friends' names? His smell is different. Before, she knew it with her eyes closed. He smelt of sugar.

She follows father and son into the dining room. Marie-Laure, perched on the sofa, seems emotional. She gets up, comes toward Nina, hugs her. She has changed. The beautiful, tanned woman has wrinkled. *How old is she? In her sixties*, Nina works out in her mind.

"How good it is to see you again, Nina."

Nina hugs Marie-Laure in return. Still the same perfume, Caron's *Fleur de Rocaille*.

"Sorry, Marie-Laure, sorry."

"Sorry for what?"

"Never having come to see you."

"I could have gone up to the shelter, too. I have plenty to be sorry for . . . When you left . . . I should have understood . . . But let's not talk about that anymore. Come on, sit yourself down."

Nina glances over her shoulder, sees Marc smiling at her, he's become rather stout, he kisses her. Formerly so reserved, he seems warmer. How often had Étienne complained of not being loved by his father? Had they finally talked, understood each other, come to some agreement?

It's Louise's turn to get up, her stunning blue eyes, a woman, adolescence gone, still radiant, blooming. The big brother, Paul-Émile, his wife, Pauline, and their two children, a boy and a girl, Louis, and Lola, eight and ten years old. A blond woman enters the room, small, slim, around forty, a vigorous handshake.

"I'm Marie-Castille, Étienne's wife."

"Good evening."

Marie-Castille eyes Nina like a rival, as if she had something to fear, it's instant. Her handshake and the way she said, "Étienne's wife," meaning: "He's mine."

*Clearly*, thinks Nina, *the moment Étienne touches a woman, a paranoid possessiveness is triggered.*

Nina takes a box of chocolates out of her bag and hands them to Marie-Laure.

"You shouldn't have."

"Yes, I should."

Nina has put on the dress she bought the previous day. She feels like she's in disguise. She'd even dashed into the supermarket to buy a BB cream, and a crimson lip pencil that she'd combined with her lip balm, just for a touch of color, and had drawn a brown line around her eyes. She thought she'd forgotten that skill, but the skill hadn't forgotten her.

"So, you look after the shelter?"

"Yes."

"That doesn't surprise me, knowing you. Do you still draw? No? What a shame. I've kept many of the portraits you did of Étienne and Louise. I had them framed. They're in our bedroom."

Louise is a surgeon in Lyon, single, no children.

"As for me, I'm still a cop," mutters Étienne. "I met Marie-Castille at work, she's my chief."

Marie-Laure and Marc are both retired. Nina vaguely gathers that

Paul-Émile and Pauline are engineers and work in Geneva. She isn't listening to anyone anymore. Just smiles. Says yes or no.

Étienne doesn't seem ill. Would Valentin have lied to her? No, not the sort of kid to lie. He takes a few photos with his mobile phone, then a selfie, asking everyone behind him to smile.

Nina senses Étienne's eyes on her, often. She senses him watching her. What's he thinking? That she, too, has changed, aged, her skin, her lines, forever outdoors, walking the dogs, accumulating cats and worries, the kennels that never empty, the open days to make them less crowded, the old animals that die there, the sorrow at not managing to place them, offer them a few months in a basket in a warm home before the grim reaper pays a visit.

*All that*, thinks Nina, *is bound to show on my face and hands.*

As soon as she looks at Étienne, tries to meet his gaze, he turns his head away. She feels once more the annoyance he used to provoke in her. Her annoyed love. Their bickering: "Don't do this, don't do that," "Stop drawing attention to yourself" . . .

Étienne gets up.

"Where are you going, darling?" asks Marie-Castille.

Étienne replies, in a thick voice:

"Where you can't go in place of me."

On his way, he stops in the kitchen. Opens a cupboard. Downs three slugs of the Grand Marnier his mother uses to flambé crêpes. Numbing the pain. He retches. Goes upstairs, locks himself in the bathroom, drops his trousers, sits down. His head is spinning.

A memory.

He's on the beach at Saint-Raphaël. He's flirting with a girl he likes, what's her name again? Camille. Yes, that's it, Camille. The others have nicknamed her Chamomile. "But believe me, buddy, she's not the kind of girl to make you fall asleep." He doesn't understand, smiles stupidly, not aware that chamomile tea is a bedtime drink. He holds her long hair in his left hand to clear her face, while his right hand roams her body, the interesting bits. To one side, a shadow looms up between him and the sun. A rigid presence. He thinks he hears his name being said. He turns his head, opens one eye, it's his mother. At that moment, Étienne wants to kill her. He hates her for intruding on this intimate moment. What the hell's she doing here? She has her back to the sun. He asks her, aggressively:

"What is it?"

"We have to go back, something serious has happened."

Beside her, his father appears, that's all he needs. His father and mother leaning over him. Camille gets up. *Nooooo, don't go, it was so good.* He's in his bathing trunks, has a bit of a hard-on, mortifying in front of his parents. What are they on about? Go back? Go back where?

"Pierre Beau has died."

In the sitting room, Marie-Laure pours Nina a second glass of champagne.

"That's my last, I'm driving."

Louis's and Lola's shrieks drown her out, as they chase each other over a *Game of Thrones* figurine stolen by one or the other.

"Well, in any case, you're having supper with us," Marie-Laure says to Nina.

Think of a lie, immediately.

"I can't, I have to collect a dog from the veterinarian before eight."

"Which dog is it?" asks Valentin.

Think of a second lie. She thinks of Romain. Then of old Bob sleeping on the sofa while she'd hastily got dressed in front of him last night.

"He's called Bob, a small griffon, you didn't see him this morning, he was already in treatment."

"What's wrong with him?"

"Heart ache."

Nina had replied instinctively. *Whose heart is aching the most around this sitting-room table*? she thinks. Time separates those who love each other . . . Nina had written a song about that at the time of the three. It went:

*Time separates those who love each other*
*Even the newlyweds whose train you held*
*All that's left of their love is wan memories*
*Time separates those who love each other . . .*

What comes next, she can't remember anymore. Neither the words, nor the tune.

One morning, her ex-husband burnt her notebooks of lyrics and drawings. He said: "We're getting rid of old stuff." Nina saw her words and sketches go up in smoke. She felt no sadness. Just let him carry on without saying a word, she was near him, like a doll whose lips have been drawn in a permanent smile.

Marie-Castille doesn't finish a single sentence without saying the name Étienne, like some bet to be won or challenge to be met: "Étienne thinks that . . ." "Étienne feels like," "Étienne doesn't really like," "Étienne says that he," "Étienne was sleeping when . . ."

Étienne returns at that moment, sits back in his place, beside his wife, on the sofa.

At the same time, Marie-Castille asks Valentin if "Daddy knows you went over there this morning."

"No. I didn't tell anyone," the boy replies.

"What am I supposed to know?" asks Étienne.

"That Valentin went to the shelter all on his own this morning."

"Mom, give me a break, I'm fourteen! And I didn't go to flog crack outside schools, I went to Nina's shelter."

"Well, in any case," Marie-Castille says, with fake complicity, "I hope Nina didn't put it into your head to adopt an animal . . ."

Nina responds, quick as a flash:

"I never do that. An animal has to be deserved."

Étienne is amused:

"You haven't changed."

"Étienne told me that used to write music, that you had a group?" Marie-Castille continues, to change the subject.

"Yes," replies Nina. "I suppose . . ."

She doesn't feel like talking about it at all.

"I love it when Étienne sits at the piano," adds Marie-Castille.

*Bravo*, thinks Nina. *You've managed to get Étienne into your last ten sentences*. And suddenly, that very Étienne asks her:

"Join me for a smoke?"

"I don't smoke," replies Nina.

"Now's the time to start."

"With her asthma . . ." chips in Marie-Laure.

Étienne gets up, Nina does the same without looking at Marie-Castille, who must, doubtless, be put out. She follows him into the room that leads to the garden.

"Put on a coat, it's freezing outside," he says to her.

"Yes, Dad."

He smiles. They meet up again in the biting cold. Hopping, from one foot to the other, on the spot. Étienne offers her a cigarette, which she turns down.

"You know very well I can't. That I never could."

She notices a scar cutting across his eyebrow.

"You've got a scar above your eye."

He smiles.

"War wound . . . If I told you who did that to me, you wouldn't believe me . . ."

"Someone I know?"

Étienne dodges the question by asking:

"Are you happy?"

"More tranquil than happy. I'm at peace. And you? Are you happy?"

"Like you with the cigarette, you know very well I can't be. That I never could be."

"Are you ill?"

Étienne stares at her. She's still just as direct. In his eyes, first anger, then dejection. As though laying down his arms.

"Who told you that?"

"Valentin."

Étienne seems stunned. A long silence falls between them. There's only their breathing, the smoke in the cold. Whenever Étienne takes a drag, it looks like his mouth is catching fire.

"Don't feel like talking about it," he finally says.

"What's your illness?" Nina perseveres.

"Don't feel like it."

"Why?"

"Don't feel like it."

He's got his stubborn look, the one he'd get on bad days. Like when something was refused him, as a child and an adolescent. You get older, change skin, but certain reflexes are never lost. It's only your hair you end up losing.

"Does your wife know?"

"No . . . But I thought that Valentin . . . He must have rummaged around. Shall we go back in? It's freezing."

She doesn't get time to reply. He's already opened the door, the warmth inside, the smell of petits-fours, the voices, the laughter.

"I must be going," Nina says to the gathering.

"Already?" Marie-Laure asks, sadly. "But you've barely just arrived."

"Yes, the veterinarian has just called me, sorry about that."

Everyone stands up, kisses goodbye to Nina.

"It's been a pleasure for us to see you."

Louise holds her two hands.

"I'll drop by to have a coffee with you before going back to Lyon."

Nina knows she won't drop by.

"Who are you with for Christmas?" Marie-Laure asks her.

"With colleagues and friends of the shelter. We get together every year, taking turns to host."

"Will you come back here?" Valentin asks her.

"Yes . . . And you, come by whenever you like. I'm up there every day."

"O.K."

"I'll come, too," says Marie-Laure, "this time I'll come."

Valentin winks at Nina.

"I'll show you out," mutters Étienne.

They both leave the house, stop in front of Nina's car.

"Lovely bodywork," Étienne can't resist saying, ironically, in front of the Citroën combi van.

". . ."

"Why are you in such a hurry to leave? You've got no dog to collect from the veterinarian's."

"No."

"Why d'you come?"

"Valentin."

"..."

"He looks like you."

"*I* looked like him, a long time ago. You, on the other hand, are still beautiful."

"Stop it."

"In the end, I should have fucked you. Like the others."

"Stop that, d'you mind?"

"I've been drinking, sorry. Sorry. I'm beneath contempt."

She feels like talking to him about Clotilde. Says nothing. Not the time. Not the place. She strokes his cheek. A beaten track, her hand on his face. Like drawing those lines of kohl around her eyes, the gestures that remember before we do. He smiles at her, sadness. He bangs twice on the roof of the combi and about-turns.

"Pleased to have seen you again."

She watches him disappear into the house. The doorstep light going out.

She drives off, hands shaking, emotions a time bomb. She turns the rearview mirror toward her, glances at her reflection. The make-up has almost gone, swallowed up by a skin no longer used to the superfluous.

Two options are open to her: going home and vacuuming while a meal reheats in the microwave; or going to find out how old Bob is doing at Romain Grimaldi's.

Unless . . . It's barely seven o'clock. Not too late to go up and see how the kitten, Nicola, is faring.

# 37

*14 August 1994*

Something from the realm of the impossible. The brain no longer registers. It isn't conveying the right information. It's light-years away: by the time you understand where the words are leading you, everything has already been dead for centuries.

It's Marie-Laure who's taken it on:

"Sit down, sweetheart, I have some sad news. Your grandfather had an accident, he was knocked down, they weren't able to save him."

Who is "they"? They, they, they, they. "They" is a neutral pronoun referring to any number of people, the subject of the sentence.

"He didn't suffer," Marc adds.

Nina can't move anymore. Everything turns to stone. She's seen that before, in a cartoon film, *Candy*, yes, that's it.

*In the land of Candy*
*Like in every land*
*There's fun, tears, and laughter*
*There are baddies and goodies*
*And to get out of scrapes*
*Having friends is very handy*
*A little love, a little mischief*
*That's the life of Candy.*

Yes, she'd seen an episode in which the young girl, afflicted by a curse, turns into a stone statue.

They are all facing her, tanned, back from vacation, waiting for her reaction. Étienne, Adrien, Louise, Paul-Émile, Marc, Marie-Laure, and Joséphine. She doesn't recognize anyone anymore.

A stone statue. With a hammer and chisel, like Isabelle Adjani in the film *Camille Claudel*, Marie-Laure carves these words into her:

"Pierre's funeral will take place on Wednesday 17 August at the church in La Comelle. He will be buried beside Odile, your grandmother. I've taken care of everything. I've chosen the flowers and the coffin, you're too young for such things. It's an accident at work. You're going to stay with us for a few days, then it will be your decision. Joséphine is looking after the dog and cats."

Nina opens her mouth to hear her voice, the sound of her own voice saying a word: if she whispers it, he'll turn up, reverse the curse.

"Grandpa?"

No one moves. Only Adrien holds his hand out to her, touches her arm, she pulls it back. Since nothing is real. Since all she's living through right now cannot be real.

Marie-Laure takes up her chisel to carve a new sentence into Nina:

"Would you like to go and see him at the funeral parlor?"

And again, Nina calls out to him. That's enough now. He must come and collect her.

"Grandpa!" she implores.

Never would Pierre Beau enter this house without announcing himself. She'll hear him, he'll ring the doorbell, like when he rings the bell of people with no mailbox, or when it's important. A parcel, a certified letter, a money order. "Blasted doorbells," he sometimes curses.

One day, when she was little, he had sat her on his handlebars, and she'd done his round with him. He was proud as he showed her the streets he went up and down, how fast he pedaled. As he said to everyone: "She's my granddaughter!"

Maybe it's the doorbell that's stopped working. Nina stands up, her legs struggle to carry her, she goes to the front door, half-opens it. No one there. She must make him react; she must get out a final sentence. Words that will make him beside himself with anger. She whispers: "Grandpa, I'm still going through the mail."

She waits. Closes her eyes in silent prayer. Expects to see him turning up to give her a slap. Nothing happens.

# 38

*22 December 2017*

I'm still working at my desk when I see car headlights shining through the glass door in my kitchen. And then turning off. The motor stops. At my feet, Nicola is playing with an imaginary bird.

I get very few visitors, especially at this hour. The doorbell rings, Nina is wearing makeup. A touch of brown lingering around the eyes. She says: "I've just seen Étienne, give me something to drink." I can't help but shudder. Just the mention of Étienne makes me reel. I'd even throw her out to stop her from speaking. So she shuts up forever. I even stifle regret for opening the door to her. Not hiding myself. Like when we were children, and I didn't want to be seen. When finding Nina at my door, both in Paris and here, is something I've long dreamt of.

"Come in."

She dives on Nicola, breathes him in, says to him: "How's this baby doing?" She glances at his bowls of food and water. That's her job. I can tell she's content, the house fits the bill.

She takes a seat on the sofa, looks around the sitting room, occasionally stopping, and then declares: "It's a charming house."

She gets back up to look at the books in my bookcase. She takes out *Blanc d'Espagne*, I recognize the novel by its cover, a close-up of a red scarf and a child's hands holding a snowball. Behind him, a window covered in *blanc d'Espagne*, that white paint that's slapped over store windows when there's a change of owner or work being done. That whitewash that means everything's closed for now.

Nina thumbs through it, looks at me, closes it and puts it back on the shelf. I don't react.

"Port, whiskey, white Martini. And I've got some Aperol and prosecco, I could make you a spritzer."

"Great, but with no ice," she replies.

"I know."

"You remember that?"

"I remember everything . . . How is he?"

I ended up asking the question. It's stronger than me. A blasted incurable disease, when my entire being refuses to know, doesn't want to, and can't bear to, hear *him* spoken of. A graft that will never take again. A rejection. Nina knows immediately that I'm referring to Étienne. She sits back in her place. Like a good girl. I find it hard to believe that she's here. At my place. I thought I'd never see her again.

"He's changed. A lot. He seems sad. He has a son of fourteen, very good-looking, adorable, who's called Valentin."

"Louise told me about him."

Nina seems flabbergasted.

"You still see her?"

"Yes. We talk about Adrien, but rarely Étienne."

She pauses a while. Looks at me strangely. As if I've just cursed.

"Are you seeing someone?" she asks me, staring at me with her black eyes, so dark they reveal nothing.

She's always had that ability to close off her eyes, like one closes shutters so that nothing shows in them.

"You mean a shrink?"

Nina laughs at my joke.

"No, a lover."

"On forms, I tick the box 'single, no children.'"

She smiles at me again as if to say: "Same here."

"Étienne asked me if I was happy," she says.

"What did you reply?"

"Too complicated a question for a reply. Especially to someone you haven't seen for fourteen years. Especially to Étienne."

"Where did you see him?"

"At Marc and Marie-Laure's. At one point, we both went out into the garden."

I take in that information. Nina had gone back there. To No. 7 Rue du Bois-d'Agland. Suddenly, I'm back inside that big house, the sitting room, the parties, the birthdays of one among us. Étienne who took up all the space, and Louise, always in a corner, seated on a chair, book in hand, like a toy with spent batteries. A blond doll with big blue eyes whose mechanism seemed broken. So emotional and vibrant inside, without anyone really knowing who she was.

"Did you see Louise?"

Nina answers yes. A catch in her voice.

"Why?"

"Why what?" she asks.

"Why did you go there? To their place? To *his* parents' house?"

She doesn't answer, becomes lost in thought, staring at a fixed point in front of her. Like that time when I came across her and she brushed past me without seeing me. But now, little by little, she returns to me.

"With Louise, do you meet often?" she asks.

"Quite often."

"Did she tell you about Étienne?"

"Tell me what?"

"Nothing."

"Tell me what?"

"That he looked sad."

"We never talk about him. Louise knows I find it hard to bear . . . I can't bear it at all, in fact," I end up blurting out.

She stares at me. I pour her another spritzer, which I stiffen by adding a generous shot of white Martini.

"Did he mention Clotilde to you?"

"No . . . Could I leave my car outside your place?"

"Sure."

"I'm going to walk home. I've drunk too much."

"We're a long way from your house, at least three, maybe four kilometers."

"I'm used to walking."

"It's freezing cold out tonight. D'you want me to call you a taxi?"

She bursts out laughing.

"A taxi . . . that's such a Parisian's thing. I'm used to the cold."

"D'you want to sleep here? I have a friends' room. Small but heated."

"Nah, gotta go home, for my cats. And since when am I your friend?"

## 39

*17 August 1994*

Many of the locals are still on vacation, and yet the church in La Comelle is overflowing onto the forecourt. An entire family for every letter box, that makes quite a crowd. From the lower district, they've all come to bid farewell to their mailman. And they don't all fit in. Like when mail spills out if uncollected.

Eyes are wiped with cotton handkerchiefs. All those years of "just a drop" in a Pyrex glass for Pierre Beau now flowing down cheeks.

Nina arrived between Étienne and Adrien. One on either side to hold her hand, Étienne on the left, Adrien on the right, even grief doesn't break habits. They followed the coffin right up to the altar. The Beaulieu and Damamme families, and also Joséphine, behind them, like an overlong veil of sorrow trailing on the ground. The opposite of a bride: disunity, disintegration.

Nina in pieces. An orphan. Already rickety since childhood, lame and one-legged, this time it's all over, she's on the floor. Grief will come later. She's in a state of shock and fear. A dizzying fear.

Pierre Beau didn't know the Damamme family, but Emmanuel's parents are there out of friendship for the Beaulieus and to support Nina, their "little summer intern." And it's one of their drivers who knocked down the mailman.

Nina knows Damamme senior, she sees him every day at work, just as she sees the others changing their behavior and voice when he asks a question or walks down a corridor. His wife looks pretty in her fine dark clothes, blond with fair skin. Something of Catherine Deneuve. Emmanuel resembles his mother, has the same grace, the same eyes, too.

Emmanuel would have wanted to support Nina, but he's only just appeared in her life, whereas the other two have been there for a long time. No doubt too long a time. You can't separate childhood friends. Seeing her in this church prompts Emmanuel to think of marrying Nina. It's strange what's going through his mind on this morning. He'd like to sponge away the darkness shrouding her, rub her down, wipe away her pain. He'd like to slip a white dress on her and make her say yes for life. Take Cinderella's fairy godmother's magic wand and never give it back. He's in love.

Nina isn't listening to what the priest's saying. She grips Adrien's and Étienne's hands. Would like never to let them go.

Sitting down, standing up, sitting down, standing up, according to the man of God's directions. She keeps glancing, in desperation, at the pale Christ hanging to one side, a little isolated, above a few dying candles, lit the previous day. What is the crucified one thinking? How many funerals has he witnessed since they hung him up there? What father can make his son suffer *that*? And the Virgin Mary, did she know? Was she complicit?

How could the same bastards take her grandfather from her? Weren't her parents enough? They had to take more? Couldn't they have allowed her just a few more years? Long enough for him to come and listen to her sing in Paris, and for her to take him on a vacation beside the sea?

Occasionally, she looks at the coffin in which Pierre Beau's going to sleep for eternity. She'd never seen one before. At eighteen, unless you live in a country at war, you've never seen anyone dead.

A photo of Pierre has been placed on an easel, a portrait his colleagues had unearthed, so rarely did he pose for one.

This morning, Nina is thinking how neither she, nor Étienne, nor Adrien had ever been to a catechism class. Pierre couldn't care less about God. "Before," he'd told her one day, "I was a Communist." Nina never really knew what "Communist" meant, except that it was supposed to protect the poor, share any money, and that it crapped on the Church. Later, she learnt at school that it could also take the guise of Stalin or Mao Zedong, and that it was an ideology as nightmarish as any other. A force that was utopian and unfeasible. Like drinkable seawater.

Even if Nina hasn't been to a catechism class, she's been inside this church before, to light a candle, make a wish, beseech heaven for a boy to fall in love with her. Dear God, make Alexandre go out with me. Sometimes, Adrien also prays. She questioned him on what he requested, as though he were placing an order on the phone to La Redoute, and, as usual, Adrien replied: "I'll tell you one day."

As for Étienne, he thinks praying is a bit like extorting heaven. He enters churches like a tourist who surveys the stones and statues without seeming entirely convinced. Never would he kneel and talk into the void. He feels it's not modern enough, that the church belongs to bygone centuries. That from now on, there's Minitel, computers, and video games. And that if there is a divinity, it resides in progress, advancement, great discoveries, like the Ariane rocket or open-heart surgery.

Marie-Laure asked Nina to choose a song for her grandfather. A song that would be played after the Mass, as a tribute to who he was. Pierre Beau never listened to music, just to RTL, on his radio. And to Joe Dassin, on the quiet.

His wife's LPs, on the anniversary of her death. Nina had caught him, hunched over her record player, which, for the rest of the year, gathered dust on a chest of drawers in his bedroom. And so, Adrien, Étienne, and Nina had listened, wide-eyed, to the singer's entire repertoire. So cheesy, so far from what they love, worship. A different world. Particularly the orchestrations. In the end, Nina had chosen "*Et si tu n'existais pas.*" Because of the sentence "Like a painter who sees the colors of the day emerging from his fingers." And she was hardly going to choose "*Aux Champs-Élysées*"—her grandfather had never set foot in Paris. He was supposed to do so for the first time in September, to move Nina into her student accommodations. Both of them were looking forward to going up to the very top of the Eiffel Tower.

As soon as she senses a ripple, some movement within the packed crowd, Nina looks searchingly at Marie-Laure Beaulieu to follow her directions.

After the song, the bearers lift the coffin, and just as when they arrived, Nina, Adrien, and Étienne follow it out of the door before it is hoisted into the hearse.

The sun is already beating down. She thinks that, for her grandfather's funeral, the weather might have made an effort, had a little decency and wept like the rest of them. Reflected the grief of humans.

They come up to kiss her. A load of people she doesn't know leave their tears and snot on her cheeks. She says thank you in return. Can't feel her legs anymore. Even during the condolences, she receives from everyone, she never lets go of Adrien's and Étienne's hands.

When Emmanuel approaches her, he clasps her nape and places a kiss on her lips. A possessive kiss. One that both repels her and soothes her. He's very handsome, his eyes full of compassion looking into hers, he kisses her in front of everyone, in front of his father and mother. He seals a pact between them. When Emmanuel kisses Nina, she feels Adrien's and Étienne's tense fingers gripping her tighter.

Now they must get into a car to go to the cemetery. Follow the hearse drowning in flowers.

Nina is in the Beaulieus' Espace, in the back, between Étienne and Adrien. Behind them, Louise and Joséphine. Almost as if they were off to Saint-Raphaël.

Marie-Laure hands her a small bottle of water. "You must drink a little, sweetheart. It's going to be hot over there and it's going to be difficult."

Thank goodness Marie-Laure is there. Since returning from Marseilles, Nina has been sleeping in Étienne's room. Marie-Laure looks after everything. Even washing her clothes. Her days are dedicated to organizing the funeral, filling in forms, for insurance companies, the bank; she's managing Nina's future, what's left of it, at least.

They park in front of the gates. It's so hot one can barely distinguish who's who, the light reflecting off the tombs dazzles the eyes, so it's mere shadows that walk over to the Beaus' vault. Nina knows the place; she's often been with her grandfather to leave flowers for Odile. Odile, that stranger for her, that great love for him, of whom he couldn't speak. Pierre Beau's parents are buried there, an uncle and a great-aunt by marriage, a little brother who died at four years old, before Pierre was born.

The priest blesses the coffin, the flowers are already starting to wilt, their stalks, suffering under this blazing sun, won't hold out another hour.

*What a strange idea to die in August, Grandpa.*

With the help of ropes, the coffin goes down to join "the others." *One day*, thinks Nina, *I, too, will go down there.*

The priest throws a handful of earth into the hole, Nina copies him, the others follow suit. And now the stonemasons will re-seal the vault.

Three plaques, "To my grandfather," "To our friend," "To our dear colleague."

Among the perspiring crowd that's beginning to disperse, due to the unbearable heat, Nina doesn't see a woman who is watching her, who hasn't taken her eyes off her since she entered the cemetery, hand in hand with Adrien and Étienne.

No one has noticed her, at a slight distance, as though visiting the tomb of someone else, when it's definitely Pierre Beau's burial that she has come here to attend.

# 40

*22 December 2017*

Nina has just left. Nicola has dozed off in one of my shoes. And I just sit there, not moving. Don't fancy working anymore. Empty spritzer glasses. Usually, I can take the silence. It's even a companion I'm fond of. But the silence after her, unbearable.

And her last words: "Since when am I your friend?"

I put on a coat and go out. The cold bites my face and hands. Nina has already disappeared, the garden is empty, dark, the big linden tree seems frozen stiff.

I brush past her car, search for her in the street, spot her in the distance, under a lamp. Just a small figure, frail and furtive, scurrying away. I follow her, mustn't lose her again.

My phone vibrates in my pocket. It's Louise. As if she could see me. She never calls after eight. To have a chat, Louise keeps office hours: 9–12 noon or 2–6.

"Hello?"

"What are you up to?"

"I'm walking."

"Where?"

"On the road, outside mine."

"It's dark."

"I can see that," I say, smiling.

"D'you want me to come over?"

"Call me back later."

"Are you with someone?"

"No."

"You seem strange."

"I always seem strange."

We're cut off. Unless Louise hung up. Don't feel like calling her back straightaway. Must follow Nina, walk in her footsteps, a few hundred meters behind her.

How often did I follow her when we were children? For the pleasure. I always loved her silhouette. Seen from the back, people are more mysterious, they tell other stories. Eyes interest me less than attitudes.

Nina doesn't continue in the direction of her house. She makes a detour toward the town center. We're alone. Not a living soul around. Wan light from a few shop windows that Nina walks past without glancing at them. She turns off and stops at Rue Rosa-Muller, then, in front of the door of a house, seems to hesitate. The windows are lit. She retraces her steps. I hide a bit further along, under a porch.

She finally goes back and rings the doorbell. A shadow opens to her a few seconds later, Nina disappears inside. I move closer as discreetly as possible and read "R. Grimaldi" written in black pen on a mailbox. Why did she hesitate to go inside there?

After ten minutes, she still hasn't reappeared. I leave, stifling a shiver. And call Louise back.

"Can you come and pick me up?"

"Where are you?"

"Outside the post office."

"I'm on my way."

I wait barely five minutes. Her car pulls up alongside me, I get in. I haven't seen Louise since last summer. She's wrapped up in a blue padded jacket, winter sports gear. She often wears blue to match her eyes. The doctor in her checks me over before the woman does. She scans me from head to toe in less than a second. A lightning inventory. Like Nina, earlier, with the kitten's food.

"Shall I take you home?" she asks.

"Yes."

"You O.K.?"

"Yes."

In the car, her perfume intoxicates me. I look at her perfect profile, determined despite all her evident gentleness.

"Thanks for being there. In my life. What would I have done without you, Louise?"

She doesn't respond, just smiles, sadly.

As we arrive outside mine, she notices the car from the shelter parked outside the house.

"Is Nina there?"

"She left."

"Why's her car here?"

"Because she'd drunk too much, she walked home."

She pauses a while.

"I didn't know you were seeing her again."

"It's very recent. We crossed paths twice in one week. I hadn't seen her for a long time."

Louise strokes my hand.

"You're trembling," she says.

# 41

*17 August 1994*

It's two o'clock. Nina is sitting on the Beaulieus' sofa, in that dining room she'd danced in so often. She looks at the few remaining people from the funeral, without seeing them. Those having a bite to eat before hitting the road again.

Which road?

Pierre only knew people from around here. His only travel had been through the postcards he delivered. The Damammes aren't there anymore. Emmanuel came by, briefly. Nina sensed he wanted to see her again that evening but hadn't dared say so. Or he had, but she can't remember it. Two places will be laid, by invisible staff, on the table in his kitchen, but she won't be going. She probably won't go back there again. In fifteen days, she'll be leaving La Comelle.

It remains to be seen who will end up with the animals. Marie-Laure and Joséphine have both volunteered. The dog and two of the cats at the house of the one, the two other cats, being older, in the apartment of the other.

Since she returned from Marseilles, Nina hasn't been back home. They all urged her to keep well away from it, as if her grandfather had mined the garden before dying. As if the scene of the crime was right there.

Only Joséphine goes there, morning and evening, to feed and walk Paola. And open the shutters and windows to air the place a little.

Now, it's time to go home. Nina wants to escape. Get back to her things, her room. She's going to do it alone. Face up to it. Slip away from Étienne's house when the time's right. So that no one notices. She'll phone the boys later, for them to join her. At first, she needs that solitude. Losing her grandfather has aged her. Just moving is so arduous, she feels like she's a hundred.

Outside, the sun is still blazing. Nina can't help thinking of her grandfather. Is he hot or cold in his hole?

Sticking to the shady side of the streets, she finds herself outside her home in a matter of minutes. She pushes open the gate, Paola is sleeping under a tree, in the basket placed there by Pierre, beside a rocking chair in which he'd relished years of naps. Nina sits in it, closes her eyes. Clutches her dog's coat. Two cats make their appearance, around her legs.

"*Life will never be the same again.*" It's a dumb sentence straight out of a dumb soap, but all the same, thinks Nina, life will never be the same again. Basically, it was a sweet, calm, spoilt life that she'd had with her grandfather. When had she seen him for the last time? The evening the three of them, including Adrien, had supper in the garden. She'd said to him: "Goodnight, Grandpa," hastily, without coming back down to kiss him. The following morning, he'd already left for work when she got up. And then there was Marseilles, the escapade with Adrien, his strength in protecting her. His strength, or his weakness: maybe he was afraid of facing Nina's sorrow on his own. So he took her elsewhere, until Marie-Laure was back to do the dirty work. She thinks she's being hard on him. But she can't help wondering: that Marseilles interlude, was it a gesture of love, or of cowardice?

As she pushes open the door of the house, she feels uneasy, dizzy, a dread. As though entering an unknown and hostile place.

When all she wanted was to be alone, just with Pierre Beau's things, to get used to the void, tidy up, sort out, reread, as she enters the kitchen, she sees that all the half-opened cupboards have been emptied. Not a trace of food anymore. Even the salt and pepper are no longer in their place. All that's left is the table, without the chairs. Out of habit, Nina opens the fridge: it's empty, too, and has been unplugged. She doesn't understand. It's as if a removal were about to happen.

Without expecting anything, probably as a reflex, it's the word she's said the most since being born, Nina calls out:

"Grandpa?"

Her voice rings out, without an echo.

She holds her breath when she goes into Pierre Beau's bedroom, upstairs. Everything has disappeared. His life has been burgled. Their life. No more LPs, no more record player, clothes, sheets, bed.

All that's left is the large wardrobe, but it has been dismantled. Even the photos have disappeared. For Nina, it's a second death. A betrayal, a coup de grâce.

But who could have done *this*?

Joséphine, impossible. Marc and Marie-Laure Beaulieu hadn't left Nina's side. And they'd never have dared. Never would they seek to harm her. It had to be strangers, a break-in. Someone had taken advantage of her grandfather's death to enter their house. Pierre had talked about them, opportunists who study death notices, find out the address of the deceased, check the closed shutters or full mailboxes, and steal everything before the will has been read. But from a small laborer's house like theirs? Aside from all the love between them, nothing under this roof had any value. Perhaps the leather-bound books, the entire works of Victor Hugo, that a "grand lady" had given him when he started out as a young mailman? The whole collection has disappeared from his room along with all the rest. He was so proud of his "treasure." But whenever he had money worries, Pierre would say to Nina: "If needs must, I'll sell Victor Hugo."

Nina hesitates to go into her own room, a few meters away, at the end of the narrow corridor. The burglars might still be there, hiding somewhere. She feels like a stranger in her own home. In a matter of days, everything has been taken from her.

Nina calls Paola, the dog comes upstairs and pushes its damp nose into her hand. She can't ever be apart from her pets again, she thinks. Not now.

She pushes open the door to her room. Nothing seems to be missing. The posters and photos are still up on the walls. The cassettes, novels, charcoal pencils, oil sticks. She opens the drawers of her chest and finds her underwear and bath towels still there. Everything has been rifled through and put, almost, back in place. It's a sort of rape. Her personal belongings have been touched. She goes back down to the small sitting room, there's no more coffee table, or television, or video recorder. Even the videos have disappeared. Her films and her grandfather's. She'd given him the entire Jean Gabin collection last Christmas.

The old sofa, so ugly that Nina had covered it in throws, vanished. The accident had stolen life itself from them, this burglary their daily existence. Nina sits on the floor, waiting for her sudden asthma attack to pass. She remains like this for a good hour until she hears Adrien's and Étienne's voices outside, rousing her from her torpor.

They find her there, sitting on the floor, Paola beside her, in the middle of her plundered house, struggling to breathe and longing, irrepressibly, to die.

# 42

*23 December 2017*

The Collège Georges-Perec is empty. The classrooms closed. Only Romain Grimaldi is working in his office. He just dropped by. Because he's alone, because he gets a bit bored at home. Walking Bob, once, twice, is nice, but it's freezing outdoors. He's placed a small heater near his feet, hasn't taken his coat off, and is reading some letters, replying to a few emails.

All the pupils must still be lying around in bed, waiting for their presents while watching TV. People are with their families. Romain's family is in Australia.

Yesterday evening, he suggested to Nina that she join him for Christmas Eve. Without thinking, she said yes. He wasn't expecting that.

Nina.

A few phone calls, including one to the departmental archives "on behalf of . . . ," and Romain had got hold of parts of her school file. Like remnants. He read the notes and assessments from her bac, which had survived the years. A diligent pupil in all subjects. He put the jigsaw together, bac with merit, fine-arts option, 17 out of 20. She should have gone on to higher education. Why had she stayed here? Some of Nina's drawings had been scanned. Portraits in charcoal, two boys, always the same two, their features captured strikingly by her. Talented, unquestionably. It's Romain's job to spot the good pupils. Must be what he sensed at the shelter the first time he saw her.

Yesterday evening, she turned up at his place. For ten days now, she's been coming by without warning. She rings the bell, and a few minutes later, they make love. He's not sure right now whether he finds these intrusions seductive, or not. His pupils call it "having a crush"—Romain didn't know the English expression, for being attracted to someone. "It's fancying someone, sir. Y'know, being turned on."

Nina is fast, rough with her hands, doesn't take her time. Her gestures say exactly the opposite of what's in her voice and her eyes, a depth and gentleness. She seems damaged, wary, tense, as though she were serving herself in Romain's bed, and doing the same back to satisfy him. Not to love him.

And yet, if she wasn't coming over this evening, the void would be horrendous.

*

Étienne opens his eyes, struggles to come to. When his head dictates that it's time to get up, something in him refuses, his body stops him from doing so. He wants to sink back into instant sleep. Escape the mornings, escape the days. Carry on dreaming a little. Waking up is being back home. And he hasn't the strength for that.

Marie-Castille has been out of the bed for ages. Grey, wintery light outside. Étienne hears voices downstairs. First his parents'. Then the sound of Valentin's, higher pitched, reaching right up to him. His son. God how he loves his boy. He never would have thought himself capable of loving a person more than himself. A smell of coffee. Of toast. Of what's for lunch. Everything's mixed up in the house of his childhood. He glances at the alarm clock, 11:15 A.M. Must get up. Get washed. Get dressed. As usual. Marie-Castille must be telling anyone who'll listen that he needed rest, that he's recuperating, that he "must be allowed to sleep, poor thing."

He thinks again of Nina. The shock when he saw her yesterday evening. She hasn't changed. The texture of her skin, perhaps, less beautiful than before, before, her skin was like satin, face powder, fine brown sand. He thinks back to what she'd said to him. Valentin knows. But how? Étienne has spoken to no one about it. And he left all the results of his medical tests in the office, in a double-locked drawer. He's never brought his illness back home. When

Marie-Castille finds out, she's going to freak out, and Étienne wants to go through it all without any fuss. He can't bear even to imagine people's eyes changing as they look at him. Empathy, pity: no way. His job is all about that, victims. Never wind up on the other side.

Only Louise knows. But Louise keeps quiet. Louise always kept quiet.

He's at stage 3. Which means "locally advanced." Translation: he's got secondary cancer all over the place. An operation to stop the damage spreading, then initial chemo treatment. A six-month procedure. To see how the tumor behaves. Whether the crab scuttles off when confronted with the enemy. A session every two weeks. As an outpatient. A catheter at the end of his arm to inject the poison into him. He'll be able to read the newspaper. If he wants to. He's already been told: "During the session, there's nothing to stop you from watching a film, or anything else you like doing." But what he likes doing is swimming against the tide, surfing, strumming the guitar, taking his son to school, secretly watching him laughing with his friends, drinking a black coffee at the bar beside the police station, the adrenaline rush of catching them red-handed, nabbing a criminal, surprising Marie-Castille as she's secretly eating an ice-cream bar so as not to tempt him, the scent of her night cream when she lies close to him, listening to music.

He won't be going for any treatment.

He'll go off to die in the great outdoors, by the sea, rather than dragging on for months while going to seed physically, until his wife and son can remember the number of his hospital room better than the features of his face.

*

"Shit Christmas present," she hisses between her teeth. A dog tied up outside the shelter. Three centimeters of rope. Terrified when Nina goes near it. Seems ashamed of having been left there. How long has it been there, choking on its rope? Young, barely a year old, soaked, starving, the lot. A sort of Pyrenean Mountain dog crossed with bad luck. Nina could weep. Sick to death of it. How much longer can she keep going? And all those idiots who'll give each other puppies for Christmas. Who's going to get them in late July when they're not "so cute" anymore? Yours truly. "What are you doing for the vacation?—I'm ditching my dog. And maybe my kids and wife if they annoy me too much. Life's short, must make the most of it." And it's you, poor twit, who picks up other people's shit.

Untie it, take it into her office, wipe it down, reassure it. It stinks, it's shaking. She looks at the state of its skin, parasites, no parasites, marks, no marks, identification, no identification.

It dives on the water and dry food she gives it.

Nina recognizes the sound of Simone's car. She's relieved, doesn't feel up to facing such abandonment on her own this morning. Simone places a box of chocolates on Nina's desk, saying: "These are for everyone!" then looks down, widens her eyes, and says:

"Well, I never. And where's that one sprung from?"

"Christmas present, tied to the gate."

"Where will we put it?"

"Good question. We'll take photos and alert the local police."

"They're still sleeping at this hour, the local police."

"I know."

"Did you walk here?"

"Yes."

"You're brave."

"Less than you are, Simone."

Simone doesn't react. She indicates the dog, chilled to the bone, now warming up under its blanket and watching them both. Like an accused man awaiting his verdict.

"What are we going to call it? Noël? Jesus? Mary?"

Simone strokes it.

"It's the caramel color of a *cannelé* cake," she says.

"Let's go for Cannelé then," Nina decides.

After walking, cleaning, and caring for all the others, it's already three o'clock. Two volunteers have joined them to take the dogs out. In cold weather, since the buildings are old, and even though she's not allowed to for some obscure sanitary reasons, Nina lays straw in each stall. She also adds a blanket in the baskets and inside the kennels.

Throughout winter, Simone cooks up scraps that the butcher puts aside for her. Nina loathes that smell of offal, as Simone browns it in large pans, but that meager sustenance warms the dogs up. Before leaving, Simone takes portrait photos of Cannelé, which Nina posts on the social networks:

Found this morning tied to gates of shelter, male, about one year old, no identification. If you recognize him, please contact us.

This kind of announcement is like pissing in the wind. What she hopes is that someone will take pity on Cannelé. Adoptions are like disappearances, the more time that passes, the less chance there is of hearing any news.

*

The car from the shelter isn't parked outside my house anymore. Nina must have come to collect it very early this morning, I didn't hear her.

I look around for any note she might have left me, in the mailbox, under the door, or in Nicola's basket. Anything, just a "Hi, see you soon, much love, Happy Christmas, I'll be back one of these days, take care of yourself, I was pleased to see you."

Yes, anything.

My head's all over the place.

I'm writing an insert to inform the paper's readers that the sonar-assisted investigations in the Lac de la Forêt have concluded. No other body was discovered in the vicinity of where the car was recovered. And no jewelry, metal objects, or weapons. It now seems certain that there is just one victim, the one found inside the metal wreck.

The only evidence confirmed to me by an acquaintance, a police officer in La Comelle: the body was at the back of the vehicle, not at the front. Suicide, an accident, murder, it's all mere conjecture. Only time will allow any certainty.

Last night, I dreamt of Clotilde Marais, she was close to me, sitting on my bed. A nightmare. I woke up in a sweat, I believe I cried out in my sleep.

"Virginie, it really is pretty extraordinary that it's you writing my story in the paper." She was mocking me, speaking too loudly. And I replied to her, trembling: "But Clotilde, it's not you in that car." She was smiling at me, the way she did when we passed in the corridors at school. She was smiling at the wall behind me, and that wall was Étienne. I turned around, Étienne was there, he was seventeen, and was crying tears of blood.

## 43

*17 August 1994*

It's 9:00 P.M. Adrien is lying on the bed in Nina's room. He's listening to her breathing, from time to time she dozes off for a few minutes, then wakes up with a start, speaks to him, throws words at him that seek to understand. "Why has this happened to me?" "What will become of me?" "Who has stripped the house?" "D'you think Grandpa can see us from where he is?" "D'you think there's life after death?" "He didn't commit suicide because we were going off to Paris, did he?" "Why didn't the driver see him?" "What was his last thought?" "My mother, how will she know that her father's dead?" "D'you think she'll come to find me?"

Questions that go around and around.

"D'you think it's because I read other people's letters? That I'm being punished?"

"You don't do it anymore."

"Yes, I do, I started doing it again."

Adrien strokes her hair, reassures her, repeats to her that he's there, and will always be there.

"And what if you die, too?" she murmurs to him.

"I won't die."

"How d'you know that?"

"I just do."

Paola is snoring noisily. She doesn't know that, soon, she'll be off to live somewhere else.

This house didn't belong to Pierre Beau, he rented it from the town council. It will have to be given back. The drama is unfolding too fast, too far, the pain is deep, subterranean. A steamroller.

Joséphine and Marie-Laure might have assured her that she'll never find herself alone, that there's always be a place for her in their homes, it remains a place, a sofa bed, or a bed in someone else's room. Adrien reminds her that, in a few weeks' time, the three of them will be living together in Paris. That life will go on. But Nina feels as fragile as a Bohemian-crystal glass placed on the tracks of a train coming at a hundred-and-fifty kilometers an hour. She thinks that disaster is unavoidable.

Marie-Laure and Marc went to the police station to report the burglary at Pierre Beau's house. The neighbors had seen nothing. In August, most are still on vacation. The burglars must have taken advantage of that. There are no signs the house was broken into, but when the policemen learnt that the key was hidden under a flowerpot outside the front door, they rolled their eyes. "And the dog? Too nice to bite."

Adrien is starting to drift off. They are exhausted. Since their return from Marseilles, they've accumulated sleepless nights and sad days. *How many times have Adrien and Étienne slept here?* thinks Nina. The empty packets of KitKats and sweets on the floor. The noise the sleeping bag made whenever one of them moved in their sleep. How many times had Pierre Beau, on discovering the state of the room, shouted: "Nina! Tidy your room! And air it, it stinks of feet!"

He won't shout anymore. Nina wonders whether, where he is, there are mailboxes. Local tax demands to deliver. And whether he's found Odile. Whether they do the rounds of paradise together.

Adrien is asleep, his hand in Nina's. The window is wide open. The temperature is starting to go down. In the distance, a family not yet hit by bereavement is having fun around a barbecue. Nina hears laughter, glasses clinking, children playing in a paddling pool. In her street, it's not like at Emmanuel's: pools have to be inflated.

Earlier, the landline phone—miraculously, not stolen—rang three times at fifteen-minute intervals. Nina's sure it was him. Emmanuel's looking for her.

Étienne must be with Clotilde. He hasn't seen her since getting back from Saint-Raphaël, giving the funeral preparations as an excuse to avoid her, but this evening, he couldn't get out of it. He wants to end their relationship for good. For her to understand that he's leaving for Paris shortly and wishes for just one thing: to be eighteen with no ties.

Nina is thirsty.

In the late afternoon, Joséphine had popped in to leave bottles of water and other provisions in the kitchen. She had been staggered to discover the house stripped bare. "This morning, everything was still in its place."

Nina is almost afraid of going downstairs alone in this empty house. It's the prowlers' ghost that's haunting the place, not her grandfather's. She puts the light on in the corridor, goes into the kitchen, an unknown perfume is wafting around the house. A shiver runs through her, she grabs a bottle and quickly goes back up to her room. She falls asleep almost immediately. She's awoken a few minutes later, in the middle of a nightmare, relieved to open her eyes. She thinks she hears a noise in the garden, the cats maybe. She leans out of the window, no one, the street is deserted, just an old blue van parked a bit further along. Moths start dancing in the light from the streetlamps. Adrien and Paola are sound asleep.

Nina doesn't feel sleepy anymore. She gets up, slips on some mules to go out onto the doorstep. Two of her cats come looking for strokes. She opens the door; they follow her out. She sits on a step, looks up at the sky, night starting to fall. She can't seem to visualize her future. Before, it was bright, unknown, full of hope. This evening, to her, it seems impossible to believe in. All her strength is anesthetized, the muscles of her life atrophied.

A door opens behind her. Her two cats run away.

But it isn't the front door that's just been opened, it's the cellar door. Nina is petrified, a horror movie, like those she watches, one after the other, with Etienne and Adrien, shut away in the dark.

There's no longer a screen between herself and terror: there, before her eyes, the shadow of a very tall man, carrying a large box full of old stuff. She and her grandfather would sell things they didn't use every year at the May yard sale. With the money, they'd treat themselves to an omelet and *fromage blanc* at the alfresco meal organized by the local community. Nina recognizes a small bedside lamp that belonged to her, and a few bits and bobs sticking out, including her Barbies. When he sees her, the man stops for a moment, then continues on his path, grumbling about something, barely audible, brushing right past her, and disappearing into the street. Nina doesn't dare move or call Adrien for help. It's like she's paralyzed. Her brain has switched off. Like when Marie-Laure told her about her grandfather's death. Incapable of doing a thing. Fear is added to her surprise and horror: someone else is coming up the stairs. How many of them are there down there, in that tiny cellar, where bottles jostle with gardening tools, chipped china and jam jars? A shadow appears, it's a woman, very slim, thin even, with shoulder-length hair. Because she's against the light, Nina can't see her face. She's carrying something heavy, awkward, wider than her. An object Nina instantly recognizes: the Singer sewing machine that belonged to her grandmother. Just before she turns off the light bulb with a nudge of her shoulder on the large switch, the woman stops as she sees Nina's seated silhouette, still as a statue, turned toward her, from the doorstep. The only light is that of the dying day. A wan light making them look like two ghosts.

Nina's mouth is so dry, she can't get out a word. The stranger pushes the door to and gives a little kick in just the right place to latch it. It seems she knows all the required movements. To tackle the switch and now the door, as if she knew the place, as if she were at home. And Nina visiting.

"Hi. Don't be scared, it's only me."

". . ."

"I've come to collect what belongs to me."

". . ."

A shaky voice. Uncertain.

"I'm going to put this down because it weighs a ton. And I'll be back."

Just like the man before, she brushes past Nina and disappears into the street. She reappears a few seconds later. Alone. Empty-handed. The man must be waiting for her out there.

"Didn't know you were here. You're really pretty. I saw you at the old man's burial."

". . ."

"Lost your tongue?"

". . ."

"You know, it's not easy . . . Life, it's not easy for anyone."

". . ."

"But then, we don't know each other. You can't remember me, you were just a tot."

She sits on a step below Nina, turns toward her while lighting a Gitane. The flame from the lighter lights up her face. She's wearing tight jeans and a red crop top showing her bony shoulders. The woman's a bag of bones. Her skin is fine, white, allowing bluish veins to show on the neck and forearms.

"I can't hang around. We have a long way to drive."

She takes nervous drags. Fingernails bitten to the quick.

"Didn't want to meet anyone, especially not the neighbors."

She stubs out her cigarette on the heel of her platform shoe.

"You've got friends here. Saw them at the cemetery, the ones holding your hands."

She stands up under Nina's stupefied gaze. Is about to say something, kisses her on the cheek, then turns, rushes off. A few seconds later, the blue van reverses and disappears into the night. Nina can see Marion's profile on the passenger side, she lowers her window for some air without looking over to her, without even a wave.

Nina stays as she is for a few minutes, transfixed.

She was at the cemetery this morning . . . They must have come to the house during the church service, cased the joint, and then the man emptied the house out while the other attended the burial from a distance.

Nina finally stands up, reeling, like after a boozy night, and vomits bile over her grandfather's hydrangeas.

Like a little old woman, she totters over to the phone and presses "recall." Emmanuel Damamme answers immediately, as though sleeping with the phone in his hand.

"Come and get me," she implores.

"Where are you?"

"At my grandfather's."

"I'm coming."

She goes back up to her room, looks at Adrien asleep. A child. Suddenly he seems very young to her. Suddenly she has turned into an adult. She needs someone older now. She wants to forget her youth, her childhood, her past. And it's much too soon for the future. Adrien and she had grown up lame, Adrien without a father, she without parents.

Nina had always really hoped, deep down, secretly, that her mother had abandoned her for good reasons. Too young, inexperienced, alone, scared, lost. That one day, she'd beg her forgiveness.

What had happened between the young girl smiling in the class photo, surrounded by her friends, and the "thing" she's just seen, her despicable behavior? The reality is, decidedly, too hard to take in. She'd have preferred never to know. Not in these circumstances. A woman who comes to rob her own father while his body's still warm. What's she going to do with those paltry things? Sell them to make a few francs? First, how did she know he was dead? And how can one care so damn little about one's own child? Speak to her like some vague acquaintance, a former neighbor? And that man with her, who's he? Her husband? Her lover? Her pimp? Her dealer?

Nina is annoyed with herself now for not saying anything, not reacting. She should have punctured the van's tires, called the cops, shopped them, hit them, insulted them, yelled. She'd remained inert as a slug. She'd wanted to ask, pose the question, the one that's obsessed her forever: "Who is my father?" She'd allowed Marion to fly off, like a bird of ill omen.

She recognizes the idiosyncratic sound of Emmanuel's Alpine; it stops outside the house.

She takes a last look at Adrien and Paola before leaving her room.

It's only 10:00 P.M.

# 44

*24 December 2017*

"Cheesy petits-fours, porcini carpaccio, La Bonne Foi vegan terrine. That's to go with our aperitif. For the meal itself, I've gone for a sweet potato and coconut milk velouté as our starter, then morel risotto and truffle ravioli. Followed by some mini pâtisseries and a strawberry vacherin glacé. Are you more red wine, or white?"

"Basically, you're a psychopath."

"Possibly."

"Or gay . . ."

"Also possible."

Nina, arms loaded with bags, puts a bottle of champagne, another of Bordeaux, chocolates, and a wrapped gift down on the sitting room table, while noticing the one Romain has laid in the dining room. It all looks beautiful, refined, and extremely appetizing. He, too, is wearing black trousers with a black shirt. Bob is at Nina's feet, staring at her and wagging his tail. She crouches to stroke him.

"Is that a present for me?" Romain asks, indicating the gift she's just put down.

"No, for Bob," Nina jokes. "It's a bit much, all this . . . that table, all that preparation . . . I thought we'd be eating an omelet by the fire."

"An omelet, on Christmas Eve? And may I remind you that I don't have a fireplace . . . Which fire are you talking about?"

Nina can't stifle a smile.

"It doesn't mean that much to me, Christmas," she admits.

"You aren't Catholic?"

"I'm an orphan, divorced, and I work at a shelter . . . I can't see Jesus getting mixed up in my story . . . He's left it too late . . . Why do you ask me that? Are you a believer?"

"Atheist. But for once I have a guest at Christmas, so I'm making the most of it."

"And your friends?"

Romain smiles as he opens a bottle of rosé Ruinart.

"They're with their families."

"And yours, your family?"

"My parents live in Australia. I go there every other Christmas. You've fallen on the right year . . . Or maybe not."

He hands a glass to Nina.

"To you."

"To you."

"Happy Christmas."

"Happy Christmas."

*

For Christmas Eve, Louise is dining with her parents, her two brothers, her sisters-in-law, and their children. She spoils everyone, particularly her mother and her three nephews. She's always had a soft spot for Valentin, but she spends the same on all of them.

It must be hereditary, having favorites in this family. She feels awkward toward Étienne when it comes to their father. "Daddy's little darling," how many times had she heard that ghastly expression.

How unfair it is to prefer one of one's children, both for that child and the others. But love isn't debatable. And Marc doesn't know how to pretend. When he wants to make an effort, decides to show an interest in Étienne, asks him a question about his work or his life in general, Louise can see that he soon loses interest when Étienne himself pretends not to notice.

"I couldn't care less, little sis, Mom loves me for two."

"And me for three," she quips back, masking her sadness.

Once everyone has gone to bed, she meets up with Adrien to spend Christmas Eve with him. In the early hours of the morning, she goes back home and slides into her bed for a few hours before the family gathers around the tree to open their presents.

Since Adrien was seventeen and Louise sixteen, they meet up at the Hôtel des Voyageurs, Room 4. It's the smallest and cheapest room, the one under the eaves, given to guests only as a last resort. This hotel in La Comelle used to say "no vacancies" when the Magellan factory was still recruiting, and its outsourced workers would lodge there. Today, a few reps and consultants stay in the hotel, but most of the rooms have been vacant for a long time. Now, Louise and Adrien are the only ones to ask for Room 4. They could choose another room, but out of superstition, they don't. Wherever Adrien might be in the world, on 24 December, he's in La Comelle for the night to sleep with Louise.

For as far back as she can remember, Louise has loved Adrien.

The first time she saw him was at elementary school, at the start of the autumn term. He was in fifth grade, she in fourth. She saw him arriving late at the cafeteria with Étienne and Nina. He was new, out of breath, red-faced, looking around distractedly, but as soon as he returned to his two friends, he seemed more focused. Louise tried not to look at him, but every time, without her really wanting to, as if suffering from some kind of ocular defect, her eyes would fall on him. Her vision was one step ahead of her thinking, preceding it.

The first time she spoke to him was two days later. During recess, she had intentionally put herself on her brother's path, in the middle of the yard, targeting the moment the three of them would pass where two imaginary lines met, a bit like a sharpshooter would, and she'd left her hopscotch game, stone gripped tightly in hand. Almost surprised to find her there, in the yard of their school, Étienne had mumbled to Nina and Adrien: "My sister, Louise." She smiled at them, said hello, and then, scarlet as a poppy, went back to her classmates. But she'd still had time to sink her blue eyes into Adrien's, while Nina and he smiled nicely at her. Louise kept turning Adrien's face over in her mind until it was lunchtime. Adrien wasn't good-looking, but love and beauty aren't remotely connected. They're put in the same bag just because it's easy. That's like lumping a star and a nail together just because you can hang something on both of them. Adrien had a mystery and depth about him that went beyond childhood. Like a kind of enigma.

And then there were the Wednesdays, the evenings, the weekends. Sometimes Louise came home and sensed that Adrien was there. In her brother's room, or in the cellar, making music. Even if his shoes weren't in the cupboard by the front door. She would hide to watch them. And there was always that tender way Adrien looked at Nina as soon as she opened her mouth. Louise wasn't jealous: it was the same tender way Étienne looked at her when he didn't realize she could sense it, when she caught him at it, the look only a brother gives a sister.

After that there had been the "Py plague." Louise didn't understand why Adrien was becoming emaciated, fading away. A shadow of himself, lost. Recesses without him. In detention every evening. She hardly ever saw him, except between two doors. One day, Étienne had said to their parents: "Py is really putting Adrien through the wringer and back," but what could "putting through the wringer and back" mean?

When Adrien went to hospital because of the teacher, Louise cycled over to Py's home several times, had a look round, and decided to spray bleach over his flower beds. Everything burnt up overnight. By dawn, the flower beds surrounding his house were the color of piss.

And then the summer vacation plunged Louise into deep despondency. The three would be starting at middle school, while she had to stay in elementary for her final year. The days were going to drag on forever and the yard shrink.

One day in July, they turned up at the house, shut themselves away in the sitting room to listen to music. They had danced, screamed. Three total screwballs. Louise had hidden in her room all afternoon. When they'd left the house, she'd gone down, and imagined, among the soda bottles left on the table, which ones Adrien had drunk from. She breathed in everything in their wake, like a dog seeking its owner's smell among others.

During the middle-school years, when their paths crossed, they greeted each other shyly. Sometimes, Adrien would ask her if school was O.K., her subjects, teachers, all that . . . To which Louise always replied yes, before dashing off. She found it impossible to hold his gaze. Every evening, she would imagine their wedding, the party, their outfits, the exchange of rings, the music, Étienne and Nina as their witnesses, but once she was in front of him, she couldn't string three words together.

Things changed when they all went together to Saint-Raphaël, in the summer of 1990. She didn't sleep for nights before their departure. For months she'd been hearing her mother say that, for the next vacation, if Étienne raised his average grade, Adrien and Nina would be joining them. Louise knew perfectly well that her bone-idle brother got his two friends to help him. She kept an eye on his grades, secretly opened his score file, and intercepted his report card before the family laid hands on it. She danced around her room when she found out her brother's average grade: 14! They'd done it! They were going to be in the same house in the middle of summer. Adrien in the room next door. Adrien on the beach, sharing meals, donuts, towels, the same view. The wall of the three, which had seemed impenetrable to her until then, had cracked open on the day she'd read Étienne's assessments and grades. She'd resealed the envelope, slipped it among the mail, and that very evening, amid the general jubilation, her mother had phoned Nina's grandfather and Adrien's mother to ask them, officially, for their permission to take their children to the seaside.

Louise was hiding in the corridor when Marie-Laure told Étienne that they'd said yes. That yes, it was the same word Adrien would one day say to her in front of the mayor.

*

Adrien arrives in La Comelle. He automatically drives past Nina's house, at a crawl, there are no lights on inside. She must be celebrating Christmas Eve elsewhere. *Good*, he thinks, *she's not alone*. Then he can't resist driving across town, along streets he knows by heart, to approach the Beaulieus' house, stopping far enough away not to be seen. Marie-Laure and Marc have hung up strings of flashing lights outside. Adrien imagines Louise at the table, observing her brother. Wondering if it's her last Christmas with him. Adrien knows that Étienne is ill, Louise told him. He can't wait to hug her tight, feel her skin, caress her. He can see shadows inside. He gets a shock when Étienne appears on the doorstep. Adrien is in his car, parked twenty meters away, but he'd recognize Étienne anywhere. Should he get out of the car and go and speak to him? Was it all "ancient history now," as they say? He doesn't allow himself time to think, does a U-turn, with headlights off like some prowler. He drives to the Hôtel des Voyageurs. Grabs his bag, containing just one change of clothes and a toothbrush for the night, and a cooler bag containing a bottle of champagne, some oysters, salted butter, and a rye loaf.

Like every year, there's no one at reception, the owner is celebrating with friends, but the entrance code hasn't changed for ages, 1820A. "Eighteen, coming of age, twenty, the best age, A for *Amour*." She's left the No. 4 key in plain view on the counter. Adrien goes up to the third story, finds once again the nineties-era red carpet, the flowery bedcover, the matching curtains, the frieze along the salmon-colored walls. The two radiators are burning hot, Adrien opens the window for a few minutes to let the icy air revive the tired fabrics, rid them of their mothball smell. He switches on the old television for some sound, a presence, and goes into the tiny bathroom to shuck some oysters and arrange them on an earthenware dish.

*

Étienne smokes a cigarette while gazing at the stars. "They're light-years away," Nina would say. "What we see of them here is truncated. Stars are like lies."

Étienne has stopped himself from thinking about Nina all day. Forbidden. Nina belongs to another life. Pointless to keep going back over it. But he can see her again now, imprinted on his retina. Her eyes haven't changed. Preserved like a precious metal wrapped in satin.

Marie-Castille joins him outside, wrapped in a shawl.

"Everything O.K., my love? What are you doing? You'll catch cold."

"There's something I must confess to you . . ." he says to her, looking serious.

Marie-Castille stiffens. She's sensed a change in Étienne for a few weeks now. He seems preoccupied. She barely dares say the words:

"What is it?"

He looks straight at her, half-smiling. His eyes make her melt. Will always make her melt. As soon as she saw him, that first time, she knew he'd be hers. She loves him stubbornly, jealously, obsessively. When she'd given birth to Valentin, she'd felt happier about presenting this gift to Étienne than about being a mother. She'd become one out of love for her husband, who's crazy about their son. And Valentin looks just like his father.

"You'll be able to keep the secret?" he asks her.

"Yes," she whispers.

"Promise?"

"Promise."

"I'm looking out for Father Christmas."

"What?"

"I pretend I'm going out to smoke, but the truth is that I believe in Father Christmas. I'm hoping to see him."

"You're so silly . . . You scared me."

"That's why you love me."

He hugs her tight. She's trembling. He regrets his bad joke. *How can you be such an idiot?* he thinks. *And such a coward.*

"I find Louise strange this evening. She seems sad," Marie-Castille says into his ear.

"She's always sad," Étienne replies, laconically. "And not just at Christmas."

"Really? Why? I hadn't noticed."

"Oh, it's an old story."

"What story?"

"A man."

"I thought your sister preferred girls."

"It's more complicated than that."

He stubs out his cigarette and kisses his wife full on the lips to shut her up and show her he loves her. He won't be able to hide his illness from her for much longer. A matter of a few weeks. On top of that, he's losing weight, his muscles are wasting too fast.

It started with an MRI of the abdomen and a scan of the thorax. He pretended to his colleagues, including Marie-Castille, that he had a meeting with an informer. Had to go alone. Considering his results and the look on the specialists' faces, Étienne asked Louise to be beside him when he came round. They had slid an endoscope right down his throat to reach the duodenum. Duodenum, never heard of it. Louise explained to him that it's wrapped around the head of the pancreas. "Like a tire around the rim of a wheel, if you like."

With the help of a probe, they had examined his pancreas from every angle and then proceeded with a biopsy of the tumor to assess what stage it was at.

Pancreatic cancer develops stealthily. Never showing itself or making a sound. A lethal diffidence. When it starts to make itself felt, it means it's serious. Advanced. It's one of the worst cancers. It's vicious.

*It's the first time I've been first in something,* Étienne thought to himself. *I've beaten my brother, better at illness than him, my father's finally going to be proud of me.*

When he came to, Louise was beside him. When he saw the look on his sister's face, he knew he was done for. She wore a fake smile on her lips while her eyes were full of fear. Even her eyelids were quivering behind the "All's well" façade.

Louise had already planned the appointments and care protocol with some oncologists.

"They're going to operate on you, apply some strong chemotherapy to reduce the tumor . . . And after that, they'll remove your pancreas, one can live without it."

Étienne had thought that he was already living without dreams and without love. Only Valentin counted among his dead stars, the only one shining in the sky of his life. The only thread still attaching him to the day. And that's why he preferred to disappear, rather than have Valentin witness his pitiful decline.

Fifteen days ago, Étienne had a consultation with his sister in Lyon. He asked her for medication so that he wouldn't suffer.

"You'll give me something strong, hey. Stuff that puts other painkillers in the shade. After that, I'll go off somewhere, you know, like in the romantic films that I loathe, and you love. I want to die beside the sea, wrapped in a blanket . . . Sitting on a bench. In peace. Without anyone else. Just imagine the sun rising on my dying-man's face."

"Stop, Étienne, it's not funny."

"You never call me Étienne . . . Are you in training for when you'll be recalling fond memories of your brother?"

Louise began to cry. He apologized to her.

"You can get better."

"Nah. You know very well I can't. Did you see what that thing looked like? It's spread all over me."

"Chemo is targeted. We can at least try to reduce the tumor."

"What I've been afflicted with since I was seventeen, no one can reduce that."

45

*17 August 1994, 10:00 P.M.*

The Beau family vault is situated on the edge of the main road, the one that runs along the wall on the left side of the local cemetery.

Pierre Beau rests beside his wife, and some ancestors with the same surname but whom he never knew. He was buried a few hours ago. A starry night, the sound of a motor, and a weak light coming from the road briefly illuminates his name etched into the marble. It's from the headlights of a blue van in which all of his meager possessions, piled one on top of the other in the back, are heading straight to south Finistère, in Brittany.

That's how life goes. That's how things go. "And that's how the little puppets go, go, go," Odile used to sing to her daughter while shaking her pretty hands.

Marion is in the passenger seat beside Arthus, a former sailor who now deals in secondhand goods and scrap metal. From Bénodet to Quimper, everyone calls him "the Wangler," because he always gets hold of the part or item needed. This can range from aluminum-alloy wheels for a Renault 5 GTL, to an English garden suite, via a bar of hash or an original 1966 Beatles album. Just one phone call, a request, and Arthus replies: "I'll see what I can do," and ends up tracking it down. Only Marion calls Arthus "my love." She leaves "the Wangler" to everyone else, seeing as he's far less good at handling her than he is antiques.

*

At that very same moment, Pierre Beau's granddaughter is also sitting in the passenger seat, but of a car. She's heading straight for the Damammes' property, just beyond the town, on the edge of a private forest. Nina doesn't know it, but when her grandparents were young newlyweds, they liked cycling around what they called "the Château." Pierre and Odile went past the gates all year round, and in winter, from a distance, when the trees were bare, through the large picture-like windows, they would count the rooms lit by fine chandeliers, and watch the shadows moving about inside. Never could they have imagined that one day their granddaughter would be just such a silhouette.

Whenever the road ahead is straight, Emmanuel looks instead at Nina in profile. Her face is haggard. The closer they get to his place, the fewer streetlamps there are. The young woman's face is plunged in darkness. Even disappearing entirely. Since Emmanuel picked her up, she's said nothing.

He was dozing when the phone had rung. He'd been waiting for that call. That "Come and get me" is a gift from heaven, the death of that grandfather a blessing. By some strange irony of fate, it was a lorry from his family's company that knocked him down. Emmanuel is Catholic. Having done his First Communion and Confirmation, he wonders whether it's a sign, a divine nudge in the right direction.

He'd feared losing Nina after the funeral. He thought he'd never see her again. Because of those two kids who never leave her side. The ones she's supposed to be moving to Paris with.

For now, she's saying nothing, seems dazed, staring at the road with vacant eyes. But later, when they'll be close, when she'll snuggle up to him, she'll speak. She'll feel assured enough to describe how the pain of a sudden death can make you suffer, enough to puncture your organs, like being stabbed with a knife and without anesthetic, how it shuts off everything, including plans for the future. She'll manage to talk about her childhood, about her mother, about that man she saw coming up from the cellar at night, carrying away, in a cardboard box, her dolls, what little they owned, she and her grandfather, and then about that woman, her cigarette, her smell, her skin, her jeans, her voice, the blue van, the things that had disappeared, right down to the salt and a half-empty pot of mustard. Marion and the tall guy—before, Nina had imagined all sorts of things without ever thinking he could be her father—had left nothing behind. Like dogs devouring some wild creature down to its carcass. Only her room had been spared. To ease their conscience? Do those who steal from a dead man have a conscience?

Nina will talk later, in bed, and Emmanuel will be able to find the answers, the right words, he'll reassure her, love her.

For now, he gives her a drink. And then another one. Neat whiskey, no ice or soda. Nina hasn't eaten a thing. She knocks them back, swift as a barfly. Her head starts spinning, almost instantly. She puts on some music, between gulps, chooses a song by The Cure, "Boys Don't Cry." Nina is relieved to be in this house that's both strange and already familiar. Suddenly, the melody and Robert Smith's voice makes her think of Adrien and Étienne. She misses them desperately. Reaches for their hands. Closes her eyes to forget them, like slamming two doors behind her. She starts to dance, right there, in the middle of the sitting room, in front of Emmanuel, who's burning with desire for her. Every time he's close to her, he suppresses violent urges. It's as if he wants to cherish her and bruise her all at once. Crush her and kiss her. He's frightened by how he feels. It's as if Nina rouses a stranger inside him. A dark being lurking in a corner. Emmanuel thinks it will pass, that he wants her so much, it's messing with his emotions a bit. Must be what they call "falling head over heels." What bullshit.

Nina sways to the rhythm, barefoot, arms out, singing "Boys Don't Cry." Emmanuel approaches her, summons up all his gentleness, presses himself to her back, follows her movements, they dance body against body, she groans, he takes her in his arms and up to the bedroom, since that's what she wanted. Since she'd said to him: "Come and get me."

*

Adrien opens his eyes; the alarm clock says it's 10:04 P.M. Nina's not in the bed anymore. Her place is cold. He calls out to her. His voice wakes Paola, who struggles up and goes down to the kitchen and her bowl of water. Adrien follows the dog; the front door is open.

He calls for Nina again, goes back upstairs and searches for her in the empty rooms. This stripped house is disturbing, like the set of some horror film. One question haunts him: who plundered it? He finds this burglar story hard to swallow. Suddenly, Adrien fears meeting Pierre Beau's ghost, he shudders. What if it was him? If he wasn't really dead? If it was someone else, over there, in the coffin? After all, he hadn't seen his face on the day of the accident. Just legs, the rest of the body was covered with a sheet. Ridiculous. It would be too easy if our dead didn't die. Spooks and mysteries belong in the cinema and in literature. Not in real life. In real life, his father's an idiot and Nina's now alone.

Where is she? He goes out into the garden, grazes his feet on the gravel. Three cats around his legs, but no one else. Has she gone for a walk? He takes stock, standing between the hydrangeas and two scrawny fruit trees. All of a sudden, he senses a presence behind him, like some threatening shadow, almost clinging to him. He turns around, screaming. Doesn't recognize him immediately. Adrien thinks Étienne scared him on purpose. He loves bad jokes. Adrien shouts at him, with genuine anger:

"You scared the shit out of me . . . You're sick!"

Normally, in similar circumstances, Étienne would be laughing, triumphant, but he remains silent, staring at Adrien with crazed eyes. A short silence. Adrien is scared of understanding.

"Is it Nina? Has something happened to Nina?" he asks, his voice flat.

"No."

Looking downcast, Étienne goes into the house. At a loss, Adrien follows him.

"What's up?"

". . ."

"Where's Nina?" Adrien persists.

"How do I know? Weren't you supposed to be together?"

"We were together. But she vanished!"

Étienne throws up his hands as if he didn't care. Adrien can't really make sense of the gesture. Finally, sounding resigned, Étienne comes out with:

"That's Nina for you."

He goes upstairs, strips down to his briefs, and throws himself on the bed, pulls the sheet over him despite the heat, closes his eyes. Adrien watches him. On top of alcohol, he smells of swamp, that whiff they all have on their skin after a swim in the lake. Usually, Étienne showers afterwards because it "stinks of rotten eggs."

Adrien doesn't understand. And Étienne is hardly ever cryptic. And now he seems to have dozed off there, blind drunk, in Nina's bed. When she's disappeared.

"You couldn't care less where Nina is?" Adrien asks.

". . ."

"And weren't you supposed to be with Clotilde this evening?"

"Come," Étienne says to him.

## 46

*24 December 2017*

At the Hôtel des Voyageurs, Louise is dozing in Adrien's arms. She mustn't fall asleep, just close her eyes, but not give in. She has to go home, like an adolescent who's jumped over the wall and must be back before dawn. Slide between the cold sheets in her childhood bedroom, and a few hours later, play the game of Father Christmas having just been down the chimney for Louis and Lola, her nephew and niece. Despite Étienne always pretending to ignore her, Louise never felt as close to Paul-Emile as she did to him. There's just a year between her and Étienne, they're a bit like twins, the same instincts, emotions, fears, concerns. And they're alike physically. How often had Étienne heard, after introducing his sister, "Well, yes, we'd guessed that."

Louise still has a hope that Étienne will change his mind, will get treatment. For that, she needs some support, she won't succeed on her own. Confined by medical confidentiality, she's not allowed to reveal what she knows. In the family, only she and Valentin know the truth. Her nephew fell on a text message Louise had sent to Étienne:

*I beg you, have the treatment, you must stay hopeful, I've seen more critical cases pulling through. You must live.*

Valentin had immediately called her.
"Auntie?"
"Yes, sweetheart."
"Is Dad sick?"
"I don't understand."
"I saw your text on his mobile."

"You snoop in your father's mobile?"

"Of course. And watch out because my mother does, too. I check first to delete stuff, to avoid dramas."

"What kind of dramas?"

Valentin sighed, then repeated:

"Is Dad sick?"

Louise came up with a lie.

"I sent it to the wrong person. I was addressing a patient called Edmond . . . Edmond, Étienne, they're adjacent in my contacts."

"How can you lie to me, Auntie? To me? Thought I could trust you."

There was a long silence. She could tell that Valentin was stifling sobs.

"Your father has cancer. He's refusing treatment. Swear to me you won't talk about it to anyone."

"I swear." he murmured.

"Not even to him?"

"I swear, Auntie. Will you treat him?"

"I'll do all I can to, if he accepts."

"Why wouldn't he accept?"

"Because he thinks it's too late, that he's doomed."

Another silence. The teenager has taken it in. "Doomed" meant it was all over. It meant he was going to lose his father. And then he got back to his questions. He wanted to understand.

"Why does he think that?"

"Because his illness is at an advanced stage."

"And you, Auntie, what do you think?"

"That it's never too late. You never know how the body might react to treatments. You have to try to find out."

"And how will you change his mind?"

"I don't know yet."

Louise has failed. Three weeks have gone by since she had that conversation with Valentin, and Étienne still hasn't been to chemo. He doesn't answer her calls anymore. He's playing dead.

One evening, she had posted herself right beside the police station, but he'd come out with Marie-Castille. Louise was waiting for him in the Nazir, a café adjoining the station. She could tell that Étienne had seen her, but he just walked past her, talking to his wife as a diversion. Grabbing her arm, knowing that Louise would never dare approach him with Marie-Castille there.

Three days ago, when she'd arrived at her parents' house and seen Étienne, Marie-Castille and Valentin in the sitting room, glasses in hands, she'd thought to herself that it was during these few hours as a family that she'd manage to convince him. She and Valentin went off to discuss it. The teenager has a wisdom that Louise finds disconcerting. Like Adrien as a child, an almost abnormal maturity. Why do some children grow up faster than others? In Adrien's case, she knows why. But in Valentin's, she doesn't.

"I think I'm going to talk to Dad, ask him to have the treatment for my sake."

"The trouble is, you're not supposed to know. And you're pretty young to carry such a responsibility."

"I can tell him I snooped on his mobile. At worst, he'll bawl me out . . . Even though he never bawls me out."

"And your mother?" Louise asked, without much conviction.

"If Mom finds out, it'll be one big drama. Dad will leave for good . . . We'll never find him again. But you, don't you know anyone who could talk to him?"

Louise didn't need to think for long.

"Yes, I do . . . Well, I think so."

"Who?"

"Adrien and Nina."

"Who are they?"

"His childhood friends."

Adrien opens his eyes and smiles at her. It's their twenty-third Christmas Eve at this hotel.

"D'you want me to make you a baby?"

Louise doesn't respond. She's forty years old, has never married. A few casual affairs, a life of freedom attached to Adrien's life of freedom.

"I've ruined your life," he says to her.

"I love my life," Louise says. "But right now, it's my brother who's ruining his. I have to find a way to take him to get treatment . . . I can't force him. I'd love you to talk to him."

Adrien recloses his eyes. Louise doesn't know what happened between her brother and him, but one thing's for sure: they're mortal enemies now.

*

Nina isn't sleeping. She's listening to Romain breathing. She's had a delightful Christmas Eve, gentle, joyous. She hasn't had such a lovely one since her grandfather. By midnight, they'd already opened their presents, chocolates and a fountain pen for Romain, a box of charcoal sticks and a large sketch pad for her. Nina didn't react, just stared wide-eyed as if she'd found the black box of a plane that had crashed twenty-three years ago.

"How do you know?" she finally asked.

"I know."

"Who told you? I haven't touched a pencil since I was eighteen."

"I saw your grade for drawing in the bac."

"Where?"

"I looked."

". . ."

"Bac grades are like medical files . . . even though lots of stuff has been lost . . . Why did you stop drawing?"

"Because I moved on to other things."

"What things?"

"Life, the real one."

"At eighteen?"

"Yes."

"Draw me."

"Now?"

"Yes."

"I've forgotten how to."

"Don't believe you."

Nina opened her pad, grabbed a charcoal stick. Her hands were shaking.

"Sit in front of me," she told him.

"Should I strike a pose?"

"No point. It won't take long."

Nina drew a few lines and handed the paper to Romain.

"There you are."

What Romain saw was the head of a stick man, like kindergarten kids draw. A circle for the head, two rings for the eyes, two dots for the nose, and a straight line for the mouth.

"I look pissed off," he observed, mischievously. "It's crazy how much I look like my father."

They both burst out laughing.

"I can't draw anymore."

"It's like love. You said your body had forgotten, and yet . . ."

"And yet what?"

"Shall we go upstairs?"

They spent the night making love. It was gentler than the first few times. They are starting to know each other. Are no longer surprised by the smell of each other's skin. On the contrary, those skins meet again, and it feels good. Mustn't fall in love, Nina tells herself, last time it had turned into a nightmare, and now that she's got herself out of it, she doesn't want to fall again. Why do we say, "fall in love"? She had expected love to lift her up. And yet she'd experienced the opposite, a dizzying fall.

Nina slips on a shirt from Romain's wardrobe. She goes down to the sitting room. Vestiges of their festive meal on the table. Wrapping paper on the floor. On the sofa, Bob is sleeping against the cat. Nina places her sketch pad on her knees and draws them. She takes her time, rubs out, tries again. An hour later, she's finished. The result isn't disastrous. She's used to sketching animals, she spent her childhood doing so, pictures of Paola and her cats. She's forgotten nothing. She stares at the drawing and feels a sadness welling up. One tear falls onto the coffee table, next to the empty champagne glasses. And then two, three, four. She lets it happen. For how many years has she not let it happen?

*

Étienne and Marie-Castille make love. Him on his back, her on him. It suits him, he's exhausted. And since arriving at his parents', he's been hitting the bottle to silence the physical and mental pain. That's the good side to Christmas festivities, when they've barely left the table, they move on to aperitifs, and then start all over again. The vintage wines brought up from the cellar. His parents, happy to see them all back together, spoiling them. Even though he's become an inspector, his father still considers him a failure. Étienne can see clearly that he even prefers Louis and Lola to Valentin. The way he looks at them isn't the same. No doubt Valentin resembles Étienne too much. With Louise, his father is different, she's a girl. Apparently, fathers go soft with their daughters. And yet, so the family story goes, it's Louise who's an accident. She's the child that wasn't expected. The last little one, like a poisoned gift. The one for whom his mother was obliged to stop working for a few years. But him, Étienne, his parents wanted him, for God's sake.

Marie-Castille had woken him during the night, he'd felt his wife's mouth on his penis. He'd stroked her hair, closing his eyes, pretending to enjoy it. To get it up he imagines improbable scenes, avoids thinking of anything else, ogling imaginary tits and cunts, inventing a masked girl, hot for it, wrists tied, that he makes come. He must maintain the erection, if he goes soft, she'll cry, whine, tell him he doesn't love her anymore. And yet he does love her. But here, now, it's difficult. He needs to be alone. When he's back in Lyon, he'll organize his disappearance. He's taken out life insurance on his son's behalf, so he never wants for anything. Even though he knows Valentin won't want for anything, except for a father. Basically, this illness suits him. It's the end of electric racing tracks, little remote-controlled cars, riding on carousels while holding on tight to his shoulders, the time when Étienne could play at being a child to be on a par with his boy has passed. Valentin will soon be the age for asking questions, man to man. What would Étienne tell him? What advice coming from him could have the slightest value?

Marie-Castille is a police chief, she's very well paid. The house is already theirs. Not saddled with a loan. She'll start her life over. The thought of his son and wife paying their respects at his tomb revolts him.

Organizing his disappearance. Even dead, he'll have to disappear. No ID on him. Winding up in a communal grave.

But for now, he's imagining himself at an orgy, with girls on top and under him, all drop-dead gorgeous, tangled bodies, mouths, the pleasure in the breasts, the panting, loads of lace, leather, and stiletto heels. He comes. He's so relieved he could cry. It's over. He kisses his wife, who snuggles up to him, whispers an "I love you" in his ear. He shuts his eyes, hears Louise parking down below, switching the motor off. The creaking of the stairs, a ray of light under the door of his room when she switches the corridor light on, taps running in the bathroom. The sounds of his childhood and adolescence. One can know everything about a house, its little ways, just from the noises made inside it. No more light. Louise has gone into her room. Like every year, his sister has spent the night with *that* one.

## 47

*18 August 1994*

Nina opens her eyes. Emmanuel, lying against her, looks at her and smiles at her.

"You talk in your sleep."

"Did I call out to my grandfather?"

"No."

"I dreamt he was dead . . . and he is dead."

"I'm so sorry."

She turns on her side and draws her knees up to her chest, in the fetal position.

"I'm all on my own now."

"I'm here."

Nina looks hard at him. Is he laughing at her? Is he taking advantage of the situation? Why would a man like him care about a kid like her? They barely know each other.

She collects her thoughts, draws up a list of things to do first:

"I must move out, empty my bedroom before leaving for Paris."

"Why?"

"Because the house doesn't belong to us, Grandpa rented it from the town council."

"I'll buy it for you."

". . ."

"What's the point of having money if it isn't to help those one loves?"

"But . . . it might not be for sale . . . And what about your parents? What would they say?"

"My love, I'm twenty-eight years old."

"You just called me 'my love.'"

"Yes, because you are my love. The love of my life. I've never loved the way I love you, Nina."

She throws her arms around him. It's the first time such a declaration has been made to her. Like in those songs that make you dream. When she'd heard "Un homme heureux" by William Sheller—"Why are those in love always a little similar?"—she'd cried.

"Adrien and I have a theory. We think that when life takes something away from us, it gives us something else in return."

"Do you mean me when you say that?"

"Yes."

Emmanuel kisses her, caresses her, plants kisses on her body as if it were a precious stone, seeks Nina's pleasure, finds it, she trembles. She thinks: *I'm not alone anymore, someone loves me. No one will abandon me anymore. He loves me.*

*

Adrien goes out to walk Paola, since Nina hadn't come back all night. As they go round the block, the old dog seems to be dragging as much sadness as him. They struggle to move forward, heads down, staring at the asphalt unable to understand what's happening to them.

*Where is Nina*? Adrien wonders. *If she'd been there . . .*

As soon as he'd got up, he'd phoned Marie-Laure. No, she hadn't seen her. She suggested he call Emmanuel Damamme. But he didn't feel like it. There's something about that man he finds repellent. He can't say what exactly, except that he's jealous of him. He finds it hard to accept Nina being with a good-looking guy, tall, intelligent, rich, irresistible. Their youth, which he thought was a strength, has been jolted, shaken.

He reassures himself with the fact that, in a fortnight, it will be over. Adrien will take Nina far away from here. This thought makes him lift his head up, walk faster. And then, like a boomerang, the anger returns. Why is Pierre Beau dead? They were so good before, all three of them. They didn't know it, dreamt of a future in Paris, not knowing that La Comelle, that Py year aside, was paradise. The base, the support they needed to take flight. The setting of a gentle and protected childhood, a cradle far removed from misfortune. Holding Paola's leash with one hand, Adrien wipes away a tear with the other one. *Étienne on the left, Nina in the middle, me on the right.* The future that seemed so bright to them when they celebrated getting their bac last July darkens. It's eight in the morning in summer, and yet to Adrien, it feels like midnight in the depths of winter.

He takes Paola back, feeds her, and the cats, fills their bowls with fresh water because Étienne won't think of it.

*Étienne . . .* Adrien goes upstairs, pushes open the door, looks at him asleep in Nina's bed, as if to reassure himself that he hadn't been dreaming. Étienne is lying on his front with a pillow over his head. Adrien thinks of Louise, stifles an urge to throw up, right there, in the house of the dead one and the absent one.

He jumps on his bike and pedals fast, very fast, breathlessly. When he arrives at the service station, he is out of breath. He opens his kiosk, switches the diesel oil and premium pumps on. A red Renault Clio pulls up. "Fill her up please, young man."

*

Nina comes out of the bathroom, she's just caught sight of her face in the mirror, distorted by grief. She wants to get back to her job at Damamme without delay. She tells Emmanuel that going home, spending days on end in an empty house, seems impossible to her. He says: "I understand." He wants to give her a lift to Damamme, but she doesn't want them to be seen together. The summer intern and the boss's son can't arrive in the same car.

"Afterwards, the other girls, they'll all be looking at me, I dunno. I'm an orphan as it is."

Emmanuel tells her that he has no intention whatsoever of hiding her.

"I want everyone to know that we're together."

And it's on the way, between his home and Transports Damamme, in the red Alpine A610 sports car, that Emmanuelle utters these words:

"You're so young, Nina, I think you need to recover. Going off to

Paris in a fortnight, it would be madness. Let a school year go by, and then join Étienne and Adrien the following autumn."

*It would be so much easier*, Nina immediately thinks. *Maybe that's the solution. To recover before leaving.* For the moment, she is disorientated, as though on a bad trip. She's already seen school friends flipping their lid after taking acid. Her head, her aching muscles, her unease, her grief, her racing thoughts make her suppose she's in the same state as some guy getting back from a rave at eight in the morning.

"And then during that time, you'll carry on working with us . . . Over a year, you can save enough money to allow you to be free in Paris . . . And as for me, I get to keep you a bit longer," Emmanuel adds.

He lowers the volume of the radio. *A summer song*, thinks Nina, *away from here it's summer, people are on the beach.*

*Eat me! Eat me! Eat me!*
*That's the song of the shroom that pleads*
*That plays with folks' souls*
*And opens the shutters of per-cep-tion . . .*

How many times had Nina, Étienne, and Adrien danced and sang along to those words while laughing like hyenas? It's Joséphine that uses that expression, "laughing like a hyena." Since her grandfather's death, all the hyenas in the world must have quit laughing. Thinking of the boys again is like summoning up childhood memories for an adult, the fun and joy seem very distant to her. *Just a month ago, I was playing Kiss in the Ring at Club 4.*

"Could you drop me off at mine at lunchtime? I need to go and check that all's well with my pets."

"Of course."

"Thanks."

He strokes her knee. His hands are big and beautiful. Nina grabs his fingers and kisses them with her eyes closed. *I'm not alone anymore, someone loves me. No one will abandon me anymore. He loves me.*

"You also need to refurnish your house, since your mother's taken the lot . . . We'll go buy some furniture together."

*My mother*, thinks Nina. *That* thing *that smoked a cigarette beside me*. Too much suffering kills suffering. Nina turns up the volume on the radio and sings, sadly:

*Eat me! Eat me! Eat me!*
*That's the song of the shroom that pleads*
*That plays with folks' souls*
*And opens the shutters of per-cep-tion . . .*

*

At that very moment, Adrien spots the red Alpine whizzing past. It's like a speeded-up scene from a movie. Adrien makes out Nina's hair flying in the wind, her profile, her nape. So, she's with *him*. She's betrayed him. She prefers the flash guy to him.

In his kiosk, where he was already brooding about last night, now he's ready to top himself. What does drinking gasoline do to you? Has anyone ever been known to commit suicide by filling themselves up? And to cap it all, he has to have lunch with his father. Who wants to discuss his move to Paris.

"We need to manage it," he told him on the phone.

That's all Sylvain Bobin knows how to do, "manage." He's not a father but an administrator. Adrien hadn't been brave enough to answer back: "No, I'm going to manage it alone."

They are meeting at the restaurant of the Hôtel des Voyageurs. Quite a smart place. Usually, they go to the Harbor Pizzeria, right beside the footbridge—given that name by the owner who's nostalgic for the Mediterranean, even though there have never been any boats in La Comelle, apart from the odd dinghy. It will surely be the last time Sylvain Bobin sets foot in La Comelle. Maybe it's to celebrate his relief at that, the end of his obligations, that he's decided to change venue.

"The restaurant at the Voyageurs? Well, I say, only the very best for your father," Joséphine commented, sarcastically.

*

It's two in the afternoon. Marie-Laure goes into Pierre and Nina Beau's garden.

Everything's parched, the flowers and vegetables already dying of thirst. When Pierre was buried only yesterday. It's incredible how fragile all that a man leaves behind him is.

How many months will it take for the rain to scatter the gravel, for the cracks in the walls to widen, for the weeds to invade, for the damp to blacken the pointing, for the wind to rough up the tiles?

Marie-Laure notices the dejected look of the tomato plants on their stakes. Normally, she'd get down to it straightaway, normally, she'd already have the watering can in her hand. But there's something more urgent. She calls Étienne several times, he doesn't answer. She enters the house, sees the empty rooms again.

But who on earth could have done this?

Marie-Laure goes up to Nina's room, finds her son asleep. At the foot of the bed, the dog opens one eye and promptly closes it.

Marie-Laure seems put out to find him alone. She lays a hand on his bare shoulder. Remembers the day he was born, his skin is the same, a particular softness, satin-like. She still loves breathing it in, as she did when he was a child. She no longer dares to, now he's almost a man, bury her nose in his neck and sniff it noisily, so she sometimes breathes in his T-shirts from the dirty laundry basket.

Étienne opens his eyes with a groan.

"Clotilde has disappeared," his mother tells him. "Her parents are worried, they're searching everywhere for her . . . They told me that you were together yesterday evening."

# 48

*25 December 2017*

"Happy Christmas, Simone."

"Happy Christmas, *mon petit*."

"No one's called me *mon petit* since my grandfather."

Simone smiles and grumbles at the same time:

"I told you not to come today!"

"I was hardly going to leave you to manage this little world on your own."

"I met a man and I like him," Simone blurts out.

Nina is stunned. Between incredulity and astonishment, she stares at Simone as if she'd just admitted a crime and told her where she'd hidden the body. Discreet, adorable, and forever elegant, Simone has been a widow for years, and is mourning the death of her son. A dead weight she keeps to herself. Nina had almost forgotten that she's still a woman.

"Yesterday evening, we celebrated together. And it was really nice. He'd invited me, and . . . I slept at his place," she admitted, smiling at Nina.

"But that's wonderful, Simone!"

"Yes, you said it, it is wonderful . . . When I thought I was done with . . . that kind of thing."

Nina bites her lip to stop herself from laughing.

"How did you meet him?"

"At the dance . . . Every Sunday, my neighbor goes dancing at the municipal club. It's a thing for old folk, with an accordion. Ghastly . . . Personally, my thing is Matthieu Chedid, or -M- if you prefer. Know who I mean?"

"Yes."

"Anyway, a dance for widows and widowers. With a meal, dance floor, and spotlights. At first, I didn't want to go along . . . But my neighbor insisted. She dragged me there, so to speak . . . And in fact, it was fun. He's called André. I immediately took his fancy. And you?"

"What about me?"

"Have you met someone?"

Nina wasn't expecting this question. Especially coming from Simone. Well, when we think we know people . . . They're busy cleaning out the kennels with a hosepipe this morning, and the temperature's below zero. Three dogs are wandering around them. They have to scrub until the cement is dry, otherwise the surfaces freeze over and that's disastrous for the dogs' pads and arthritis. They've got hours and hours of work ahead of them, shivering side by side, wrapped in their padded jackets, hats firmly on their heads.

"No, I don't have anyone," she finally replies.

"Oh really? I thought you did. You've got that loved-up look about you."

Nina blushes like a schoolgirl.

"I haven't met . . . Let's just say that . . . I had a lovely Christmas Eve, you're right."

"I was sure of it," gloats Simone. "Who is it?"

"The man who adopted Bob," admits Nina, blushing even more.

"Ah, yes, I know . . . Good, very good. And how's Bob?"

"Good, very good," Nina quips.

"He's happy?"

"Very happy."

"Well, I'm going to have Cannelé. I'll take him home later."

Nina is flabbergasted.

"I thought you didn't want any more dogs at your place!"

"That's what I thought, too. You know, Nina, one thinks something, and then one's wrong."

*

Louise goes into Etienne's room, closes the door very quietly behind her. After the opening of presents, her brother went back up to bed, claiming to have a headache. He's sleeping. Louise sits on the bed to watch him, and gently places two fingers on his wrist to take his pulse.

She's still imbued with Adrien. She wears him like a coat that she'll take days and days to take off. Then she'll place it on a hanger until some day soon. As she watches her brother sleep, she remembers Saint-Raphaël. The summer of her vacation with the three. The first time Louise watched a boy sleeping, it was Adrien. Like this morning, she'd slipped into his room. Nina and Étienne had gone off with Marie-Laure to do some diving. Adrien had opted to stay at the house. With his terror of snakes, he feared a close encounter with some similar underwater creature. Louise remained beside him for a long time, and then he opened his eyes. In the half-light, it took him a few seconds to see her, make her out, sitting in a rocking chair a couple of meters away. He smiled at her, asked her to come closer to him. She sat on the edge of the bed.

He said:

"You know, I'm not a boy like other boys."

She replied:

"That's why I love you."

"You love me?"

"Yes, I have since I was really little."

"You still are really little."

"No, I'm thirteen. Have you ever kissed a girl?"

"On the mouth?"

"Yes."

"No. I've never kissed anyone."

"Have you ever made love?"

"Well, no, seeing as I've never kissed anyone."

"D'you want us to try?" she asked him.

"Making love?"

"No, kissing."

Adrien nodded yes. She slipped under the sheet beside him, laid her head on his shoulder. Her heart was beating fit to burst, but that morning, she felt bold as brass. She could have just stayed like this forever, in this room, with the window open, the louvered shutters closed, the streaks of brilliant light, the chirping of the cicadas outside. They got going at ten in the morning, as soon as the sunlight hit the pines, that was their starting signal. Louise sat up on the bed and got undressed, she was wearing a yellow-cotton strappy dress, with nothing underneath. Adrien was in boxer shorts. He took the dress, and breathed it in.

"You smell good."

She found herself naked against him. Adrien drew back to look at her. He scanned every part of her body, as though fascinated. As though admiring an old-master painting.

"You're beautiful, Louise."

Then, very lightly, he touched her with his fingertips. Her face, mouth, neck, breasts, tummy, pubes, thighs, down and back up the length of her body several times. With only his fingertips. She still remembers her shivers, her skin turning to gooseflesh, a warm wetness between her thighs. Like an urgent need to pee in her abdomen. She ended up closing her eyes. Said to him: "I often caress myself thinking of you, d'you want to see how?" Yes, said Adrien.

She lay on her front, turned her head toward him, looked into his eyes, and caressed herself. He had laid her dress against him, as if to breathe her in without touching her. Then he, in turn, turned onto his front and mirrored her. They came together, holding hands.

Only silence in the room, Louise looking deep into Adrien's eyes. They drew closer and kissed on the mouth, finding each other's tongue. After, they fell asleep, in a shared warmth.

"You're thinking of him," mutters Étienne.

Louise jumps.

"No, I'm thinking of you. We need to talk."

Étienne pulls a pillow to his chest.

"Get out of my room, I saw it in your eyes that you were thinking of him. You never could lie."

"It's true that, when it comes to lying, you're the expert."

"What do you want?"

"To get you to hospital."

He turns his back on her.

"Won't go."

"That's ridiculous. If you don't do it for yourself, do it for Valentin."

"So, he sees me suffering? Being butchered? Losing my hair? Throwing up after chemo and not being able to stand anymore? You want my son to see that?"

"At least he'll see that you're fighting!"

Marie-Castille comes into the room.

"What on earth are you doing? Why are you shouting?"

Louise smiles at her.

"No, it's nothing . . . I wanted us to go and see an old friend together."

"What friend?" Marie-Castille asks, suspiciously.

"Let's quit talking about it," Etienne cuts in, "I won't be going. Ladies, would you be so kind as to leave my chamber? I'd like to get up and I'm butt naked. As you know, my modesty is legendary."

Louise gets up to go, devastated. She tries to smile at Marie Celeste but can't. For just one moment, she turns back to tell her the truth, seeking the help she desperately needs to make her brother give way. Étienne, who senses it and can hear her think, cries out, coldly: "Louise! No!" Stifling an urge to scream, she swallows her tears, and leaves the room.

Behind the door, she hears Marie-Castille and her brother arguing. "Calm down . . . Everything's fine . . . Don't make me mad . . . A school friend . . . don't feel like seeing him . . . Louise insists . . . You're all wearing me out . . . I want to be alone . . . please . . . I'm tired . . . You're hiding something from me, Étienne . . . Yes, my dick . . . I don't like being seen butt naked . . . Don't cry . . . It's Christmas . . . Peace . . . pity's sake . . . peace . . . we're on vacation . . . Coming to bother me, even in my own room . . ."

Valentin finds Louise. With one look, she lets the teenager know that she's failed yet again.

*

I come into my house laden with packages. I'd had them in the trunk of my car for several days but was waiting for Christmas to give them to him. That's it, I've tipped over the edge: gone nuts. I'm giving presents to my kitten. Unless it's the first sign of premature senility.

I place a new ultra-cozy basket against the radiator, a cat tree beside the sofa, when, in a few months' time, he'll have all the countryside round here to frolic in. I shake a few toys in front of his tiny pink nose, nasty plastic things. He places his paw on a little ball and makes it roll. Watching Nicola reminds me of how I hated being an only child. What if I went and picked another one? A kitten, too, so they grow up together and are on the same wavelength. Nicola will be less bored with one of his four-legged kin than with me, one of the gloomiest, most solitary people on the planet. With me, even plants end up committing suicide, refusing to eat, falling out the window, self-destroying. Thank goodness my linden is aged, had time to grow before I arrived, to get close enough to the sky.

There must be someone on duty at the shelter. Even on Christmas Day. If I don't go now, I never will. I'll have time to think. And if I think, Nicola will grow up alone and end up depressive and neurotic, like me.

Ten minutes after this sudden thought, urge, this renewed pessimism or optimism, I'm not sure which, I'm parked outside the gates of the shelter. Two vehicles are already there, including Nina's Citroën combi. I enter the place for the second time in my life. When Nina caught me sliding that envelope of money into the mailbox, and offered me a coffee in her office, it was dark, I saw nothing of the shelter itself. This morning, I discover it in daylight. Not great. A hodgepodge of buildings. Cement sheds, prefab huts. To the right, a large black griffon-type dog barks without conviction. To the left, three isolated kennels, two of which are empty, with the label "Dog pound." A dog stares out at me, sadness, I lower my eyes, ashamed, as if it were me who'd abandoned it. I push open a second gate and am in the main kennel area. There are signs everywhere saying don't put your hands through the bars. My entrance here causes a din, all the dogs start barking as I pass, and don't stop.

A little lady finally emerges from somewhere inside.

"Good morning."

"Good morning . . . is Nina here?"

"She's out walking one of the dogs. Can I help you?"

"I adopted a kitten and . . . I'd like to pick a playmate for him."

The little lady smiles at me and leads me to the cattery. It smells of shit and detergent.

"The litter trays haven't been cleaned out yet," she tells me.

A few cats watch me, warily. Others approach, sniff me. One or two dare to rub themselves against my legs.

"We don't do any adoptions on Christmas Day," the little lady informs me.

"Why not?"

"Our offices are closed."

"But Christmas . . . that's exactly the day one should be able to adopt."

"Not untrue," she replies. "What's your name?"

"Virginie."

The little lady stares at me as though searching for something on my face.

"What's your kitten like?" she asks me.

"Small. Very small. Black. With a pink muzzle. Does one say muzzle for a cat?"

"Nose."

Nina comes into the cattery. She looks chilled to the bone. Blows on her woolen gloves.

"What are you doing here?" she asks me, seeming fearful.

"Happy Christmas, Nina."

The little lady doesn't allow her time to respond.

"It's for adopting a cat," she says, softly, as if to apologize for allowing me in.

"You've lost Nicola?" Nina exclaims, in a panicky, almost aggressive way.

"Not at all. I'm afraid he'll get bored on his own."

"You think that you'll be able to care for two cats, you? That you can handle that?"

Nasty, cutting. Her small personal revenge. I can't blame her.

"Yes, well, I think so."

"Follow me."

We go along a corridor and into an overheated room.

"This is the nursery and infirmary. It depends on the day and the arrivals."

Three tabby kittens are sleeping, all curled up together.

"I could give you one in a fortnight. For now, they're recovering."

"Can they be separated?"

Her beautiful dark eyes search mine. Instantly, the words she'd sung at the end-of-year party at middle school come back to me.

*We'll see each other every day, once we're back*
*Where are you off to, dark eyes, you're heading for nowhere . . .*

Étienne and Adrien behind their keyboards, Nina on the mike. We were all in our last year. They had organized a concert in the Vieux-Colombier schoolyard, under the awning. I can still see the banner, the word THREE attractively written by Nina onto white fabric. Three was the name of their group. As a tribute to the Indochine album, *3*, from which Nina had sung "Tes yeux noirs," "Canary Bay," "Troisième sexe," and "Trois nuits par semaine." She had followed on with some original songs written by her and Adrien to music composed by Étienne. Slightly weird lyrics. Old-fashioned melodies. But Nina had a lovely voice. I adored listening to her.

"Life's all about separation. They have to grow up . . . Can't stay stuck to each other," she says to me, without batting an eyelid.

There was an awkward silence, one that lingered. During this protracted lull, as if we'd just said, "Let's play the silence game," I watch the sleeping kittens. Empty cages, packets of food, a pharmacy cupboard, medicines locked away, an old poster of a dog behind bars with these words: "Guilty of what?"

Nina finally breaks the silence:

"There are two males and one female. Which d'you want?"

"The female."

# 49

*January 1995*

Five months, now, that Pierre Beau has been lying in the cemetery.

Nina is a personal assistant. She works with the administrative and financial director, Yves-Marie Le Camus, a charming man. She deals with his correspondence, his phone calls, the sending and receiving of his faxes, researching potential clients' financial security on Minitel, writing reports of meetings. She earns 9,000 francs a month, over 13 months. She doesn't make spelling mistakes, doesn't draw, doesn't write songs.

At Damamme, she's appreciated by all, her youth is endearing, her eighteen summers prompt kindness. She's pretty and plays the role of ideal employee to perfection.

During the week, she sleeps at home, lives with Paola and her cats. One of the gardeners from the Damamme property takes care of outside. And from Friday to Monday morning, she weekends at the Château.

In the space of five months, the mechanics of her life have been well oiled by Emmanuel. He purchased her grandfather's house from the council for peanuts, refurnished it to Nina's taste, found her a good job, presented her to his parents, who think of her as their daughter-in-law. She has lunch with them every Sunday.

Emmanuel drowns her in flowers, care, gifts, and loving words.

Nina's daily life is unbelievably charmed, so charmed that it sometimes gives her a hot flush. This must be what happiness is. No longer being afraid, no longer feeling anxious. A lovely carpet, a big bath, anything she fancies in store windows turning up, as if by magic, in her dressing room. While her school friends are in Dijon,

Autun, or Lyon, living off tinned food and slaving away in fifteen-meter-square studios, heads buried in books, she feels free. It's like she's ten years ahead of them.

Once a week, she goes up to the cemetery to talk to her grandfather and tell him how things are going.

"I'm doing fine, don't you worry. Emmanuel is kind to me. We're so in love. I like my work; the days go by fast. Your garden's looking good. The pets are well. At the weekend, it's Joséphine who sleeps at ours. She likes looking after the house, it makes a change from her apartment. She says she's going to her second home. Adrien and Étienne phone me often. They're waiting for me in Paris."

This life, it's like when she'd play storekeeper as a little girl. She'd display fruit and vegetables out in her garden, sell them to imaginary customers, and ring up her sales on a plastic cash register.

*

Vincennes, RER train A, direct to Auber, change, take metro line 7, get off at Poissonnière. The Lycée Lamartine, 121 Rue du Faubourg-Poissonnière, 9th arrondissement. This is Adrien's routine from Monday to Friday. Backpack, sandwich, pasta, or salad in a plastic box. Those wan lights, those long corridors, those people crammed together, those doors closing, those loudspeaker announcements: "Your attention please, the A line of the RER is delayed due to a suspicious package . . . due to a passenger incident . . . due to strike action . . . due to . . ." The begging of vagrants who sleep on the floor, on benches, under old newspapers, the buskers, the hawkers flogging dodgy Eiffel Towers, fruit, cigarettes, flowers, the smell of piss, plonk, some aggressive looks, punks with dogs, suits-and-ties going right up to La Défense, all these people rushing, running, jostling, together but not together, in the same direction, not looking at each other. The masses. Since living in Paris, Adrien has an overwhelming desire not to move, to stay in his room in Vincennes, in the apartment where he lodges that smells of scented candle.

Going out to attend classes costs him. He'd like to sleep all day. Close the windows. Find silence. And yet he sets off an hour early, and when he reaches Auber station, he sits in a corner, where there's little traffic, to read, to forget this underground world and dive into words the way he dived into La Comelle's municipal pool with Nina. Since he's been living in Paris, he feels as if he no longer really sees the sky. As if he's eating concrete. Before, he saw green everywhere, now he sees gray. No one ever mentioned that particular assault to him. They talk about global conflicts, prisons, love stories, petty crimes, the enlightened, the old, prostitution, the unemployed, car manufacturing, but never has he heard any accounts of how a provincial feels upon landing in Paris. Everything seems vast, you get lost, you feel lost even if you aren't, no one talks to anyone, sees anyone, greets anyone. All eyes are turned inwards to a great labyrinth of loneliness. As if a collective sadness was stuck to the soles of metro users.

Paradoxically, despite the oppression, the throng, Adrien feels freer. Lost in the crowd. Being anonymous reassures him. Here, there's no gossiping, slandering, or condemning. Here, when it comes to others, no one gives a damn. When you die in Paris, no one knows about it. When you die in La Comelle, there's an article in the newspaper.

To his great relief, he didn't end up in the student hostel. Finding himself surrounded by other students without Nina seemed unbearable to him. He lodges with Thérèse Lepic, a piano teacher and friend of his father. Unbelievable: how can his genitor, that taciturn, cold, and dull man, be the friend of this funny, cheerful, astute woman, artistic to her fingertips? In her home, there are candles and there's lace, many paintings, portraits of muses and a drawing by Salvador Dalí, given to her by the artist himself. This woman of seventy-five has more youth in her veins than Adrien has, her way of moving, nimble and agile, of enthusing, of laughing. She smokes like a chimney, but only in the sitting room she entertains in, where she leaves a window open day and night. Even in winter. Her pupils sometimes end up playing the piano in their coats, so chilly is it.

Adrien has never dared ask her how she knew his father. He thinks she was his mistress. Framed sepia photographs in Thérèse's bedroom testify to her former beauty.

The musician is slight as a sparrow, living on only fruit and almonds. She doesn't eat, she nibbles. For Adrien, she buys ready-made dishes at the delicatessen down below.

It's Sylvain Bobin who pays for his board and lodgings, but Adrien doesn't know how much it costs his father and doesn't want to know. He hates the thought that Thérèse might be making money out of him because he likes her. And what if his father stopped paying her, would Thérèse still keep him there, close to her?

What is the market value of this son, this godsend from the sticks, who has the Bobin name, but that Thérèse had never heard of before?

If he forces himself to get up every morning and brave public transport, that cornucopia of solitude, to reach the Lycée Lamartine, it's because his father warned him: "I'll pay if results are good, if you fail, it's the student hostel for you."

Adrien has a room of about seventeen square meters, with adjoining bathroom. Everything is clean, white walls, bed with quality linen. Washing and ironing done once a week. No hanging around in the local Laundromat like everyone else. A large desk to work at, a window looking out onto the street, third story with no elevator—which doesn't stop Thérèse from going up and down several times a day with no problem. For thirty-five years, she's lived in this apartment of around eighty square meters, paying a paltry rent. "Just as well," she says, "I've got no savings, I've spent it all." Her income is from the lessons she gives. Thérèse had married very young, to a career soldier. Widowed at twenty-five, she'd had a daughter, but she doesn't get on with her, and has lived alone for decades. A few lovers have shared her bed—"It's them who ruined me," she likes to say. Thérèse's and Adrien's habits were immediately in harmony. An early supper in the kitchen, then, at around 7:30 P.M., Adrien retires to his room to study and Thérèse to hers to read, listen to the radio, or watch the latest literary program. Thérèse belongs to Vincennes's library and goes there every two days to return and borrow the books she devours. What any other student would find off-putting about this monastic life suits Adrien perfectly.

Twice a week, Adrien phones Nina. He listens to her voice with his eyes closed. They chat about his life in the big city, his lessons, the others in his class. He tells her he misses her. "It's horrid without you, whenever I do anything, I think of you." As he's not very talkative, he doesn't have many friends in Paris. Just good morning, good evening.

As for Nina, she talks about her work, Emmanuel, her colleagues. Soon, she'll visit Adrien. In the spring, she'll have some leave, and the weather will be nice. He can show her the Eiffel Tower and the Champs-Élysées. To which Adrien replies:

"In any case, you're joining me in September. We'll come to an arrangement with Thérèse. You'll sleep with me, and my mother's agreed to move into yours and pay you a small rent."

"Yes, perfect, can't wait."

On Saturday evening, Étienne insists on Adrien meeting him at the Bus Palladium club. Adrien wonders why he's so emphatic about it. And until he gives in, Étienne doesn't hang up.

"It's agreed? We're meeting up? I'll wait for you outside?"

"O.K."

Is it some promise he made to Nina or his sister? Along the lines of: "Promise me not to abandon Adrien when you're in Paris . . . You're cool, for him it's difficult, he's shy."

Every Saturday, Étienne turns up with a different girl. He never arrives alone, but rarely leaves with the girl first accompanying him. Étienne is sharing his apartment with a roommate, Arthur, a student attending the same college as him, and also preparing for the entrance exam to the national police academy. "That way we can study together. We're on identical paths. It makes life simpler." *You bet it does*, thinks Adrien, *like that you can crib from him.* Adrien admires Étienne in every way but has no illusions about his ability to use other people, to suck them dry with a straw so that he can do only what interests him.

At the Bus Palladium, the pretty girls hover around Étienne. Sometimes, he disappears into the restroom or out onto the street. Then, as if by magic, he reappears on the dance floor, brimming with confidence, smiling like a king. Adrien likes watching all the maneuvers of seduction, the attraction of bodies, the games of those testing each other out. He stays in the background, observes the moves, the outfits, the gesticulating, the cigarettes held between fingers, the smoke inhaled and exhaled, the boosted cleavages, the looks that catch each other, absorb each other.

Adrien writes even when not writing.

He has started drafting a novel and fills pages of his notebook between classes.

He dances only rarely but loves electronic music. It feeds his mind with images. The sensations it produces in his body are positive, colorful, joyous. Akin to those from listening to classical music, especially Bach. Electronic music puts him into a state of torpor that eases his tormented mind. It releases the crazy bird flapping away inside him.

Sometimes tipsy girls come and sit next to him, he breathes in their perfumes, is intoxicated by their body odors, but never touches them. Süskind's novel, *Le Parfum*, had fascinated him, a quill dipped into a bouquet, and that character Grenouille, chilling.

Étienne thinks it's because of Louise that Adrien doesn't dare pick up other chicks in front of him.

Last Christmas, Étienne caught them out, saw them leaving a hotel in La Comelle together. He was returning from Club 4; it was six in the morning. Nina and Damamme had just dropped him off in the town center, they'd wanted to take him home, but Étienne had declined the offer, preferring to walk and sober up. So his parents wouldn't see him in that state.

Étienne thought he was hallucinating when he saw them both. He'd spent Christmas Eve with his family, with Louise, a few hours before. At midnight, Nina and her swell had picked him up to take him to Club 4. On the phone, Adrien had said he wanted to stay with his mother.

*Oh, sure, his mother . . . it was to meet up with my sister in secret.*

His sister, a minor, and Adrien, hand in hand, coming out of the Voyageurs like two thieves. A hotel: no doubt about it, they were sleeping together.

Étienne could have put them on the spot, given Adrien the willies and a slap to his little sister, but he did nothing. He turned a corner so as not to cross their path or be seen by them. At least Louise wasn't having it off with schmucks. And it didn't seem that crazy, those two, weird as each other, being together. Always staying silent or speaking really quietly, reading without being forced to, never blowing their top, always starry-eyed at "the beauty of the world." Going into ecstasies over a flower, a butterfly, or a painting in a museum. Well-behaved children. Like the surface of a rather dreary lake. As for Étienne, he prefers waves and turbulence. The wind and the hail.

After Clotilde's disappearance, just before moving to Paris, Étienne had gone to the police station. The girl's parents were looking for her, unable to understand why she had left overnight, without telling anyone. A woman had recognized her at La Comelle station on the evening she was supposed to meet Étienne at the lake. The witness was due to catch the last train, the 10:17 P.M. for Mâcon. And Clotilde was waiting for it, too.

Interviewed by the police at Clotilde's parents' request, Étienne went along with it willingly. Asking the two police officers taking his statement questions about their careers. Explaining that, on the evening of 17 August 1994, he and Clotilde were supposed to meet up at nine at the Lac de la Forêt. Admitting that he'd drunk while waiting for her, stressed out because that evening he was planning to tell her that he was breaking up with her.

"Why?"

"Because I didn't love her anymore."

"Had you argued?"

"No. I hadn't seen her alone since 15 July, before going on vacation."

Now, already five months have passed without anyone hearing from Clotilde. She left no note. Never phoned, or even sent a letter. When she disappeared, Clotilde was eighteen. And all legal adults have the right to disappear without being investigated. Clotilde had vanished taking only her purse containing ID and some money. She had worked as a waitress during the summer and pocketed around 15,000 francs. She had emptied her savings account, which had 30,000 francs in it, two weeks before disappearing into thin air. Everything led them to believe that she had planned her departure.

Clotilde's mother phoned Étienne several times, begging him to let them know if she contacted him. He promised he would.

This disappearance turned Étienne's life upside down. Caused a radical change in him. He feels at fault. A guilt that's heavy to bear. As if to redeem himself, he started to study. Really study.

Sharing his apartment with Arthur, a serious student, helps him. This time, he wants to understand on his own, climb the rungs.

He allows himself one night out a week, and some music on Sunday, but otherwise he works relentlessly. He wants to become a cop. And not just an officer. First, he'll do a law degree. Then the entrance exam to be assigned to a police station.

*

Étienne and his roommate Arthur have been renting a two-room apartment in the Nation district since last September. Nation is one stop on the RER from Vincennes. On Sundays, Adrien sometimes meets up with them at their apartment.

Étienne has brought the two synthesizers to Paris, his own and Adrien's, and set them up in the sitting room. They play them together, but with no great conviction. Stop often to chat, drink beers, watch TV. They tinker with music Étienne composed before Paris. Add a rhythm, an instrument, change tempos, bars. But without Nina's voice, it just sounds desolate. An absence with the nasty taste of eternity. She's still there but without actually being there. As though she were dead. Their music without her voice is incomplete, lame. They don't compose anymore, haven't the time.

Adrien is expecting Nina to join them, whereas Étienne no longer believes she will. But he says nothing to Adrien.

On that Christmas Eve at Club 4, he saw clearly that Damamme wasn't letting Nina go. Even when she went for a pee, he followed her, like a little dog, to the restroom door.

He'd never let her leave. Or then he'd come with her. Or then Nina would do a runner. Take drastic action.

They would doubtless never be three again. But playing music is like guarding some treasure, maintaining the link that unites them. It's carrying on as if you still believed in it.

Étienne has taken up the bass guitar without telling anyone. He's plugged it into an amplifier in his room so Adrien doesn't notice. Like a child dropping a friend because he's found a new one but won't admit it. He's had it with the synthesizer. Whereas Adrien listens to popular French singers, or "singers of texts," as he calls them, he prefers alt rock.

He feels like a traitor.

The phone rings. Adrien and Étienne are busy cooking pasta in the kitchen. It's Arthur who answers it.

"Hi, it's Nina, is Étienne there?"

"Yes, I'll pass him to you," Arthur replies. "Adrien's here, too," he adds.

"Oh, great! I called him at Madame Lepic's, but no one was there . . . Hello, boys?"

"Yup," says Étienne.

"Can you put it on speakerphone, so Adrien hears me?"

"Yup."

Étienne switches the microphone on. Nina's voice fills the small sitting room. She sounds strange, as if she's been drinking. She seems overexcited, is breathing heavily.

"What are you doing?"

"We're cooking pasta."

"Are you well?"

"Yup, fine."

"Can you hear me?"

"Yes," reply Étienne and Adrien in unison.

*That's it*, they think, *she's coming. She's leaving La Comelle and might even be calling from a phone booth at Gare de Lyon*.

The two boys look at each other, with a hopeful smile in their eyes. They hold their breath. She's like that, Nina, no brakes.

"Are you sitting down?"

". . ."

"I'm getting married!"

# 50

*25 December 2017*

Half an hour, now, that Valentin has been nagging:

"We'll go there together. Please, Dad . . . Before leaving for Lyon tomorrow."

Étienne finally hears himself saying:

"O.K."

"But we say nothing to Mom, or she'll want to come with us."

"So?"

"So . . . don't want her to, she's not that keen on animals."

"Neither am I that keen on them."

"You, Dad, you just pretend."

"Pretend?" asks Étienne, stiffening.

"Not to like them."

Étienne looks hard at his son. He'll forever surprise him.

He tries to visualize him in ten, twenty, thirty years' time. Gives up. Doesn't have the strength to hurt himself anymore.

First, take a shower. Étienne lets the warmth of the water engulf him. A nice feeling, it's been a long time. After his row with Marie-Castille in the bedroom, he's gone overboard, overdone it on the meds his little sister prescribed him. The painkillers soothe him, stop him from thinking. He closes his eyes, lovely images flood in, he sees himself on his skateboard again, gliding over the asphalt, then the swimming pool, its blue coolness in summer, the fries, the tears welling up because he's emptied the mustard pot onto his hot dog, the three of them in hysterics, the Nesquik sandwiches, the horror films, Nina's hand in his, digging her nails into his skin, the parties, the music, the cellar, the synthesizer, the smell of rotting fruit in Nina's garden, the tobacco, the alcohol, the lake, Clotilde. He reopens his eyes. Turns the water off. Comes out of the shower. Looks at himself in the mirror, can't see himself because it's misted up. *Just as well.*

He passes his father on the stairs, they barely glance at each other.

"Your mother and Marie-Castille have gone off to find a Yule log," he mutters.

*Phew*, thinks Étienne.

Right now, having his wife on his back would just be too much.

He spots his brother and sister-in-law in the garden, playing with their children, Louis and Lola. Paul-Émile is a stranger, thinks Étienne. When you have a brother who's a life ahead of you, you never catch up. Almost a ten-year gap. Few shared memories. When Paul-Émile left home, Étienne was eight. He'd come back during the school vacations, but would immediately go off with his friends. He was very young when he met his future wife. There are only a few photos of them as kids in which they seem at all close. Étienne sitting on his brother's knees. He must be around three, and Paul-Émile is already a teenager. He was there in Saint-Raphaël every year. But always hanging out with older boys. Basically, Étienne thinks of his brother as a vacation buddy. A guy he played volleyball with on the sand. A kind of role model, a family icon flirting with excellence. Top of the class. His father's pride. While still ogling porn mags left in his bedroom.

This morning, Étienne realizes that he's never exchanged more than a few words with his sister-in-law Pauline. "Hi, are you well? And the kids? And work?" She always answered yes. Yes to everything. Ticking the right answers to avoid any other questions. Pauline is very beautiful, discreet, intelligent, affectionate. Probably a shame to have missed out on her.

How many people do we miss out on in a lifetime?

He dispels his gloomy thoughts, pulls on his parka.

Valentin is already waiting for him in the car, earphones in. When he sees his father approaching, he takes them out. Étienne is just starting the car when Louise slides onto the back seat. Étienne glares at her in the rearview mirror.

"What do you want?"

"To come with you."

"What's this? An ambush?"

". . ."

"You know where it is, Dad?" asks Valentin.

"Yes, son. I know where it is."

On the radio, they hear that Christmas presents are already being flogged on the net. Didn't hang around, the disappointed.

Like every year, Étienne had done nothing, and it was Marie-Castille who'd organized everything. It was Rêve d'Ossian for Louise, that perfume she adores, and he loathes. It reminds him of the smell in La Comelle's church when Nina was lighting a candle. A drone and wireless speaker for Valentin. And for him, a weekend in Venice for two, all inclusive. Even love, going by the hearts drawn on the box.

Marie-Castille is incredible, a weekend for two. Étienne imagines her face if he went without her. "I'm going with another woman. Bye, have a nice weekend, see you Monday."

*How cruel I am*, he thinks. *Even in thought*.

"What are thinking about, Dad?"

"Nothing in particular, son."

Étienne observes Louise in the rearview mirror. He feels like annoying her. Like when they were little, and he'd provoke her. It's stronger than him. A brother and sister thing. And it will be a kind of revenge for her intrusion into his bedroom this morning. It was her fault that Marie-Castille flipped her lid.

"Did you have a good night, then?" he asks, sarcastically.

Louise blushes.

"You got in late, I heard you. Where were you?" he continues.

He knows she was with Adrien. She doesn't reply. Turns her head, studies the empty pavements. Changes the subject.

"Valentin, are you sure Nina will be at the shelter?"

"Yes, she's there. I sent her a text. Have you been over there before, Dad?"

"When we were little. Nina had found a dog, with Adrien, and we took it there."

"Who's Adrien?"

Louise's blood freezes.

Étienne sniggers:

"Louise, answer Valentin, who's Adrien?"

"You're being a pain now," she snaps back at him.

"Who is he?" insists Valentin.

"A childhood friend," replies Étienne. "And a *very* good friend of your auntie."

"You're not funny," Louise shouts at him.

"Auntie, why's Dad saying that?"

"I'll explain it to you one day."

"You'll explain to me why you're not married? You're so beautiful."

"Thank you, my darling."

Louise is on the verge of tears. Marrying Adrien . . . how she'd dreamt of doing that. And yet she'd always said no.

They reach the level of their old school. Étienne slams on the brakes.

"Shit! They've razed the Vieux-Colombier!" he exclaims.

They just sit there for a few seconds, brother and sister each reliving their memories of heavy schoolbags, straps over shoulders, pulling on their backs.

Louise gazes at the wasteland. *Exactly like my love life*, she thinks. *A deserted site, contaminated by asbestos. Not even able to give life to a tomato plant. At least I save a few lives. Basically, I'm of use to others' lives. But not to my brother's. What will I do without him?* Discreetly, she wipes away her tears. Étienne looks intently at her in the rearview mirror. Once again, he's heard her thoughts. The look in Étienne's eyes right then, in that rectangle of mirror: despair. He's let go. It's over. He'll let himself drift away. She can see in her brother's beautiful blue eyes, the same as hers, that he's already gone. Nothing and no one will be able to hold him back.

Étienne drives off again, puts the turn signal on and follows the SHELTER signs, a red arrow painted on a rickety panel at a junction.

He parks alongside a wall, a few meters from the gates. Immediately spots Nina's car, along with two other cars, one of which is reversing to leave. He takes no notice of its driver.

The first time he came here, he must have been thirteen or fourteen.

The same age as his son today. Nina had found a small Brittany spaniel. No collar, scrawny. They had spent all afternoon going door to door, like traveling sales reps.

"Is this your dog?"

"No."

At 9:00 P.M., Pierre Beau, mad with rage and anxiety, had given them a roasting. Seeing his granddaughter cradling the mutt, he'd exploded:

"This time it's over. We've already got Paola and four cats! This isn't Noah's Ark here! You'll kindly take it straight to the animal shelter!"

"But it's closed at this time, Grandpa!"

"I don't want to know."

Nina had turned her beautiful, sad eyes to the boys.

"I won't be able to bear leaving it at that place."

Étienne had taken the little creature in his arms to carry it home, where he, too, was greeted by his parents' hollering:

"What is that?"

"A dog. We found it in the street. I'll take it to the shelter tomorrow."

"And in the meantime? What exactly were you thinking of doing with it?"

His parents had insisted that he put it back on the street. The animal would find its way home on its own.

"Oh, sure it will . . . we're not in some cartoon movie."

But Louise had stepped in. Two children against two adults, it wasn't really a match, he and his sister had won the battle but not the war. They'd made it a makeshift bed with a blanket found in the cellar, and they'd fed it. Louise had slept on the sofa beside it. The following morning, it had crapped all over the sitting room. Marie-Laure was almost apoplectic, and his father, red with rage, had launched into him:

"Didn't I say that you're completely hopeless!"

"It's O.K., it's only shit," Étienne had answered back.

He loved answering back to his father in front of his mother, because he knew that, whatever he said, Marie-Laure would stick up for him.

That morning, Adrien came to collect him at nine, and they walked up to the shelter with the little dog merrily following them. A lady greeted them curtly, took the dog, grumbling unintelligibly, and disappeared, slamming the gate in their faces. That pleading look the dog gave them. Two traitors. Ashamed, Étienne and Adrien didn't dare cry in front of each other.

They walked back in silence, and each went to their own home to sob, hidden from view.

For ages, Louise begged her parents to let her go and fetch the spaniel. Nothing would make them give in. Secretly, Étienne rang the shelter twice to know whether the dog had been reclaimed. Both times, the phone was slammed down on him.

Why is he back here this morning? Why had he said yes to his son's request?

For two reasons, to please Valentin, and to kiss Nina before leaving. One last time.

# 51

*Saturday 1 July 1995*

The town hall, which is packed to the rafters, gradually empties. Essentially, it's members of the Damamme family and their close friends. On Nina's side, the guests come down to the Beaulieus, Adrien, and Joséphine. But they're what's essential to her. As she's hugging, in turn, the boys' mothers with her puny arms, she thinks that, actually, they are her surrogate mothers. When the mayor had congratulated the newlyweds' parents, she had thought of Marie-Laure and Joséphine, not of Marion.

It was they who went with her to Dijon to choose her outfit: it's like a ballet dress, ivory in color, the bustier in silk and lace, fanning out in a corolla of tulle from waist to ankle, matched with pretty strapped shoes, a bouquet of pale-pink roses in her hands, and a band of fine pearls in her hair. Nina looks splendid. All eyes are on her, a light brighter than the rest, dazzling. Because she looks younger than her age, she could be a mere girl attending her first ball. Emmanuel, as elegant as his young wife in a dove-gray Dior suit, has all the distinction of an English lord. No one could remember ever seeing such a handsome couple outside La Comelle's town hall before.

Étienne and Adrien are Nina's witnesses, they have just signed the register. It's as if they have signed their friend's death sentence while mustering a smile for the hired photographer's flashes. "Young men, look at me, heads up a little . . . Yes, that's it, like that, less wary, more cheerful, please."

Two days before, they had both organized the "burial" of Nina's life as a young girl. It had annoyed Emmanuel, but he'd not let on. *The day after tomorrow, she'll be mine forever*, he told himself.

He, too, had gone out for a drink with some old school friends who had come especially for the wedding. He pretended to have fun, thinking only of Nina, almost to distraction.

Following tradition, for the two nights preceding their marriage, Nina had slept at her home and Emmanuel at his. From this evening onwards, Nina will live in the Château all year round. And Joséphine will live in Nina's house.

"Are you sure about leaving the apartment, Mom?" Adrien asked her. "This marriage, it won't last."

"You're being a bit pessimistic, son."

"No, Mom, optimistic."

"It's reassuring for Nina. And if I have to leave, I'll leave. I'll easily find somewhere else to rent. And since you've been in Paris, I can't bear going past your dark room . . . It feels like you've died."

"Mom . . ."

"It's true. I need to move on. Have a change of air."

On the evening Nina's life as a young girl was being "buried," Étienne and Adrien came to collect her at 8:30 P.M., at her house. They were surprised to find Emmanuel there, "a whirlwind visit to kiss my future wife." They all shook hands vigorously, but their body language and looks betrayed a reciprocal animosity. After asking them a few polite questions about their studies in Paris, Emmanuel finally left, with a patronizing parting shot: "Be good . . . Don't make my little woman do too many silly things." Étienne managed to stay cool, but Adrien wanted to smash his face in. Like he'd done to Py.

Once Emmanuel was out of the door, Nina seemed almost relieved. As though allowing herself to be an adolescent again. The three began by greeting each other again *properly*.

They hadn't seen each other since Christmas. Seven months. An eternity. And they'd only had two days together. When Étienne and Adrien had returned to La Comelle on 24 December, Emmanuel had sprung the surprise of whisking Nina off to an island in the sun, from 26 December, to celebrate the New Year. "He did that on purpose," Adrien had railed. "He knew we were coming home." Étienne had played it down: "It's her first New Year's Eve without her grandfather, maybe it's just as well that she's not here."

The three all gave each other a long hug. Adrien cracked, weeping on Nina's shoulder. Whispering to her:

"It's really tough in Paris without you . . . Life without you."

Étienne watched them without saying a word.

The boys saw Nina's house refurnished and redecorated for the first time, the new paintwork, and the PVC windows. They barely recognized Pierre Beau's old home.

"Emmanuel really bought the house for you?" asked Adrien.

"Through the company."

"Does that mean it isn't yours?"

"What's his is mine."

Glances were exchanged between Adrien and Étienne, and the latter said:

"That's all very well, old bean, but now, we must be off, it's time for your burial."

They tied a black blindfold over her eyes, guided her to the car, and sat her down in the passenger seat. Adrien got in at the back. They drove for about five minutes.

Marie-Laure had lent her Clio to her son. During the five-minute journey, all Étienne said was:

"The car's brand new and the tank's full."

"Where are you taking me? Tell me."

"You don't really think that we bothered to blindfold you just to tell you where we're going, do you?"

Étienne switched off the engine, grabbed something out of the trunk, the sound of metal.

"You're going to kill me and hide my body, is that it?"

"Yup," Étienne replied, through gritted teeth.

"Are you annoyed with me?"

Étienne and Adrien again exchanged glances. Just as they had when Nina had said, about her future husband: "What's his is mine."

"No," Adrien finally replied, "it's myself I'm annoyed with for not managing to take you away by force."

"I'm happy here," Nina said, apologetically, as if to reassure them, or excuse herself.

They took her by the hand, Nina in the middle, Étienne on the left, Adrien on the right, and walked a few meters. Étienne unfolded a metal ladder, Adrien went in front, took both of Nina's hands, and helped her over an iron gate. Nina first felt grass under her feet, then smelt chlorine.

"We're at the swimming pool!"

She pulled off her blindfold. Daylight was fading. At that time, the municipal facility was deserted, closed to the public. The blue water in the pools now wavered between navy and purple. Heat clouds were still reflected in it. They took off their shoes, the tiles were cold, the air soft.

"Are we allowed to be here?" asked Nina.

"Well, no, that's the fun of it," Étienne replied, pulling a bottle of Malibu and some pineapple juice out of his backpack. "I brought your girly drink for you."

He carried on emptying his bag, packets of chips, plastic glasses, whiskey, Coke, towels, *pains au chocolat* (Nina's favorite brand), sweets, a swimsuit borrowed from Louise, which he handed to Nina.

"I think it should fit you."

Nina raised her arms to the sky and cried:

"You're the best!"

"Shush, no one must hear us."

In three minutes they were all together in the big pool, plunging into the water, again and again, touching the bottom, timing their speeds, dunking each other in turn, Nina on the boys' backs, arms clamped around their necks.

From time to time, Étienne got out to refill their glasses. His little cassette-player was on quietly in the background. He'd carefully taped the favorite songs of all three of them. Those they'd listened to the most over the past ten years. Every one of them, even those he didn't like. A-ha, "The Sun Always Shines on TV"; Cock Robin, "The Promise You Made"; Étienne Daho, "Le Grand Sommeil"; INXS, "Need You Tonight"; Mylène Farmer, "Ainsi Soit Je"; The Christians, "Words"; Nirvana, "Smells Like Teen Spirit"; Depeche Mode, "I Feel You"; The Cure, "Charlotte Sometimes"; David Bowie, "Rebel"; Indochine, "Un Jour Dans Notre Vie"; 2 Unlimited, "Let the Beat Control Your Body" . . . an unlikely mix, rather like them, in the end.

They swam for a long time in the black water. Occasionally, they scared each other, Étienne humming the music from *Jaws* while circling Nina, who screamed into the water so no one heard. They got out only once to climb up to the five-meter diving board, then all held hands and jumped into the night, unable to see the pool down below.

They returned to Nina's house, all three blind drunk, at four in the morning, shivering, laughing, three chumps belting out the songs of their young lives.

"I've just enjoyed the best burial of a young girl's life of all the young girls in the world . . . Thank you."

She started to think of her grandfather, cried every tear she had on their shoulders. They took a scalding hot shower to warm themselves up, stretched out on Nina's bed, all three of them, and started reading comic books. The two boys smoked a joint. At the bottom of each page, Adrien or Étienne would say "Finished." And Nina would turn to the next one.

At around five in the morning, starting to doze off, Nina asked:

"Have you ever fancied me?"

"Shut up," Étienne replied.

"You can tell me everything, I'm getting married."

"We can tell you everything?" Adrien said. "O.K.: the tank's full, the car's new, tomorrow morning we take you far, far away. And in September, you come with us to Paris."

"But . . . I'm getting married."

"Well, what Adrien's trying to tell you is that you can still cancel it."

"And my dress?"

"We'll sell it."

"But I can't do that to Emmanuel."

"Run away, Nina, come with us. We'll look after you," Adrien pleaded with her.

"And my house?"

"My mother's moving in, you don't need to worry."

"I can't abandon Emmanuel, I love him. He's wonderful."

"It's life that's wonderful. If he loves you, he'll wait for you."

"You can't understand . . . Couldn't you just be happy for me? For once? You're both jealous!"

"Jealous? My poor dear, your life of luxury, it means fuck all to me!" said Étienne, getting carried away. "Who is it that left us in the lurch? Weren't we supposed to live in Paris, all three of us together?"

"You're just a schmuck who understands nothing!"

"Schmuck yourself!"

Adrien stepped in:

"Have you both gone mad?"

"It's her, getting on my nerves," said Étienne, annoyed.

"I didn't get on your nerves when you needed me!"

"What? What? Go on, explain!"

"Who got landed with your homework while you did fuck all at school?"

"Oh sure, you were only too happy to make the most of my money!"

"Your money? What money?"

"You were pretty spoilt when we took you on holiday!"

"Calm down! Calm down!" said Adrien, soothingly.

"Oh, you, don't start!" Nina retorted. "We never know what you're thinking!"

"Oh yeah? What I think is that you mustn't get married."

"Why? Give me one good reason."

"You're too young."

"What you don't understand, Adrien, is that the day my grandfather died, I stopped being young. And that the person who held his hand out to me, who looked after me, was Emmanuel . . . When you two went off to Paris, it suited you, him being there. You didn't have to cope with my grief. He did."

They went quiet. Calmed down. Looked at each other. Regretted their row. Étienne rolled another joint. Nina went down to the kitchen to fetch the dregs of the whiskey and three glasses. They stayed just like that for more than fifteen minutes, not saying a word to each other. Dawn was starting to break. It was Adrien who broke the silence:

"I must tell you something."

"Well, it's about time," Nina snapped. "You prefer boys, is that it?"

"No, he prefers my sister," Étienne jumped in.

Adrien blushed.

"I've started writing a novel."

The other two looked at him, baffled.

"It's easier to write than to say," Adrien added.

"Are you going to talk about me in your book?" Nina asked, testily.

"If I talk about myself, inevitably, I talk about you."

"And about me, too?" Étienne asked, anxiously

"Why? Are there things I shouldn't say?" Adrien asked him.

The two boys looked daggers at each other.

"Am I missing something here?" Nina asked.

No response.

"What am I going to be called in your novel?" she continued.

"What would you like to be called?"

"Angélique."

Étienne burst out laughing.

"God you can be corny!"

"And you?" Adrien asked Étienne. "What would you like to be called in my novel?"

"Kurt. Like Kurt Cobain."

*

"I do."

"Nina Beau, do you take Emmanuel Jean-Philippe Damamme to be your husband?"

"Yes, I do."

"You are now united before God. You may kiss each other."

The organ, Johann Sebastian Bach, signs of the cross, congratulations. Glancing at the pale Christ, Nina can't help thinking of her grandfather, buried eleven months ago; she stops herself from thinking that maybe it's her being buried now. Étienne and Adrien have sown a bad seed in her mind. A seed she wants to destroy before it grows. What she doesn't know is that it's too late: cutting off the head of the plant doesn't pull up the roots.

It's 4:00 P.M., the guests are all gathering for the group photo.

Then drinks are served, courtesy of the Damammes and in honor of the newlyweds, in the presbytery gardens. Three hundred people, at least, nearly all of La Comelle, out of whom a large number have been selected for the dinner.

People whom Nina doesn't know come to congratulate her. Repeating to her: "You look so beautiful," "You look stunning," "You'll make lots of girls envious" . . . To all of them, Nina serves up the same response: thank you.

The Beaulieus, Adrien, and Joséphine are reunited. Louise smiles, seems happy, doesn't stop admiring Nina. Marie-Laure and Joséphine drink glass after glass of champagne while gaily chatting. Marc is discussing something with Adrien, whose mind seems to be elsewhere, as usual. *But what is he actually thinking about*? Nina wonders. *Adrien and Louise. I noticed nothing. We think we know everything about our friends, when really we know nothing.*

"How's Madame Damamme doing?" Emmanuel asks her, while kissing her on the neck.

"She's happy . . . And how's my husband doing?"

"Delirious. I love you."

"I love you."

*This is unreal*, thinks Nina. She goes to sit a little to one side, in the shade. Someone brings her a glass of champagne. *I'm at my wedding*, she says to herself. *Today is my wedding day*. She surveys the gathering once again. Lots of Emmanuel's friends, people of his age, approaching their thirties. The girls are attractive, tall, slender, two are pregnant, others tend to their little ones, babies, and toddlers. The strollers and chairs for the elderly stand side by side. From time to time, Emmanuel's friends give kind looks to Nina, favor her with knowing smiles. Nina has won the jackpot, Emmanuel Damamme has made many hearts swoon, and it's this little thing that's ensnared him. You have to admire that. A number of his closest friends were surprised when Emmanuel announced to them that he was marrying Nina. It had all happened so fast. They had never seen their friend in love. The best looker in their group would go from one affair to the next, never committing for long.

For the last few minutes, Nina doesn't understand her uneasiness, it pervades her gradually, something is disturbing her, tightening her stomach. Or someone. His face among all those strangers. Nina grips her glass, she identifies him, zooms in on him as if with a camera. What was blurred becomes clear. She recognizes him. He's there, at the buffet, stuffing himself with *saucisson*. He's in a badly cut suit, chatting to his wife as if nothing was amiss. Who had invited him? Who had dared? How could her parents-in-law have been that tactless? Nina struggles to her feet, her legs barely carrying her, and searches for Emmanuel in the crowd. Feels an urge to escape.

"The car's new, the tank's full." The boys' words have a different ring to them all of a sudden.

Someone grabs her arm, grips it almost too tight. It's Emmanuel.

"You O.K., my love?"

"No . . ." answers Nina. "*He* is here."

"Who?"

"The man who killed my grandfather."

For a moment, Emmanuel doesn't seem to understand what his wife is on about.

"Ah . . ." he said, finally. "I invited him to the drinks, it gives the staff such pleasure to join in with our celebrations."

"Y*ou* invited him?"

"Yes . . . Sorry, I should have told you."

"But . . . he killed him!"

"Darling, it was an accident . . . That poor Monsieur Blondin, it's not his fault . . . Come on, smile . . . You're not allowed to sulk today."

Nina can't speak anymore. "That poor Monsieur Blondin!"

"Go check on your two witnesses," Emmanuel whispers in her ear, "they look bored."

Nina looks at him now. Searching for something in her husband's lovely eyes, something she doesn't find. Doesn't see. The shadow in the painting.

"Is it because Étienne and Adrien are my witnesses that you invited the criminal?"

Emmanuel's face clouds over. His eyes roll skywards.

"What are you talking about?"

"You were against it. You didn't want it to be them. Admit that you don't like them, that you're jealous of our friendship."

"You've had too much to drink. Control yourself, please."

After the accident that caused Pierre Beau's death, Blondin had taken early retirement. The police hadn't been able to establish which of them was responsible for not giving way, Pierre Beau or the truck driver. The latter, arriving on the left, was obliged to give way to the bike on the right, but he claimed that Pierre Beau arrived from Rue Jean-Jaurès, on the left of the square. But Nina was always convinced that her grandfather had arrived from Rue Saint-Pierre to the right of the truck driver. Since the truck had dragged the poor mailman's body several meters, the police and insurance experts hadn't been able to prove anything. And no one had witnessed the accident.

A few weeks later, Nina had gone to question the people living on those two roads, to find out whether any letters had been delivered into their mailboxes on that day. All said yes, they had. With which of those two roads had Pierre Beau started his delivery? No one will ever know. But Nina still blames Blondin, considers him a criminal. She attempted to question him, followed him in the street once, he'd quickened his pace. So, Nina had been to his home. It was his wife who opened the door. Supposedly, her husband wasn't in. Nina was sure he was hiding inside. She hadn't pushed it any further. What was the point? It wouldn't get her grandfather back for her. What's more, if she did manage to prove the driver responsible, the Damammes would take the flak, a family that's now hers.

*

A few hours later, the newlyweds are opening the dancing with a waltz. It was Emmanuel's mother who had taught Nina the steps. Lightheartedly, Gertrude had explained to her future daughter-in-law that she couldn't possibly go by that ostrich's name, so she was called Gé. But *never* Gégé. They practiced in the large dining room. Gé barefooted and Nina in sneakers. "One two three four, one two three four, one two three four." That's how Nina really got to know her future mother-in-law: by treading on her toes. They'd come together in a joyful musical bubble.

Intimacy is almost nonexistent at the Château. On Sunday, there are always at least ten around the table, surrounded by staff. In Gé, Nina discovered a woman who was funny and kind, the opposite of how she first seemed—reserved, almost cold. Gé had asked her questions about her childhood, her grandfather. Not to know but to understand. No intrusive questions, just interest. Nina left out the episode when Marion came to steal, to take back what belonged to her, on the evening of the funeral. Nina just told Gé that she didn't know her mother. That she'd never seen her. Had no memory of her, and that her grandfather had raised her with only love.

When Nina talks to her parents-in-law, she weighs her words, thinks them through. Allows for no spontaneity. These people are not from her world. They'd attended elite universities and were born "with a silver spoon in their mouth"—a strange expression her grandfather sometimes used. Nina is wary of Henri-Georges, Emmanuel's father. She hugs the walls when she comes across him. He's cordial enough, but far from friendly and so haughty that Nina feels obliged to look skywards when he addresses her. They both make polite small talk, and that's all.

This morning, as Nina was putting on her bridal gown before the admiring eyes of Marie-Laure and Joséphine, who kept saying: "How beautiful you look, how very beautiful!" Gé had turned up. She had exclaimed: "Goodness, how beautiful my daughter-in-law is!" While Marie-Laure made coffee for everyone, Gé had opened her elegant handbag. "Tradition says that the bride must wear 'something old, something new, something borrowed, something blue' on the day of her wedding." And she had presented Nina with a sapphire, a white-gold bracelet still in its box, and a splendid antique ring set with diamonds, and finally, had taken off her own engagement ring to lend it to her.

Nina looked around at the three women supporting her, caring for her. Why had her mother never wanted her?

The party is taking place about seven kilometers from La Comelle, in a property equipped to host around a hundred, with the kitchens, the large reception room, the gardens, the dance floor, and the adjacent buildings with several apartments and dormitories for those staying overnight. The setting is sumptuous, with flowers everywhere. As if white roses had taken over the walls and ceilings for centuries. And it's entirely lit with candles. A fairy-tale décor.

It was Emmanuel's parents who had organized everything. Gé asked the young couple to choose the menu and the music they would like. The dancing would be traditional to start off, with a band and violins. From midnight, a DJ would do the mixing and tequila would be served.

For now, gazing into each other's eyes, the newlyweds swirl around as the flashes go off around them. Nina is drunk. Only Étienne and Adrien know what the rest will never see. What's shining in her eyes isn't joy, but champagne. A few couples join them on the dance floor, they continue for about twenty minutes, then everyone returns to their tables. The choreography is perfect, it's smiles all around, except on Adrien's face. Étienne is in the same state as Nina. He's been knocking it back all afternoon. Right now, he drinks some water to clear his head: it's him who's got to read the speech that he and Adrien prepared for the newlyweds. It was mainly Adrien who wrote it. As he refused to speak in public, he did a deal with Étienne: "I write, you read."

The tinkle of a silver knife against a crystal glass. Silence. Nervously, Étienne stands up, clears his voice, has a sudden urge to laugh, which he stifles. *This isn't the moment.*

*How handsome he is, that rascal*, thinks Nina, swallowing a gulp of champagne.

While the one is so shy, the other is equally reserved but would rather die than show it. Nina's emotions take over before Étienne even opens his mouth. Emmanuel puts his hand on her knee, she feels the pressure of his fingers against her flesh, as though he were trying to crush her turmoil.

"Dear Nina, Adrien and I have written this speech in your honor . . . though you can be pretty sure he's the one who worked on it . . . Me, I just watched . . . Like when we did our homework and studies together. Between us two boys, it's me who's the dunce . . . And of us three, it's definitely me. But I digress . . ."

Étienne searches for his father's eyes with defiance, then unfolds a piece of paper he'd slipped into his pocket.

"Our dearest Nina, we have no memories before you. And yet we met when we were ten years old. But before you, the memories don't exist. You are the beginning. Nina, you are the good student, the friend, the artist, the laughter, the sister, our light. Not torchlight, no; you are the star, the asteroid, the one-and-only, the river, the link between us. Three. That's how we grew up. The expression goes 'they're like the five fingers of a hand.' Until today, our hand had but three fingers. But that didn't prevent us growing up together. Me on the left, you in the middle, Adrien on the right. We grew in the same rooms, streets, schools, cellars. We grew in the same dreams. Do you know what the three-fingered salute is? The thumb, the index finger, the middle finger. It's a gesture symbolizing a pledge of loyalty. We will always be loyal to you, now and forever. You, by definition, are the middle finger, even if it's onto your third finger that your fine husband slipped a ring symbolizing your love, your union. But let's get back to you, Nina, an artist first and foremost. Vivacious and spirited. A full-time genius at drawing, a part-time singer. Time we now give back to you. Our songs will join our memories, those of our childhood and adolescence, you have a new life to build. Without your voice, our compositions will decompose. But it's no big deal. Our fans won't miss us because they don't exist. The Christmas fairs and music festivals will be all the better off. Today, we're losing you a little, but it's doubtless for your happiness. You've never done anything like everybody else. You've always been an epoch ahead of us. You're the girl and we're the boys, quite simply. A boy is so small, next to a girl. He always seems to have one less life. Didn't the poet say that woman is the future of man? Dear Nina, before, you had two families, ours. From today, you're joining a third. Again, that figure reappearing, like the Holy Trinity. The Father, the Son, and the Holy Ghost. The story of your life. You're starting a new family with Emmanuel. Today, your happiness belongs to him, to you both. Emmanuel, this evening we entrust our sister to you, and there are certain things about her you don't yet know, that you will discover as the years go by, such as her sunny disposition. Smiling is second nature to her. We've compiled a non-exhaustive list for you—because lists can change—in three parts: what Nina likes, what Nina doesn't like, and finally, what we don't like about Nina. Nina likes *pains au chocolat* and black coffee, dogs, cats, pigs, calves, cows on the loose, never on her plate. She can weep in front of a *boeuf bourguignon*, Emmanuel, we have warned you . . . And she's often made us feel ashamed in front of some salami. She also likes vanilla essences, on her skin and in her food, piña colada and Malibu, the salt on fries, mustard, tomatoes, rummaging in drawers, dancing, swimming, *Columbo*, ugly sneakers, apple tart, creamy desserts, *sauce au poivre*, spuds, cheese, sandwiches, cherries. She doesn't like the bitterness of grapefruit, waiting in line, people with a limp handshake, ice cubes, and hot desserts. Never give her a fur coat, unless you want to be rid of it—not the coat, your wife. What we don't like about Nina: she draws us all day long, even when we've just woken up, even when we're sleeping, when we've got acne and bags under our eyes, she makes us pose for hours, she's rubbish at video games and tennis, but is *determined* to join in, a nightmare, and she asks weird questions, too. All the time. Like 'Why are bananas yellow?', 'Where does saliva come from?', 'Why didn't he look at me?', 'Why are tears salty?', 'Why are some people quiet?', 'Why do folk generally not give a damn?', 'Why do we say "*tomber dans les pommes*" for fainting, why apples, do you think?', 'What does an earthworm think about?' . . . Emmanuel, we have warned you. It was always said that she had no sense of direction, that she got lost at the drop of a hat. This isn't true. And today we have the irrefutable proof, seeing as she met you. We wish you both a world of happiness, your world. The rest will sort itself out."

Étienne sits back down, everyone applauds, Nina stands up to kiss the two boys. Modestly, Étienne tells her: "I did nothing, it wasn't me, I didn't write it." And Adrien whispers in her ear: "For you, we'll always have a new car with a full tank."

# 52

*25 December 2017*

My blood froze. I recognized his 4x4, with 69 on its license plate. He didn't see me as I drove past him. Not a glance. At the back, I could make out Louise, her blond hair. She didn't notice me, either. How could she have guessed, imagined that I'd be there? What's the likelihood of us meeting in front of the shelter on Christmas Day? I slowed down while they were getting out of the car.

I watched them in my rearview mirror. I took my time to really study them. My hands were shaking, clutching the steering wheel as if my body was hanging in the void.

I had just told Nina that I was reserving a sister for Nicola. "You can come and collect her in three weeks' time." She consulted a calendar. "19 January. A Tuesday. Tuesday's a good day for adopting." I don't know why she said that to me. I tried to find some Tuesdays in our childhood memories but came up with nothing.

I felt like getting out of the car, following them into the shelter, listening. Hearing their voices.

Étienne was wearing a bulky parka and a hood over his head. The way he walked hadn't changed. I glimpsed his nose, his mouth, I didn't see his eyes, his head was down. And the teen next to him, his son, a carbon copy. And then Louise had appeared, too. She looked worn out.

There I was, unable to drive off, unable to cut the engine and get out. Suddenly, I imagined that Étienne was going to take Nicola's adoptive sister. That Nina was going to take revenge that way, by giving away my 19 January cat. That they were coming to collect the litter of three kittens, so as not to separate them. And I started to cry. I've no idea how long I stayed like that, sobbing on the steering wheel.

I looked up, and saw them again in my rearview mirror, with the little lady who had greeted me, led me to the cats. She had a dog on a leash and was surrounded by Nina, Étienne, his son, and Louise. They looked over in my direction. Nina said something. Étienne turned his head, it lasted forever, that moment of him staring at my car. He had hesitated, then approached, alone. I didn't move. Impossible to drive off. I waited. My heart was pounding, fit to burst.

When he reached my car, he knocked on the window. He said: "Police, your papers, please."

On the surface of his eyes, I saw our childhood reappearing, like dead skin. In his eyes, a cocktail of laughter and despair. Seventeen years without seeing each other. Fourteen without speaking.

The last time, we'd almost come to blows. Never have I hated someone as much as him.

And there he was, on that icy morning, leaning toward me.

I lowered my window. The cold rushed in. I gazed at him for a long time, as he did me. We must have sized up our wrinkles, the frown lines and the "vale of tears," our sagging eyelids, the furrows at the corner of our lips, who had we kissed? How many times?

"Why are you crying?" he asked.

"Because you're going to take my cat."

# 53

*May 1996*

Ten months, now, that they've been married.

It's seven in the morning when Emmanuel kisses her on the neck before leaving. She moans with pleasure and instantly falls back to sleep. Every morning, she opens her eyes for the first time at around 10:00 A.M., goes back to sleep, reopens them at around 10:15, 10:20, 10:30. Doesn't feel up to it. Returns to her dreams. Finally gets up at 11:15, at the latest. So she looks fresh when Emmanuel comes home for lunch. As if she'd got up at eight. She takes a shower while listening to the radio. She likes the voices of the presenters.

When she goes into the kitchen, Nathalie, the housekeeper, is already there. The invisible staff of the early days have made their appearance, much to Nina's despair. She preferred cooking and cleaning herself but didn't even attempt to suggest that to her husband, who would have ruled it out immediately. Nina doesn't like this woman, but since she's worked for the Damammes forever, she daren't say a thing.

Nathalie prepares all the meals. Emmanuel gets in at around one, to spend some time with Nina, saying that the days feel less long like that. Except when he has meetings or is away on business. Since last September, that's his routine.

Two days after their wedding, Emmanuel asked Nina to hand in her resignation.

"You can't work as the finance director's PA now you're my wife."

"I like what I do . . . It's fun. And Monsieur Le Camus is charming."

"I know. But you must find yourself other activities. Nina, next year I'll be in charge. It wouldn't be right for the boss's wife to work in the offices as an assistant. You don't need to earn your living anymore."

"But what will I do all day?"

"Look after your husband, make yourself beautiful, and spend our money . . . I don't want you worrying about anything anymore. Do whatever you please, Nina. I love you. I'm here to spoil you. To make life better for you. Bigger. Just relax."

Nina chewed her thumbnail while thinking.

"Well, I'll go back to my studies then.

"What for?"

"To learn. I can do it by correspondence."

"If you feel like it . . . Your wish is my command, my love."

She signed up to do a distance-learning course in graphic design, bought herself a computer. She lasted until the winter. Three months. Working at home, motivating herself, having to send homework regularly, getting her tutorials on floppy discs, she didn't have the heart for it all. So now she lingers in bed, puts on some makeup, changes dress and hair color, has lunch with her husband, watches TV series, listens to music, reads, goes shopping. Sometimes even makes herself go back to her old house, to have a coffee with Joséphine and see her cats. Paola had died in her sleep of old age. Nina had her cremated and scattered her ashes on her grandfather's tomb. *You'll be taking your naps together, like before.*

Only the two elderly cats remain, barely venturing out and sleeping on a bed all day. Nina could have taken them with her to the Château, but Emmanuel is allergic to animal hair. He promised Nina he would get himself desensitized but couldn't guarantee anything. "Sometimes it works, sometimes it fails."

On Sundays, they join the rest of the Damamme family in the large dining room, the very one in which Nina had learnt to waltz with Gé. They have lunch and talk politics, business, and local news. Nina listens, rarely saying anything. Just once, when the conversation turned to the latest nuclear tests in French Polynesia, she had spoken out, outraged at Chirac's decision, and fired up by a 1989 red burgundy selected by her father-in-law. Surprised, the family had reacted with polite smiles, not really understanding her outburst. The Polynesians and the Coral Reef are so very far away from Burgundy.

Returning home from these Sunday lunches, always a little tipsy,

Nina phones Adrien and Étienne. It's the Sunday-afternoon ritual. While Emmanuel takes a nap, she talks to them, listens to them, asks them questions. They tell each other about their lives, theirs in Paris, studying hard for their entrance exams, hers leisurely and happy.

"You're not bored?" Adrien is forever asking.

"No, I'm making the most of it."

"Making the most of what?"

"Of life."

She says she will come and visit them soon, with Emmanuel, as soon as his schedule allows. They talk about next summer, the boys must come and swim at the Château, the pool's fab, they'll have barbecues and dinners with the grass between their toes. Adrien and Étienne promise, in turn, to come.

She doesn't draw anymore. As though her art belonged to her former life. The one with her grandfather. One morning, she sketched Emmanuel dozing, he laughed when he saw himself on the drawing paper, made fun of her a little, didn't think it was a good likeness.

"My love, I fear that you're no Renoir."

At the time, Nina was deeply hurt, but then she told herself that that's what love is, that honesty, telling the truth to the one you love. That she'd been misled when young, humored with illusions as to her talent. She looked at her sketch of Emmanuel, realized that her work was mediocre. Since then, her folders, charcoal, and paper slumber at the bottom of a closet.

In the evening, Emmanuel gets home at around seven, they drink, have a late supper, make love. Emmanuel tells her that he's never been so happy, that she gives him the life he dreamt of. When he finally drops off, she puts the TV on, and watches talk shows until two in the morning. *Bouillon de culture*, *Comme un lundi*, *Ça se discute*. She listens, fascinated, to these people, sometimes in makeup, a wig, and dark glasses, telling their story to the presenter, Jean-Luc Delarue.

When signing her marriage certificate, Nina had signed up to a never-ending vacation.

*

"Monsieur Bobin?"

"Yes."

"Monsieur Désérable awaits you."

With a dry mouth and tight throat, Adrien enters an office full of books lined up on cherrywood shelves. He'd sent his manuscript to several publishing houses. All had replied that his novel didn't fit in with their editorial direction. All but one, a famous imprint with prestigious authors.

One evening, Thérèse Lepic told Adrien that someone had phoned.

"A certain Fabien Désérable from the publishers . . . the publishers . . . I've forgotten."

"What did he say to you, Thérèse? What precisely did he say to you?"

"Nothing in particular, you just need to call him back."

Adrien immediately thought this was a good sign. Those kinds of people don't phone if they're not interested in you, they send a form letter. Unless it was to insult him, or remonstrate out loud, considering the nature of what he'd written.

It was 8:00 P.M. when, feverishly, Adrien dialed the number. Answering machine. He didn't sleep all night, stared at the ceiling conjuring images in his mind, each one crazier than the last. The following morning, he took the RER and metro as usual to his school. At lunchtime, he went out to find a payphone, dialed the number Thérèse had scribbled on a scrap of paper. A woman gave him an appointment but said nothing else. Adrien hadn't dared ask a question. And now here he is, facing a man of about forty-five, small, with a mischievous look in his eye, warm, a deep voice, bald as a coot. Firm handshake.

"Do take a seat. Tea? Coffee? Water?"

"No, thank you."

"Are you related to Christian Bobin?"

Adrien considers. He has no idea who Christian Bobin is. His father's name is Sylvain. Might he have an uncle or cousin by marriage called Christian? After all, he knows nothing about the family of his genitor.

"I don't think so . . ." he finally replies, sheepishly.

Fabien Désérable looks intently at him. Adrien feels uncomfortable.

"I'm not going to beat around the bush, your manuscript is good, very good, even. Profound, fascinating, forceful. I've never read anything so . . . Original. Forgive me if I speak out of turn . . . In no way do I want to be rude."

". . ."

"You garnered almost unanimous approval from our reading committee. Only one or two expressed reservations . . . But I think that's down to its originality. The text could be disconcerting. Did you send it to any other editors? Any other contacts? Offers?"

"No."

"Thank you for your candor. Would you be interested in joining our outfit?"

Adrien musters a barely audible yes. As though hesitating, when in fact his heart is pounding.

"The title, *Blanc d'Espagne*, is excellent."

". . ."

"What do you do in life?"

"Literary studies. I'm in my second year of preparing for École Normale."

"How old are you?"

"Twenty."

"Ever written anything previously?"

"No. Well, a few songs, now and then. Nothing special."

"I won't hide from you that I'm really impressed by the very nature of your text."

". . ."

"Are you already working on something else? Another novel in the pipeline?"

"No."

"Well, then you must think about doing so."

". . ."

"I have a question that you're not obliged to answer: is it autobiographical or fictionalized?"

Adrien takes a while before answering.

"I think that in every novel there are certain truths, roots that feed off the real, and that in autobiographies there are many lies."

Smiling, Fabien Désérable again looks intently at him.

"You come across very well . . . I'll get your contract drawn up. As soon as we're ready, we'll be in touch again . . . There will be some corrections, very few, some cuts, we'll do them together, and only if you agree to them. I will be your editor; we will work together. Welcome."

Fabien Désérable stands up and holds out his hand.

Five minutes later, Adrien is in the street, lost. He can't quite grasp it. His writing is going to be like a bomb dropping on his circle. His words are doubtless going to change his life. His novel, it's going to be edited, published! Everything had moved so fast. He's not walking, he's flying, carried by a tortuous pride. Those words he'd thrown down on paper are tinged with deep pain, and those people liked them, or understood them. He feels recognized. He exists for the first time. Emerging into the light, and through the biggest door. It's like a waking dream. He must ring Nina and his mother. Must tell them the great news.

He stops dead, on the pavement. Of course not. He'll say nothing. Except to Louise. There'll be no champagne or drumrolls for this event.

Adrien forgot to let Fabien Désérable know that he wishes to remain anonymous. That his name mustn't appear on the cover.

*

Louise hangs up. Adrien has just told her that he's going to be published. She'd said: "That's marvelous, but it doesn't surprise me." She's the only one to know. Had read the manuscript before Adrien sent it to several editors. She promised to keep the secret. Before hanging up, she whispered to him:

"I love you."

"Me too."

She lives in Lyon, where she's doing her first year of medicine. She's bored without the Three. Misses her twit of a brother. Nina has stayed where she was born, and Adrien is going to shine elsewhere, she's sure of it.

Whenever Louise returns to La Comelle, she says to herself that she must pay Nina a visit, and on Sunday evening, just before leaving, she thinks: *Darn, I forgot about her.*

*

Étienne leaves the lecture hall of his university. More than a year to go before his roommate Arthur and he take their entrance exam for the police academy. Two years at university before the exam are mandatory. They must have their diploma under their belt.

Étienne is almost crossing off the days on a calendar. He's eager to be at the academy, getting to the heart of the matter, the heart of his existence. Law school is the worst, like a punishment. Compared with it, even hell must be cushy. Civil law, private law, constitutional law . . . a nightmare. But he perseveres, joining the police has become his obsession. If he passes his entrance exam, which would be great, he'll enter the Cannes-Écluse police officers' academy, and if he's up to scratch, in eighteen months' time, he'll be a police lieutenant. Eighteen months of training, including six internships at police stations, where he'll take part in searches, custody cases, surveillance.

Depending on what's available, his grades will allow him to choose his posting. He'll have to work really hard, be among the best of the class of '96. He's paying for help from a woman who's an assistant professor at the Sorbonne, whom he sees three times a week. At first, he was so hopeless that he was sometimes reduced to tears. Remembered what Nina was forever telling him: "Understand what you're copying, one day I won't be there anymore."

Nina isn't there anymore. She isn't dead, but she might as well be.

When his training is over, Étienne will request Lyon as his first choice. Paris doesn't interest him. Paris was part of a dream to make music, the dream of before. Lyon is a good compromise, the city, the sea not far, mountains close by, Louise.

He already knows that he meets all the physical-aptitude requirements and that he's an excellent marksman. He no longer smokes at all. And if, at the rare parties he attends, a joint is circulating, he moves over to the window, or to another room.

He's got his sports kit in his backpack. Three times a week, he takes the metro, line 9, to go running, circuiting the upper and lower lakes in the Bois de Boulogne, with Sonic Youth from his earphones.

He doesn't run too close to the water, and if, unfortunately, he's forced to swerve near its edge, he feels anxious. That silent water that invariably reflects the sky, that mirror he imagines as an eye scrutinizing him takes him right back to the Lac de la Forêt. To that evening when he'd waited for Clotilde. Almost two years ago, now, that she disappeared. Apparently, her parents want to appear on that TV show about missing people, *Perdu de vue*.

Étienne remembers his mother watching it when he still lived in La Comelle. At the time, he would roll his eyes at the dramatic music used to heighten emotion. The point of the show is to appeal for witnesses in the context of a concerning disappearance or following an unsolved murder. There's a voyeurism to it that gets Étienne down. And more importantly, that shows the police in a bad light: "You're not capable of solving a case? Then we'll turn to the media."

Should he be a witness? He won't be able to get out of it if he's asked to be one. Or he'd seem suspicious. Running clears his head. Keeps him fit, too.

Today, he's going to circuit both lakes. Take different paths through the wood. Since he's been imagining Clotilde's parents requesting help in front of the TF1 cameras, he avoids looking at the water, like avoiding meeting someone's eye. As soon as his mother had told him: "Titi, Clotilde's parents have been in touch with the presenter Jacques Pradel, the TV show is studying the file," the lakes in the Bois de Boulogne seemed like a face, a terrifying mask.

He watched the latest show with Adrien. Didn't feel up to doing so on his own. It was a Monday evening. Usually, they meet up on Saturday or Sunday, never during the week. But Étienne said it was important. He'd ordered in pizzas, which they ate side by side, their synthesizers behind them, permanently switched off, now used as somewhere to sling coats and empty pockets onto. Like two adored bodies, worshipped for years and now forgotten.

"Why d'you want us to watch that?" Adrien asked, surprised.

"Because journalists are sure to call me, my mother told me that Clotilde's parents had decided to appear on the show."

"Are you serious?"
"I wouldn't joke about that."
"What are you going to say?"
"What else would I say? That I waited for her, and she never came."

# 54

*25 December 2017*

Étienne grasps his cup of coffee with both hands, takes a gulp, pulls a face. "Happy Christmas," he finally says to us.

He looks tired. He's taken off his hood but is still wearing his parka. I find it hard to believe that I'm in the same room as him. Sometimes, one lives things that one has so often imagined, or dreaded, that when they happen, one can't grasp it, one remains outside of what's going on.

Nina never takes her eyes off Étienne. In this tiny office, he seems like a giant. He lights a cigarette without asking if it's allowed. She says nothing. Looks for her words the way one looks for a path when one is lost.

Louise and Valentin went off with Simone to see the litter of kittens in the nursery. Louise had rallied them, so we'd be left alone.

When she saw me getting out of the car, she became translucent. And she was pale enough on arrival. She didn't expect to see me, here.

I approached them, with Etienne by my side. I got another shock when I saw his son up close. The resemblance.

I didn't touch or kiss anyone.

When young, Nina was very tactile. She needed to touch other people to connect with them. She kissed and took hold of hands, stroked faces as if she were sculpting the people before her. I admired her because I was incapable of doing that. I've always feared touching others.

Now, I'm alone facing Étienne and Nina. My hands behind my back so they don't notice that I'm shaking.

"You don't have something stronger to drink?" Étienne asks Nina. "Your coffee's disgusting . . . A brandy to toast Christmas?"

"It's eleven in the morning," Nina retorts. "And I don't think it would be a good idea considering your condition."

Étienne smiles. He looks at me. "Did Louise tell you about me?"

"Tell me what?"

My voice is flat.

"That I'm going to die."

Nina steps in. I'm relieved. I'm not obliged to reply to him.

"If you don't get treatment," she snaps, "that's for sure."

"You're not starting, too, are you . . . Leave me in peace . . . There's nothing to treat."

"What do you intend to do?"

"Nothing."

"What d'you mean, nothing?" Nina insists.

"I'm going back to Lyon tomorrow."

"And?"

"And . . . I'll get lost in the sun. I want to see the sea before . . . Louise has given me what's needed. I won't be in pain."

"Where do you want to go?"

It's me who asked that question. When I desperately wanted to stay out of this conversation. It just burst out. There are some words one can't to hold back. Words kept silent for years that suddenly escape from us.

"I don't know yet . . ." he replies to me. "Italy or Greece . . . something like that . . ."

Nina and Étienne carry on as if I was no longer there:

"Have you spoken to your son about your intentions?"

"Not yet. I'll do so before taking off."

"When are you planning to leave?"

"Soon. Very soon. Next week probably. I don't have much time left."

"How do you know that?"

"You haven't seen the state of my tumor," he replies, bitterly.

"You can be operated on. And there are chemo treatments that work," Nina counters, without seeming that convinced.

"You sound just like my sister! Did she coach you?"

"Not at all. I have friends who've come through it."

"Which friends?" Étienne asks.

Nina doesn't answer.

"Joséphine?" Étienne persists, almost aggressively. "You think I don't know how much she suffered?"

"You didn't even come to her funeral!"

I've just shouted louder than I would have wanted to. I'm still reeling. Feel like running away as fast as I can. I've already heard too much. Unbearable. I left my car out of love for Louise and Nina, not for Étienne. Let him just die, anyhow. For me, he died a very long time ago. I turn toward the door to leave, Étienne stops me.

"I visited Joséphine's grave . . . the day after the funeral . . . When everyone had gone away. At the time, I didn't want to cross anyone's path."

# 55

*6 September 1997*

Two billion people are in front of their TVs, following the cortège with their eyes, mesmerized. The young princes, under a blazing sun, weighed down by grief like two reeds by clusters of birds. The world can't bear to see its crowned heads suffer. Even less so, two children losing their mother.

And that same world has also just learnt of the death of Mother Teresa. One can picture them both before Saint Peter, the princess of hearts and the princess of the poor, hand in hand. Both with soft voices. Does one lose one's voice when one dies?

*So what is this late summer trying to say*? thinks Adrien.

Elsewhere, a son is burying his mother, without an ocean of flowers or floods of people. A woman who did her best. With hands covered in felt pen and modeling clay under fingernails, she spent her life wiping down other people's children, greeting the parents in the morning, returning their kids in the evening. Arms hired by the day. A break. Her daily routine is making them play, laugh, dance in a ring, eat, sleep; cuddling them, wiping their snot, sorting out security blankets, reading them a story, keeping them busy before they start elementary school. Twenty years of kindergartens and municipal day-care centers. Blond and dark-haired tots, some stubborn, some docile. She was there for first teeth and first steps. Forever bending down to catch them when they were about to fall.

It's 11:00 A.M. when Nina, Adrien, and Louise enter La Comelle's cemetery. Louise on the left, Nina in the middle, Adrien on the right. It's the first time Louise is standing in for her brother, detained at the police academy. Louise, Nina, and Marie-Laure all helped Adrien to organize the funeral. As if Marie-Laure was in charge of others' deaths. Those of her son's friends' parents.

There's an interval of three years between Nina being hit by grief and then Adrien. Of course, Sylvain Bobin insisted on paying for everything. He, too, is present that morning.

It took no more than two months for Joséphine to be taken away. One morning, her doctor made her have a blood test because she felt rather more tired than usual, the following day, she learnt that she had generalized cancer.

They tried chemotherapy, but Joséphine died before her hair fell out. It's Nina who looked after her, accompanied her to the hospital at Autun, until she passed away right there, surrounded by Adrien, Nina, and Marie-Laure. Right to the end, Adrien came every weekend, overburdened by his heavy school schedule.

The truth is that Adrien didn't sit the entrance exam. The truth is that he lied to everyone: since *Blanc d'Espagne* was published, in March 1997, five-hundred-thousand copies of the novel have already sold in France, and it has been bought by twenty other countries. A real phenomenon, its subject matter fascinates people. And the fact that its author wishes to remain anonymous contributes to that. Sasha Laurent is the pseudonym Adrien came up with.

Was that a woman or a man? Speculation was rife, with famous names being bandied about. Some even imagined that the writer had died long ago, that it was an exhumed manuscript.

The advance for his second novel was so big that Adrien left Thérèse's apartment in Vincennes and moved to Paris's 6th arrondissement, into a comfortable sixty square meters overlooking a courtyard, right next to his publishers. A clandestine life, dealing in contraband. He says he's a student to avoid admitting to his loved ones that he's the author of *Blanc d'Espagne*. He also leads his editor to believe that he's working on his second novel, when in fact he hasn't an idea in his head. He's stumped. His daily life is a blank page. *Blanc d'Espagne* had been an outlet. And behind the lie, more lying. It's his second skin for good now.

Without noticing it, like the IV drip his mother was connected to in the last days of her life, Adrien has changed. He has gained in confidence and is starting to look at himself in store windows to tidy his hair. A former ugly duckling who has become handsome thanks to glory. A glory he reaps no benefit from, apart from in his bank account.

He goes out every evening with his editor, Fabien Désérable, who introduces him as one of his young prodigies, but adds nothing else. To those who are curious to know what he has written, he merely replies: "We're only at the correction stage, a little patience . . ."

Adrien and Désérable go to all the shows, always in the front seats. Adrien ends his nights in trendy clubs. He sips expensive cocktails through straws while watching the wild things dance.

For the first time, he's conscious of being appealing to people. It must be to do with his attitude. The blushing kid is dead and buried forever. Success has made him walk tall. On these Parisian nights out, he always positions himself so he's overlooking the dance floor and can feast his eyes. Not for one moment does he think of himself as having lived in Burgundy. He invents a past for himself in which he grew up around Saint-Germain-des-Prés. Sometimes the son of artists, sometimes no one's son. Born in Buenos Aires or New York, he creates a life for himself depending on whom he's just met. He no longer uses public transport, rarely leaves his neighborhood, and when he has to go somewhere else, hails a taxi. He doesn't keep in touch with Thérèse, his "landlady," as he now calls her. After all, she'd taken him in for the cash.

He doesn't see Étienne anymore, he's now at his Cannes-Écluse police academy in Seine-et-Marne.

It wasn't Joséphine who told Adrien about her illness, but Nina. Joséphine didn't want to worry him. Told herself that she'd soon get rid of this cancer and would confess everything to her son once she was all better.

One evening, Nina phoned Adrien to tell him that he should come, his mother was ill. When she said the word "cancer," he froze.

The following day, he took the high-speed train to join them directly at the hospital. As he opened the door to her room, he was shocked: his mother had lost weight and her face already looked like a death mask. He took it as punishment, he had written *Blanc d'Espagne* without saying a word, and life was taking revenge. He had admitted everything on paper, but in silence. Nina looked totally different, too, her face was puffy and her body was someone else's. She had gained ten kilos, maybe more. Adrien thought she was pregnant. He felt like running away from this former life, legging it to return to his glamorous invented lives. Nina went off to use the coffee machine, and when he found himself alone with Joséphine, he felt like confessing everything to her: "Mom, I'm the one who wrote *Blanc d'Espagne*, forgive me." But he didn't have the courage.

She died not knowing.

Apart from a few old school friends and work colleagues, there wasn't a big crowd in the church. People had stayed home to watch Princess Diana's funeral on the TV. In the cemetery, only a handful of people are there for the burial. Louise and Nina hold Adrien by the hand. Stiff as a board, Sylvain Bobin is behind them. Adrien could feel his genitor's breath on his nape if he moved back a centimeter.

Adrien asked the two girls to take him somewhere far away after the funeral. Not a drink at the home of one or the other, just being alone with the two of them. Nina winced. Tricky not going back home, Emmanuel hates her being far away from him, but in such circumstances, impossible to abandon Adrien. She lied, told Emmanuel that everyone was getting together to remember Joséphine after the ceremony.

"Where? Until what time? D'you want me to go with you?"

"No, it's O.K."

She even dared to say: "I'd prefer to be alone, Étienne won't be there as it is."

After Joséphine's death, Louise had phoned her brother:

"She's being buried on Saturday."

"They do burials on a Saturday?" was all he said.

"Must do."

"Can't come. My captain refused me leave. I'm stuck."

"Phone Adrien, at least."

"O.K."

Étienne hung up, and remembered Joséphine. She was cool. Never raised her voice. Always having fun. Cig in mouth. Her hand ruffling their hair. Only great memories in her little apartment. He thought of Adrien's grief. Of Nina's loneliness. Her youth wrecked. He and Nina had died on the same day and no one knew it. He thought that he'd give everything to go back to his adolescence. His typically carefree self.

The following morning was Sunday. He bought a ticket at the station in Lyon, caught a high-speed train. As he alighted onto the platform, he caught sight of Adrien and Louise, sitting side by side in front of a drinks dispenser inside the station. They looked lost.

No doubt he was returning to Paris, she to Lyon.

Étienne hugged the walls so they wouldn't spot him, like on that Christmas Day when he'd seen them coming out of the Hôtel des Voyageurs.

*What an odd couple. Look like they've been together a hundred years. Little old folk in youngsters' bodies.* Why didn't they live together? Why did they still hide away?

Étienne caught a bus to La Comelle, walked up to the cemetery under a blazing sun, looked for and found Joséphine Simoni's grave among those that were most recent. He realized that he was just discovering her maiden name.

For him, she had always been Jo, or Adrien's mother.

He sat down just beside her, on a bench, and began to talk to her. He started by thanking her for all the chocolates and sandwiches. Then digressed to the evening of 17 August 1994. He'd never spoken about it to anyone. From where Joséphine was, she couldn't tell a soul. Just listen to him. The need to ease his conscience.

It was the evening of Pierre Beau's funeral. Étienne, his head in a whirl, had arrived early at the Lac de la Forêt. He'd brought along some savory biscuits and a good bottle of whiskey, swiped from his parents' bar. He was dreading this reunion with Clotilde, whom he hadn't seen for more than a month. Just fleetingly that morning at the funeral and that afternoon at his house, but only briefly because he hadn't let go of Nina's hand.

A reunion that would end in separation. His little speech was ready: "I love you but I'm off to Paris in a fortnight, we'll meet again perhaps, probably, in a few years' time, later, we'll end up getting married, you'll see . . . But right now, let's have a break, or we'll be too miserable." The word "break" was less harsh, more cowardly but less definitive than "It's over." He wanted to avoid the shouting and the tears. Melodrama, not really his thing.

He'd already made a good start on the whiskey, and had dozed off, knocked out by the strain of the past few days and the alcohol, when Clotilde arrived. He got a start when he saw her, all dolled up.

She threw herself at him. Étienne let himself be kissed. Then she stared at him.

"You didn't get my letter?" she asked him.

"What letter?"

She smiled strangely before shrugging her shoulders. He noticed that she looked drawn, as if the summer had aged her. She wanted to have a swim, right there, right then. "It's just too hot . . . And all that with Nina's grandfather, that funeral, it got me down, the poor girl . . ."

She didn't think a word of it. Bad actress. She was jealous of Nina, of the Three's closeness. Étienne heard the opposite: "Couldn't give a damn about Nina Beau."

He despised her. Almost left there and then. Clotilde sensed it. She completely changed her behavior.

"Shall we find a quiet little corner? Like that we can strip right off," she said, suggestively, while stroking his crotch.

The flesh is weak, especially Étienne's. He said to himself that he wouldn't mind getting laid one last time. After all, that's why he'd gone out with her for so long. He said O.K.

They jumped on the motorbike, drove deep into the forest, found a shady spot, far from prying eyes, with no embankment. The other swimmers were on the other side, on jetties crudely camouflaged with quarry sand, where some youngsters were grilling sausages.

Étienne and Clotilde would leap straight into the lake from a small bank covered in tall grasses burnt by the summer.

He got undressed. Dived in. The water was muddy. He watched her getting undressed, with her back to him. She was wearing some kind of strapping, the things old folk wear to support the lumbar region. She just turned her head in his direction and smiled at him, a strange smile. Once again, he felt uneasy, felt an urge to get away, instantly lost his hard-on. Didn't want to fuck her anymore. *What an idiot to come here . . . What a total idiot.*

He swam, away from the edge. Already the muddiness had gone. The water was clearer. And being cold had sobered him up. When he turned round, Clotilde was in the water, swimming toward him and laughing too loudly. When she reached him, she whispered, "I have a surprise," and then disappeared. Étienne thought she was going to do some kind of underwater fellatio on him. But she resurfaced and floated on her back. A rounded belly. Like some growth. A nightmare. He'd never seen a pregnant woman's belly. Beneath clothes, yes. But never bare. The belly button protruding slightly.

He scrolled back over the whole affair in a flash, he should have suspected it, sensed it: she hadn't had an abortion.

And yet he had gone with her to Autun. Waited in a café opposite the hospital. She'd come back out mid-afternoon.

"Did it go alright?" he'd asked her, rather ashamed.

"Yes, it's better this way," she'd replied.

Right now, impossible to get a word out. And her, on her back, gazing at him and smiling, almost proud of her good, or bad, joke. He closed his eyes, ducked his head under the water and swam, to reach the shore and get out of there. He would have liked to cancel this moment. Like on his computer, with the "delete" arrow.

She followed him, swimming the crawl. An exceptional swimmer. He'd forgotten that detail. He felt her hands grabbing his ankles. He kicked back and scrambled out of the water. He saw her strapping thrown on the ground, beside her clothes.

*A madwoman*, he thought.

She struggled to climb out, asked Étienne to help her, he didn't move, looked at her, coldly. She caught hold of the root of a tree and somehow pulled herself up. He felt like pressing her head back down so she'd disappear to the bottom of the lake.

Once out of the water, she started bawling:

"Don't you worry, I'll ask nothing of you. No one knows, not even my parents."

She took wads of banknotes out of her bag. Several thousand francs.

"See I've got plenty of cash, I'm going to leave."

"Leave to go where?"

"Don't know yet . . . This evening, this meeting between us two, it was to dump me, wasn't it?"

He didn't reply. She started crying, letting out strange yelps. Again she spoke of a letter that she'd supposedly sent him. Hatred and pity. He took the bottle of whiskey out of his backpack and downed several glassfuls. Alcohol had always soothed him. He became calmer. Felt dizzy, sat down in the grass.

"Fuck's sake, I'm not even eighteen . . . Why d'you do that?"

"I wasn't brave enough to have the abortion."

"I don't believe you, Clotilde. Just say you wanted to trap me. But don't make me swallow your bravery crap."

She got dressed without a word, sniffing now and then. Without bandaging her belly. He rolled a joint. Kept on drinking. She sat down close to him.

"When our parents find out, they're going to flip their lids . . . yours as much as mine."

"I'm going to leave before they know," she said.

"But where will you go, for God's sake?!!"

She smiled.

"I've always worked things out."

"I don't want a kid. I've never wanted one. I never will want one. You've cheated me. It's disgusting."

"And you, you're not disgusting for wanting to leave me?"

He closed his eyes. A living nightmare. This morning, Pierre Beau's funeral, and now, this one rolling up with her big fat belly. He could have wept. But never in front of a girl. His head started spinning. He stretched out, eyes still closed. Against his back, dry, prickly grass. From time to time, he'd brush away an ant from his arm or neck. Clotilde put a hand on his stomach, a hot, deft hand. He pushed it away once, twice. The tenth time, he gave in. What was the point of fighting? And fighting against what? She'd trapped him. Might as well get some kind of pleasure out of it. She stroked him, she'd always known how to handle him. He came, dozed off, lulled by the warmth and the whiskey.

Night was starting to fall when he was woken by a dull noise. He called out to Clotilde several times, no reply. Her clothes and strapping had disappeared, not a trace she'd ever been there, as if he'd had a bad dream.

He stood up, felt queasy, too much alcohol, legs unsteady. He stank of slime.

Two hundred meters away, maybe three, he thought he saw something sinking into the water. Finally, Étienne realized that it was no figment of his imagination, a car was going under before his eyes, swallowed up by the lake. He made no attempt to dive in. To find out if there was anyone inside and, ultimately, save them. He told himself that it must be to do with trafficking, a stolen car. Around here, there had always been shady characters, small-time dealers, and dope smokers. That evening, Étienne made no connection between Clotilde and that old wreck.

He got onto his motorbike and, without looking back, drove to Nina's house.

After all, what the hell. That kid, it was her problem, not his.

The following day, he learnt of Clotilde's disappearance.

A witness had formally identified her as being at La Comelle station, at around 10:00 P.M. The train schedules tied in. So Étienne had lied: Clotilde hadn't come to their meeting place. Much simpler. By saying he hadn't seen her, he convinced himself that nothing had happened. He was going off to Paris and no one would stand in his way. He'd become a cop, and apply the law to stop any other Clotildes, or cheats, from trapping men.

## 56

*25 December 2017*

"How are you doing?" asks Étienne, leaning against the shelter's railings, as if we'd just met by chance on a street corner. Further off, there's the barking of the dogs, as Simone, Louise, and Valentin walk past them.

"I live here. I came back."

"Why?"

"Because I know it. I bought a small house."

"The truth," he insists.

I don't understand what he's getting at. As if he wanted me to own up to something, or someone.

"Nina, perhaps . . . I . . ."

Right then, Nina joins us.

"Can we go to your place?" she begs me.

"Yes."

"I'll ask Louise to give Valentin a lift. I've only got two seats in my car, can you take us in yours?"

"Yes."

I understand then that she fears Étienne will slip through her fingers. She expects my help. She's tense, wastes no time. She's ready to go now. Simone comes out of the shelter with a dog in her arms, followed by Louise and Valentin, hand in hand. I think to myself that I'd rather they were getting into my car than Étienne and Nina.

"I'm taking Cannelé home and I'll be back late afternoon," Simone tells Nina.

We're all frozen stiff. Tips of ears and noses red. Nina watches Simone settling Cannelé on the back seat of her car. Adopting means having a project, making plans for the future, when up until then she thought Simone had one thing on her mind, dying. Valentin watches her, too, enviously.

"When I'm grown up, I'll have a dog," he says.

Étienne smiles at his son, without saying anything. He couldn't even be bothered to give him a mutt.

"You'll come and get it here, I hope," Nina joshes him, to ease the tense atmosphere.

"Dunno . . ." Valentin says, sadly. "It's terrible choosing one and leaving all the others."

"Don't worry, I'll choose for you . . . Louise, we're leaving with Étienne. Can you take his car?" Nina asks.

Resigned, Étienne hands his car keys to his sister.

"Don't worry, I do know how to drive your great big car," Louise preempts him.

He gestures toward Nina and me.

"If I'm not home before one, call the police. With those two, you can never be sure," he jokes, without smiling.

Nina gets in at the back, he gets in beside me. I smell his cologne. He lowers the window, lights a cigarette.

"I'd remind you that I'm asthmatic."

Étienne throws away his cigarette and winds the window back up. He leans his neck against the headrest and closes his eyes. Nina grips his shoulders. He takes one of her hands in his.

He only reopens his eyes when we've pulled up outside my house.

"That's where you live?" he asks me.

"Yes."

Inside, we're greeted by Nicola. Étienne looks at my desk, my computer. He does a tour of the place as if about to buy it, or conduct a search of it.

"You live alone?"

"With my cat."

"You're going to stay here?"

"Yes."

"Forever?"

"Yes, well, I think so . . . Who'd like a coffee?"

Étienne sits on the sofa. He picks up Nicola, puts him on his knees to play with him. He seems out of it. He closes his eyes in spite of himself, as if he were drugged.

After knocking back an espresso and coming back to life, Étienne addresses Nina:

"Why did you make me come here?"

"If you're going, we're going with you."

# 57

*12 July 1998*

Tonight, it's the final of the football World Cup. Adrien and Étienne will be there. Nina pushes her cart along the aisles of the supermarket, selecting the ingredients that Nathalie, the cook, will prepare for supper.

Once a month, Emmanuel's friends come to their house. As a rule, it's a lemon-chicken tagine, everyone's crazy about it. They're around ten at the table, all alumni of the same European business school in Lyon. They sleep in the outbuildings and leave at dawn.

When they arrive, Nina never feels quite at ease in their trails of perfume, the city scents of women who work, a smell of independence. After a few glasses of champagne, Nina relaxes. She's read the newspapers, is well-informed, can join in the conversations like a pupil who has learnt the lesson off by heart. One thing that's a relief to her is that they never bring their children. It's *their* date night.

Emmanuel is becoming obsessed. He wants a baby from Nina. He dives on all the kids they come across, the strollers, saying to her: "Look how beautiful the baby is!" He keeps track of her hormonal cycles, makes love to her morning and night, stays inside her for a long time, hoping so hard she can almost hear him. Next he'll be saying a prayer while his semen spreads inside her. Nina feels as if her body doesn't really belong to her anymore, that, little by little, it's disappearing.

Every month, when her period returns like a curse, Emmanuel becomes morose. For a few days, he leaves early for work and comes home late. Skips lunches with her.

They've been married for three years, trying to procreate for one year, next month they will consult an infertility specialist.

Nina is scared of becoming like her mother. She's scared of not loving the child. Of abandoning it. These thoughts stop her from falling pregnant. From falling altogether. The truth is, she takes what's required for it not to happen.

After shopping at the fresh-produce counter, she lingers a while in front of the diet products, hesitates between two, one slimming, the other draining, what's the difference? What's the difference between happiness and joy? Hope and desire? Sadness and melancholy? Love and habit? Fear and despair?

As well as Emmanuel's friends, tonight Adrien and Étienne will be there. She repeats those words to herself like a litany. She hasn't seen them since Christmas.

She picks three free-range chickens at random. She won't be eating any, as usual. Will pretend to help herself to some, as usual. Ever since he's wanted a child, Emmanuel reproaches her for not eating meat.

"It might be because you're anemic that it's not working."

"I've never been anemic."

"You don't know, my love, a human must eat meat."

"Absolutely not."

"Yes, it's natural."

Lemon, onions, garlic, ginger, coriander, white wine, red wine, champagne. Her cart is full.

Nina thinks back to the last time they'd got together with Emmanuel's friends, the evening had taken a strange turn. Everyone was pretty tipsy, it was warm, they were all beside the pool, candles flickering on the table. After dessert, Emmanuel suggested a game, you make three statements that are either true or a lie. The rule: not to reveal a thing. It was up to the others to guess.

First of all, Emmanuel said he'd been to San Francisco, second that he consulted his horoscope every morning, third that he'd read all seven volumes of Proust's *A La Recherche . . .* Then everyone else joined in, enthusiastically: "I stole my mother's purse," "I haven't smoked a joint today," "I'm scared," "I'm happy," "I'm stressed out," "The day before one of his trips, I stole my brother's passport so he couldn't leave," "I love children," "The future scares me," "My husband has never cheated on me," "I haven't made love for six months,"

"I made love this morning," "I carved my ex's phone number on the door of a public toilet in a shopping center with the message: 'Call me any time, I'm horny as hell,'" "I gobbled an earthworm," "I swallowed a fly," "I ate a butterfly," "I stole and read other people's letters," "I'm crazy about mutton tripe in sauce," "I love Malibu," "I've walked on embers," "I won a European chess tournament in 1990," "I got hypnotized to quit smoking," "I urinated in a broken-down elevator." "I was supposed to be named Juliette," "My favorite film is *Jeux interdits*," "I had a drink with Bono and The Edge in a hotel bar," "I danced the 'Macarena' naked on my bed" . . .

Once they were alone again, Emmanuel asked Nina which, out of what she'd said, were her lies and which her truths. She tried to dodge the question:

"No, the point of the game is not to say . . . otherwise it's not funny."

"It's not funny to read other people's letters . . . Especially for the granddaughter of a mailman."

Nina blushed.

"And I'd have liked you to say, 'I love my husband,' or 'I long to have a child with my husband' . . . Believe me, it's serious. You could go to prison for that."

"What's 'that'?" Nina responded, drily. "For not having said that I love my husband?"

"You don't love me anymore?"

"Of course I do."

"Maybe you don't get pregnant because you don't love me anymore."

"You're talking nonsense."

"You're getting fatter by the minute. A woman in love doesn't get fat."

Feeling hurt, Nina closed her eyes, as if not seeing him anymore would mean not hearing him anymore. He pushed her back on the bed and made love to her, aggressively. It was a first, this almost-violence. In her head, Nina spoke to the universe. She could have said that at the table, earlier, in her husband's stupid game: "I speak to the universe."

*Infinite universe, before dying, I'd like to be happy.*

That evening, Emmanuel fell asleep inside her. Repeating to her: "I love you, Nina, I love you too much."

On her way to the cash registers, she walks along the book aisle. A mix of comic books, recipe books, and fiction. The last time she'd done the shopping, she'd bought Nancy Huston's novel, *L'Empreinte de l'ange*. She'd devoured it over two nights. In the first year of her marriage, Nina and Gé would swap novels, but now, Emmanuel's parents are living in Morocco. The Château itself is inhabited by staff in charge of its upkeep. That departure had isolated Nina. Since Joséphine's death, she feels increasingly lonely. Reading allows her to break out of that loneliness. When reading, she does drawings in her mind, sees the characters, imagines them posing for her. She creates her own pictures. Through reading, she finds Étienne and Adrien again in her dreams. She still phones them every Sunday. Étienne has started at his academy, he tells her about his intern days, about searching properties and questioning people.

Adrien is quieter. Prefers to listen to her than to speak.

Back at the book display, Nina sees *Blanc d'Espagne* by Sasha Laurent, the novel everyone's talking about. She reads the back cover:

*'Blanc d'Espagne' is that chalky whitewash often used as a cover-up on the windows of stores undergoing renovation or a change of proprietor.*

Nina isn't hooked, but finds the front cover appealing. And she's seen somewhere that the book is highly rated, so ends up adding it to her caddy.

She continues to the tills, repeating to herself, like a mantra: *This evening, Étienne and Adrien will be there.*

*

At that very moment, Adrien adds the final period to his new work. Months he's been laboring on it. Since his mother's death. With his words, he brings her back to life in a different way.

He won't write any more novels. He knows it, but hasn't yet confessed it to his editor. Since writing is now part of his life, he'll try his hand at drama. He's just finished a play in five acts entitled *Les Mères*. The story of five friends who are talking about their own mothers and, especially, the mothers of the others.

The first mother resembles Marie-Laure, the second Joséphine. The three others he conjured up by taking the character traits of Thérèse Lepic, Louise, and Nina as inspiration. Truth was his starting point to fictionalize these mothers, who were at once crazy, hard, flighty, fantasized about, irresponsible, capricious, loving, selfish.

A color chart of motherhood.

He already has the staging in his head: five small houses juxtaposed, the ten characters, five children and their mothers, evolving side by side, loving each other, tearing each other apart, gathering together, asking questions, sharing feasts. The acts follow the rhythm of the events they each live through over ten years. Those who leave and those who stay, those who return. Stories of love and separation. Ten lives that brush against each other and rub shoulders. Without husbands or fathers.

Adrien has a meeting with a theater director in a few days' time. A man he met at a dinner party, who doesn't know that he is Sasha Laurent. Adrien will sign his play with his real name.

He's in an express train taking him back to La Comelle. He's been invited, this evening, to the home of Nina and her swell. He's dreading it. Étienne will be there, too. No bad thing. Football-match dinners, not his thing. But Nina had been so insistent.

Although Adrien used his "former life" to write his play, he senses that he's increasingly less keen on it. That he's growing away from it. He's better off in Paris. With his anonymity. And now that Joséphine is no longer there, nothing attaches him to La Comelle, apart from Nina and Louise.

# 58

*25 December 2017*

Étienne didn't react when Nina told him: "If you're going, we're going with you." Nicola plays with the zipper of his parka, gets bored and finds refuge in Nina's arms. Étienne stands up, walks around the sitting room, looks at my video collection, my CDs and records, falls on a few cassettes, including one of Three, recorded in 1990 at school.

"You kept that?" he says to me.

"Take it if you like . . . For your son."

"These days, kids don't dream of starting their own pop group, they just want to be famous YouTubers."

"What's a YouTuber?" Nina asks Étienne.

"YouTube is like a TV channel, but on the Net. People post videos that everyone can watch."

"Videos of what?"

"Music, comedy, clothes, games . . . Geez, no one would ever guess that you're the one who stayed in La Comelle . . ."

"Get lost."

"That's all I ask, but you kidnapped me outside your shelter."

"Where are you planning on going to . . . die?" she whispers.

"Haven't decided yet . . . I told you, I'd like to see the sea . . . It's not very original as a closing shot."

He sits back down, close to Nina. They're side by side. Me, I'm standing against the kitchen door, a few meters away. As if they scared me.

"You're not saying anything?" Étienne suddenly asks me.

"What d'you want me to say to you? Louise has spoken to you. It's killing her that you're refusing to have treatment."

"And you? Are you going to have treatment yourself?" he snaps back at me.

My heart skips a beat.

"Get out of my house, Étienne."

"Please, I beg you, stop that, both of you, now!" Nina steps in.

I breathe deeply, try to calm the storm raging inside me. What Étienne triggers in me. I hate myself for still allowing his words to affect me.

"We're getting nowhere, now," he says, annoyed. "If you asked me here to beg me to have an operation, it won't work."

He gets up from the sofa.

"Could you give me a lift home?"

Nina bursts into tears. Étienne sits back down. He grips his coffee cup so tightly, his hands whiten. He swallows hard several times.

I walk a few steps over to her, touch her shoulder. She doesn't push me away. No longer has the strength.

"Nina, why did you want me to bring you back here? What do you want me to do?"

"I want us to go with Étienne," she manages to articulate.

I turn toward him. Still rigid on the sofa. A scary look on his face.

"Do you want us to go with you, Étienne?" I ask.

"If I get to drive."

# 59

*1999*

Four years of marriage.

Nina is just twenty-three, she looks more like thirty. Two years, now, that Emmanuel keeps trying to give her a child. But she still doesn't want one.

She takes hormonal treatments to increase her fertility and nothing happens. Strong medication that makes her put on weight. Makes her feel nauseous. She has a puffy face. Doesn't look at herself in mirrors anymore. She and Emmanuel have been through a battery of tests, nothing seems to be malfunctioning. Except them.

Nina doesn't phone Adrien and Étienne once a week anymore. Things had gradually spaced out. You miss one Sunday because you're away, then a second one because you forget or feel ill. Life's words for absence. When separation becomes a habit. And you say: "What's the point, after all, we're not kids anymore."

And wherever you live, you always make new friends. For Étienne, they're colleagues. For Adrien, actors, directors, authors. His play, *Les Mères*, was a success. Since then, he has written two more, one of which was bought by the Théâtre des Abbesses. It will be the big event of September 2000.

So when the phone rings at Nina's that morning, and she recognizes Adrien's voice, she thinks it's something serious. Why would he call her during the week otherwise?

"Are you well?" he begins.

"Yes. Fine."

"Why are you speaking so quietly?"

"Because the cook listens at doors."

"Why?"

"Because she doesn't like me."

"Everyone likes you, Nina."

"Everyone liked me when I was young."

"You're still young."

"Everyone liked me when I was little, if you prefer. Why are you phoning me? Are you well?"

Nina holds her breath while waiting for the answer.

"Yes."

"And Étienne?"

"Yes, I think he's well, too."

"So why are you phoning me then, Adrien? It isn't Sunday."

"Last night, something came back to me."

". . ."

"I hid a bag at Damamme's."

"What bag?"

"Your grandfather's."

". . ."

"I found it on a bench, the day of the accident. In the panic, someone must have put it there. I took it. And when I got to Damamme's to take you to Marseilles, before going into your office, I hid it in a room, on a shelf."

"Adrien, that's five years ago, why didn't you tell me before?"

"I'd forgotten. But last night, I dreamt of it . . . Such a strange dream. As if . . ."

"As if what?"

"I dreamt of him . . . Pierre was speaking to me."

". . ."

"And in my dream, he was telling me to tell you about it. So you could get it back."

Adrien's directions—"A door smaller than the others, not far from the office I found you in that day. There were boxes everywhere, cardboard ones, too, I remember a poster pinned to the wall, mountains or a lake, a landscape, anyhow"—were good. Nina doesn't have to look for long. Perches on a table and sees it.

No one has touched it. Five years it's been sleeping there, in the dark and the dust, on the fifth shelf against the wall to the left. It's partly crushed.

Now that Nina is holding it in her hands, she's shaking, and thinking. She feels overwhelmed, doesn't dare to open it. Occasionally, the naked bulb had probably shed light on it, but no box of archives had ever been stored in that inaccessible place. How had Adrien managed to stick it up that high?

Later, he would tell her how he'd thrown it there with all the energy of despair.

Nina strokes the leather. At the time her grandfather had died, he still had a few streets left to deliver to. So the bag must still contain mail. She presses it to her body, covers it with her coat, and leaves the offices, under the curious gaze of Claudine, a former colleague. The only one she'd bumped into when, with heart pounding, she'd arrived at Damamme's. Nina had told her that she needed to find an old bag forgotten on a shelf, just before her wedding, when she was working with Yves-Marie Le Camus. Nina had said that without stopping, while Claudine just stared at her. She'd seen in Claudine's eyes that she'd struggled to recognize her at first.

"Did you find what you were looking for?"

Nina jumps. She'd almost forgotten that Claudine was around.

"Yes, thanks a lot . . . Just don't tell Emmanuel . . . I mean my husband, that I came by, I'm preparing a surprise for him."

"Won't breathe a word . . . How stunning you both looked on your wedding day . . ."

Nina can feel Claudine assessing her, from top to toe . . . What's left of that slender, young swan? Nina doesn't even know where her lovely ivory dress is now. No doubt lost between two cardboard boxes, two redecorations, two rearrangements, two new wardrobes. It's an obsession with Emmanuel, changing the décor, buying, throwing out, or moving furniture around. Building bonfires in the garden to burn "the dated stuff."

"Oh, sweet Jesus, you're pregnant!" Claudine exclaims, staring at Nina's bulges, including the bag that she's concealing against her chest under her long coat.

Nina is incapable of responding. She turns pale, lowers her eyes, muttering: "No. Goodbye." Then rushes away like a thief, gets into her car, starts it, and quickly leaves the car park, for fear of meeting Emmanuel. No reason she should, he's away on business.

Before, when he'd be traveling, she'd pine away. Now, she's thrilled to pack his suitcase for the week. The prospect of some rest and relief. The weight on her stomach lifts. Nina doesn't work, but she's tired all the time.

She had put the mailman's bag on the passenger seat. She feels as if her grandfather is close to her, all damaged, as if flattened. Here's what's left of the man, proof of his tragic demise. Since her mother took away everything, Nina has nothing left of his, except her own memories. Not even an item of clothing. Luckily, she had slipped a sepia photograph into a box: a picture of her grandparents' wedding.

Back in 1994, Pierre would set off on his round with two bags, one for certified mail, the other for general letters. It's the latter she has in the car. The one she'd sneak letters out of, to read in secret.

Basically, what her mother has passed down to her is theft. Nina doesn't dare look at the bag anymore. Normally, she should go to the post office or the police to hand it in. But no way will she do that.

*

Étienne is a long way from conducting his first interrogation. It's Captain Giraud who is doing this one. Although he is qualified, Étienne remains in the background, observing.

A banal pickpocketing case. Two teen girls who look as if butter wouldn't melt in their mouths, minors, angelic faces, stolen property on them. One who stops a passerby to ask the way or the time. The other who's busy rifling the victim's pockets or bag. Money, cigs, leather wallets, watches. That's all they're after. No interest in IDs. Dump them in trash cans. However, for the past two years, people are increasingly using mobile phones, and as these have proliferated, so a thriving black market has emerged in Lyon. The captain is hoping that the two girls will enable them to trace the network they sell those phones to.

They were caught by an undercover store detective in a high-end store. Hand in a Louis Vuitton bag. They'd tried to run away, fought back, struggled. It was coming to blows until two burly security guards grabbed hold of them and handed them in on a silver platter.

They're denying the whole thing, playing the old "You've got the wrong person" card.

And yet for months, they've been plaguing the area around the Parc de la Tête d'Or. They've been identified and their Photofits match up. Émilie Rave and Sabrina Berger.

Émilie seems to be the brains of the duo. Insolent, she keeps smirking when the captain asks her questions, and looking defiantly at Étienne, ever since he entered the interrogation room. Sabrina is reserved, says nothing, lowers her eyes, remains in the background.

Because they are minors, an attorney is present on their behalf. Not the same profile as the little louts they're used to nabbing. Two spoilt rich kids playing at being Arsène Lupin, the gentleman thief, for fun, and behaving like high-class hookers. Two faces just asking to be slapped.

Their parents will be along soon.

Since joining the police, Étienne has heard it all:

"It wasn't me, mister, I didn't do nothing. It's the fault of them voices in my head, controlling me. Nothing to do with me. Didn't do it on purpose. You've got the wrong person. It's my twin, you're mixing me up with my brother."

"You haven't got a brother."

"I have, mister, I swear I've got a cousin who's like a brother, he's my double, everyone'll tell you I've got a double, I'd been drinking, I can't remember anymore, my mind goes blank, I'm a sleepwalker . . ."

And always: "I swear I'll never do it again." How many times had Étienne heard that sentence.

"I'll admit to everything" Émilie finally blurts out, "but I want to be alone with him, over there."

She indicates Étienne with her hand. All eyes turn to him. He immediately retorts:

"I don't think you're in any position to decide a single thing."

"When it comes to positions, I've got my own ideas," the kid throws back at him.

"Drop all that, you're barely out of diapers."

"You drop it, as I say, I've got other ideas."

"That's enough!" shouts Captain Giraud. "We're not playing some game here! You're both looking at a prison sentence, young ladies!"

"We're minors," snaps Émilie, rolling her eyes. "We don't risk a thing."

"You're dreaming, my girl," Étienne responds. "Minors have been thrown into jail before . . . Usually, teens like you are kept separate from the adults, but believe me, the cells are one on top of the other . . . If I were you, I'd come clean . . . Unless rubbing shoulders with bitches who'll teach you all about life turns you on."

"I would ask you to temper your language," the attorney interrupts him.

Étienne pays no attention to the man of law, just keeps his eyes glued to the girls. Darting from one to the other. Giraud lets him carry on. He has total confidence in his young recruit, who has a way of getting even the toughest nuts to come clean. So these two girls, for him, will be a walk in the park. Étienne has a ruthless side. Never loses his temper. It's all down to his steely blue eyes, two iceboxes, when he's confronting a suspect.

"Who do you sell the mobile phones on to?" he asks.

Émilie isn't smirking anymore, but doesn't lower her eyes, still looks defiantly at Étienne.

"My father will never let me go to prison . . ." she finally says.

"Your father doesn't get to decide," Étienne snaps back. "Leave that to the juvenile-court judge . . . a shrew like you can't imagine, she won't put up with your little smirk . . . Attorney, you need to explain to your clients that they're taking a big risk. We've got a hundred witnesses who saw them at work, and they're ready to identify them. They've been up to their tricks for months now. We'll start with a little search of their homes, and then we'll make them face their victims until they buckle. It won't be pretty . . . Unless they give us the name of their fence."

An hour later, it's all wrapped up. As usual, Étienne will get the report typed up by a colleague, an arrangement between them. He has a visceral loathing of anything administrative. In exchange, he does favors, makes calls to informers.

He likes doing searches and tailing, not typing. Their station might be equipped with a few computers, but it's the street for him. Lurking in bars, asking questions, observing, laying low. That's where he belongs.

Right now, Étienne is sipping a beer on his sofa and listening to "Where Is My Mind?" He loves that Pixies song. Listens to it non-stop, thinking of Nina, of past musical dreams. Of dreams, period.

He opens another can, musing on his own way of tackling any female suspects before him. Those who wet themselves are rare, but such fun to squeeze. No need for any amateur psychology, he knows it's all about Clotilde. His personal revenge, repeated over five years.

The image of the car sinking into the black water of the Lac de la Forêt hasn't left him. That car, did he dream it or really see it? If the latter, who could it have belonged to? Was there anyone inside it? Who shoved it in? Her? Clotilde didn't have a license or a car. Had he glimpsed someone behind the wheel? A shadow, perhaps. Why hadn't he told the police, in La Comelle, that they'd swum together that evening, and he'd dozed off beside Clotilde, due to the whiskey, fatigue, and emotions after Pierre's burial that morning?

Just said that he'd seen a car in the water. And that rounded belly.

## 60

*25 December 2017*

Adrien has just filled his car up with gas. He's sitting on a bench, outside, in front of ashtray-trash cans. In the distance, a swing, abandoned by children, is rocking, buffeted by the wind. Wrapped in a thick coat, he smokes a cigarette in the biting-cold air. He swiped the packet from Louise's bag this morning. And just found it, deep in his pocket, with a candy-pink lighter tucked inside. Long time since he's had a drag. Disgusting and exhilarating.

Staring into the cold, Adrien thinks of Étienne. Of his cancer. Of this death prowling around him. One's never prepared for the death of friends, even when they've ceased to be friends.

Adrien remembers.

January 1997. It was just over a year since he and Étienne had moved up to the capital. Him in Vincennes, Étienne in Nation—he hadn't yet got into his Cannes-Écluse police academy. For the second time, Étienne asked for his help.

"I can't watch on my own. You must come to my place. Must be with me. It's happening, they're going to talk about the Clotilde Marais case."

Strange that Étienne uses her surname. As if to distance himself from Clotilde, keep her at a distance.

He was talking about that TV show, *Perdu de vue*, broadcast in prime time on TF1.

"Did Clotilde's parents ask you to be a witness?"

"No," Étienne replied, sounding like a child caught with his finger in the jam.

Adrien arrived at his place at 7:00 P.M. Étienne had ordered in two pizzas, their favorite ones, ham and mushroom for Adrien, a calzone for himself, which he'd drowned in chili oil, as usual. Despite the circumstances, his nervousness, he was hungry. Adrien has always known Étienne to be ravenous.

Adrien was bowled over to be the one Étienne had called. So he did consider him a friend, then. Even without Nina, he really mattered to him.

Why had this doubt always lingered?

Étienne opened a bottle of rosé, turned on the TV, cut the sound, so they saw, without actually watching it, a report on Yasser Arafat, and then on Bill Clinton. They chatted about everything and nothing.

Adrien had finished writing *Blanc d'Espagne*, but didn't mention it. And Étienne didn't ask him a thing about the novel he'd spoken about on the night of the burial of Nina's life as a young girl.

Then the program began.

Étienne upped the volume while lighting a cigarette. His eyes were glistening, as if he had a fever. A mix of terror and excitement that surprised Adrien.

Something disturbing about even just the intro. Something warped about appropriating others' misery to turn it into a TV show.

The Marais couple sitting under the lights of the projectors, side by side, just like them on their sofa, glasses of rosé in hand.

The teary eyes of those parents, as if shipwrecked, resigned. The father, wracked with anxiety, caught in a vise between propriety and shame at being used by the media, but resolute. "Our last chance," the mother murmured.

Pictures of Clotilde scrolled past.

First the parents were questioned about their daughter: "What was her personality like? A bit secretive, or did she open up easily?" "Did she seem different to you toward the end? Had anything changed in her behavior? Irritable?" "Had she ever gone off for a few days, without telling you, before? A witness says she saw her at La Comelle station at around ten that night. Where did she go? What direction might she have taken?" "Another very important point: Clotilde had emptied her savings account two weeks before leaving, why do you think she did that?"

Then the presenter, Jacques Pradel, spoke straight to the camera:

"You may possess crucial information and, thanks to you, the mystery of this disappearance could be solved. If the slightest thing comes back to you, don't hesitate to contact us. And if, by any chance, Clotilde is watching our program, if she would like to reassure her loved ones, she can dial the phone number that will appear at the bottom of your screen, anonymity will be respected."

A background report followed:

"La Comelle, an ordinary little town in Saône-et-Loire. It's here, in the heart of tranquil Burgundy, that Clotilde Marais, eighteen years old, vanished on 17 August 1994. It's been two-and-a-half years now that her loved ones have been without any news. Not the slightest sign of life."

The streets of La Comelle were filmed, then the Maraises' house, and finally Clotilde's bedroom. When he saw the dolls arranged on the patchwork bedcover, Étienne went to the bathroom to throw up his pizza.

Adrien didn't know what to do. Couldn't find the right words to say. On his return, Étienne merely muttered:

"Too emotional for a future cop, got to toughen myself up."

"Shall we turn the TV off?"

Étienne held his head in his hands.

"No, leave it on . . . Fuck's sake, what the hell did she do?"

"Who?"

"Clotilde."

*How can I be such an idiot*? Adrien asked himself. *How can I have asked such a stupid question*?

Adrien didn't like Clotilde. The two of them barely spoke when they met in the school corridors, or at parties. For Clotilde, Adrien was a common maggot, and she wasn't remotely his type. Too sophisticated and did everything too loudly. Laughing, talking. Sound system at full volume. Hard eyes, pinched lips. Devoid of any gentleness or the beauty of intelligence that both Nina and Louise had.

Basically, Adrien couldn't care less what had happened to her. He was sure she was the kind of girl to vanish just to get people talking about her. That she'd reappear one day on the arm of a prince, or a guru, or at some hippie commune. Adrien had never imagined that something serious might have taken place. That this disappearance could be linked to a drama. It was just another far-fetched attempt to show off. She must be gloating right now, in front of her TV set.

What got Adrien down about the whole event was the state it put Étienne into. Adrien hadn't realized he was that fond of her.

And then, suddenly, things took a turn. The presenter announced that a witness, who wished to remain anonymous, had informed them that on the evening of 17 August 1994, Clotilde was with "her boyfriend at the time." This allegation had to be verified, since it contradicted the witness who had seen her at the station waiting for a train.

So, who was this boyfriend who'd been pulled out of the hat?

Clotilde's mother stepped in: "That boy was due to meet up with my daughter that evening, he waited for her but she never came." The questions came thick and fast: Why hadn't she joined him there? Had she met someone on the way? Might Clotilde have found herself in the wrong place at the wrong time? And yet the first witness was positive: she was alone at the station.

On the set of the show, floods of tears.

Adrien wasn't listening anymore, couldn't see a thing anymore. His hands were shaking. Étienne had turned to jelly when the presenter had mentioned Clotilde's appointment with her "boyfriend." And since then, Adrien felt something starting to form in his mind. The shadow of a doubt at first, then certainty.

Étienne had seen Clotilde that evening. Something had happened. Something irreparable. Otherwise, Étienne would never have had that terrifying and terrified reaction. His whole body tense, his face contorted by fear, dread.

"Étienne, what did you do?"

"Nothing. I did nothing. I swear."

"But . . . you saw her . . . that evening?"

"Yes."

A long silence. The two boys stared at each other.

"Did you argue?"

"We had a swim . . . messed around. I fell asleep. And then . . . nothing more."

"Nothing more? What d'you mean, nothing more?"

"When I woke up, she was gone."

"Are you lying? Étienne, are you lying to me right now?"

"No!"

"Did you hurt her?"

"No. I swear to you."

"An accident?"

"No!"

"But . . . this is a nightmare."

"Yes . . . At the time, I thought she must have cleared off, gone God knows where. But she never got in touch."

"Who is she, this witness who saw Clotilde at the station?"

"No idea."

"What time was it when Clotilde arrived at the lake?"

"Dunno . . . Didn't have a watch on. I'd say between eight and nine."

"Anyone see the two of you?"

"Don't think so."

"Have you talked about it to anyone else? Nina?"

"No one. Just you. I've never said that I saw Clotilde that evening. And even under torture, I wouldn't say it."

"Why?"

"Why what?"

"Why didn't you say anything?"

"I don't want to end up in jail."

"Why would you end up in jail?"

"I'm the ideal suspect . . . The boyfriend, always the ideal suspect . . . especially when . . ."

"Especially when what?"

"Nothing."

"Especially when what, Étienne?"

Adrien felt a great vacuum around him after asking that question. What was Étienne about to admit to him?

For the first time, Adrien felt the strongest of the two of them, the least vulnerable.

"She was pregnant."

## 61

*1999*

Nina gets home. No one there. A relief. The "cook"—that's what she calls Nathalie now—is out doing some shopping. Emmanuel won't be back for two days.

She places the bag of mail on the kitchen table. It's like treasure coming into a dead house.

At the beginning, Nina was amazed to find the floors and carpets cleaned, her washing ironed and put away in the wardrobes, and piping-hot meals waiting on the table. But that luxury has another side to it: no privacy. The cook comes and goes in their home without knocking. Nina can come across her in the middle of a room at any time. How often had she jumped when suddenly coming face to face with that one clutching a dust cloth? She can't stand her anymore. Sometimes, she even wishes her dead. Nathalie has reached retirement age, but Nina knows she will never stop clinging to her rock: Emmanuel Damamme.

Nina is convinced that her husband asks Nathalie to keep a close eye on her when he's away: "I'm counting on you, I'm entrusting Nina to you, she's so young." Young or hopeless? Which word did he use?

Nina did try to tell Emmanuel that she'd like Nathalie to knock before coming into their rooms, but he smiled and just brushed her off: "She's part of the furniture, she's faithful, a pearl, we're so lucky to have her, stop being difficult, basically, you're too spoilt."

Nina imagines her life if she fell pregnant. And that prospect chills her. The cook would be breathing down her neck all day long if she had a baby. She couldn't bear it. And anyway, having *his* child, that would be locking herself up for ever and ever. Now, deep inside, she has a glimmer of hope, that of escaping one day. Not just leaving, but *escaping*. This thought terrifies her, but it exists, it's the chance of an island. Even if, today, that island seems inaccessible to her, the voyage unfeasible, maybe one day . . .

To keep going, she drinks at least three glasses every evening. She knows she's destroying herself, but can't find any other palliative. Alcohol makes the unbearable bearable, it helps her to be ready for Emmanuel's return. She downs the first glass after five. A full glass. The second at six. The third half an hour later. That way, when Emmanuel arrives, Nina, sucking on a sweet, seems radiant.

Supper, cheery banter, a smiling mask on her face. Convince him that all's well, that life's great thanks to him. Then they go up to bed, always together, him following in her tracks, and once in their bedroom, she knows he watches her as she takes the medication that awaits on her bedside table. To stimulate her ovulation.

She waits for the sound of Emmanuel's electric toothbrush to take one of her contraceptive pills. She never keeps the packaging. She gets a repeat prescription every quarter from a doctor. The one furthest from the center of La Comelle. A doctor that doesn't ask questions. She pays for her appointments in cash and doesn't claim it back. Once out of the pharmacy, she takes the pills out of the packaging and slips them into a little bag containing her homeopathic remedies, aspirin, and lip balm.

It's this unlikely mix of hormones and alcohol that disfigures and stiffens her, day after day. She fights while destroying herself. But she fights all the same.

She can't talk to anyone about it. She has no more friends. Étienne and Adrien have left. Louise, too. Before, there was Joséphine, a cup of coffee together, it was uplifting, but now that's over. Marie-Laure and Marc Beaulieu are away all day, busy working. And since Emmanuel has taken up the reins of the company, her parents-in-law rarely return from Morocco. Gé phones Nina every week, they exchange a few hollow words, the titles of some novels worth reading, all at a polite and warm distance. But how do you say to a mother that her son is a touch unhinged? So possessive that it's killing his wife?

All that's left are those weekends once a month when friends come over from Lyon, but they're Emmanuel's friends, not hers. They're pleasant, nice to have around, always kind to her. But once they've gone home, she never misses them. Unlike Étienne and Adrien.

She strokes her grandfather's bag again. Finally opens it, noticing, as she does, her swollen fingers. How could she have fallen so low? Accepting to swallow those treatments that treat nothing but the emptiness of the couple that she and Emmanuel make.

The white envelopes have yellowed slightly. More than a hundred letters and postcards. All bearing the postmark of 11 August 1994. The day before the accident.

Five years, now, that words have slumbered inside that bag. The sentences we send each other in summer, on vacation. She must go and deliver them, one by one. Finding mail in your box that's five years late, it's probably never happened before.

The first thing to do is hide the bag. So that neither Emmanuel nor the cook come across it. Somewhere in her bedroom, behind her clothes in the dressing room? No. Too risky. The only place in the house that Nina can lock herself in is the bathroom adjoining her bedroom. Her haven of peace, as she reads while soaking in a bath. She has the idea of emptying the contents—apart from the bills, which she doesn't care about—into three large bath towels, which she then refolds and carefully hides behind others, on the shelf above the bathtub. She then returns to her car to stow the bag in the trunk, which she locks.

She feels as if she's living like a prisoner on parole.

She wonders now whether her grandfather would allow her to read the letters. Has enough time gone by? They were destined to end up there, on a shelf at Damamme's. Never to be delivered, let alone read. How to receive a sign from him? Where to look to find out whether he consents or not?

The phone rings. It's Adrien again. Two calls on the same day, when she hears the sound of his voice increasingly rarely.

"Did you find it?" he asks, impatiently.

"Yes."

"No one had touched it?"

"No."

"Extraordinary."

". . ."

"Where have you put it?"

"In the trunk of my car."

"Is there mail inside it?"

"Yes, lots."

"Are you going to read the letters?"

"Dunno. I'm not a kid anymore . . . And it's theft."

"It isn't theft, it's borrowing."

". . ."

"It's like borrowing an old story from someone before returning it to them . . ."

"That's not what you said before."

"Before, that's over. It's a present your grandfather's giving you now. Otherwise I wouldn't have dreamt about it."

"D'you think?"

"Yes."

"If I ended up coming to Paris, would you help me?"

"Why? Is your marriage on the rocks?"

He asked that in a smug tone. Meaning: "I told you so."

"No, I was just asking . . ."

Adrien remains silent. An awkward silence that Nina finally breaks:

"Can you believe it, it's going to be 2000 soon . . . I think you and I are starting to lose touch, Adrien."

"Not at all, Nina, stop fretting over nothing," he replies, almost annoyed.

"I'm not fretting over nothing. D'you think we'll be together for New Year's Eve?"

"I don't know yet . . . I must get back now, I'm not on my own."

"O.K. But Adrien, swear to me we'll be together for New Year's Eve 2000."

"I swear to you, Nina."

"Is that true?"

"True."

"Big kiss."

"Kisses."

She returns to the bathroom. Locks herself in. Turns the bath taps on, gets hold of one of the three towels, unfolds it. Dozens of letters tumble onto the tiled floor. She picks one at random. Waves the back of the envelope over the hot-water tap, manages to unseal it without tearing it.

Nina finds a 20 franc note slipped between two sheets of paper.

> "My little poppet, happy birthday, you can buy whatever you fancy. I hope the sun's shining. Here, it's stifling, and my legs are killing me. Outside, don't forget a bowl of water for the birds.
>
> Your loving Granny"

Nina recloses the envelope and puts it to one side. She'll go later to slip it into the mailbox of Rachel Marek, 6 Rue de la Pépinière. Since Emmanuel won't be back this evening, she'll deliver what she reads gradually, once it's dark. Apart from any bad news. Five years late, there'd be no point.

Nina opens and recloses other envelopes. Builds up a pile for delivery that evening. She reads the letters out loud as though her grandfather were beside her and she were sharing the words with him. Pierre Beau did sometimes read letters out to people who asked him to, those who couldn't read, or didn't understand some official document. "Mister Mailman, what does that mean?"

It's 9:00 P.M. when she starts up her car, with twenty-odd envelopes lying on the passenger seat. She knows that, the day after tomorrow, the cook will tell Emmanuel that she went out after supper. So, to pre-empt any sly questions, between pear and cheese, she told Nathalie that there were drinks at her gym class for a trainer's birthday. Her gym class, what a joke, she hasn't set foot there for more than two years. But she still pays her subscription for two sessions a week. She parks outside the gym and goes for a solitary walk along the river.

Right now, she's retracing the route her grandfather should have done on that day. She starts from Place Charles-de-Gaulle, where he met his death. Her intuition was right, Pierre was arriving from Rue Saint-Pierre, and not from Rue Jean-Jaurès. It was the lorry that had cut him down. The driver had lied.

*But don't we all lie*?

Only one addressee has moved house. The name has been torn off the mailbox, the shutters are closed, and the weeds have taken over the gravel. All the same, Nina pops in the postcard that Jacques Laurent should have received on 12 August 1994.

> "My dear Jack,
>
> On my way up from the Midi, I'll stop off to see you in your burrow. I'm keen for us to go fishing, seeing as that's all there is to do around yours. Get the beers in the fridge and clean out the barbecue. I'll bring my guitar, like in the good old days.
>
> Big hug, bud,
>
> Sergio"

At eleven, Nina stops her delivery round. She drives home with an aching heart. She's just made the very gestures her grandfather would have made that day. Gestures annihilated by a goddamn lorry.

She still has around a hundred envelopes to deliver. In the meantime, she goes upstairs to bed, soothed by Emmanuel's absence.

Before, when he was away on business, he would phone her every hour. "Are you well, my love? What are you up to? What are you wearing? I miss you, and . . ."

Now, he calls to say he's arrived safely, and that's it.

Last Christmas, he gave her a mobile phone. "So we can reach each other at all times."

A nightmare. Being reachable at all times, who on earth could want that?

She would have preferred him to bring her back a dog. Answer: "No, with the baby it wouldn't be hygienic. And Nathalie has enough work to do as it is. Can you imagine dog hair around the house? Because with you, the dog would be allowed onto the sofas."

After Joséphine's death, Emmanuel sold Nina's grandfather's house—"It serves no purpose anymore."

And her two cats went off to the Beaulieus—"*No question of having them here, you know I'm allergic.*"

Marie-Laure promised Nina she'd take care of them.

Lying in her bed, Nina is tempted to pay another visit to the bathroom. Unfold another towel, let the envelopes tumble onto the floor. Summon up her grandfather's spirit. Go back to August 1994. When Étienne and Adrien still held her hands.

# 62

*25 December 2017*

I dropped Étienne and Nina back outside the shelter. We're going tomorrow morning.

I said yes to going with them, accompanying Étienne "to the seaside."

We all amount to yes and no. For a long time now, I've been saying no to everything. But Nina needs me. She smiled at me when I said yes. That smile, I've waited years for it.

I drive around aimlessly, thinking about how I haven't entrusted my keys to anyone since I moved back to La Comelle. Not once.

Nina gave me the phone number of a volunteer who does pet-sitting. "Someone trustworthy," she assured me.

I'm meeting with her late afternoon. Like almost everyone, today she's celebrating Christmas with her family.

*

Marie-Laure and Marc Beaulieu are busy in the kitchen.

Marie-Castille is laying the table, lighting the candles, placing Christmas figurines and crystal glasses on the golden paper tablecloth.

Through the window she sees Louise arriving at the wheel of her husband's car, with Valentin beside her.

*Where is Étienne?*

Valentin enters the house like a whirlwind and doesn't give her a chance to open her mouth:

"Dad's back later, he's with friends."

"What friends?"

"Nina and someone else."

"Who?"

"No idea."

"Where is your father?"

"I told you, he's having a drink."

"Where?"

"No idea, Mom," Valentin exclaims, exasperated.

Marie-Castille looks questioningly at Louise. She looks down while hanging her coat on the hook.

"Where is Étienne?" Marie-Castille persists.

"He's coming back."

"Why were you arguing this morning?"

"Because I wanted him to see someone again."

"Who?"

"Am I obliged to answer your questions? We're not in your police station now," Louise snaps, on edge.

She'd spoken more aggressively than she'd meant to. Marie-Castille stares at her, taken aback. On the verge of tears, Louise goes up to her room.

Marie-Castille tries to contact Étienne on his mobile phone: voicemail.

"Valentin! Where were you?"

Valentin emerges from the kitchen.

"At the shelter, I begged Dad to go."

"Why?"

"I wanted him to see something."

"What thing? I said no animals in the house!"

Valentin looks at her as if she's lost her mind.

"It's a surprise for Gran," he mutters.

"What surprise?"

"A cat for Christmas," he whispers in her ear.

Marie-Castille looks unconvinced, and finishes laying the Christmas table.

She doesn't like coming to La Comelle, prefers their life in Lyon. Back there, she knows Étienne's friends, all cops, colleagues he gets on well with. She doesn't like Étienne seeing Nina again. She doesn't like not being in control of things. And her husband's memories, she can't control them. Those charcoal portraits of Étienne that Marie-Laure has hung everywhere, she'd happily tear them down.

"Valentin! Is it Nina who's bringing back your father? Is she lunching with us?" Marie-Castille shouts.

"No. She'll be with her lover," the adolescent replies.

"Oh, really? She has a lover?"

"Yes."

"She told you that?"

"No. Simone did."

"Who is Simone?"

"A lady who works at the shelter. She adopted a dog today. Called Cannelé. Like the cake."

Marie-Castille is so annoyed, she breaks a glass without meaning to. She feels like crying, but swallows her tears in front of her boy. He helps her to pick up the pieces.

"Take care, darling," she says, calmly.

She must get a grip on herself. And she mustn't be jealous, either. Her husband only went for a drink with some childhood friends. She watches Valentin. He looks sad. She finds him pale. Indigestion?

"You O.K., sweetheart?

"Yup."

"Do you have tummy ache?"

"No."

"My love?"

"Yes, Mom."

"It's not that I don't want a dog . . . but as you know, your father and I aren't at home all day. A dog would be too miserable with us."

"I know."

"Unless . . ."

"Unless what?"

He blows a stray lock off his forehead. His beautiful eyes stare at her. She can't chicken out. In the end, what does it matter to her?

"Unless we find someone to look after it."

"Don't understand."

"A bit like a nanny. They must exist, nannies for dogs, surely? She can stay with it for the day, and you can take over when you're back from school."

"Are you serious?"

"I think I am."
"We're going to have a dog?"
"I must discuss it with your father first . . . When he gets back."
*Will he get back*? Valentin suddenly thinks. What if he were to leave today? Louise is scared he might just disappear without saying a word to anyone.
Marie-Castille sees her son's eyes clouding over again when she'd expected unprecedented gratitude. She's really disappointed.
*Crappy Christmas*. And now it's too late to backtrack. When she's so very scared of animals.

*

Étienne is silent.
"You O.K.?" asks Nina.
"Yup."
"You're not in pain?"
"No. Louise gave me what's required."
Nina parks a hundred meters from the Beaulieus' house. She doesn't want to go into Marc's and Marie-Laure's home. And see Étienne's wife again. *Poor woman*.
"See you tomorrow, then."
"Yup."
"You must talk to your son."
"I know. Blasted Christmas."
"I'm sorry . . . And your wife, will you tell her?"
"Impossible."
"Why?"
"Impossible . . . I'll write to her. Are you sure you can go, with your work? The dogs, they don't take themselves for a walk."
"I'll have someone replace me."
"In any case, it won't be for long . . ."
He kisses her on the cheek and leaves the car, muttering: "See you tomorrow."
Then abruptly turns back.

"Nina, you promise me that it won't be sad? That we won't spend our last days together blubbering?"

"I promise you," Nina replies.

Before going home, Nina stops at the baker's. He's just closing up. He recognizes her, "the girl from the shelter." He likes her, adopted a cat from her last year. She apologizes profusely for coming so late, asks how the cat is doing, buys a round loaf and his very last Yule log, one with exotic fruit.

*Yuck*, she thinks.

"Merry Christmas."

At home, she turns up the heat and vacuums. Opens a tin of sweet corn, makes a vinaigrette. She puts asparagus on one plate, and two cheeses on another. Then dashes up for a shower. Impatience is coursing through her veins and her body is charged with electricity, with promises. She changes the sheets and sprays perfume over her bed. It stinks of stale deodorant. She laughs to herself, despite not feeling like smiling. She's torn between past and present. Losing and seeing again. Sadness and joy. Dread and love. Losing Étienne and seeing Romain again. Now, in a few minutes' time.

She remembers what they used to say to each other, Adrien and her: "When life takes away, it gives back in return." But sometimes life gets it wrong. Deals the cards out dishonestly. Sometimes life lies to us, swindles us.

She hears the gate outside closing. Romain knocks on the door, she opens it. At the sight of Bob, Nina's cats spit and scarper.

"They're going to have to get used to it," Romain concludes.

"Why? Are you planning on coming back often?"

"Of course."

"Just wait till you've tasted my cooking and you'll change your mind."

Romain notices the sweet corn and asparagus.

"I'm not very hungry," he jokes.

"But there's a Yule log! With exotic fruit!" she exclaims.

"Yuck," says Romain.

Nina bursts out laughing. She covers her mouth with both hands as if she's just said something stupid, outrageous. When all she's done is let her joy be unconfined.

## 63

*Big kiss from Nice. Fond thoughts from Cyprus. Hello from Portugal. Sending you all our love. I'll close now with a hug for you. Hoping you're in the best of health. From your Joseph. Greetings from all the family. Sunny but windy. Georgette joins me in wishing. A risk of showers. Swimming every day. Tons of love. Great weather. We miss you. All best wishes. Yours. I love you. Kind regards.*

*May 2000*

The arrival of five-year-old letters in the mailboxes of La Comelle caused plenty of ink to flow at *Le Journal de Saône-et-Loire*. France 3 regional TV even covered the issue at the end of last year. Over the past six months, no less than a hundred-and-sixty-four envelopes bearing the 11 August 1994 postmark have been recorded. The day before the accidental death of Pierre Beau, the mailman at the time.

Where was that mail for all those years? Why has it reappeared like that, just before the turn of the century? A mystery that baffles the locals. Who knows who will find one of these envelopes in their mailbox next. Banal missives and postcards that turn up sporadically, as if they've fallen from the sky.

Their delivery coincides with Emmanuel's absences. And Nina always slides them in at night, impossible to do so in broad daylight.

She's holding the last three envelopes in her hand. It feels like the end of something. She dreads it. Once she has popped them in where they belong, she repeats to herself that she'll leave. For where she doesn't know, but she will leave La Comelle.

She hasn't read them yet. She'll read just two. Because the third is addressed to Étienne. She'll hand it to him in person. Lyon isn't far. She'll go there and back in a day.

Étienne had come to celebrate the festive season in La Comelle. Christmas with the family and New Year's Eve with his friends, he'd informed Nina. No way were the three not going to be reunited to welcome in the year 2000.

"Louise will be there, too. My parents are lending us the house. We're going to make it a DVD, music, and vodka night."

But, on 23 December 1999, Emmanuel said to Nina:

"Darling, pack your suitcase, it's a surprise! Take only light clothes, and don't forget your swimsuit and sun cream."

"But . . . we're supposed to be celebrating the New Year with our friends . . ."

"Our friends will be where we're heading to . . ."

"Even Étienne and Adrien?"

"Oh, no . . . Not them . . . But all the others will be there."

"Which others?"

"The Lyon gang."

The thought of wearing a swimsuit in front of those blond nymphs left her reeling. An issue that seemed insurmountable to her.

She recalled having made Adrien promise that they'd spend this New Year's Eve together.

"I'd rather stay here . . ." she finally managed to say, with tears in her eyes. "The two of us for Christmas, and with my friends for New Year."

"Don't be childish, we're leaving in two hours' time."

Just before catching the plane at Lyon-Saint-Exupéry airport, Nina couldn't bring herself to tell Étienne, so, with a heavy heart, she phoned Marie-Laure Beaulieu:

"Tell them I won't be there on the 31st . . . Emmanuel is taking me on a trip."

"Happy holidays, make the most of it!" Marie-Laure responded, distractedly, not noticing Nina's distressed voice, too busy tackling a work problem.

*Other people are working*, Nina thought as she hung up. *But me, I'm good for nothing*.

Emmanuel had been organizing everything for months. While Nina was already looking forward to spending the New Year at Étienne's, and Emmanuel watched her selecting old cassettes and CDs to take along with music to dance to, he already knew that a big villa on an idyllic beach was booked in Mauritius. The whole "one weekend a month" gang would be there, and this time with their flock of children. They'd be celebrating Christmas and the New Year all together. Killing two birds with one stone.

During the ten days following their departure, Nina's handsome husband, all smiles, swam, sunbathed, ran along the beach, played ball excitedly with the others' children, fucked her every evening, staying inside her sterile belly for ages, endlessly repeating: "I love you, I love you so much."

Nina saw almost nothing of the Indian Ocean, starting on the cocktails, and anything else alcoholic, at breakfast time. She ended the century in a state of semiconsciousness without anyone noticing. The others were all engrossed in their own happiness.

And yet the light was beautiful, the Mauritians radiant, the food divine, but no room with a view can replace a friend.

She plucks a random book from the bookcase in her bedroom to slip the three envelopes inside it. Looks at its title, *Blanc d'Espagne*. She'd forgotten to read this novel. Bought a long time ago. She has a vague look at the back cover and replaces it among the other books, some forgotten, some already read, some abandoned halfway through.

The radio alarm shows five o'clock. Time for her first glass. She hides her bottles inside her boots. She's skilled at concealing. She's not proud of it. But concealing means giving herself intervals of freedom. Those moments, those actions belong only to her. Nina pours the alcohol into a china mug, sipping tea isn't suspect.

The cook is downstairs. Nina can hear her clattering in the kitchen.

*Daddy's downstairs, making cocoa, Mommy's upstairs, making a cake, it's sleepytime, Nicky, my little brother . . .*

She's asked Nathalie a hundred times not to arrive too early to prepare supper. But that one doesn't give a fig about what Nina asks.

She turns up at four, when they're never at the table before eight. She used to stay on to clear the table. Not anymore. Good riddance.

"Those are rich people's problems, my love," Emmanuel is forever telling her, "quit complaining . . . You do nothing all day, quit complaining. We live like millionaires, quit complaining . . . We're fortunate, very fortunate, quit complaining . . . Force yourself a little, eat some meat, quit complaining . . . You've got even fatter, haven't you? I could cheat on you, you know, plenty of pretty girls hovering around me, quit complaining . . ."

*

*August 2000*

Apart from Fabien Désérable, no one knows that Sasha Laurent, author of the best-selling *Blanc d'Espagne*, is Adrien Bobin. He had set that story down on paper in order to live, to continue living. But he made nothing of it. He carries, and will forever carry, something clandestine deep inside him. Something clandestine that enabled him to become financially independent at twenty, an absurd irony of fate.

The dress rehearsal of his play, *Des enfants en commun*, will take place in a fortnight. Posters stuck up all over Paris announce the play's opening at the Théâtre des Abbesses.

Adrien attends the final rehearsals, seated three rows behind the director. He watches the actors trying things out, moving about, and listens, with a thrill, to them making suggestions. It's like entering into a dream. The kind that mesmerized him as a child, on TV. Hearing them speak his words electrifies him. Words that belong to him, that come out of his head.

Adrien's inspiration for writing his play came from a Sunday when he'd just arrived in Paris, and was living at Thérèse Lepic's in Vincennes. That day he had accepted to go and have lunch at Rue de Rome, his father's place, because his genitor did, after all, pay his rent and provide for him. And because, for Adrien, living at the student hostel without Nina is unthinkable. Other students didn't interest him. Terrified him, even. Thérèse's apartment was his only solace, a clean and cozy refuge.

"The code is 6754C, sixth floor," Sylvain Bobin had told him over the phone. Adrien discovered a fine Haussmann building. In the elevator, with its wrought-iron cage, he gazed at himself in the antique mirror. As usual, he had prepared some ready-made questions and answers, to avoid any of those lulls in the conversation he so dreaded.

It was the first time Adrien was entering the world of his "old man." Usually, the two of them lunched at a restaurant.

He found his name on the door. The same name as him, something that had always astonished him. The father and son had only their name in common.

A woman opened the door to him. A blond bob, quite pretty, something of Isabelle Huppert, around fifty, affected. Adrien felt himself blush and hated himself for it.

"Hello, I'm Marie-Hélène."

"Hello, I'm Adrien."

"Yes, I know," she said, laughing.

He held his hand out to her, she took him by the shoulder and kissed him clumsily. He smelt her perfume, that Laura Ashley stuff that always made him gag. In the metro, he dodged any women who'd doused themselves in it.

He followed behind Marie-Hélène, she was wearing a white silk blouse and a tight black skirt that stopped just below the knees, with a small slit at the back. Adrien thought she had nice legs, slender and toned. He also thought of his mother, who had never worn that kind of skirt. Just long fuchsia or turquoise things.

Adrien passed close to the kitchen door. The aroma of something cooked in a sauce simmering.

"It's *coq au vin*," Marie-Hélène told him, as if she'd read his thoughts.

In the corridor leading to the sitting room, Adrien saw some photos. A younger Marie-Hélène in front of a Christmas tree or an ocean. In a sarong or a skiing jacket. And always with Sylvain Bobin by her side. Other pictures of people he didn't know, kids in football strip and elderly people posing, glass of wine in hand, at a banquet table.

His father was a stranger to him, and Adrien felt keenly that he was entering his private world for the first time. An entire life that had begun long before his birth and was just following its course.

But why had his mother slept with this married man? All of a sudden, he wanted to know how these two people, so seemingly different, had ended up in the same bed. It's meeting Marie-Hélène that made Adrien feel the need to know. He'd often seen his genitor turning up at their apartment in La Comelle, drinking a coffee in silence, with Joséphine nearby, keen for him to leave. But he'd never asked himself any questions on the mystery of that union. Had she made him laugh? Had they loved each other? How had he seduced her? What had attracted them to each other? Him, the caricature of an accountant, who counts the peas he's just been served to calculate the price per square centimeter of the dish of the day, and her, wacky, a disciple of Buddhism and natural remedies.

On the table in the sitting room, flutes of champagne and bowls of savory snacks. On the sofa, Sylvain Bobin beside two young men. Aged about twenty-five and thirty.

All three of them stood up to shake his hand. Adrien had never kissed his father.

"Hello, I'm Laurent," said the younger of the two.

"Hello, I'm Pascal."

"Hello . . . Adrien."

They sat back down. Pascal and Laurent asked Adrien where he was living, what studies he was pursuing, where exactly was La Comelle.

Sometimes, one is so disconnected from reality that it takes time to understand the obvious. Adrien had always been labeled as "the shy one who lives in his own world." And that day, removed from his world, it took him two glasses of champagne to understand that Pascal and Laurent were his half-brothers. Half-brothers who had the same surname as him, who had been legally recognized like him, with the only difference being that they had grown up with their father. When he realized that they were all chatting naturally, about the global silence over the Rwandan genocide and Tom Hanks's performance in *Forrest Gump*, Adrien thought to himself how mad people are, and felt like throwing up those cheesy little snacks.

They all moved to the dining table. Marie-Hélène went to fetch the starters, preceded by Pascal.

"I'll help you, Mom."

Adrien observed his brothers at length, wondering if they suffered from the same pain as him. But how could one tell? This pain was invisible. And the two strapping lads opposite him bore no resemblance to him. His father had definitely had to go and plant his seed elsewhere to produce the puny young man that he was.

He left the paternal apartment at around four, slightly tipsy. Promising Marie-Hélène that he'd return.

He did return there, but only in his thoughts. He carved up and dissected every minute of that Sunday, a stranger in his own family, to create a play out of it that those in "the trade" describe as "masterly."

He saw his father every now and then but always in packed brasseries, during the week and at lunchtime. Sylvain Bobin never again brought up his other life to Adrien. Why?

He can't have made a good impression. Too reserved, too pallid, not enough.

As if that Sunday had never existed.

*

*August 2000*

Étienne hangs up. Hands and mind clammy. This business has dogged him for far too long.

It's the police officer, Sébastien Larand, who warned him. An old school friend. A man had again called the police station at La Comelle to assert that Clotilde and Étienne were together on the evening of her disappearance. "No doubt the same person who phoned Pradel's program in '97," Larand had added.

Three years of silence and here it is, catching up with him again.

The file had been closed. But the police can't ignore these anonymous calls from a phone booth in the lower district of La Comelle.

It's as if someone has got it in for him. But who? Clotilde's parents? How could he find out? By talking? Saying what he saw? That car that sank to the bottom of the lake, any connection? An accident? The thought makes him shudder.

What if he began by questioning the witness at the station, that woman who allegedly saw Clotilde on the platform that evening?

He calls Sébastien Larand straight back:

"I've a favor to ask you."

## 64

*25 December 2017*

Étienne is sitting on his bed. Thinking about his disappearance. After Clotilde's, it's his turn.

Marie-Castille is a police captain. His wife will find him in five minutes if he doesn't plan everything meticulously.

She mustn't know anything about the car in which he'll make his getaway, or be able to trace his cash withdrawals. He took out quite a sum from the bank last week, enough to cover motorway tolls and hotels, in cash.

He still doesn't know where they're going to go. And with what vehicle.

First solution, hire one. But not in his name, or Louise's, or Nina's. They'll have to go and pick up a car in Autun, but using someone else's ID, not theirs. That of a neighbor or a distant cousin who won't say anything. So Marie-Castille can never connect it to them. Second solution: borrow one from a stranger. "Hello, could you lend me your car? It's to go off and die quietly . . . It will be returned to you after my burial. Sorry for the inconvenience, you will be compensated."

Dying. Right now, he views this prospect like a voyage. As though catching a plane to discover as yet virgin territories. Panoramas that don't feature in any magazine.

He refocuses on his planning. Mustn't allow his thoughts to wander, or to make him sad.

All their mobile phones must be switched off. Shut them up, day and night. Make any important calls with prepaid cards. He considers any urgent calls to Louise. In case she needs to send a prescription to a pharmacy for him. Although, with all the meds she's prescribed him, he's already got enough to self-administer a lethal dose.

Knowing Marie-Castille, she'll tap everyone's phone within twenty-four hours. From Nina's shelter to his parents' house. She's going to go crazy. And when Marie-Castille goes crazy, the whole world takes the rap. She shrinks from nothing. If she knew, she'd have him arrested and handcuffed on the spot, to take him to hospital by force. Even if it meant inserting the drip herself to get the chemo inside him.

He hears her voice from downstairs, rallying the family for Christmas lunch: "Dinner's ready, everyone!"

Before going down, Étienne sends a text message to Nina. He then deletes it from his phone. Between his wife and his son, he can't be too careful.

This evening, he will talk to Valentin.

*

Ringtone. Nina reads Étienne's message several times.

> We need a car nobody recognizes. Or my wife will have every police force in France after us. If you need to contact me, send to Louise's mobile.
>
> See you etc.
>
> E

Nina doesn't hang around. She's been like that since childhood. Maybe a bit more since her grandfather's death. Those early days with Emmanuel, daily life with Emmanuel, being resourceful, she knows all about that. At the shelter it's the same thing. She's used to getting out of impossible situations. For Nina, there's no such thing as impossible. She replies immediately on Louise's mobile:

Tell your brother all O.K. Thanks.

Nina.

"I'm going away," she tells Romain, gazing at his fine profile.

They are lying on Nina's bed, with Bob at their feet. Watching a really dumb Christmas movie while nibbling chips.

“Where to?”

“I don’t know yet. I’m accompanying a friend. My childhood friend.”

”For how long?”

“I don’t know. He’s terminally ill. Won’t hear about chemo.”

Romain takes that in.

“When are you off?”

“Tomorrow. And I need a car . . . His wife is a cop. She’ll search all over for him.”

“Why isn’t your friend going with his wife?”

“Because she wants to force him to have treatment.”

Romain switches off the TV. Brushes a crumb off Nina’s cheek.

“You want to take my car, is that it?”

“Yes. That’s it,” she replies, with both assurance and distress.

“Is it one of the two boys you did those drawings of, at school?”

“Yes.”

“You won’t forget your sketchpad and charcoal before leaving, will you?

*Why have I only met you now*? thinks Nina. *Why is my life so tardy*?

“Thanks.”

*

Louise reads Nina’s message. Watches Étienne pretending to relish his foie gras on toast. She’s not duped. Knows that in five minutes, he’ll go and spit it all out into the toilet. Nina hasn’t managed to convince him to have treatment. But knowing that her brother isn’t going off alone reassures her. She mustn’t cry. Mustn’t watch him. Mustn’t let Marie-Castille suspect a thing. Must drink champagne, but moderately. Just so it goes to her head a bit, but not too much. When it’s too much, it lets the sadness spill over.

Chat with her nephews and niece, Valentin, Louis, and Lola. Ask them questions, not caring about the answers. “So what is *Game of Thrones* exactly? Tell me the story.” And find the right moment to whisper what Nina’s just texted in Étienne’s ear.

*

"Louise" comes up on my mobile. I answer straight away. It isn't her.

"What are you doing?" Étienne asks me.

"I'm packing my traveling bag . . . And waiting for someone."

"Who?" he asks, as though jealous.

"The young girl who's going to look after Nicola."

"Who's Nicola?"

"My cat. You saw him this morning."

"Oh, yes . . ."

A long silence follows. I hear him breathing.

"You're not with anyone for Christmas?" he finally asks.

"I'm not a great fan of festive meals. I'm listening to music. I'm fine."

I try to guess what he's doing. There's no one around him. Suddenly, I panic, tell myself that he's gone away on his own and is phoning me for that reason. To announce it to me.

"Where are you?"

"At my parents'. Hiding in the john."

I feel instant relief. He hasn't gone without us.

Étienne adds:

"The only place I'm left in peace."

Silence once again. As if he wanted to say something to me but didn't know how to go about it.

"Why are you calling me, Étienne?"

"I've written a letter for my wife . . . I'm not great at grammar, formulas, waxing lyrical . . . all that . . . Can I send it to you on email?"

". . ."

"As you're a whiz in French . . . Can you sort it for me?"

"I don't know your wife."

"You don't need to know her to know what I must say to her. Because me you do know."

"I knew you, a long time ago."

"Can you help me, please?"

"O.K."

I receive the letter, sent from Louise's email account. I send it back to him a few minutes later.

Étienne, I've corrected two spelling mistakes. As for the rest, I haven't touched it. Because words belong to those who write them.
Especially those words.

Marie-Castille,
I've gone. You have every right to be angry with me.
Maybe you'll think me selfish, disgusting, horrid. And that's your right.
But it's my choice.
There's no other woman. I've not met anyone.
I'm ill.
Louise will explain it to you. Don't reproach her for anything. I forbade her to talk about it.
I refuse to let Valentin and you see me suffering like some creature in a lab. Degrading myself. I don't want your last image of me to be that of a bedridden invalid. You know I hate hospitals and am as proud as Artaban. You're always saying to me: "My love, you're as proud as Artaban." So I'm both too proud and, no doubt, too cowardly to die before your eyes.
Don't look for me, I beg you. At first I'll be with two childhood friends, who'll accompany me toward the final journey.
Not seeing our son grow up and not growing old with you is goddamn painful, but I have to accept it.
You know I don't believe in God, and that for me, it's unthinkable to be locked in a box that's blessed by a priest then carried off by guys I don't know. Or worse: by our colleagues. I'd rather hurl myself into the water, take the initiative. And that's what I'm going to do, hurl myself into the water when I feel the time is right.
I'm not going to weep over my fate. I beg you, never wear black in memory of me. Put your sweater on, the one I like, with red diamonds. Buy plenty like that. Blow our dough. Don't be my widow. Meet other guys and have fun. Yes, have fun, burn the candle at both ends, and make the most of the sunshine. Do that for me. Étienne

# 65

*September 2000*

Monday morning. Nina has two weeks ahead of her. Emmanuel has just left with a large suitcase. Enough to make her reel. Alleluia.

The cook is on vacation. A package tour to Madeira.

Dream and reality synchronized. Alleluia.

A ten-hour time difference between France and Australia, a twenty-hour flight separating her from Emmanuel. He'll fly from Paris late evening. Two days without him being able to phone her.

Emmanuel hadn't been away since last November, leaving her no room to breathe. Inconceivable for him to come home and her not be there. Otherwise, it was always the same old story: "Where were you, who with, why? I was worried sick, what's the point of giving you a mobile phone if it's forever switched off? I love you."

He announced his departure for Sydney to her two days before flying off.

"My love, I have bad news, I must go away for a fortnight. I'm so sorry. I tried to cancel right up to the last moment, but I can't get out of it. It could bring us an enormous contract. What bothers me is it falling when Nathalie is on vacation . . . I don't like leaving you all alone."

At first, Nina thought it was hoax. She really thought he was going to end his diatribe with: "Ta-da! I got you there! Of course I'm not going anywhere! We're staying together, just the two of us . . . my little wife and me. And this time, it's going to work, we're going to get that child of ours."

But when Nina saw the plane ticket inside the passport placed on the bed, beside the shirt he'd just taken off, she realized that it was true. That he was going.

*Don't show my elation.*

She stared wide-eyed and replied, innocent as you like:

"Don't worry, my love, a fortnight goes by very fast."

"It would still have been nice if you'd begged me a little to stay."

He was smiling at her, half-amused, half-accusingly.

That look of the misunderstood victim that he assumed all the time. And always that jokey tone, to seem like a cool guy.

A desire to hit him. Increasingly often. The love she'd felt for him had turned into disgust. Not constant hostility, more intermittent. Sudden bursts of hatred that rose up and could vanish just as quickly, or grip her for ages. Like poison in her veins. She, all empathy, and kindness, was turning into a witch. She was becoming her own enemy. Sometimes she even imagined her husband's murder. Pushing him down the stairs. Burning him alive. Knocking him out, putting him behind the wheel of his sports car and pushing him over the top of a ravine. Monstrous Hitchcockian scenarios that chilled her. Especially in the morning, upon waking, when he'd fuck her before leaving for work. Just a quickie, to plant his little seed. *He can drop dead*, she'd think, closing her eyes while he screwed her.

But right now, he absolutely mustn't change his mind. This trip to Australia was a godsend.

*The chance of a lifetime.*

She hugged him tight, closed her eyes, thought of her grandfather, Étienne, Adrien, and burst into tears, whispering into her husband's ear:

"You leaving is a blow, but don't worry about me, I know how hard you fight for us . . . for the company . . . I love you . . . I'm so proud of you."

And then she lay on their bed, summoning up all her tenderness and docility. She often thought that there was no difference between her and a hooker. Only that, for her, it was the same client every day and she slept between sheets embroidered with the crest of an estate. We become what is done to us and what we accept.

Nina takes *Blanc d'Espagne* from her bookcase. She grabs the three last envelopes, dated 11 August 1994, including the one addressed to Étienne. Why take it to him in Lyon? Since the New

Year fiasco, he doesn't speak to her anymore. He holds it against her that she'd preferred to go to Mauritius to see in the year 2000.

When she'd returned from her trip, she'd phoned him, he hadn't answered. She'd left him a voicemail: "It's me, it's Nina . . . Happy New Year and new century . . . I miss you. I went round to yours, but your mother told me you'd just left . . . Let's get together soon . . . Love you lots . . . And again, happy new year . . . Arrest all the naughty thieves and nasty murderers."

Étienne had replied to her three days later by text, words that were cold and detached:

Happy New Year to the family. Kisses.

The family? What family? The Damammes? In the word "kisses" she'd read Étienne's raging fury more than the slightest kiss.

Just like when he sulked as a child.

She unseals the first envelope, addressed to a certain Julie Moreira, and discovers a postcard featuring a drawing of the cartoon character Marsupilami.

"My dearest Juju,

I've left François. Two years with a psychopath! I've lost the 100 kilos that were weighing on my stomach. I can breathe! Since I left, I feel as if I've been connected to an oxygen mask. He'd become so jealous, couldn't even tolerate someone's shadow brushing against me. So much time wasted. I regret it so much, you wouldn't believe. Even though it's pointless. I eat sandwiches every day and haven't a bean left, but I so don't care.

Can't wait to see you again, next week we'll jump from the five-meter board at the pool, like when we were kids, and we'll suck candies. Better than the dicks of bastards.

Big kiss, chickabiddy,

Lolo"

Nina reads and rereads the postcard. The words "psychopath"

and "breathe" combine in her mind. It's as if this Lolo was giving her directions for how to leave. It all appears so easy. And it seems so exhilarating, to go, to leave.

She unseals the second envelope, addressed to the "ADPA." It takes Nina a while to realize that it's the official name of La Comelle's shelter for animals. She's never set foot there. Always avoided the place, for fear of being traumatized. She remembers the little spaniel they found when they were still three, and going door to door to try to find its owner, and the rocketing from her grandfather when he saw them return carrying the dog. No question of keeping it. The two boys decided to take it to the shelter, while Nina wept every tear she had.

"Dear Sir or Madam,

I would like to alert you to a Labrador/golden retriever type dog that spends its days and nights locked on a balcony overlooking a private inner courtyard. It lives in its own excrement and I doubt it is regularly fed. Its owner is very often away.

For verification, the address is as follows: Cristelle Barratier, 10 Chemin des Cent-Pas, La Comelle."

The letter isn't signed. No sender's name on the back of the envelope. Is it a troublemaker's revenge over some dispute between neighbors, or a real report of ill-treatment? This letter is six years old. What has happened in the meantime? Was the animal taken away? Whatever the case, it's probably dead now.

She reseals the two envelopes without leaving the slightest tear.

She slips the letter to Étienne back inside *Blanc d'Espagne*, and puts the novel back among the others.

She dials 12 on her landline phone. An operator promptly answers.

"Hello, I'd like the phone number for the Théâtre des Abbesses, A - B - B - E - S - S - E - S, Paris, 18th arrondissement."

She jots down the number, calls the theater, and books a ticket for the following evening. Since it's the premiere, all the good seats are sold out, just a few left at the back. It doesn't matter. What counts is being there. She will watch *Des enfants en commun*, the play written by Adrien. She's going to surprise him by just turning up, with no warning.

Later, she'll go and buy her train ticket at the travel agency. And she'll wait for it to be dark to find the mailboxes of Julie Moreira and the ADPA.

She has a shower listening to *Corps et armes*, the Etienne Daho album. It's Emmanuel who gave it to her, explaining: "In memory of the concert that never was on the night I kissed you for the first time."

Nina knows the words of "La Baie" by heart. It's a song that's like traveling without moving. She follows the road along the sea, as described by the singer, the path taken by the person leaving.

She dries her hair and starts packing her suitcase.

This time, she's leaving.

*

Monday. It's at 9:00 A.M. that same day that Étienne arrives in La Comelle. He has a meeting with Sébastien Larand, his old school friend who became a policeman.

Étienne left Lyon at 6:00 A.M. He won't be visiting his parents. He's told no one he's coming. Like the day he went to pay his respects at Joséphine's grave. He thinks of Nina. No doubt alone at home, vegetating in her wife-who-doesn't-work daily life. He could drop by for a coffee, surprise her, but doesn't remotely feel like it.

Not feeling like seeing Nina to this extent makes him queasy. He never would have thought it possible. He still hasn't gotten over the blow she'd dealt him at New Year's. Going away at the last moment when they were all supposed to be together. He knows that it's not her fault, that everything starts with her husband, but she could have refused. Étienne is annoyed with her for meekly putting up with whatever that guy imposes on her.

This morning, Étienne should finally meet the witness who said she saw Clotilde on the station platform the evening she disappeared. She's called Massima Santos. Sébastien Larand has asked her to come to a bistro, less formal than the police station. Less daunting, too.

Étienne needs to know what this woman saw. And how she knew Clotilde.

Six years later, what will she remember? Sébastien Larand sent him Massima's statement by email. A statement recorded five days after Clotilde's supposed departure.

On 17 August 1994, Massima closed the notions store she worked in at 7:00 P.M. She went home to pack her suitcase and give her keys to the neighbors, so they could water her flowers and feed her cat. She then walked to the station to catch the last train for Mâcon, the 10:17. Clotilde Marais was sitting on a bench, on Platform 2, holding a traveling bag. She greeted her and got onto the regional train. Did she see Clotilde getting on, too? Impossible to say for sure. When Massima returned to La Comelle five days later, her boss told her that Clotilde Marais was the subject of a concerning missing-person alert. So she phoned the police.

Étienne enters the bistro. Some men are playing cards at a table by the window. They barely look up on his arrival. Sebastien is already there. With his kepi under his arm, he's having a coffee at the bar and chatting with the owner. Étienne knows the chap by sight. In La Comelle, everyone knows everyone by sight. It's the first time he's entered this café. It's an old-folks place, a bit gloomy, still stuck in the fifties. No video games or rock music here.

Étienne and Sébastien both take a seat at the back of the room. They each order a coffee and a glass of water. They're fifteen minutes early. They talk about their respective careers. Sébastien is impressed by Étienne's. Police lieutenant, no mean feat. Those entrance exams, with all that studying, are damned hard.

Then they get to the Clotilde case. Before disappearing, she had worked as a waitress. A summer job.

"At the time," says Sébastien, "I was still a student, but colleagues who conducted the inquiry told me the girl had serious mood swings. That wasn't mentioned on Pradel's TV show. It's the boss of the pizzeria she worked at who told us. On her last few days, apparently, she was forever looking outside, as if waiting for someone."

Étienne takes this in. Allows no emotion to show. He learned that control for the oral entrance exams. Putting on a mask, that of listening and thinking.

"Clotilde didn't come to our meeting that evening . . . so I just left . . . Who on earth keeps phoning you to claim the opposite?"

Sébastien grimaces.

"Denouncements like that, we get them all the time . . . One day, for peace, the friend you stayed with that night should testify. You never know."

"You never know what?" Étienne jumps in.

"If it carries on, you could be in trouble. The only person to show up after the TF1 program is the guy who keeps calling to grass on you . . . Who might have it in for you?"

"But when he calls you, he doesn't accuse me directly."

"No, but he might as well . . . He says you were together, you and her, at the lake that evening, and then hangs up."

When Massima Santos pushes open the door, they both look up.

She seems intimidated. Maybe not a good idea, this place. She's not the type to frequent bistros. The card players, who barely noticed Étienne when he came in, now put their cards down, on the baize, as if caught in the wrong. They all greet her, looking sheepish. Massima manages to nod back and orders a *café crème*, as if apologizing for being there.

Étienne knows her by sight, too. He remembers her dark clothes, fine clear skin, deep-set little black eyes, and the gold crucifix around her neck. A thin woman with a slight limp. He must have gone to the notions store occasionally with his mother, or passed her, like all the other locals, on one of the town center's four pavements.

Sébastien and Étienne both stand up to offer her a chair, which she settles down on, looking awkward. She places her thin, white hands on the Formica table. Étienne instantly thinks of chicken feet.

Sébastien asks after her health and introduces Étienne to her, "a top police lieutenant in Lyon." Massima seems both scared and impressed. Étienne swiftly reassures her by speaking as gently as he can. Just as he does whenever he wants to reassure a witness, or get them to talk. He manages a big smile, although the acidity in his stomach is killing him. Too many coffees at highway service stations between Lyon and La Comelle, too many sleepless nights, too many nightmares seeing Clotilde sink into the brackish water.

"I knew Clotilde Marais." Étienne begins. "We dated at one time . . . and on the evening you noticed her at the station, I was waiting for her. We were meeting up. Can you tell me what you saw exactly?"

"Well, as I've said, she was at the station. Sitting on a bench."

"Was she alone?"

"Yes."

"What was she doing? Was she reading? Listening to music? Did she have her Walkman headphones on?"

Massima screws up her eyes as she wracks her brain.

"No. She was looking straight ahead."

"Did she look annoyed? Happy? Tired?"

"She looked like she was waiting for her train."

Étienne goes quiet. Reflects. Asks himself the same questions that have obsessed him, constantly, for years: what time was it when Clotilde met him at the lake? Did she have time to go off to the station? How? Who was in that car he saw sinking into the lake? Did he really see it? He'd drunk a lot that evening.

Massima stirs her milky coffee, staring into the cup.

Étienne knows that many witness statements are worthless. People forget, are mistaken, mix things up. They are full of certainty and don't remember faces, think only of themselves and care so little for others. It's easy to change their minds in a flash. Photofit pictures are irrefutable proof of that. How often had he pursued the wrong individual after being led down the wrong track? "He was blond." "Are you sure?" "Yes, really sure." "But someone saw a brown-haired man who seems to match . . . Look at this photo." "Oh, yes, maybe, it was dark . . ." How often had he heard that?

*It was dark!* Étienne immediately withholds two questions that the police, thinking it just a banal case of a teen running away, probably never asked Massima Santos: "Was it dark when you say you recognized Clotilde at the station, and do you wear glasses?"

*The sun must start setting at around nine in August. So after ten, it's dark*, thinks Étienne. *The old woman can't have seen Clotilde clearly . . . There is lighting on a station platform . . . And me, when I woke up, when I saw the car sinking into the water, it was already dark. Must have been later than nine-thirty.*

Étienne looks at Massima again. She must be well into her sixties.

So she was over fifty-five in August 1994. Who still has excellent sight at that age?

Although, as things stand, Massima's testimony clears him of the slightest blame, Étienne wants to know if the pious old woman is mistaken or telling the truth. Then another idea comes to him. Who, in La Comelle in 1994, might *resemble* Clotilde? Same shape of face, same general appearance, tall with blond hair? Several girls, inevitably. Did Clotilde have any distinguishing marks? Just thinking about it gives Étienne a violent pain in his stomach, like being hit with an iron rod. His memory focuses on Clotilde's face, searching for a beauty mark, a tattoo, a birthmark. Nothing. Unblemished skin. He avoids thinking about her belly.

Sébastien jolts him out of his ruminations.

"How do you know Clotilde Marais?" he asks Massima.

"She came to the store with her mother as a little'un. And sometimes on her own. She liked to sew."

Étienne jumps in without intending to—one can't control everything.

"You must be mistaken . . . She wasn't the kind of girl to sew."

The woman eyes him scornfully.

"Yes she was. She even made her own nightdresses. Pretty ones. My boss always told her to make a business of it. That she'd be a big hit. Yes, she used to say that to her, 'a big hit.'"

*And what a hit*, thinks Étienne.

Most of the time, they would meet at his place. Very rarely at hers. He doesn't recall seeing a sewing machine in her bedroom, or any other room. And she'd never talked to him about clothes or sewing. She was feminine, but more a sportswear girl. Étienne tries to remember which bac she was doing, which options, she was due to leave for Dijon to do a sports degree, not to become a fashion designer, or anything like that.

"We'll check at her parents' house whether there's a sewing machine," says Sébastien, signaling to the waiter. "Would you like something else to drink?"

"No, thank you."

*What on earth are you doing*? Étienne asks himself. *Now you're just getting yourself in deeper. If this woman's testimony collapses, all eyes will turn to you. Especially Clotilde's parents' eyes. It suits others to believe she went off to live her own life somewhere else. But not her parents. And who is it that's ringing the police station to say I was with her at the lake that evening? It might be time to ask Adrien for some help.*

*

Adrien opens his eyes.

What should he wear to appear on the TV program *Vol de nuit*?

That's the first question he asks himself.

Last night was the press preview of *Des enfants en commun*. Adrien's head is still spinning.

The Parisian elite giving it a standing ovation. Actors, authors, journalists—those on TV, or who write for the top weeklies and monthlies.

Adrien never tires of reading the good reviews he's been showered with ever since his first play, *Les Mères*. He hopes old Py reads them, too. But no, what a strange idea. Old Py belongs to another life.

"Adrien Bobin, the little prince," "Adrien Bobin dazzles us. His majestic, fluid writing goes straight to the heart," "There's a touch of Shakespeare in young Bobin," "Adrien Bobin makes a splash," "Adrien Bobin blows the cobwebs off contemporary theater" . . . He keeps reading and rereading these headlines, hasn't really come down from cloud nine. He collects the cultural magazines he appears in. Looks after his secret garden.

"Is there someone who shares your life?"

"Yes, but I won't be sharing that with you."

In the street, he's starting to be recognized. Especially by students and budding actors.

Thierry Ardisson was at the press preview, preparing for *Tout le monde en parle*, the country's most watched program, on which the three main actors will be appearing.

Patrick Poivre d'Arvor, who adored the play, is also planning a *Vol de nuit* on playwrights. He wants to invite Adrien onto his show, along with other writers for theater, to discuss their different styles:

"What draws someone to writing?" "Why the theater?" "What part is fiction and what personal experience?" "Do you think of an actor or actress to inspire you?" "How do the scenes appear in your imagination? And how do you feel when you hear your words coming out of the players' mouths?"

When people say to him: "Your parents must be very proud," he makes a sad face and, clutching a handkerchief, replies, "Mommy is dead." Nothing more. People don't push it any further. Don't dare to enquire about the father. Particularly those who have seen a preview of *Des enfants en commun*.

Adrien hasn't been in touch with Sylvain Bobin for several months. What for? To have lunch in a brasserie stinking of fries and Madeira sauce, and watch the flies buzzing around? Make small talk to fill in the gaps? Put up with the glum, blank way his genitor looks at him?

Tomorrow evening, it's the premiere of *Des enfants en commun.* Time to face up to a real audience.

Adrien has invited no one.

Neither his father nor his stepmother, not to mention his half-brothers.

He used them, as dramatic material, to weave his plot. End of story.

The publicist asked him if he'd like to invite some loved ones. Adrien told her that he'd lost them. He could have invited Louise, but that would mean also inviting Étienne. Étienne at the theatre, how incongruous. As for Nina, she goes nowhere without her play-boy, who would never come to see one of his plays. Adrien hadn't even tried to suggest it to them.

He stops himself from thinking of Nina, otherwise he feels uneasy. A sense of having abandoned her, despite his promise: "For you, we'll always have a new car with a full tank." And that old line keeps coming back to him: "There's no love, only proof of love."

He stops himself from thinking that maybe he should have made an effort. And ends up telling himself that everyone has their life to live, that it's impossible to save the entire world. And that it's also up to people to save themselves.

Fine, but Nina isn't just people. Having said that, how many times had he suggested she come and live with him at Thérèse Lepic's?

"And that lady you lodged with when you arrived in Paris, any news of her?" Désérable had asked him one evening when they were dining together at L'Arpège, to celebrate all his success and bury forever any hope of a second novel.

"She rambles on," Adrien had replied, drily.

But, thanks to the delicious wine they had been savoring since the start of the meal, the editor was emboldened. He'd never risked mentioning Adrien's private life. Had maintained a certain reserve regarding the mystery of Sasha Laurent, Adrien's pseudonym.

"And the people you talk about in *Blanc d'Espagne* . . . have they read it?"

"*Blanc d'Espagne* is fiction."

Désérable looked hard at him. And for the first time, dared to say "I don't think so." Adrien blushed, raising a 1984 Montrachet to his lips.

"Think what you like."

Adrien is still lying on his bed. It must be around nine, going by the light filtering through the blinds from outside, and the street sounds.

Today, he's free. No doubt he'll go to the movies. He likes the late-morning sittings. He hasn't yet seen *Harry, un ami qui vous veut du bien*.

For a few months, he's been unable to write like he used to. Now, he observes himself and hears himself searching for fine phrases. Through wanting to impress people, he's conscious of losing all sincerity.

Writing *Blanc d'Espagne* was a necessity. Today, writing means shining in the eyes of others, not saving his life anymore. And what he used to find a great pleasure is now but a chore.

It must be fatigue. He hasn't stopped, since living in Paris. Six years already.

How times passes. He thinks of Louise and Étienne. He likes seeing them in La Comelle, not in Paris. The thought of meeting them at Gare de Lyon irks him. He's already gone there to fetch Louise. As soon as he sees her appear at the end of the platform, he feels uncomfortable. He has the awful feeling of not knowing what to do with her. He shows her around like a tourist, from restaurants to museums. Feels like a cold-blooded monster, and, when she leaves, is relieved.

# 66

*25 December 2017*

Nina opens her eyes. Romain is sound asleep, head buried under pillow. They had fallen asleep in each other's warmth. Christmas-lunch leftovers on the bedside tables and the old dresser.

It must be around five in the afternoon. The cats are dozing on the chairs, while lying in wait for Bob, blissfully sprawled on the duvet.

Nina gets up without making a sound.

She gathers her thoughts: phone Simone, and go up to the shelter to organize everything for her departure. But first, she takes the sketchbook Romain gave her the previous day, grabs some charcoal, and starts drawing his profile. She can only see part of his face and his tousled hair. She rediscovers the desire in her fingers. Thanks to the movements of her hand, she reconnects to her body. To her sensuality, too. Her wrist brushes against the paper, her eyes flit from the lines on Romain's face to those she's making. Her pleasure is obvious, one she hasn't felt for years, that of capturing an individual by drawing their nose, their mouth, their eyes, their forehead. She writes "Christmas 2017" at the bottom of the sheet of paper and places it beside him on the bed.

Nina thinks back to what Simone told her that morning about adopting Cannelé and her amorous night with her budding dance partner: "You know, Nina, one thinks something. And then one's wrong."

*A hundred years since I last packed a suitcase*, she thinks, contemplating her clothes. She's kept her grandmother Odile's suitcase. The ugly imitation-leather and cardboard one she'd taken to Saint-Raphaël in 1990. And that she'd packed again in September 2000, for the premiere of *Des enfants en commun*, Adrien's play. She could have taken one of the suitcases Emmanuel had given her, bigger, more robust, on wheels, but she was determined to carry her grandmother's for *leaving*.

When Nina had arrived at Gare de Lyon, she'd stored it in a locker. Inside it, what was left of six years of married life with Damamme, sorted and ironed.

It was the first time she was coming to Paris.

From Gare de Lyon, clutching her metro map, she took the new line 14 to get to Madeleine. She walked up to Rue des Abbesses, cutting across Place Blanche, had to ask her way twice, and discovered, en route, that the Moulin-Rouge was tiny. Like a movie set.

In Rue des Abbesses, she sat at a table in the Saint-Jean, the café right beside the theater. On the night of a premiere, she knew Adrien would attend, and he might have a drink or meet friends at this bar.

It was six o'clock when she sent him a text message:

Drop into the Café Saint-Jean, Rue des Abbesses, I've had a surprise left there for you.

For two hours, she'd scanned the street, the passersby, the clients, jumping each time a new shadow appeared behind the door. At eight o'clock, she went to the theater's box office, not having heard a word from Adrien.

Nina told herself that he must be backstage with the actors. That he didn't have his phone on him. That they'd meet up later. That she'd tell him, at around eleven, over a glass of champagne: "I've left La Comelle, I'd like to stay in Paris, could you hide me at yours while I find my feet?"

Adrien would be happy, relieved. Nina often thought of what he'd whispered in her ear on her wedding day: "For you, we'll always have a new car with a full tank." After all that time waiting for her.

Six years had gone by, between the day the boys had left and this premiere. It had taken her six long years to leave Emmanuel. He'd had to go off to Australia for her to find the courage to run away. She'd said nothing to anyone, not even a phone call to her parents-in-law. Emmanuel was capable of anything, especially the worst. And by the time he got back to France and realized she wasn't there anymore, Adrien would have found a way of hiding her for a while. He had contacts now.

In Rue des Abbesses, seeing her reflection in the store windows, Nina had told herself that she must lose weight, stop drinking every day and stuffing herself with hormones. And most of all, get back to drawing . . . and maybe singing.

Between La Comelle and Paris, she'd been dreaming while watching the scenery pass by: why not go back to music? Now that he was famous and recognized, Adrien would write lyrics for her and she'd sing them. And if they pushed a little, Étienne would join them. Was he truly happy in Lyon, in the police? Nina would know what to say to get him to join them. To be Three again. They were still young, and life, the real one, after a six-year delay, was about to start.

At the box office, she picked up the ticket she'd booked by phone the previous day, then walked around the foyer, in the midst of quite a crowd.

She was buoyed with pride, the joy of being the friend of the person named on the poster. She was apprehensive, too, hadn't seen Adrien since the day France won the football World Cup.

She was just working it out, two years—twenty-six months to be precise—when her eyes met his.

In twenty-six months, his way of looking had changed. At others, maybe not, but at her, definitely. First, he had blushed. Realizing that it really was her. Nina, his Nina. Just a few meters apart.

He looked around for who she was with. Étienne, hopefully. Étienne, obviously. He finally accepted that she was alone. But he didn't move. Didn't take a step toward her. It's Nina who went up to him, smiling. She threw herself into his arms. Felt him stiffening.

Too much emotion. Adrien's reserve. His immense shyness.

They stared at each other, exchanged a few words.

"Are you well?"

"Yes."

"Are you nervous?"

"A bit."

Faced with his silence, his slightly forced grimaces saying, "This isn't the right time," his well-cut clothes, new Tod's, and fancy hairstyle, she came out with some trite remarks that didn't belong in this non-conversation, just as she didn't belong in this place, which suddenly seemed cavernous and glacial to her. She stammered something like "I came by train, I sent you a text, right, I'm off to my seat, see you later."

He looked around, as if checking no one was watching them, or as if looking for someone. Nina couldn't tell which.

"See you later," he replied, gracing her with a small, knowing smile.

*Poor thing, he's terrified, that's why he's not his usual self.* So she told herself as she settled into her seat.

At the end of the play, she was among the first to stand up to applaud. She was happy, had loved it all: the acting, the staging, the words, the scenarios, telling herself she'd be back to watch it every evening.

She remembered that Adrien had been for lunch at his father's place and had discovered his "other family," two older brothers and a stepmother who seemed to appear from nowhere. Adrien had phoned her upon leaving them: "Nina, you can't imagine what I've just been through." After they'd talked for about ten minutes, Emmanuel had become impatient. Had started signaling to her, pointing at his watch: "Can you hang up?" So she'd closed her eyes, not to see her husband anymore, and covered her left ear with her hand. She'd chatted with Adrien for more than an hour. Afterwards, she'd had a furious row with Emmanuel. Had drunk more than usual to silence her body's pain. She mellowed with alcohol. Everything went quiet inside her. She turned hell into a false paradise.

Ten minutes of applause.

Adrien had an outstanding gift for narration. The way he'd transcribed those few hours of his life was amazing. The actors got the director and Adrien to come up on stage. The applause and bravos increased. Seeing Adrien among those "great" people, Nina let her emotions take over. He had *arrived.*

Then a curtain closed or the stage went dark, she can't remember.

There were voices and the sound of feet moving toward the exit. Nina found herself back in the foyer, among strangers. No one to talk to. She waited for Adrien in a corner, pretending to be interested in the flyers for various shows.

Once the foyer had emptied, she didn't dare ask the remaining employees where Adrien could be found. She returned to the Saint-Jean to wait for him there. She sent a second text message:

I'm waiting for you at the café next door.

Her phone rang, she jumped. At last, he was calling her back. At last, he would ask her to join him in the dressing rooms, introduce the actors, wardrobe staff, technicians to her. She must be there to share their triumph.

A phone number she didn't recognize. She answered, heart thumping.

"Hello?"

"Is that you?"

"Sorry?"

"I don't recognize your voice."

"It's Nina."

"Sorry, I've made a mistake. Forgive me."

Why are some mistakes crueler than others?

Nina bit the inside of her cheek so as not to cry in front of everyone.

After two hours and four glasses of white wine, she walked back down to Madeleine, took line 14 again to return to Gare de Lyon. She retrieved her grandmother's suitcase from the locker. It was past midnight. The next train for Mâcon wasn't until 6:30 A.M.

She walked the streets behind the station, found a hotel with no stars, a single room for 394 francs. She struggled to get to sleep, kept replaying the evening, over and over again, clutching her phone, waiting for Adrien's call. When, at four in the morning, it finally rang, she thought, with heart racing and breath short: *It's him, he's just got home, where he'd forgotten his mobile, he's just seen my messages, he looked for me after the show, he's going to apologize to me, ask me to join him at his place, he must be out of his mind with worry.*

"Hello?"

Emmanuel's voice. Sounding ecstatic.

"My love, I'm in transit! I can't talk to you for long. I love you. I'm thinking of you. Be good."

And he hung up.

Basically, she was alone in the world. So she might as well be alone in the world at home. Might as well go for the easy option. Two hours later, she took the first train for Mâcon. Got back to her house late morning. Unpacked her suitcase. Put her things away. Took *Blanc d'Espagne* from the shelf again to slip the last letter into it, the one addressed to Étienne.

And then thought no, after all. She placed *Blanc d'Espagne* on her bedside table and unsealed the envelope . . .

"Are you dreaming?" Romain asks her.

Nina jumps, lost in her thoughts.

"Memories coming back."

Romain has just found her downstairs. With an open suitcase on the kitchen table, gazing outside, as if watching someone walk into the garden. He kisses her on her neck.

"You smell nice."

"I smell of dog. With a touch of cat," she jokes.

"No, with a touch of me . . ."

He sniffs her neck.

"You smell of warmth, as if forever out in the sun . . . I love your smell."

"What's wrong with you?"

"Everything," he deadpans.

He moves off, pours himself a coffee.

*What is this handsome guy doing in my kitchen*? Nina wonders. *My scruffy old kitchen that hasn't been repainted since François Mitterrand was first elected. Guys like him don't exist in real life. Especially in mine. He's an engine tuned for others than me. Those who are beautiful, clean, and cheerful. Or maybe he's heaven-sent. Like in that bad movie, earlier. Tomorrow, Santa Claus will pop him right back into his sack, to give him to some other broad next year.*

"I don't think I've had a nap like that since kindergarten." he says, gulping his coffee.

He goes up to her and hugs her. She lets him, can feel armies of ants in her tummy. She says nothing, closes her eyes. He adds, in her ear:

"No one has ever drawn my portrait. Thank you."

Just as Romain is whispering that "thank you" into her ear, Nina hears Simone's words again: "You know, Nina, one thinks something. And then one's wrong."

*

I've just handed a copy of my key to the cat-sitter, a pretty, gentle young girl called Élisa. She went into raptures when she saw Nicola's little face. And yet she's supposed to be used to cats. At the shelter, she sees cute faces like my cat's every week. Battered faces, and old limping cats, too, but it surprised me. Maybe sensitive souls never get used to anything.

From tomorrow, she'll sleep at mine, until my return. She knows I'll be away indefinitely and hard to get hold of. She also knows that Nina will be with me on this trip.

Élisa is a fifteen-year-old schoolgirl, doing her first official exams this year. She's at the new Collège Georges-Perec. It's the school the guy sleeping with Nina is in charge of. Well, I imagine they sleep together. The very R. Grimaldi whose name I saw written in black pen on the mailbox of the house Nina entered last week. One doesn't just enter people's places like that, at eleven at night. Particularly since I've looked into it. He's a guy living on his own. He's called Romain Grimaldi and, according to one of my colleagues at the newspaper, he was apparently suspended from a school in Marnes-la Coquette over inappropriate conduct. An underage pupil who allegedly made a complaint about what he was up to. But since no one was able to prove anything, he was transferred, not sacked. Given a new post here, among the bumpkins, far from town. Out in the sticks, they'd be only too happy with him. Especially since they've got a brand-new school.

Does Nina have a talent for attracting psychopaths?

I asked Élisa how she found her headmaster. She seemed surprised by my question.

"Nice," she replied.

Just that. So I persisted:

"Nice in what way?"

"Normally nice. I think everyone at school likes him. And as a bonus, he's a pretty good-looking guy."

I dropped it there. I'm jealous. Everything to do with Nina makes me stupid and nasty.

Élisa asked me what I did in life. I explained to her about my translations and shifts at the newspaper.

"What language do you translate?"

"English."

"That's great, that is . . . Would 15 euros a day be O.K. with you?" she asked.

"Yes, perfect."

"When I'm back at school, early January, I'll bring my evening meals. D'you have a microwave?"

"Yes."

"Can I ask you a final question?"

"Yes, of course."

"Is it your choice to be with no one on Christmas Day?"

"A choice I'm perfectly content with."

"O.K. Otherwise, you could come and have supper at mine this evening. Mom's making an onion soup for the whole neighborhood."

"That's kind, but I'm having an early night."

A girl who invites me for Christmas without knowing me is bound to take good care of my cat.

As I close my bag, I remind myself that I must also inform the newspaper. I'm supposed to be available until 2 January, when the person I'm replacing is back from vacation. I'm going to lie. Say I need to have an urgent operation. Circumstances beyond my control.

I didn't hear her coming into my house. Neither the sound of the car, nor the front door. Louise hugs me from behind. I'd know her smell anywhere. Her breath on my neck.

"Happy Christmas."

"Are you well?"

"My brother's going to die."

"You know all three of us are setting off tomorrow?"

"Yes."

"Something to drink?"

"Yes."

"Are you sleeping here?"

"No. I'd rather be at home tomorrow morning when Marie-Castille discovers that Étienne has gone. And I'll also have to manage my parents . . . My poor darling mom."

"You'll tell them the truth?"

"Yes. I don't feel like burdening myself with lies anymore. And it will be better for Valentin, clearer."

*

He's sitting on the rack, his father's pedaling fast. The child clings to his T-shirt, a white one with Jim Morrison on it that he'd wear for years. His father's back, his hair blowing in the wind. His first memory of him. Of this tall, strong, and handsome man. His hero. The one who protects him, never tells him off, always smiles at him. Valentin shouts at the top of his voice: "I'm five years old today!" And his father pedals on, bursting into laughter, inventing humps, and screaming: "Happy birthday, my son!"

They're on holiday. A road fringed with pines on the isle of Porquerolles. Every now and then, glimpses of that sea playing hide-and-seek behind the trees. Then they arrive at a beach. A kind of bleached cove, the water's lost its blueness, is transparent. They scramble down a path of white sand, throw their towels on the beach and run into the water.

His father, his tanned skin. This man others gaze at. The child is conscious of that very soon, of that singular beauty, that Daddy doesn't look like ordinary mortals. And all those people repeating to him: "You're the spitting image of your dad."

*So, later, I'll be like him.* That's how Valentin had bolstered his own character, forever telling himself: *Later, I'll be like my father. I'll do everything the same.*

*But there's no such thing as doing everything the same. Because he's him and I'm me.*

*This proves it.*

It's 6:00 P.M.

They are sitting face to face, in the room Valentin has when sleeping at his grandparents'. A bed perched on the mezzanine floor.

"Why don't you get treatment?" the teenager asks, staring at the tips of his sneakers. "It's 2017 . . . not the Middle Ages."

Étienne wonders right then why we come into the world just to end up living through such a moment. Is it a punishment? Is he going through this nightmarish scenario because he dumped Clotilde twenty-three years ago? Because he swam back to the edge, telling her she was crazy?

Having to say to his son on Christmas Day:

"I need to talk to you, I'm ill . . . but you already know that . . . And there are some illnesses that can't be treated."

"No such thing," Valentin says, fighting back tears, fists clenched.

"Yes, darling, there is such a thing."

Étienne takes his son's hands in his. Valentin lets him, biting his lip. He likes his father's skin. Wonders right now whether, later, he'll have a bristly blond beard like him. The one he allows to grow on days off.

"Auntie says you don't *want* to have treatment, not that you can't."

"Auntie's mistaken . . . I refuse to lull you with illusions."

"I'll never see you again?"

Étienne would like to lie, to reassure his son, but what for? They've got together to tell each other the truth. Étienne doesn't trust the truth. He sometimes finds it underhand. With its various paths, nuances, ways. It's not as simple as it might seem. He knows a bit about that, in his job. But here, now, he owes it to his son.

"Today, you see me as I am. When the illness gets the upper hand, I . . . I don't want . . . I want to go before that happens. It's so important for you. Much more important for you than for me."

"You're going to commit suicide?"

The question is so blunt, Étienne recoils.

"I don't know . . . No. No. I'm not going to commit suicide. Auntie gave me some medication so I don't suffer."

"Are you scared of death?"

"No. I'm scared for you. Leaving you alone . . . But Mom is great. With a mother like yours, you'll never be alone. Do you hear me, Valentin? Never."

"So why are you going without telling her anything?"

Étienne doesn't answer. He looks down. Then looks straight into his son's eyes. They stare at each other, understand each other. Have always understood each other.

"I've written her a letter to explain everything . . . It's going to be difficult for her, but I'm sure she'll understand in the end."

"Are you going on your own?"

"Nina will be with me. And the person you saw outside the shelter, earlier."

"Why not Mom and me?"

"Because it's simpler like that. Simpler for me. Simpler for you."

Again, a long silence falls between them. Down below, in the sitting room, the muffled voices of the family playing tarot.

It's Valentin who finally speaks again:

"I'll say nothing."

"I'll phone you often. I'll make sure I can join you every evening. When you're alone in your room. I swear to you. I swear to you, do you hear me? Concealed numbers, mobile numbers you don't recognize, you answer all calls, O.K.?"

"Where are you going?"

"I've no idea. We'll decide once we're on the road. I don't want you smelling that hospital smell on me . . . those medications . . . They stink."

He hugs his son tight.

"I want you to keep the smell of your father, the memory of the man who loves you. Not of a sick man."

## 67

*10 August 1994*

Étienne,

The first time I saw you, I knew that one day you'd be mine. I knew it, or I wanted it.

Knowing, wanting, what's the difference? The result is the same: we're together.

I'd never have imagined that you'd make me suffer so much. And even if I had known, I'd still have jumped straight into bed with you.

I've just read in a magazine that the more your guy makes you come, the more you suffer when he's not around. The loving fuck is highly taxed.

It's so easy to fall for you, my stupidity makes me sick. You're the typical looker in every way. I melt at your smile, and the rest just follows. So easy . . .

How stupid I look. 'Thick as a brick,' as my grandmother used to say.

Working the whole of July meant I didn't have to think too much, once you'd gone on vacation. And as for tips, the Harbor Pizzeria is great.

I filled my piggy bank with money and tears every evening after work.

I'd run up to my room to see if there was a letter or postcard waiting on my desk.

Not a word from you since you left on 15 July. Before you went, I'd sensed you were more distant with me, but put it down to us being apart for the vacation. I told myself you had the jitters over leaving me.

Then, last weekend, I went to Fréjus to join a friend. I didn't stay long, but those few hours in the Midi were very revealing.

Fréjus-Saint-Raphaël, barely three kilometers between the two. And I knew the name of the beach you've been hanging out on since you were a kid. A good way to see you. To surprise you. And see you I sure did. Although to see you properly, I'd have had to remove the girl lying on top of you. I didn't know that you doubled as a beach towel for pushy blondes. I felt humiliated, seeing you feel her up. I even threw up my hotdog, into a trash can. Love's hard. Hard to stomach. Jealousy can really kill you. Believe me. I spied on you for a long time, unable to move. It was worse than a nightmare, when you scream, knowing you're dreaming, but can't wake yourself up. I thought of gouging your eyes out right there, but because of my 'condition,' I just left.

What a shit you are.

How two-faced.

I suspected, no, sensed that your boat trip around Corsica was a load of crap.

I got back to La Comelle yesterday evening.

I crawled back, my eyes red.

This morning, several questions are jangling in my head: Will you dump me when you get back? Will you look me in the eye? Or will you ditch me over the phone? Maybe you'll even lie low until term starts, since you're meant to be going to Paris and me to Dijon.

Unless I come and wreck your plans.

Before deciding on that, I have something to tell you. Something that will help you weigh up the pros and cons.

I was eighteen on 27 July. I waited for your call, your 'Happy Birthday.'

I even went and lit a candle to ask the Blessed Virgin for a sign from you. Me, an atheist! You see what I've been reduced to.

Reduced, yes.

But I'm still eighteen. That's it, I'm an adult. I can do what I want, although I didn't wait to be eighteen to do what I wanted, my darling.

The first time I saw you, I knew that one day you'd be mine.

So, let's go back to 25 May. When you accompanied me to the hospital. Well, 'accompanied' is a grand word for it. Let's say you delivered me to the door the way you'd leave a parcel on the doormat because you daren't ring the bell. Because, supposedly, you can't bear the smell of the corridors, you faint at a whiff of ether. So you went into a café, opposite the hospital, drank 'the worst coffee in the world,' and waited for me.

Leaving me on my own.

To present myself, alone, at reception. Go up in the elevator to the third story, the obstetrics department, alone. Lie on a bed, alone. No one to hold my hand.

The three questions I was asked: 'Have you fasted properly? Do you have your social-security card? Are you on your own?'

'No, my boyfriend is waiting for me across the road.'

For how long will my boyfriend wait for me? I wondered. He's there today, but tomorrow?

When I came out a few hours later, you saw me open the café door and you changed color. A mix of shame and relief in your beautiful clear eyes.

It was over. You could get back to your normal life. Do your bac. Next.

As for me, I was heaving due to the smell in there, a fug of cheap wine and cigarette smoke.

Wretched nausea.

Apparently, as soon as you abort, it goes away. But that I'll never know.

Because, in fact, I left my room before they came to get me. I hung around the cafeteria for a couple of hours. Through a window, I watched you eating a sandwich and drinking beers while waiting for me. Like during halftime of a soccer match.

Next, we got back on your motorbike, and I clung to you and closed my eyes.

I saw my life flash by. The one to come. My future life with our baby.

I asked you to stay with me that evening, telling you I was

'tired.' You didn't dare say no. You phoned Nina Beau, I heard you telling her a fib, because you were supposed to be studying with her, and you slept at mine. Against me. That night, I loved carrying that secret in my belly. I was the only one to know that we were going to have a child.

*Hasta la vista*,

Clotilde"

*October 2000*

On the day she read Clotilde's words, Nina knew that never again would she open a letter that wasn't addressed to her.

In the meantime, should she hand it over to the cops? But Étienne was himself a cop. And it could cause him problems. Just destroy it, then?

No, unthinkable for Étienne not to know.

Nina asked her grandfather out loud: "Granddad, what do I do with it?"

Slip it into Marie-Laure and Marc's mailbox in La Comelle? As she'd done with all the previous envelopes? Or deliver it by hand to Étienne in Lyon? Did he know Clotilde was pregnant? Was she bluffing? Had he seen her, or not, on the evening she disappeared?

Nina had been sitting beside Clotilde and Étienne on 17 August, when they had arranged to meet at the lake. When Clotilde had got up to leave the post-funeral drinks at the Beaulieus', Étienne had said to her:

"I'm staying with Nina for a while, but see you this evening?"

"O.K. I'll see you at the lake, under our tree."

She'd leaned over to kiss him. He'd responded to her quick kiss on the lips.

"See you then," he'd muttered.

Nina remembered it because when Clotilde had said the words "under our tree," it had reminded her of her grandfather's tree in the garden.

And still that question with no answer: why had her grandfather been run over on the day he should have delivered this letter? So, it never reached the person it was addressed to? Who was pulling the strings of their lives? Which God, or fate, indulged in all that? That dark farce?

What had become of Clotilde? Did Étienne have a six-year-old child somewhere? Why had Clotilde acted like that? How could one do such a thing to a man just to keep him? Étienne was forever saying that he'd protect himself. Repeating that his generation had grown up "with condom on cock." Nina hated it when he spoke like that.

"Étienne, you're gross!"

"It's the truth that's gross," he would say, after one too many.

It was true that they had lived with the specter of AIDS since birth. All the commercials, the posters instructed them not to go out without covering up.

"AIDS won't happen to me." The three of them were eleven when the public-awareness campaigns had started being endlessly broadcast on TV. If old people in ministries were discussing the sexuality of the young, it must be serious. In the end, Étienne was right, they were part of a generation that screwed with condoms.

Having read Clotilde's letter, Nina had instinctively thought of phoning Adrien, to ask his advice.

Unthinkable, after the way he'd treated her.

She still had a bitter taste at the back of her throat. A mix of feeling disillusioned, abandoned, and humiliated. Waves of grief kept breaking over her, her tears never stopped flowing. Nina had even contemplated letting herself die. When she was in the train bringing her back from Paris. Just lying on her bed and rejoining her grandfather, Joséphine, Joe Dassin, Paola, and her cats. Until she'd read this last letter addressed to Étienne.

An electric shock.

Three weeks, now, since she'd opened it. During which she'd read and reread it without knowing what to do with it.

She still didn't know.

Adrien hadn't phoned her back. Not the next day, or the day after that. Or the week following her Paris interlude. Her grandmother's suitcase had returned to its old ways, alongside the others in the dressing room.

When Emmanuel had got back from Australia, a fortnight after the premiere of *Des enfants en commun*, Adrien still hadn't phoned. Not even a word, a card, to thank her for coming.

Not even.

*

Adrien is meeting up with Étienne.

Who had sent him a text message:

Passing through Paris, we must meet.

Adrien had read it several times before writing:

O.K. Brasserie La Lorraine, Place des Ternes, 8:00 P.M.?

Yes.

Adrien wonders what that "we must" means. The last time he saw Étienne was on New Year's Eve, to see in the year 2000. On the afternoon of 31 December, he had joined Louise, Étienne, and around twenty of their friends, medics, trainee cops, and old school friends. Marie-Laure and Marc Beaulieu had gone off to party somewhere else, and Nina had let them down at the last moment. They'd had two great days. On the menu, smoked salmon on stale *biscottes* "because we forgot the sliced bread," pizza, a plate of oysters and tinned peas, alcohol, dancing, music—Larusso's "Tu m'oublieras" on repeat—TV series, video games, and siestas. Like teens whose parents have handed over the house. Adrien, despite being so far removed from this former existence, had agreed to join them at Louise's insistence, and had rather enjoyed it: no more having to pretend, or come up with witticisms to impress an elite gathering. Two days of hanging around in old slippers, eating any old thing at any old time.

When they all turned in, on the morning of 1 January, Adrien almost left for his mother's place, a reflex or habit when back in La Comelle, to get back to his own bed. Louise joined him in one of the guest rooms a few minutes later. On 2 January, she dropped him off at the station before driving back to Lyons. Since then, he's seen neither Étienne nor Louise all year, and it's already mid-October.

Adrien arrives first. He notices his reflection. He's always surprised by the image mirrors throw back at him. A fine navy overcoat, well cut. He isn't scared anymore to enter a place and calmly announce, in a steady voice:

"Good evening, I've booked a table in the name of Bobin, I'm early."

"Please follow me," says the hostess, a pretty redhead who looks a bit like Julia Roberts.

Adrien has booked a table in the smoking section for Étienne. It's the first time just the two of them are meeting at a restaurant. Adrien usually eats out in his neighborhood. He has his favorite haunts. But he thought Étienne would be more at home in this beautiful seafood brasserie.

"Would you care for a drink?"

"A bottle of Chateldon water please."

While waiting for Étienne, Adrien briefly wonders whether his friend has read *Blanc d'Espagne*, or any of his plays. *But has Étienne ever read a single book? Yes, inevitably, for his entrance exams. But not novels, let alone plays.*

And right then, because of this meeting with Étienne, like a ghastly flashback, Adrien sees Nina again, in the Théâtre des Abbesses, searching for him in the middle of the crowd.

He had received her messages after the performance. Had immediately deleted them, the way a husband deletes the words of a bothersome mistress. That evening, a dinner was planned with the director, Fabien Désérable, the actors, and a few select journalists. The theater had booked a private room at the Café de la Paix. Adrien told himself he'd phone Nina the following morning. When it would all be over. One couldn't just turn up like that without warning. He'd worked relentlessly to get to where he was. With this premiere, his future was at stake. For him, introducing his old life to his new one was out of the question. The following morning, racked with shame, he told himself he'd phone later in the day. And then the following week. Then he'd wait for her birthday. But by 2 August, his silence had become so deafening, he'd felt unable to pick up his phone and speak to her. He quickly banishes that thought, raises his hand and orders a glass of champagne.

He blocks out anything that reminds him of how Nina had looked at him, trying to find, once more, behind his mask of coldness and vanity, the young man she had loved, her almost brother.

Étienne pushes open the door. Adrien had forgotten about him, so busy was he brushing the dust of the past under the carpet.

Étienne is on time. Adrien observes him from a distance. Doesn't wave at him. Allows himself time to examine him, from head to toe. Leather bomber jacket, jeans, sneakers. The perfect getup of the cop. Each to their own, his is that of the successful writer. Dark, stylish clothes, the dress code for all occasions.

Étienne's beauty is breathtaking. He's lost weight. Shadows under the eyes, a gaunt face and two-day-old beard. His hair has got slightly darker. The eyes of the other diners all converge on his beautiful blue ones, and his sporty, youthful charm.

Étienne speaks to the Julia Roberts at the bar, and even she seems to blush and smile beatifically.

*I'll never make anyone blush like he does,* thinks Adrien.

The hostess points the table out to him, Étienne turns around, and, when he sees Adrien, smiles at him. Adrien stands up, they kiss on the cheek. Étienne's are cold and prickly. He's wearing a heady cologne, a mix of vetiver, spice, and citrus. Adrien hides its effect on him.

"Are you well?" Étienne asks, taking off his jacket and lighting a cigarette.

"Yes."

"Hey, things are going great guns for you. I even read an article on one of your plays last week."

"Oh really, which one?"

Étienne shrugs. No idea. Adrien smiles at him. Doesn't feel like talking about his work with him.

"How's your sister?"

"She's working like crazy. Studying medicine, it's insane."

"And you?"

"I still like what I'm doing. The searches, inquiries, the car, there's no routine, it's made for me. Apart from all the paperwork . . ."

A waiter asks Étienne what he would like to drink.

"Whiskey no ice please."

"And for me, another champagne," Adrien adds.

They both dive into the menu. Adrien orders sole and seasonal vegetables, Étienne a vol-au-vent with fries and a green salad.

"Would you like a few oysters, prawns, or shellfish to start? We could share a small platter?" Adrien suggests, bolstered by the two champagnes downed in one gulp.

"No thanks."

Adrien takes this refusal to mean that Étienne doesn't want to linger too long. He's adored seafood since he was a kid. In Saint-Raphaël, and on last New Year's Eve between two slices of Yule log, he'd eaten nothing but.

"Do you fancy some wine?"

"A glass of red with the vol-au-vent. I'll let you choose for me; you seem to be in the know now. Pretty classy here, isn't it."

Adrien doesn't react. He detects a hint of irony in Étienne's voice.

"Does it bring in loads of dough, writing your stuff?"

"It depends. What's really changed my life, well, things, is my novel."

Étienne frowns while buttering some warm bread.

"What novel?"

"*Blanc d'Espagne*."

Étienne pauses for a moment. Stares at his friend. Adrien can see in his eyes that he's already heard something about the book. That the title rings a vague bell. But what's he heard? When? Where? He's searching, seemingly to no avail.

Adrien doesn't know why he's just admitted to being the author of this now famous book. He never even told his mother. Until now, only Fabien Désérable and Louise were in on the secret.

Adrien smiles as he thinks that, tomorrow, Étienne will have forgotten everything, even the title of the novel. And since it's signed Sasha Laurent, he won't be able to make the connection. Or he'll give him a ring: "What's the title again of the book that made you a packet?" Or then he'll question Louise, who will feign surprise. Who would never betray him.

Adrien asks the question he's been dying to ask ever since Étienne set foot in the brasserie:

"What are you doing in Paris?"

"I came to see you," he says, between two gulps of whiskey.

"To see me?"

"Yup. I'm going to need you."

"Need me?"

"Clotilde . . ."

"A new development?"

"Not yet. But there will be."

". . ."

"They're just realizing that the witness statement doesn't hold up."

"What witness statement?"

"The old woman's, who supposedly saw Clotilde at the station. On the evening she disappeared. And so I'm going to take the flak."

"How can I help you?"

"You must say that you were with me. First at the lake, then at Nina's."

"I was at Nina's with Nina. You joined me later that evening."

"I know."

"You're asking me to lie?"

"Yes."

"Will Nina lie?" Adrien asks.

"Nina is in a permanent daze since she's been married. And she'll say whatever I ask her to say. Anyhow, she must be left out of all this. That evening she was at Damamme's."

"No, not quite," Adrien insists. "That evening she was with me at her place, well, her grandfather's place. It was just the two of us. She left before you arrived."

Adrien can see that Étienne is put out, like when, as a child, he didn't get his own way. It's imperceptible to anyone who doesn't know him. A shadow in his eyes, a line across his forehead, the slightest quiver of the top lip.

*Looks like the three signs of disharmony are in harmony*, thinks Adrien.

"But no one needs to know that," Étienne objects, annoyed. "Nina must be left out of this business."

Adrien says nothing more. He removes the skin of his sole without crossing his cutlery.

"I saw Nina yesterday," Étienne says, suddenly.

Adrien looks up.

"Where?"

"Lyons. She did a day trip to bring me a letter."

"What letter?"

"An old letter from Clotilde . . . Did you know she used to go through her grandfather's delivery bag when we were kids?"

"Yes. But I don't see the connection."

"Well I do see it. I'm a cop."

"Are you going to arrest her?" Adrien asks, sarcastically.

"She told me about the Théâtre des Abbesses . . . How you didn't appreciate her being there."

Adrien blushes and remains silent.

"Know what I like best about my job as a cop?"

"The handcuffs?"

Étienne smiles strangely at Adrien's answer.

"Playacting when questioning people. I've become a superb actor. Belmondo himself had better watch out. Nasty, nice, two-faced, stupid, gullible. I've got the whole range. I could just sail into drama school."

"I'll hire you to act in one of my plays then."

Étienne sniggers.

"Adrien, you *really* think I haven't read *Blanc d'Espagne*? You *really* think my sister didn't tell me? When your book came out, I sensed something was up. And as for worming stuff out of people, I'm the best. So, when it comes to my sister . . ."

Adrien's blood freezes. He's reeling. As if he were naked, exhibited on a platform at a fun fair for all to see, and Étienne was whipping up a crowd: "Roll up, ladies and gentlemen, come and see who Adrien Bobin really is! Come and admire this fairground spectacle!"

"You've read it?" mutters Adrien.

"Yes," says Étienne, biting into his bread without taking his eyes off him.

Adrien takes it in.

"Did you tell Nina?"

"Yes. I came out with it yesterday when she told me how you'd treated her. I was trying to find mitigating circumstances for you, so I mentioned your book to her."

"What did she say?" whispers Adrien.

"That your novel had been on her bedside table for a long time, but she hadn't read it."

Adrien is horrified. It's a nightmare. He'd like to wake up at home, stretched out on his sofa. For someone to tell him that all this isn't true, just a figment of his vivid imagination.

"I know what you think. That I don't read. That I'm a dimwit. But you're wrong, buddy. I've read everything you've written. And that article, last week, it was about your latest play, *Des enfants en commun*."

Étienne goes quiet and seems to relish finishing his food. Adrien, feeling sick and in a cold sweat, watches him. *When he's the one in deep shit over the Clotilde affair, I'm the one who feels guilty.*

"What do you want, Étienne?" he finally asks.

"You to be my alibi. You to say that you were with me at the Lac de la Forêt on 17 August 1994, that you waited for Clotilde with me, and that we went back to Nina's together."

"And no one's going to find it strange that I never mentioned it before?"

"No, because before, no one thought I could be linked in any way to her disappearance."

"Did you harm Clotilde?"

"No. I swear to you."

"Why would I believe you?"

Étienne pauses for a while, then blurts out:

"I think I saw something that evening."

"What thing?"

"A car sinking into the lake."

Étienne raises his hand and orders another glass of wine.

"What car?" Adrien persists.

"No idea. A red car. I think it was red. But it has nothing to do with your testimony. All you're going to say is that you were with me."

"And if I refuse?"

"Why would you refuse?"

"False evidence."

"Only half. I'd remind you that we did end that night together. O.K., we were young and everyone groped each other, but . . ."

Adrien stands up, Étienne stops him with his hand. A firm hand. Almost twice the size of his, crushing his fingers. His clear eyes aren't clear anymore. They are veiled by two grey shadows. His top lip isn't quivering anymore. Étienne has gone from annoyance to determination.

"Sit down. I haven't finished. Do you remember when Nina used to say to me, 'You never know'?"

"What are you talking about?" Adrien asks, pouring with sweat and on the verge of tears.

"I used to copy your tests, your homework, and she'd insist that I understand what I was writing. She'd say, 'You never know.' And I'd ask her, 'You never know what?' And she'd invariably reply, 'You never know.' She was right, Nina. I owe her everything. Because, thanks to her, that's what I ended up doing. Understanding what I cribbed from you."

". . ."

Étienne lets go of Adrien's hand and mellows.

"We can go home together if you like."

". . ."

"I imagine you have a very fine apartment. As fine as the gear you're wearing."

". . ."

"We could play doctors and nurses if you felt like it."

Adrien flings the water in his glass at his face, and instantly regrets it.

"I love your sister."

"That's a shame," Étienne says, wiping his face with his napkin. "I wouldn't have forced myself, I'd have shown my gratitude. D'you want a dessert?"

Adrien is incapable of saying a word. Doing a thing.

"I did something stupid," Étienne continues. "A month ago, I met the witness. and I ruined everything. I raised doubts in the minds of the La Comelle cops. It can't be Clotilde that the old woman saw on the station platform."

"Why?" Adrien managed to ask.

"Because she confused her with another girl."

"How do you know? Had you already killed her?"

Étienne shrugs, as if to say, "Stop being ridiculous."

"It's to do with sewing. A sewing machine."

"You've lost it, Étienne. You're talking nonsense."

"I'll stop you right there. Of the two of us, it's you who's unhinged, not me."

Adrien absorbs that. He'd like to smash Étienne's face in. Right here, right now. He feels waves of hatred engulfing him. The Py plague resurfacing.

"I never want to see you again."

"Same here. But before writing me off, be nice and go tell the cops that we were together for that entire evening."

"Or else?"

"Or else I'll tell the whole world who Sasha Laurent is. And believe me, I won't hold back on the details. My sister's going to love knowing that it's actually me you're writing about in *Blanc d'Espagne*."

Adrien gets up and grabs him by the collar. Julia Roberts runs over to them. The few clients sitting at neighboring tables fall silent. Étienne shoves Adrien roughly away, and he loses his balance, falling back onto the chair.

"My treat," says Étienne.

". . ."

"I insist."

He heads for the cash register and pulls out his credit card. Adrien remains slumped on his chair, like a rag doll.

# 68

*26 December 2017*

Marie-Castille reads Étienne's letter several times.

Usually, it's she who questions, roughs people up. It's she who passes judgment on the pathetic lives of the accused. Their misdemeanors, mistakes, madness. This morning, it's life that's putting her in custody, judging her harshly.

She places it back on the bed.

She always knew he'd be passing through, that he wouldn't stay. Not due to illness, but to another woman. She always thought she'd have to fight off rivals.

Étienne, *sick* . . . How did he leave? Their car is parked outside. Probably in Nina's. Or then they're in a train. Maybe even a plane. No doubt already far away.

Marie-Castille's whole body is shaking. She realizes that she'll never see her husband again. That he's just orchestrated his departure. Instinctively, she tries phoning him. Voicemail.

How could Étienne have had so little faith in her? Leaving with just a letter of apology and explanation placed on the pillow.

*It's like that guy who wants me to get treatment*
*And who abandons his dog in August in Spain . . .*

This morning, she feels as alone as a dog thrown onto the edge of the vacation freeway. Scrap. A dead battery.

"We're as old as the 9/11 attacks," they would say, when asked how long they had known each other.

They had met in front of a TV set. Belonging to a dealer and his two accomplices, just arrested by their respective squads.

Étienne belonged to Lyon 6th arrondissement station, and she'd just been posted to the 1st.

Since the individuals in question were armed and dangerous, reinforcement had been requested.

Just as she was leaving the apartment, Marie-Castille had pushed open a door and discovered a man sitting in an armchair in front of a TV. He was alone. He was wearing the POLICE armband. He didn't see her coming into the room, as if hypnotized by the apocalyptic images.

When he had sensed her near him, he just said:

"I've cut the sound, it's unbearable."

Without even knowing who he was talking to.

And right then, when part of the world was crashing down, when there was nothing but smoke on the TV screen, Marie-Castille fell in love.

Fell in love on the day thousands of innocent people were dying and would die, over there, here and elsewhere. It should have been prohibited by some kind of internal law. An ethical code of the heart. It was too bad an omen. Bad karma, bad start, bad encounter. When she should have been closed to any kind of intrusion, her love was well and truly born on the day of the 9/11 attacks.

Her mobile phone was vibrating nonstop in the pocket of her jeans, she should have answered it immediately, but she settled down beside him, on the arm of his chair. Almost against him. His shoulder was brushing against her arm. She breathed him in. Stopped herself from touching his hair. She watched him watching the images on TV. While the owner of the premises was in a cell, waiting to be questioned.

"What's your name?" she finally managed to say.

"Lieutenant Beaulieu."

"Captain Blanc."

"Are you the new one?" he asked her, with no awkwardness, despite the fact he was addressing a superior.

"Yes."

He was speaking to her without taking his eyes from the screen, like a teenager engrossed in a video game with a catastrophic scenario.

They emerged at around 9:00 P.M., still gripped with horror, only to discover, in a daze, that the streets were deserted.

It felt more like a Sunday in January. Everyone had gone home. The bars, usually very busy, were closed or empty.

They had a quick sandwich and a beer, eyes glued to the screen of a TV brought out specially and placed across the bistro's bar. Every channel kept broadcasting the image of the two planes plowing into the glass walls. Four clients were watching, without flinching, the symbol of the United States's economic might collapsing like a house of cards.

Marie-Castille asked where Étienne lived.

"A small apartment not that far from here. And you?"

"I'm renting a furnished one while waiting for you."

She blushed.

"Sorry, while waiting . . . I'm too scared to go home alone tonight. Can I stay with you?"

Étienne didn't believe her. This woman was scared of nothing. You could tell by the way she'd eyed him up on the sly. He liked her. A bit boyish but, paradoxically, very feminine. Rings on her fingers, no wedding one, less than ten years older than him. Blond hair cut short, a sensual mouth, green eyes. A look both impish and curious.

"I warn you, my place is a mess. All my cleaning ladies end up on tranquillizers."

She followed him in like a little dog follows its master. Looked around Étienne's bachelor pad. No trace of a woman or children.

Single.

She immediately told herself that she must capture him before another woman saw to it. Cleverly, on tiptoe.

Marie-Castille slips on a gown and goes into Louise's room without knocking. Louise is awake, drinking tea, sitting on the window ledge and staring out at the street, as though waiting for her sister-in-law.

"Has he been sick for a long time?"

"Yes, no doubt too long."

"Did you know Étienne was leaving?"

"Yes."

"Is that why you had a row yesterday?"

"Yes. I wanted him to talk to you about it."

Marie-Castille clenches her fists while swallowing her tears. Rivers of despair and bitterness engulf her.

"And Valentin, does he know?"

"Yes. He fell on an exchange of text messages between Étienne and me."

Marie-Castille takes in this new blow. It's as if everyone had conspired behind her back. As if she were the enemy or the weak link. The one who can't handle the truth.

"Is there really nothing more that can be done?"

Louise crumples. She seems exhausted. Like a valiant soldier who has lost his weapons on the battlefield.

"There's always something that can be done, tried. I'm not saying he would have been cured, but treatment could have prolonged his life."

"Does he know that?"

"I told him a hundred times. He didn't want to hear a word of it."

"He decided to die," Marie-Castille says, as if to herself. "Do you know where they are?"

"No idea."

"I think I deserve the truth."

"I don't know where they are. I swear to you. The three of them left during the night."

*

We went to pick up Étienne at 4 A.M. He was waiting for us at the end of his street, with a traveling bag hanging from his shoulder.

"Whose car is this?" he asked Nina.

"My lover's."

"You have a lover?"

"Yes."

"A normal guy?"

"Yes."

I didn't bat an eyelid. Sitting at the back, I pinched myself to keep my mouth shut. Not to reveal what I'd been told on the subject of Grimaldi.

We drove to Mâcon. Étienne was biting his nails while studying a map of Europe, spread out on his knees. He was torn between Italy and Greece.

"How long can you stay with me?" he asked us.

"Since I started working at the shelter, I haven't taken much time off."

"How long does that mean?"

"As long as necessary."

Étienne turned round to me.

"And you?"

"Same."

"In any case, we're not going to drag it out forever."

He didn't allow his voice to crack. Immediately got a grip on himself.

"I wanted to say to you . . . thank you. And . . . sorry, too. To you both."

Nina and I remained silent while Étienne traced possible routes on the map. In the end, he rummaged in his pocket and took out a euro.

"Heads we go to Greece, tails to Italy."

He tossed the coin, slapped it onto the back of his hand.

"Tails."

# 69

*October 2000*

It had been a long time since she'd come out with the whole truth to Emmanuel. He was waiting for her, uptight, on the sofa in the sitting room. It was eight thirty. The cook had made a shepherd's pie and a green salad. Since Nina didn't eat meat, she would scrape the potato off the top, but it disgusted her all the same. The employee rolled her eyes when Nina discussed meal plans, no longer attempting to disguise her disapproval—to her, being vegetarian was a fad. Just a whim. She'd sometimes grumble: "If she was really hungry, she'd eat her steak, it's obvious she never went through the war."

*You never went through the war either*, Nina would think, but pretended not to have heard her.

"I spent the day in Lyon," she begins. "I had to give something to Étienne."

"What thing?" Emmanuel asked, annoyed.

"An old thing I came across."

"And your mobile? I tried to call you all day."

"I forgot to charge it."

She sees him clenching his fists. Emmanuel could never stand Étienne. Too good looking and too arrogant, no doubt, and with a calm strength that irritates Emmanuel. And Nina still loves Étienne, whereas for her husband, all she feels is repulsion. Despite forcing herself to smile all the time, her body can't lie anymore.

For how long, now, has she been pretending to come? How many women just pretend, period, when profound boredom or disgust overcomes them?

*How many*, she thinks when faking an orgasm, *how many are doing the same as me at this very moment*?

Nina can't *bear* her husband anymore. Even his smell makes her nauseous. She's learnt to breathe only through her mouth when he's around.

She spoke about it to Étienne, once she'd given Clotilde's letter to him: "I'm going to leave Emmanuel."

Upon waking that morning, her decision was made. *I must go and see Étienne. I owe him the truth, and Clotilde's letter.*

First she'd tried, a few times, to get hold of him on his mobile. On her third attempt, Étienne finally answered.

There was a coldness in his voice when he realized it was her. He was still sulking over New Year's. Nina didn't let him get a word in. She said it all in one breath, with urgency:

"I have something for you. I'm bringing it to you today. I'm leaving La Comelle in five minutes. I'll explain everything to you when I see you in Lyon."

There was a long silence.

"I'll be expecting you. Fetch me at the police station. We'll go and have a bite together."

Étienne gave her the address.

"You'll see, it's easy to find, there's a car park right beside it. What d'you drive again?"

Still that obsession with cars.

"A black Polo."

"O.K."

Now, Nina detected a joy in Étienne's voice at seeing her again. Even when sulking, he couldn't pretend. When she arrived, she found him anxious. Before even kissing her hello, he said: "What have you got to give me? A school photo?"

"Hello, first of all."

"Sorry, hi."

Unlike Adrien, Étienne hadn't changed. Still rough and ready. He hadn't gilded his true nature. She felt happy to see him again, and hugged him for a long time, murmuring:

"What happened to us? Why did we lose each other?"

"I'd remind you that it's *you* who dropped us like trash at New Year."

"If you had any sense, you'd have understood that I had no choice."

"One always has a choice. Divorce isn't for dogs."

He led her outside. "Come, let's get out of here." They walked along a few roads, side by side. She'd slipped her arm through his. When they were children, he hated her doing that. "Don't, people will think we're going together." Adrien, on the other hand, was only too happy.

"There's a good Lyonnais restaurant near here, but it's all calf's head and lamb's brain, not sure it's quite your thing," Étienne said ironically.

They both laughed at the same time. Finally, at ten past twelve, they entered a brasserie.

"I mustn't stay too long or Emmanuel will kill me," Nina said, glancing at the clock on the wall.

"If he ever lays a finger on you, just call me."

"He's far too clever. If he ever lays a finger on me, it'll be too late."

They settled down in a corner, and Étienne ordered a bottle of wine.

"A cop's allowed to drink?" Nina asked, amazed.

"I'm on vacation."

"Since when?"

"Since you phoned me this morning."

"I'm so pleased to see you. As you can see, I'm ugly."

"You're not ugly, you've got a big ass. Like married women have. You all end up producing fat."

Nina spoke of her daily existence with Emmanuel, without pathos or self-pity. She could see the end of the tunnel, was emerging from a sort of darkness after allowing herself to be trapped in an infernal spiral. Her every act and deed scrutinized by her husband and the cook. No privacy, even in her own bedroom, that woman just barged in without knocking to put linen in the cupboard. Emmanuel's obsession with having a child. The contraception she was secretly using. No money of her own. Even the car didn't belong to her, and anything she bought was passed off as expenses, analyzed, item by item, by the Damamme accountant.

"There was I thinking you were rolling in it."

"Everyone thinks that."

"And your grandfather's house?"

"Emmanuel sold it ages ago."

Yes, she was going to leave, find a job, she was only twenty-four, even if she looked thirty. She'd lose weight, regain control of her body and mind.

She would probably need him to protect her, because she was alone in the world. Because she didn't dare talk about it with Marie-Laure, and taking refuge in Étienne's parents' house seemed like the worst idea. It was the first place Emmanuel would go. She must leave La Comelle, run away. Otherwise her husband would find her. In January, he was away for three weeks on a business trip, she'd take the chance to disappear. Waiting another three months would be no big deal after the years of hell she was dragging behind her. And she had to admit to Étienne that, to survive, she drank every day, so her gilded prison became bearable.

"Fucking hell," Étienne swore, "it's straight out of Zola. Do you remember, at school? We had to read *L'Assommoir*, *Nana*, *Germinal* . . . It did my head in so much that you read them out loud to me, in your room. Well, what you're telling me sounds just like that."

They laughed a lot. Laughed at themselves, at their bad choices. Then Nina turned to the subject of Adrien. She told Étienne how she had left for Paris, to take refuge with him. That he'd ignored her so thoroughly that evening, at the theater, she'd almost died of sadness.

Étienne tried to defend Adrien:

"Maybe it's because of what he said in his book."

"What book?" Nina asked.

"*Blanc d'Espagne.*"

"What are you on about?"

"I thought you knew."

"Knew what?"

"Adrien wrote that book."

Nina took this in. *Blanc d'Espagne.* The novel she'd hidden the envelopes in. How was it possible that she hadn't known? That Adrien hadn't told her?

"You must be mistaken. It's Sasha something or other who wrote it."

"That's a pseudonym."

"Did Louise tell you?"

"Yes."

"And what's it about?"

"You'll see."

Second betrayal. Nina felt tears welling up, swallowed them. She swept aside the image of Adrien snubbing her at the theater. She'd thought he was her friend, her brother, the one who'd sworn eternal love to her. He was nothing at all anymore.

Nina deliberately changed the topic, asked Étienne some questions—without forgetting what she'd just discovered for all that. How was Louise? Life in Lyon? Was he in love?

"Do I look like the sort to be in love? Seriously, Nina. Not really my thing. But, to be honest, I made the right choice. When I have three spare days, I go skiing or surfing, I have the sea and the mountains nearby. My colleagues are nice, the cold coffees, the fear in the belly, the post-interrogation exhaustion, nabbing the same little thug every month because an idiot judge decided to give him one last chance. Arriving at crime scenes. And then, until you arrest the culprit, you stop at nothing. You don't even sleep anymore."

"Have you ever looked into Clotilde's case?"

Étienne turned to jelly.

"Yup. Why do you ask?"

"When I was little, I used to steal letters from my grandfather's bag. That's why he gave me a hiding at school, d'you remember?"

"Of course I remember. I've always wondered why."

"When he died, I felt guilty. I thought it was my fault. That God was punishing me."

"You know I don't believe in that kind of bullshit."

"I know. It's a long story. But last year, I got back the bag Granddad was carrying the day he died. It was full of mail, which he hadn't been able to deliver. No one knew about it. I read every letter, resealed the envelopes and delivered them all to their rightful mailboxes. Five years later."

"Are you serious?"

Nina looked down without responding. Étienne was trained to

detect other people's lies, it was part of his everyday life, he realized that she wasn't making any of this up. And why invent such a thing? He thought back to that day, in the schoolyard, when Pierre Beau had turned up like a madman to hit his granddaughter. Étienne had been deeply affected by it. He hadn't been able to protect her. Like today. Like with that other moron who was supposed to be her husband. He was able to defend people whose identity he didn't even know, but not his childhood friend.

"In that mail," Nina continued, "there was a letter for you. A letter from Clotilde."

Étienne wondered whether he was dreaming, wondered how this conversation could have turned into a nightmare. Nina observed his distress, saw the panic in his eyes.

"When does it date back to, this letter?"

"To 10 August 1994. Two days before Granddad's accident."

Étienne turned pale as a corpse.

"But you surely didn't open it."

"I did. On the night Adrien betrayed me, I was livid with him, with you. And for days I wondered whether I should give it to you, or not."

She took out the letter and handed it to Étienne, who read it several times in silence. Occasionally looking daggers at Nina. He was mortified, cut to the quick. Apart from Adrien, he'd never admitted to anyone that Clotilde was pregnant.

He slipped the letter into the inside pocket of his bomber jacket.

"You know I could arrest you for theft? You know it's punishable by prison, what you did?"

"I'm really sorry. I won't do it again, I—"

Nina didn't get to finish her sentence. He stood up, threw some banknotes onto the table—"For the check and your gas"—and left the brasserie like a madman. Nina called out his name, but he didn't turn around.

Alone in the world. She returned to her car, in the car park, and went back "home."

From the sofa, Emmanuel is still watching her.

"Shall we sit down to eat? All this nonsense has made me ravenous. Is Étienne well?"

"Yes," Nina replies, as she scrapes off the top of the shepherd's pie. "I've contacted an organization to adopt a child."

"Excuse me?"

"You heard very well."

Usually, by this time, Nina has already downed a few glasses of wine to be able to tolerate Emmanuel. But right now, she's sober. She realizes that she's never sober anymore when he's around, and it's been that way for years.

"You went and did that without speaking to me first? To me? The mother?"

As she says these two words, "the mother," Nina spits her mashed potato out onto the table, before her husband's horrified eyes. She can't believe it herself. Grabs some paper towel, cleans it up, ashamed.

And then, out of nowhere, has an irrepressible fit of the giggles.

"Have you been drinking?" Emmanuel asks her.

This question just makes her laugh even more. She tries to say, "For once, no," but can't get it out. She's bent double on her chair. How long is it since she last laughed like this? She remembers Étienne's words: "Your life's straight out of Zola." Impossible to shake off this phrase, this damning observation.

She sees herself, in her ludicrously expensive kitchen, near the husband everyone dreams of, scraping off her mash because she hates meat and the cook serves it on purpose, and learning that he's applied to adopt without mentioning it to her.

"Your life's straight out of Zola."

What should make her cry rivers has the opposite effect. Her nervous laughter bounces off the elegantly wallpapered walls of the house she inhabits without living in it.

Nathalie appears, looking perplexed, and for Nina, seeing her there is like an electric shock.

*What the hell is she still doing here?*

Nina is struggling to breathe. She's on the verge of an asthma attack. She sits up straight in her chair and isn't laughing at all anymore. She starts screaming at the cook:

"Get out of my house! I don't want to see you anymore! Get lost! Get out!"

Dumbfounded, the cook looks at Emmanuel to know what she should do.

"Stop eyeing my husband like that! It's me who's talking to you, leave immediately!"

Nathalie grabs her coat in the hall and slams the door without a backward glance.

"What's got into you?" Emmanuel asks his wife.

"What's got into me is that I don't want a child. I never will want one. I've misled you on that. What's got into me is wondering how the hell you've begun adoption proceedings without talking to me about it!"

She starts to shake. She's just let out words that she's held back for too long. They came out wrong, like everything one lets escape in the grip of anger. Emmanuel's reaction is as unexpected as her fit of laughter: he smiles at her with contempt. Sure of himself, he eyes her disdainfully, as if she were less than nothing, or an object that had started to talk, something untoward. So she throws herself at him, to hit him. First the shoulders, then the arms, the back, the stomach, she hits out, blinded by rage, hits again, kicks him. He smiles at her even more. When she realizes what she's actually doing, she starts screaming. He just watches her, still smiling. A smile that's scary, terrifying even.

"My poor girl. I picked you up from the street. Believe me, we're going to have this child. And you're going to care for it day and night. But right now, you're going to do me the pleasure of phoning Nathalie to apologize to her."

"Never."

"Think very carefully. I have the power to get you locked up on the spot. Asylums are full of people like you, alone, depressive, idle and alcoholic. I have plenty of influence. One phone call to our respected family doctor and you'll spend the rest of your life in a straitjacket. You won't even know your own name anymore. Never forget, never, that you are my wife. It's me who signs any proceedings—adoption proceedings, divorce proceedings, sectioning proceedings. And don't count on your so-called friends to come and get you, your cop and your fag couldn't give a damn about you. They'll let you sink into your shit without lifting a finger. The only person on this earth who loves you, and you can always count on, is me. But you're far too dumb to understand that."

Emmanuel goes up to the bedroom, leaving Nina to clear away the remains of supper.

*

A few minutes later, Nina herself goes upstairs. She gets undressed, has a shower, thinks again of Étienne's anger and the word "adoption" uttered by her husband. She smears cream over her body without even looking at it, lies obediently against Emmanuel. Like a dog that's just chewed up its master's slipper and seeks his forgiveness.

She lets it be done to her, groans to order.

Once her husband has fallen asleep on top of her, she waits about twenty minutes, staring into the darkness. Then pushes him gently aside, gets up without a sound, switches on her bedside lamp, and seizes *Blanc d'Espagne*, which is right there, and has been close at hand since the day of the football World Cup final of 1998. She remembers clearly the moment she'd placed it in her caddy. It was a happy moment. Since that morning she'd been repeating to herself: *This evening, Étienne and Adrien are coming to the house for supper.* And they had arrived together. And she'd stifled her tears so Emmanuel didn't see that she loved her two friends much more than him. The Lyon gang was there, too. They had all screamed with joy in front of the TV.

It had been the last lovely day of her life so far. After that, the three lost touch. She had pined for them. That was exactly the word.

Lulls, silences, and absences had crept in between the phone calls and reunions. And she had put the novel away, on the shelf, its back-cover blurb having left her pensive, hesitant. It's as if she had passed Adrien by without realizing it. There are some books we miss, like some encounters, we pass by stories and people that could have changed everything. Due to a misunderstanding, a book's front cover or bland blurb, a preconception. Thank goodness that life, occasionally, perseveres.

*

*"Appearance is nothing. It's deep in the heart that the wound lies."*
*Euripides*

*I'm three years old. We stand in circles holding hands in the school yard. There are balls, hoops on the ground, outlines of games drawn in chalk. Sometimes, we're separated. Girls with girls, boys with boys. I stay in the group of girls. They have so much fun. I devour their laughter as I do the marshmallows we get after our nap.*

*I'm six years old, I tell someone for the first time. I open up. He's an old man I don't know and don't particularly trust. I remember he smells bad, has bushy gray eyebrows and a waxen complexion.*

*I have a really sore throat, I'm shivering with fever on the examination table. My mother is in the waiting room. It's the first time I'm on my own with a grown-up.*

*"A doctor is there to make you better when you have a pain somewhere."*

*I have a pain somewhere.*

*For the past five minutes, I've been deciphering, with fascination, two posters pinned, side by side, on a wall next to a height rule. Illustrations of a prepubescent boy and girl. All the parts of their bodies, including their organs, are named. They are identical. Digestive tract, liver, kidneys, stomach, arms, legs, feet, heart. It's only in the groin area that the names are different. I have difficulty reading "genital organs" and haven't the faintest idea what it means.*

*Captivated by these images, I let my secret out of its cage for the first time:*

*"I am a girl."*

*"What?" the man asks, concentrating on his blood-pressure gauge.*

*"I am a girl."*

*The doctor frowns and his messy eyebrows give him a kindly appearance. But suddenly, he looks like a clown, the sort that terrifies me but makes other children laugh at circuses and birthday parties. He doesn't reply to me, just lays one of his rough hands on my forehead.*

*"You're burning hot, you're delirious, young man."*

*"What does 'delirious' mean?"*

*"You're crazy. It's a symptom of fever."*

*I'd like to swallow back my secret, but my next words come out of their own accord. When you release something that's been captive too long, it makes the most of its freedom.*

*"But my willy, at what age will it go away?"*

*He stops frowning and grabs me by the shoulders. He's hurting me. Gone is the waxen complexion as all the blood in his body seems to rush up to his head. He's the color of a bottle of wine.*

*"Who's been telling you such claptrap?"*

*I understand then that I must wall up the girl inside me. Shut her away in silence. So I lie. I pretend. I start laughing, my throat burns.*

*"No one. I heard a friend say that at school."*

*"We don't talk about such things, do you hear me? Your parents, they made you the way you are: a little boy. You were born a boy, you'll die a boy. Don't imagine anything different. Such ideas are depraved."*

*"What does 'depraved' mean?"*

*"It means the devil . . . And we must chase the devil from our mind . . . From our head, if you prefer. To do that we must work hard at school and do plenty of sport."*

*He returns to his seat behind his desk, prescribes me antibiotics, aspirin, a spray, and throat pastilles.*

*I hand him the check my mother had already made out, and say to him:*

*"Goodbye, sir."*

*I don't talk about it anymore.*

*

Emmanuel wakes up. He tells Nina that he has an early start tomorrow and the light is stopping him from sleeping. Nina closes *Blanc d'Espagne* and switches off the lamp.

She's trembling.

Switches off. Yes, she has switched off the light like those people who don't want to see anything anymore. Closing the shutters, double-locking the doors.

She hugs the book to her chest, breathes it in. She seeks Adrien's smell between its pages, the perfume of his skin, or that of the *other*. How could she have never smelt her, made her out?

For eight years they had eaten together, walked, slept, showered, done their homework, swum, sung together. They'd phoned each other every evening before going to sleep. "What are you doing, what are you watching, what are you thinking about? . . . Good night, love you, see you tomorrow."

"*Why do you never say anything, Adrien*?"

"*I'm fine, I listen to you*."

For eight years they were never apart. From elementary to high school. They made plans for the future, mingled their blood, cried, laughed, trembled. Held each other's hand, anticipating or sensing what the other was doing, going through, even when they weren't together.

Having discovered what Adrien was hiding, stifling, Nina feels as if she doesn't know herself. Who is she? Who is this naïve and blind person?

She feels like one of those women whose husbands are war criminals or serial killers and they know nothing about it.

Because they are in denial.

Because their subconscious doesn't want to know.

They wake up one fine morning, like all the twits in the fairy tales—Snow White, Sleeping Beauty, Little Red Riding Hood—and are flabbergasted when confronted with reality.

At first, Nina saw this novel as an accusation. A finger pointed at her: "You didn't understand a thing. You didn't love the girl in me."

But after rereading *Blanc d'Espagne*, Nina had finally understood that the boy and the girl were the same person. The person she had been so close to for eight years.

That person's love of reading, writing, movies, blue, rum babas, *galettes des rois*, Louise, boiled eggs, and summer, and loathing of snakes, clowns, and carnivals all amounted to just one single human being.

# 70

*26 December 2017*

I'm stretched out on the back seat, gazing at the clouds through the glass in the car's roof. Raindrops splash down, seem to cling on for a few seconds, then get swept away by the wind.

Étienne is sitting in the front seat.

Nina is driving slowly, which seems to annoy him, but he says nothing. Nina and I know that he's champing at the bit. He glances furtively and despairingly at the speedometer, which reads 110km/hour, when we're on a freeway.

We'd agreed as we left La Comelle: Nina and I would take turns at the wheel, and we'd stop every two hundred kilometers for coffee and a snack.

"I agreed to you coming with me on the condition that I got to drive . . . I'm not disabled. I have cancer."

Nina gave in.

"Two hundred kilometers each. We'll split the journey into three."

We'd also agreed on our choice of radio station, it would be RTL2, a mix of pop rock that chimed, more or less, with us all.

*On the earth every night*
*With you*
*On your arm everywhere*
*I know all about your life*
*God said to me*
*My friend, come, I know all about you . . .*

It's on the final notes of "Karma Girls," an Indochine song, that I decide to speak.

"I went back to see Py."

My statement, tossed inside the car, is like a bomb going off. Nina brakes suddenly, I'm thrown off balance and grab hold of her headrest. She cuts across to the right, between two trucks.

Étienne, who's looking a bit pasty to me, switches off the radio while staring at me in the rearview mirror.

"When?" Nina asks me, without taking her eyes off the road.

"When I moved back to La Comelle."

"Where?"

"At his house."

"How old is he now?"

"Dunno. Around eighty . . ."

"What made you do that?" Étienne asks.

"I needed to look him in the eye with my grown-up eyes. I rang his doorbell, he opened it. He immediately recognized me. He wasn't able to utter a single word. We just looked at each other, for one, maybe two minutes, in silence, and I thrust *Blanc d'Espagne* into his hands. He took it, mutely. I got back in my car. When I looked out as I was driving off, he'd closed his door."

"What was it like, seeing him again?"

"I sealed something up. For good. It soothed me."

"D'you think he read it?"

"No idea. But today, I couldn't care less."

*

*I'm ten years old. I'm in fifth grade. I've just met my two childhood friends, a boy and a girl. Thanks to them, I don't feel alone anymore. I like them.*

*To others, I'm a skinny kid of no interest. None of them know that I have a girl hidden inside me.*

*A family secret kept all to myself.*

*Like someone's bastard daughter. The one hidden in the cellar, who must only go through secret doors and corridors, so she's never seen by anyone.*

*The illegitimate daughter repudiated by religions and public records.*

*Who won't be baptized or receive any last rites. In short, the daughter who will never be named.*

*No, no one will ever call me by my real name.*

*Later, I will find myself, will name myself.*

*I make lists. Élodie, Anna, Marianne, Lisa, Angèle, Virginie.*

*I'm ten years old. My two friends and I are inseparable. Sometimes I'd like to tell them who I am, that girl is on the tip of my tongue, but I don't dare. I swallow her back down.*

*I'm scared they'll reject me, judge me.*

*With us, it's three or nothing. It's three or loneliness.*

*If they cast me aside, I'd be back in exile. The one I lived in before I moved. When others, silently, found me strange.*

*Shyness is a bag into which everything gets shoved, to avoid asking oneself any questions.*

*In class, I spend hours gazing at my friend's back, her shoulders, her long dark hair, her nape when she has braids or sweeps her hair up with her hand.*

*One morning, she's wearing a new barrette. When she sits at her desk and bends down to get something out of her school bag, I spot a little red butterfly with white polka dots, just above her ear. I'm so disturbed by this bit of fabric attached to her hair that I forget everything else. Even where I am. I don't listen to the teacher anymore. Between my fingers, my pen is lifeless. I'm bewitched by this barrette. Now and then, my friend readjusts it. I feel like taking it from her. Snatching it out of her hands.*

*Just before recess, the butterfly falls onto the classroom's tiled floor, soundlessly. As if the ground were covered in powder snow. The teacher leans over my blank sheet of paper, pinches my arm—"Are you dreaming, or what?"—and keeps me back in class to copy out the lesson written on the blackboard.*

*We call him "Sir," this bespectacled monster squeezed into a gray scrim smock. He's a snake that slithers stealthily between the desks.*

*Everyone leaves the classroom except me and the teacher's usual whipping boy. I'm in the second row, he's in the front one.*

*The snake had left the room with my classmates, whom I can hear laughing and chatting loudly outside. I imagine their games. And return to the silence of the empty classroom.*

*For a few seconds, I watch the dunce leaning over his sheet of paper, his tongue darting around his bottom lip, as if lost. Writing demands considerable effort from him.*

*As for me, I glance up, read a sentence, copy it down with ease onto a double page with big squares. But I keep looking at the butterfly on the floor, almost at my feet.*

*I turn around several times, no one there.*

*The other pupil is ignoring me. When you're forever being persecuted, you forget the other people around you. I know what I'm talking about. Before meeting my two friends, others viewed me as one might a spelling mistake.*

*I finally bend down and pick up the barrette. It's a small clip glued to a piece of satin, one of those tiny slides that grip just a few strands. I open it carefully and place it above my ear. Just to know, to understand how it feels to wear it, to sense it in my hair.*

*I finger the barrette for a long time, as if it were a tiny creature that had just settled on me. I'm disappointed, I realize that being a girl is about more than just wearing a hair accessory. I discover that it's more complex, deeper, no doubt. I'm lost in thought when my eyes meet two hate-filled ones: the snake has silently come back into the classroom. I tear off the butterfly, the satin comes unstuck, taking several hairs with it.*

*The teacher says nothing. I'm ashamed and proud at the same time. I don't look down, I stare right at him. I'm covered in hatred, his hatred. His small eyes spit their contempt straight into mine.*

*At that moment, the teacher changes whipping boys.*

*From now on, it will be me.*

## 71

*October 2000*

Nina is in the fruit-and-vegetable aisle of her local supermarket when someone places a hand on her shoulder. She's just weighing some red apples, Emmanuel's favorites, crunchy, sweet, and organic. When that hand touches her, Nina is no longer wondering how she's going to escape, to put a stop to this life. She can see no way out. And yet it is urgent, she must leave before her husband shows up with a brat under his arm. He's capable of anything, even stealing one. And the more time passes, the more she realizes that his obsession isn't so much about having an heir as about locking her down. She'll never be able to leave again if there's a baby. Nina's head is spinning, she feels nauseous. She's been drinking already. Three glasses of wine at lunch. As a rule, she starts later. But today she's decided to drink until she drops. Because yesterday was the final straw.

Lyon, Étienne storming out of the brasserie because she'd read Clotilde's letter, the cook she'd fired, the adoption, *Blanc d'Espagne . . .*

In her cart, hidden under slabs of vacuum-packed smoked salmon, two bottles of whiskey. Combined with tranquilizers, enough to end up in an alcohol-induced coma one never comes out of.

She's going to join her grandfather in the Beau burial plot.

The look on Adrien's and Étienne's faces, beside her tomb. How they will both regret having abandoned her.

Or won't. For them, Nina belongs to the past. After all, it's the friends you make *afterwards* that count, not those you shared middle and high school with.

Since yesterday, she has been trying to contact Étienne, in vain. He hangs up on her every time.

Adrien? How could she ever forgive him? And how forgive herself? Retracing her path seems unfeasible to her.

*A person who ceases to be a friend never was one.*
*And the more my heart dwells on it, the more it hurts.*

Yes, she must leave.

And there's also the threat of being committed. Nina is sinking deeper every day and it won't be hard to get her locked up. Emmanuel is capable of that, too. He'd always prefer her in a drugged-up straitjacket than free.

Whatever happens, whatever she does, she won't escape from him.

Everything's muddled up in her head.

Even Adrien's words, which she discovered last night, in *Blanc d'Espagne*. She returned to the novel this morning. Finished it in one sitting, crying every last tear inside her. Until Emmanuel phoned her, to know whether she'd called Nathalie to apologize.

"No."

"Call her immediately."

"O.K."

The cook answered the phone at the first ring.

"Hello Nathalie, it's Nina. Please forgive me for yesterday evening. It's the medications I'm taking to have a baby. I think they go to my head . . . I'm really sorry. Please come back to the house. We need you."

Nina could hear the jubilation merely in the woman's breathing. She said nothing to her in reply.

So, yes, when that hand is placed on Nina's shoulder, while she's been searching for the price of Pink Lady apples for a good five minutes, she's in a desperate state. Which is why the woman has to try several times to get her attention.

"Is it you?"

Nina jumps.

"Sorry?"

"Yes, I'm sure it's you . . . I recognize you."

The woman is radiant. Around sixty, she's wearing black leggings that do nothing for her and a sporty top with a garish diamond pattern. She must weigh about eighty kilos. Her badly dyed hair is gathered up in a pink scrunchy. Her teeth are white and straight. Her complexion darkish. Her green eyes sparkle. Nina has never seen her before. In her cart there's a pyramid of tins of dog and cat food.

"How did you find that letter?"

Nina feels the ground give way under her feet.

"I don't understand," she stammers.

"It's you who came to the animal shelter, three weeks ago."

Of course it's her. She'd slipped that anonymous letter, reporting the appalling conditions of a dog living on a balcony, into the mailbox. It was the day before she went to Paris. Nina feels unwell. The woman notices and grabs her arm.

"Come with me, we'll have a coffee."

It's said in a tone that is gentle but firm. Permitting no dissent. Nina has no choice but to go with the stranger. She doesn't understand. But she's sure there was no one at the shelter that evening. They go to the cash registers, pay for their goods in turn, and the stranger sees the two bottles of whiskey on the conveyor belt, but doesn't blink. Merely smiles. A kind smile. With no agenda or falseness.

The two women find themselves face to face in the mall's small cafeteria, right beside a gaming machine labeled: OUT OF ORDER.

"So, tell me, how did you find that letter?"

Nina doesn't reply. She must go. Get home before her husband. Get rid of this fat woman.

"How old are you?" she continues.

"Twenty-four."

"You have your life ahead of you."

". . ."

"My name's Éliane, but everyone calls me Lili."

"Like in Pierre Perret's song."

Nina doesn't know why she said that, mentioned that singer.

"Well, no, Lili isn't Pierre Perret, it's Philippe Chatel. Pierre Perret's song is '*Mon p'tit loup*': '*T'en fais pas, mon p'tit loup, c'est la vie, ne pleure pas . . .*'"

Nina starts to cry. She hides her face behind her hands. One morning, she had caught her grandfather murmuring the words of this song when it was on the radio. When, apart from his wife's records, he never listened to music. It had surprised her. She hadn't dared ask him why he knew the song by heart.

Lili summons the waiter.

"Bring us two pick-me-ups with our coffees."

"What kind?" he asks.

"The kind that clears the mind."

Lili contemplates Nina.

"Things don't seem too great, my dear."

"How did you know it was me . . . with the letter?"

"I saw you. I live opposite the shelter. Whenever I hear the sound of a car in the evening, it's bound to be leaving a box of kittens for us outside the gates . . . I got up to have a look. I didn't expect to see a young woman slipping a letter into the box at eleven at night. And if you knew the effect the letter had on me . . . you can't imagine . . . Because that letter, it's me who wrote it."

*That's weird*, thinks Nina, *sending yourself a letter, it's like sending yourself flowers*. She remains silent, doesn't react. Sips her coffee and pear brandy while staring at the woman without seeing her. Lili is disturbed by the despair of the young woman in front of her.

"Where do you live?" she asks her, the way one questions a small child who is lost and looking for his or her parents.

"At my husband's home."

"Your husband's home isn't your home?"

". . ."

"Would you like something to eat?"

"No, thank you. I must get back."

"To your husband's home?"

"Yes."

"I'm pleased to have found you."

". . ."

"I wanted to thank you . . . because—"

"I must go home . . ."

"Hold on a second . . . Is your husband waiting for you?"

Nina seems to think before answering.

"No. He gets home at around seven."

"It's barely two o'clock, you have time."

"But I have things to do, before."

Lili senses that she must play for time. Like when she's trying to save a pregnant stray cat circling a trap. This young woman seems to be on the edge of some kind of precipice. And anyhow, Lili has never believed that things happen by chance.

"Six years ago, when I sent that letter to the shelter, two months went by without anyone doing a thing, until the owner went on vacation, leaving the dog on its own. I went to the shelter, had an argument with the woman in charge at the time. I asked her what she was waiting for to do something. She knew nothing about this case of cruelty, hadn't received my letter. I didn't believe her. I'll spare you the details, but it was tricky getting hold of the dog. After that I grew to like the woman in charge, became a volunteer, starting with walking, cleaning, a little accounting and admin, and when she retired, she asked me to replace her. Basically, if she'd received my letter, I'd never have gone to the shelter. Before, I avoided such places like the plague. Those who care about the suffering of animals are wary of shelters. They think they won't be able to bear it. They're wrong. The first time you blub, and then it passes."

"Well I wouldn't be able to bear it," Nina whispers.

"Of course you would. What's unbearable is doing nothing."

Nina gets the feeling that Lili isn't talking about animals anymore, but about her.

"Why do you live over there?" Nina asks.

"Whether there, or elsewhere . . . And you? Why do you live at your husband's?"

"Because I have nowhere else to go . . . It's complicated. He would find me. I'm alone."

Nina angrily slaps three tears off her cheek.

"Please forgive me."

"It's more those one never cries in front of whom one should ask for forgiveness. It touches me, your blubbing in front of me. It's fear that stops one. Paralyzes one. But believe me, one can always leave. What's your name?"

"Nina."

*

It's all unofficial, but the rumor is already circulating: next May, the play, *Des enfants en commun*, should make a clean sweep of the Molière awards. New discovery, best actors and actresses in leading and supporting roles, direction, and, most importantly, as Adrien keeps repeating to himself, the promise of a nomination in the Molière's own category of best playwright.

*The Molière for best playwright. The Molière for best playwright. The Molière for best playwright.*

The ceremony is in seven months' time. Mustn't think about it. And nothing's official.

But Adrien does think about it.

The imagined event wakes him up every night.

*What if I'm called up onto the stage?* 'The Molière is awarded to Adrien Bobin!' *And what if it's Isabelle Adjani who hands it to me? Oh, no, it's bound to be this year's winner. Who was it again? Dario Fo, for his* Mort accidentelle d'un anarchiste.

He imagines the thunderous applause. Himself standing up, looking like he can't quite believe it, leaving a pause for the surprise, a few seconds, smiling to himself, just to show he realizes it's his name that's just been called, closing his eyes, shaking his head, kissing the actors, the director . . . "No, really, I wasn't expecting it." Expressing that by his whole demeanor. Walking slowly, shaking hands on the way, going up on stage, accepting his Molière and thanking everyone. He thinks of his speech. The truth is, he's already written it and knows it off by heart.

He's interrupted by the phone ringing. He was getting ready to go out. Dinner at the home of the director Danièle Thompson. He'd loved her movie, *La Bûche*, watched it three times. He'd spread the word and she'd invited him through a mutual friend.

Annoyed, he answers the phone.

"Where is she?" screams Emmanuel Damamme.

"Excuse me?"

"Where is Nina? Don't take the piss, I want to know where she is!"

"Has something happened?"

"Yes, what's happened is that she hasn't come home since yesterday . . . Is she with you?"

If someone had just punched him in the stomach, Adrien couldn't have felt worse. Suddenly, he realizes that Nina has left home without phoning him, without asking him for help. And for a very good reason. Nina is somewhere without him, and he may never see her again.

He silences this pain immediately. Knows how to control it. Like he knows how to control all the rest: what he is. Since writing *Blanc d'Espagne*, his heart is frozen. He has padlocked his identity and thrown away the key.

All he allows to be seen of himself is the taciturn, gifted young man. A little prince who is sure to receive the Molière for best playwright.

He has neither lover nor mistress. He flirts, seduces, lets himself be seduced, but always finds an excuse to return home alone.

Except when he meets up with Louise.

"I've not heard from her," he finally replies to Damamme. "The last time I saw Nina was a month ago, in Paris."

"She was in Paris a month ago?" Emmanuel repeats, in a chilling voice.

Then, menacingly:

"Be careful, Adrien, if you're lying, I'll know it."

Adrien lets out an involuntary snigger. He feels only contempt for Emmanuel Damamme, and no one scares him.

"I ended things with Nina a long time ago."

Adrien hangs up. The phone rings again, insistently. He doesn't answer it, just slips on a coat and pops into the bathroom to check how he's looking before leaving. His taxi awaits.

*

*Nina had read Clotilde's letter . . .* Étienne hates her for that. It's like a rape. He will never forgive her. Her opening strangers' letters since she was a kid, he couldn't care less. But not his.

How disappointing.

He doesn't know what pains him most. Nina finding out that Clotilde was pregnant by him, or her trashing his privacy. A mix of anger and shame that won't leave him.

That letter, what a shock. Unthinkable that he only gets to receive it now. Those words seeming to come back from the beyond.

He tries to remember Clotilde on the morning of Pierre Beau's funeral. How did she look at him, thinking he knew, when in fact he knew nothing about this pregnancy? Impossible to recall. There were so many people inside the church and out on the forecourt. And all that grief he didn't know what to do with. Nina's limp hand in his. At that time, he probably avoided meeting Clotilde's gaze; he's sure, at any rate, that he didn't seek it.

As far as he remembers, Clotilde wasn't at the cemetery. She had joined them later, at his house.

For the millionth time, Étienne thinks of Clotilde's pain. How she must have suffered because of him and his fecklessness. He still can't believe she went all the way to Saint-Raphael without saying a word. Only to see him in the arms of another girl.

At work, how often had he been confronted with men who assaulted their wives? Who, in the interrogation room, sought a kind of solidarity with him, or complicity, along the lines of: "Between men, we understand each other, sometimes a good beating does them no harm." Or: "I didn't realize my strength, she kept on at me until I cracked, you know how it is."

Étienne feels the utmost contempt for them. But isn't he worse?

Cops are required to be upright, but is a man in uniform irreproachable? Who could believe such nonsense? Are they a little less disgusting than the others just because they've taken the oath? Wasn't day-to-day life far more complex than that? How often had Étienne, or one of his colleagues, hoped for the death of certain bastards? Don't they mentally condemn some individuals before they've even been to court?

The image of the car sinking into the lake will haunt him forever.

And, to the end of his days, he'll wonder whether Clotilde was inside. Sometimes he feels like returning to the lake and diving in, alone, at night, to know.

But he's far too scared. An irrational fear.

He'd seen a movie with Harrison Ford and Michelle Pfeiffer that had terrified him. The story of a mistress killed by the husband, lying at the bottom of a lake near the couple's home. The ghost of the dead woman, trapped in a car, her blond hair dancing in the water, coming back to haunt them.

Étienne hadn't been able to watch the movie to the end.

His phone rings, it's his mother.

"Are you O.K.?"

"I'm O.K."

Marie-Laure's voice is her grim-day one. The one for bad news.

"Nina has gone."

In shock, Étienne has to sit down. His legs won't carry him anymore. For the word "gone" he hears "dead." Just as he does for the word "disappeared," which he associates with Clotilde.

Never, since that evening in August 1994, has he thought that she could be alive somewhere, raising their child alone.

Sensing her son's distress, Marie-Laure continues:

"She sent a farewell letter to Emmanuel."

*A farewell letter. Nina is dead . . .* He should have answered her calls. What she'd told him the day before yesterday should have alerted him to her vulnerability. Her life had become unbearable with that half-wit.

Étienne is shaking. Unable to cry, to say a word, he just sits there with the phone pressed to his ear.

"Emmanuel came to ours this morning. He's looking everywhere for her. He seemed demented."

". . ."

"The farewell letter, she wrote three copies of it. One for Emmanuel, the other two for you and Adrien."

*

Emmanuel is going around in circles at home.

She'd vanished, taking nothing with her. All her belongings were still there when he got home from work. And Nathalie was back in the kitchen. At his request, Nina had phoned the employee that morning to apologize.

An aroma of stew, delicious. Oh, what a lovely evening they were going to have. He was hungry, he was in a good mood. He'd stopped at the jewelry store to buy a solitaire diamond for his little wife.

The previous day they'd had a fight, she'd told him that she didn't want to be a mother, but they'd patched things up on the pillow. Nina loved fucking, that was his hold on her. Every evening, she asked for more.

Nina? No, Nathalie hadn't seen her. When she started her shift at two, her car wasn't there.

Where could she be all this time?

The day before, she'd gone to Lyon and back. Today, she should have kept her nose clean.

The hours went by. And her mobile was still on voicemail.

At 10 o'clock, Emmanuel thought of an accident. He went to the cops to report his wife's disappearance but was told it was far too soon.

"Do you know who I am?"

"Yes, Monsieur Damamme."

"I keep part of La Comelle alive, so kindly launch an inquiry immediately."

All that night and the following day, the town and surrounding countryside was combed in search of the black Polo, but no trace of it was found.

Then Emmanuel received a letter from Nina, posted in La Comelle the previous day.

He piled up all her clothes, books, cassettes, videos, down to her toothbrush, in the garden to burn the lot. A giant bonfire, minus the fun.

She had kept the credit card. But no withdrawal had yet been made. On the day she'd disappeared, she'd bought some things at the local supermarket, and then nothing more. What had she bought? Emmanuel had asked the cashiers, they could no longer remember.

Her phone was permanently switched off. Impossible to get hold of her.

Had she known for a long time that she was going to leave? For whom? For what reason?

Emmanuel ended up contacting two private detectives: "I'll pay whatever it costs, but you will find her for me. Alive, if possible."

He asked them to station themselves outside the homes of Étienne Beaulieu and Adrien Bobin. But not a sign of Nina, either in Lyons or Paris.

For the moment.

Because the bird's wings aren't large. She's bound to reappear or make a blunder. Come back with her tail between her legs, begging him. And then he'll really sort her out.

He rereads Nina's letter for the thousandth time, already knowing what it says:

> "Adrien, Emmanuel, Étienne,
>
> I'm leaving. It is my decision, I am leaving of my own accord, nobody is forcing me to.
>
> My two friends, you brought sunshine into my childhood. It was wonderful thanks to you.
>
> I was so happy to meet you. And just as unhappy to lose you.
>
> But that's how life goes, apparently.
>
> My husband, I wish you all the happiness in the world with someone good. Which I no longer am, neither for you, nor for me, nor for anyone.
>
> With love to all three of you.
>
> Nina"

At first, Emmanuel thought it was a trick. She was addressing the three of them together to put the other two beyond suspicion. But he had looked into it, and Marie-Laure confirmed to him that Étienne had also received this handwritten letter. Posted at the same place, Rue de la Liberté, on the same day as his letter, before the 4:30 P.M. collection.

He tried to contact Adrien, to know if he'd received the same letter, but he didn't reply.

Emmanuel went to the police station to report a desertion of the marital home and submit an application for divorce by proxy to an attorney: when one person in a married couple disappears of their own accord and without leaving an address, that's the usual procedure. Because there was no question of her getting a cent from the Damamme family. She could ask for a compensatory settlement, he'd been warned, despite their having married with a separation-of-property agreement. If that did happen, he would do everything in his power to ensure she never got anything.

The only thing that can make Emmanuel feel any better is imagining Nina starving to death somewhere.

Worst of all is picturing her in the arms of another man. Never would Emmanuel have believed it possible to hurt so much. A deadly pain. Since she left, he's been on antidepressants. His doctor gave him no choice. He looked a sorry sight. He wasn't eating anymore and only slept in bursts. When he woke up, he reached around for her, in their bed. Now he sleeps on the sofa in the sitting room.

He told his parents, made his mother promise to phone him immediately if Nina contacted her. Gé promised. Thinking all the while that if Nina asked her for help, she wouldn't tell a soul.

# 72

*26 December 2017*

Louise is sitting near Marie-Laure in the kitchen. They are both drinking tea, lost in their thoughts.

Valentin and Marie-Castille have just left for Lyons. Paul-Émile, Pauline, and their two children for Geneva.

And so the house has emptied. Just like every year, they all leave to resume their lives again. But this time, Étienne will never return. On top of the post-festivities melancholy and sadness, there's the terror and horror of the unthinkable.

As usual when anything concerning Étienne is going on, Marc is in the garage, where he's set up a workshop for himself. He must have found something to repair.

*If only he could repair our son*, thinks Marie-Laure.

She's furious with herself, for seeing nothing, understanding nothing. She thought Étienne was just tired. And at this time of year, everyone looks pasty. We don't go out much, eat too much, drink too much, do a lot of things too much. Wrapped up in the joy of having her children and grandchildren under her roof, she hadn't paid any special attention to her boy.

*My boy*, she thinks.

Our children remain small in our hearts as mothers. They take up all the space, and yet they remain small. We think of them as just being born. She can see herself again, kissing him yesterday evening, almost distractedly. "Good night, darling, see you tomorrow." Étienne knew he wouldn't see his mother again, but the hug hadn't lasted that long. Two pecks on the cheek and off to bed.

"And you really don't know where they've gone?" Marie-Laure asks Louise again.

"No. I know Étienne longed for light and water. I imagine they're heading to the sea."

"Maybe they're in Saint-Raphaël. All three of them."

"Maybe."

"Étienne loves Saint-Raphaël . . . Do you think he'll phone us? Get in touch with us?"

"Yes, probably."

Louise lays her hand on her mother's hand.

"And you're sure he won't suffer?"

"Yes, I'm sure, Mom."

Marie-Laure watches her tears drop into her cup. Then looks at her daughter, so beautiful, so alone. Is she happy? Brilliant studies, demanding work, and a solitude she seems to have chosen. Or "owned," as they say these days.

"Why did you never marry Adrien?"

Louise can't believe her mother is bringing this subject up. They've never broached it before. The relationship she's had with Adrien since she was nine, everyone seems to know about it but no one talks to her about it. Admittedly, at the merest allusion to it, she clams up.

"Is it because of you brother?" Marie-Laure persists.

"No, it's me who never wanted to."

"Why?"

"Because of her."

"Her, who?"

"Adrien."

*

*The first time I see her is in the yard of my new school. Instinctively, I know I'm not coming across her by chance. I sense that she's planted herself on my path, like a flower, on purpose.*

*She is holding a stone. Has just left a game of hopscotch, is out of breath, it's September, it's warm, a few strands of blond hair stick to her face. In fact, they're not blond but almost white. Bleached by the summer. That's what she is, a little schoolgirl with silver hair. Her cheeks go pink when her eyes turn to me.*

*She is called Louise. Is nine years old. But she's no child.*

*She's the sister of my new friend.*

*They look alike. Same blue eyes. But their eyes say opposite things. He's all about adventure, she about accomplishment.*

*No one has ever looked at me like Louise does. And I know as I write these words that no one ever will. That look is lucky, my luck.*

*She sees who I am, despite my appearance.*

*Her brother introduces her to us: "My sister."*

*She says: "Hi." I give my name and, already, she doesn't believe me. There's doubt in the way she stares at me, stumbles on my first name. I sense it. It's immediate. There's no hanging back when it comes to us.*

*Louise is silk. It's precious. Louise is also porcelain and metal. An alliance of daintiness and strength. She is indestructible, gentle and delicate.*

*I see her again, often, in the schoolyard, on Wednesdays at her brother's, during the vacations. She's part of my life. She often holds herself like those decorative dolls placed on sofas. Louise is also lace. And silent when engrossed in a book. She likes learning. It's in her nature. Most of all she likes discovering.*

*When she senses my presence in a room, she looks up and smiles at me, without lowering her eyes, and her cheeks always turn pink, then she returns to her book but her smile doesn't fade. I seem to be Louise's sun, and when someone sees you as a star, you seek to get closer to them. To stay right beside them.*

*But there's a wall between her and me that, for years, prevents me from feeling her warmth:* we three. *My two friends and I never go anywhere without each other. Our focus is entirely on our trio. We have no other perspectives. We form a bloc.*

*In summer we all go on vacation together. Louise, lying under her parasol, often smiles at me. Her beauty disconcerts me. But I'm busy hiding the girl that I am from the others. In my gait, my gestures, my voice, I "act the boy." My voice will probably break soon.*

*That particular year, I'm fourteen and can think of only one thing: my Adam's apple. When is it going to appear? It still isn't prominent, but how long will that last? I shave despite being smooth-cheeked, so that my beard finally grows. When, paradoxically, I dread it like a kind of death. Why am I so ashamed of the girl I am? Why am I obsessed with hiding her? In hindsight, I think that, without my two childhood friends, she would have pushed me to suicide.*

*And that without Louise, I would never have known amorous love.*

*During that month of vacation, one morning, when I wake up, Louise is sitting in a rocking chair in my bedroom. A beautiful apparition.*

*The house is empty. Everyone has left for the day, except us two. It's the first time we're alone together.*

*"Do you love me?"*

*That's the first question I ask her. Because I can't believe that someone could love me.*

*"Yes, since I was very little."*

*"You still are very little."*

*"No, I'm thirteen. Have you ever kissed a girl?"*

*"On the mouth?"*

*"Yes."*

*"No. I've never kissed anyone."*

*"Have you ever made love?"*

*Her question staggers me.*

*"Well, no, seeing as I've never kissed anyone."*

*"Do you want us to try?" she asks me.*

*"To make love?"*

*"No, to kiss."*

*I say yes. She slips under the sheet, close to me but not touching me.*

*"Can you feel how hard it's beating?" she asks, taking my hand and placing it on her breast.*

*I feel the beats of her heart. Her body is hot.*

*She gets undressed, with no false modesty. She offers me her nudity but I grab hold of her dress. I can't take hold of* her, *embrace* her. *We're too young, awkward, terrified. A certain distance must be maintained. I cast my eyes over her body. She is beautiful. I envy her. I allow myself to touch her with just my fingertips, to take her in. She closes her eyes, trembles, groans, arches her back. I still have her dress in my other hand, I grip it very tight, I cling to the fabric as to a rope, so I don't fall into the void caused by fear.*

*After a long while, as if at the end of a lengthy corridor, Louise says: "I often caress myself while thinking of you, want to see how?"*

*This again staggers me. How can a young girl be so daring and, above all, trust me?*

*I say yes.*

*She lies on her front, turns her head toward me, and gazes at me. I've never had the privilege of seeing someone so beautiful.*

*I lay her dress against me. As if laying her on top of me. Then I, too, get undressed, take Louise's hand, we never take our eyes off each other. She reconciles me, reconciles us. I no longer know. I feel so good, I don't know who I am.*

*Louise is in love, but who does she love? And who of me desires her?*

*I'm overwhelmed by my attractions because I don't have any. My "sexual preferences," as they're called, don't reveal themselves. Since I'm a girl, I should like boys. It's in the order of things. But nothing is as it should be. No love story is. And Louise moves me, deeply. She turns me on.*

*We doze off together.*

*When I wake up, she's holding my penis in her hand.*

*I push her hand away: "No, don't touch me there, it isn't mine."*

*

Last night, as we were about to leave, Louise said to me:

"Since you're accompanying my brother to his death, I'd like you to make the most of it and kill off Adrien, once and for all."

"That's too violent, what you're saying to me, Louise."

"It's life that's violent, and that's not my fault."

Louise became a surgeon because of me. She always corrects me when I say that: "Not because of, but thanks to you."

She's trying to convince me to go through a hormonal and then surgical transition.

To become what I am.

I've been dodging it for years.

Dodging, procrastinating, rejecting, leaving for later, lying, compromising. I know all the subterfuges by heart.

I'm scared.

I know that I'm a woman, it's just my roommate. Louise has never wanted to live with me *because of him*. She says I'm lying to everyone, starting with myself. That she'll like me just the same with "tits and a pussy." When she uses this language, I immediately close up again. I can't bear vulgarity. She knows it, uses such words to provoke me. She has tried everything.

I've never gotten along with my body, but I've never managed to take the plunge. This transition that, today, is available to "people like me," that's spoken of in the media, that seems almost easy, I reject it. Louise has tried to take my hand countless times and accompany me on that path, but in vain.

She's introduced me to psychologists, endocrinologists, but I don't manage to speak, to decide. She gets annoyed when I mention the doctor I saw at six years old, or Py. "That's all in the past. You need to move forward."

She can get so annoyed she ends up in tears. Once, worn out, she hit me, telling me she hated Adrien, that she wanted to see him die. She called me a coward.

Our biggest argument. We didn't see each other again for eleven months.

*

It's eight o'clock. The three of us, Nina, Étienne, and me, are all sitting cross-legged, side by side, on a large bed. We've just found a *pensione* in Savona, close to Genoa in the north of Italy. We're exhausted.

We've placed a tray in front of us, and are spreading fresh pesto onto bread and savoring some white wine, all bought in haste. Étienne insisted that we sleep in the same room. The owner of the place didn't bat an eyelid when the three of us moved in. We immediately agreed: me in the single bed and them in the double.

Nina has already taken a shower. She's wearing some ghastly pink-cotton pajamas. Étienne made fun of her when she emerged from the bathroom: "Wow, that getup sucks, like some gift in *Santa Claus Is a Stinker*." We laughed like before. Like when we were kids, and slept at Pierre Beau's, and loved each other.

Nina told Étienne that she'd lived alone for so long that she slept with nothing on, but she wasn't going to wander around stark naked in front of us.

"Tomorrow we'll buy you some clothes . . . and some prepaid phone cards," says Étienne. "I must call Valentin."

"And I my lover," adds Nina.

"If you've got a lover, burn those pajamas. And what's he got that others don't, eh?"

"He's normal and kind. And handsome to boot."

"What do you know about him?"

I couldn't stop myself from saying something. Étienne and Nina both look at me, questioningly.

"Why? Do you have something to tell us?"

"No."

Nina changes tone.

"You're lying. I know when you're lying. Well, now I know. I read *Blanc d'Espagne.*"

". . ."

"Do you have something to say about Romain?" she persists.

"Ask him why he left Marnes-la-Coquette."

She looks confused, not understanding what I'm getting at.

"How do you know that he worked in Marnes?"

"I just know."

"Basically, you're a monster. You want to sabotage my life, is that it?"

"Not at all."

"No? Well why are you hinting at something?"

"Because I've been told things."

"What things?"

"That he was sacked from that school because, apparently, he had problems with a female pupil. And that the whole affair was, more or less, hushed up."

"Who told you that?"

"A colleague at the paper."

"He just told you that, out of the blue? 'Oh, by the way, the new headmaster at the Perec school, he had problems with a female pupil . . .'"

"No, I asked some questions about him."

Things are getting heated. I can see in her eyes that she's angry with me. That nothing will ever be as it was before.

"Why did you ask questions about him?"

"Because I saw you going into his house."

"You followed me?"

"Yes."

"Psychopath!"

Étienne tries to calm things down.

"Whoa, cool it, comrades."

"Phone him," I say. "That way he can tell you what happened . . . And you'll have peace of mind."

"Peace of mind? What's that got to do with you? Which of us has peace of mind?"

"Done?" Étienne asks, to smooth things. "Can we watch a TV series?"

"Which one?" asks Nina.

"*Breaking Bad*?" suggests Étienne.

"Never seen it."

"Me neither," I say.

"You're both hopeless . . . It's brilliant."

Étienne disappears into the bathroom after swallowing a ton of pills. Nina and I gaze at each other for a long while. How we had loved each other.

"I've never apologized to you for Paris, the Théâtre des Abbesses . . . My self-important and intolerable behavior. I'm still ashamed today."

"And me, I've never apologized to you for not having seen the real you. Me who thought I knew you . . . me who thought of you as my brother, when you were a silent sister. A girl you'd been gagging."

"Well now that's done."

"Yup."

Nina gets up, slips on her sneakers without tying the laces, puts Étienne's parka around her shoulders and leaves the room.

"I'll be back," she tells me.

*

She goes downstairs and finds the owners of the *pensione* in front of their TV. They get a start when they suddenly see her behind their sofa. She joins her hands to apologize for disturbing them, holds out a twenty-euro note to the man, miming that she'd like to use the phone. Étienne had asked them not to switch on their mobile phones or withdraw any cash because he was paranoid that his police captain of a wife would track them. "For no reason whatsoever. Or I'll be dead," he said, with a smirk.

"Keep your money," the woman says, in perfect French, to Nina.

They both point toward the landline phone in a small room adjoining the kitchen. Nina dials Romain's number, while the man, remote control in hand, turns up the volume of the TV.

Romain answers immediately. What will she say to him? Will she talk to him about this sordid story just to have "peace of mind"? She feels good with Romain. Doesn't feel like knowing more about it. When, for once, someone had made her swoon a little, when she no longer believed it possible.

"It's me," she told him.

"How are you? Where are you?"

"In Italy . . ."

# 73

*December 2000*

Two months not knowing where she's hiding. Emmanuel has searched everywhere for Nina. Even in ditches, under beds, and inside all the cupboards of the house.

Enough to drive you crazy.

He had walked up and down all the surrounding country roads. By day and by night. He had knocked on random doors, showing her photo, no one had seen her. He had asked the *Journal de Saône-et-Loire* to publish, for a fee, her portrait with the caption DISAPPEARED.

Which is a lie. Nina had written that letter to Adrien, Étienne, and Emmanuel to indicate clearly to them that her departure was her choice.

The two detectives hired by Emmanuel are now certain that she didn't find refuge with one of her two friends.

Around Adrien Bobin, not a trace of Nina. Neither in his apartment, nor within his circle. Same scenario in Lyon: Étienne lives alone and sees few people outside work, apart from some colleagues and one-night stands.

What was left? Who could have harbored her?

As a last resort, Emmanuel considered Nina's mother. He doesn't know much about her. Just that she's called Marion Beau and was born on 3 July 1958 in La Comelle. "I should be able to find her with that . . . With her social-security number," one of his investigators told him a few weeks ago.

And it's with a racing heart that Emmanuel discovers the address he's just received in a text message:

*I've found her: Marion Beau, 3 But au Vilain, 14640 Auberville.*

Emmanuel immediately checks on a road map, Nina's mother lives in Normandy. The village is close to Deauville. He knows the resort well, having vacationed there several times.

There's another text from the detective:

*Would you like me to go there?*

*No.*

Emmanuel leaves his office and informs his colleagues that he's going to be absent.

"But . . . the phone conference and your meetings on—"

"Sort it out yourselves," he snaps, to shut them up.

He has never disrespected them before. Since Nina's departure, he's losing it. He's unrecognizable. Forever staring into space. Behind his back, they're whispering that "it's not going to end well."

He covers five hundred kilometers without a thought, at full speed. He stops twice to fill up the car, have a coffee and a candy bar.

When he arrives at the address he's been given, he finds around twenty terraced prefab houses. It's almost midnight. The road is empty. A few lamps cast a pale light on the wet asphalt and the social housing. An icy drizzle falls on his windshield. *Here, even in summer it must feel cold*, he thinks.

At No. 3, behind a nylon curtain, a large TV emits flashes of light. Marion doesn't seem to be sleeping. Unless it's Nina. Will she open the door to him in a few minutes' time? If it is her, he'll hit her. He can feel it in his fists. He won't let her speak, let alone apologize. He'll drag her by her hair. She can scream, can struggle as much as she likes, once he's got hold of her, he'll never let go of her again.

He leaves his car, unsteadily. His legs can barely carry him, probably the exhaustion of these past weeks. He's still taking antidepressants, otherwise he'd do himself in pronto. But before taking his own life, he has just one obsession: taking Nina with him. He won't be leaving on his own.

He pushes open a weather-beaten gate—it looks unlikely that its latch ever worked. Rings the doorbell. Waits for a minute. A bleary-eyed woman opens the door, must have been asleep.

"Are you Marion?"

She doesn't answer. Wonders what this dish, this classy young man, with his new shoes, is doing on her tatty doormat at midnight. She glances at the sports car parked under a streetlamp, just behind him. Is it a candid-camera stunt? Patrick Sabatier and his team would sometimes turn up at the house of people like her to give them a surprise and prizes. What was that TV show called again? But that stuff's not on anymore.

"Is Nina here?" the dishy young man finally asks.

The question takes her so much by surprise that Marion Beau can barely get out:

"Which Nina?"

"Your daughter."

No one has ever spoken to Marion of *her* in those terms: "your daughter."

When she left her to her old man, the little one had just been born. Whenever she thinks of her, that's what she calls her to keep her at a distance. Never "my daughter." Because nothing is hers, nothing belongs to her.

She'd been dispossessed a long time ago.

When asked if she has children, she says no. That way she doesn't get asked any more questions. In any case, she interests no one, never gets asked any questions.

"Can I come in?"

Marion hesitates for a few seconds. Then remembers that it's clean inside, that she'd done the housework that afternoon, the mopping and dusting. So she nods him in. "Come on then."

The smell of stale cigarette smoke.

The TV takes up all of the main room. Fake-leather sofa right in front of it, low table, and in the background, a kitchen dominated by a microwave.

"I'm your daughter's husband," Emmanuel says, wearily, as he sits on the sofa.

He closes his eyes. He can tell, just from glancing around the room, that Nina has never set foot here. He feels tired. Would like to stop moving forever. He's just clocked up more than five hundred kilometers for nothing. Just to find himself facing this woman, who Nina had told him was thin and common. She isn't thin anymore, but more bloated, bulging, and seems despondent, in her drab slippers.

"Oh, I didn't know she'd got married," Marion says, pulling on a cardigan. "Would you like something to drink?"

"If you join me."

Marion smiles. Opens the door of a kitchen cupboard containing started bottles of Teisseire syrup, pastis, port, and Suze liqueur.

"Otherwise, I've got some muscatel in the fridge."

"Let's go with the muscatel."

She serves Emmanuel and then pours herself a little of the sweet, fortified wine.

"Where are you from?"

"La Comelle."

"Ah . . . It's strange to hear of that place."

"Do you live alone?"

"Yes. And why are you looking for her?"

She can't bring herself to say either "Nina," or "my daughter."

"Because she's disappeared."

"Disappeared in what way?"

"She just left, out of the blue."

"Why did she leave?"

"That's what I'm trying to understand."

Emmanuel downs his wine in one.

"Wouldn't mind a drop more of your muscatel."

Marion pours him some straightaway, and some for herself while she's at it. An almost-full glass. She hasn't suggested it to him, but Emmanuel has decided that he's going to sleep on this sofa. He has neither the will, nor the strength to find a hotel around here at this hour. Marion, sitting on a chair in front of him, observes him as she sips. That's good, he's found the weak spot, like mother like daughter. She's almost finished her second glass.

"Mind you, dogs don't have kittens. I myself left, too."

"Has your daughter been in touch recently?"

"No," she replies, as though regretting the fact.

She seems sincere.

"What do you think, where is she?" he asks, with the energy of despair.

Marion looks at him as if he's crazy. Or had got the wrong person. Doesn't he know that she abandoned her when she was two months old?

Didn't abandon, actually. She had *entrusted* her to the old man. And when she wanted her back, it was too late. Time had gone by. She was walking and talking like a crazy doll that had grown up too fast.

She went back twice to see her, kissed that little stranger, felt nothing. The kid belonged to the old man, and by entrusting her to him, Marion realized that she had lost her.

What would she have done with her, in any case? That kid was much better where she was.

The young man sitting in front of her, who is starting his third glass, does he know that she's never seen her as an adult?

The last time was on the day of the old man's funeral. Marion can feel the alcohol warming her up. It always has that effect on her. A desire to talk, to let it all out.

"Before, I was a nice girl. Pretty and all. I was cheerful, too. Laughed all the time. Worked hard at school . . . mustn't just go on appearances. I knew fine words, all that. Got good grades. And then my mother, she fell ill. For months I begged her to get treatment, but my old man never wanted that. And she, she said: 'No, no, don't worry, it'll pass.' He didn't want her to go out the door, to leave, to go to hospital. He wanted to keep her all to himself, for her to be treated in her own bed, at home. He'd call the family doctor, who was stumped, gave her the wrong medication. And me, I was begging my parents. I'd say to my old man: 'Take Mom to be treated where they know what they're doing.' Stubborn as a mule. If I had my time again, I'd have taken her myself. That went on for a year. When he did make up his mind, it was too late. She died in hospital. On arrival. Didn't even have time to unpack her suitcase. When I lost my mother, it did my head in. It . . . it killed me. I lived badly. I lived badly and put up a wall. I became unmanageable. My old man used to say that, 'unmanageable.' People, the neighbors, they said that, too: 'That Marion, she's unmanageable.' Everyone felt sorry for the old man. 'Poor thing,' they'd all say. Poor bastard, more like."

"Who is Nina's father?"

She lights a cigarette. A dark-tobacco one that stinks.

"I'm trying to quit . . . but it's not working. Would you like another glass?"

"Gladly."

"Her father . . . he went off, far away. I had her on my own. As I told you, I was living the life, but not the good one, the bad one."

"Why didn't you keep Nina with you?"

"Couldn't. Incapable of doing so. Can I ask you something?"

"Yes."

"Do you have her phone number . . . Nina's?"

"Yes."

"Can you give it to me?"

"Her mobile is permanently switched off. There's no point."

"It's just to have something that belongs to her. Even if it's only numbers."

Emmanuel stretches out.

"Could I sleep a little?"

"Do."

She stubs out her cigarette. Looks at the man lying on her sofa, which she purchased in ten interest-free installments from Conforama when she left Arthus. He'd become too heavy-handed by the end. When she kept getting hit, she finally quit.

Like Nina. Why had she taken off? When he seems like a nice guy, her husband.

Does such a thing exist, a nice husband?

*Now*, thinks Marion, *I have peace. I feed the stray cats in the neighborhood, water my geraniums in summer, work part-time in a cafeteria and get a little welfare, not the high life, but life all the same. And no one bothers me anymore. Men, don't want 'em anymore, not in my bed, not in my kitchen. I've burned my assets . . .*

*But what about her, why'd she left?*

*

Five in the morning. A dog wakes her.

As the weeks have gone by, Nina has learned to recognize them. To distinguish them, one from the other. It's Paprika that's just barked, an old spaniel-cocker cross. He has the hoarse voice of one who's shouted too much. She glances at the radio-alarm clock, why is he barking so early? Has he heard something or someone? Usually, the dogs start to stir later, when Lili arrives, followed by staff and volunteers.

The fear machine goes into overdrive: it's *him* and the dogs can smell him.

It's beyond her control, her hands, muscles, stomach all clench, tighten, close up. Frozen with terror, she lies there for a long time, eyes wide open, studying the ceiling, senses alert, waiting for the slightest unusual noise. She even ends up hearing *someone* fiddling with the latch of the front door.

Nina gets up with difficulty, it's 5:35 A.M., she doesn't switch the light on. She does everything in the dark, she's got into the habit of never switching on the ceiling light. Living in obscurity.

She drags herself over to the narrow window in the bathroom, climbs onto the toilet, pulls back the curtain. Not a living soul. Her legs shake so much she almost falls. She boils some water, drinking an herbal tea will calm her down.

She raises the radiator's thermostat a little, covers her shoulders. Then climbs back up onto the toilet and gazes out for a long time, peering into the night, the kennels all shrouded in darkness. Paprika must have smelled another creature, a fox or a rat.

Lili was right. At first it is disturbing to see the animals in kennels. And then you end up getting used to it. The first time, they look at you as if you might be a chance of escape. Unless they've had such a hard time that they hide all day behind a screen, sheltering them from the cold and people's eyes. Later, they see you as the person who is going to walk them or feed them.

The animals arrive from all over the place. Mainly from roadsides, forests, and trash cans. Last week, five were saved from a dysfunctional breeding kennel.

Two months, now, that Nina has been sleeping alongside them.

The difference between her and the animals is that she's not waiting for anyone to come and collect her. All she wants is peace. And as soon as she hears the engine of a car, instead of being pleased, she hides. Disappears inside her own body. She know that Emmanuel is looking everywhere for her. She can smell him. She wakes up every night in a sweat because she has his smell in her nostrils. As if he were in the same room as her, leaning over her bed.

Lili showed her the DISAPPEARED insert, with photo, that Emmanuel had published in the local newspaper. She saw, with horror, that old picture of her. He must have searched through all her things. Looking for tracks the way you snare a wild beast on a hunt. He's so demented, he probably sniffed her underwear.

He's capable of anything.

She'd known that for a long time, but distancing herself has made her even more aware of it. She has taken her husband's perversion on board.

She can't stop blaming herself, occasionally: "He was nice when I first met him. It's because of me that he became like that." When she comes out with that kind of thing, Lili retorts, jokingly: "I'm going to give you a good slap to get your ideas straight again."

The one thing Nina regrets is never going back home to collect a few of her things, her favorite T-shirt and sweater, her books, and her small box of photos. She had one of her grandparents on their wedding day, and many of Étienne, Adrien, Louise, Joséphine, and Marie-Laure.

On the day she left, everything moved so fast that Nina didn't have time to sort herself out. She wiped the slate clean by leaving everything behind her. Like someone who dies in a road accident, and then his mug of cold coffee and breakfast crumbs are found on the table at home. The bare hanger slightly askew from when he'd grabbed his coat as he left.

That was what was needed. No thinking about it.

On the day Nina and Lili met, after leaving the cafeteria in the mall, they returned to the car park, where they had left their cars. They looked at each other.

Lili said to her:

"Are you sure you want to go back to your husband's home?"

"Do I have a choice?"

"You have no family?"

"No one."

"Friends?"

"I could go to Étienne's parents . . . that is, a friend's parents. But my husband knows them, he'd find me in five minutes."

Lili loaded the tins from the cart into her trunk, looked up, and said:

"I rescue dogs and cats. I've also, occasionally, saved guinea pigs and hens . . . But never a young woman."

Nina smiled for the first time since Lili had approached her in the fruit-and-vegetable aisle.

Half an hour later, the Polo was hidden in a padlocked garage to which only Lili had the key, and Nina settled in her guest room. And then, nothing else. A resounding silence.

"And now, what am I going to do?"

"Wait," Lili replied. "As long as it takes."

It was like being in prison, locked between four walls. Except that in prison, you're allowed to have visits, in a parlor, once a week.

So that the cops didn't search for her, Lili advised her to write a farewell letter to her husband. Nina wrote out three copies of it. The same letter for Emmanuel, Adrien, and Étienne.

When she handed the three envelopes to Lili, for her to go and post them, Nina felt as if she were chucking her past into the trash. All that was left was the void of the present. Everything to build.

A fortnight after her arrival, the time it took to clean everything, Lili moved her into a small studio within the shelter, right at the back, hidden from prying eyes. All eyes, even those of the employees.

"That way you'll have your privacy. And in the evening, you'll only have to cross the road to come and have supper with me."

Nina is living in twenty sparsely furnished square meters with two windows facing away from the shelter and looking out onto the countryside. Only one narrow window in the bathroom looks out onto the kennels. It was in this studio that the founder of the shelter, Annie-Claude Miniau, had lived a long time ago.

"Here you'll really be at home. There's television, lots of books, and food in the fridge."

"I have nothing, Lili. Not a bean to repay you."

Nina pulled off her wedding ring, her sapphire one, and her diamond-set one.

"By selling them, I could keep going for a while."

"Keep your trinkets," Lili told her. "We'll see about that later."

But when was later? How long would she have to hide? She put her jewelry away in a drawer.

When she goes out to stretch her legs, she slips on a hooded jacket and jeans. She has already lost ten kilos. No more need to drink to survive, or to take those hormonal treatments that knocked her out. Just something to sleep, or she has too many nightmares. Lili had bought her some clothes and toiletries. She does all her shopping for her. For two months, Nina hasn't left the shelter.

"It's as if you were hiding an illegal immigrant . . . Or a war criminal."

"On this earth, there are two places for hiding in: cemeteries and animal shelters. No one hangs around our place. People are too scared of diseases or getting bitten."

The shelter is far from the center of town. Between two disused buildings. Lili is the only employee who stays all day. In the morning, a dozen or so people work there, from nine to one. And visitors rarely turn up without phoning first. As for those who come to get rid of their mutts or a litter of kittens, they hang their heads and scarper like thieves, so no risk of them saying that they saw a hooded figure wandering around the kennels . . . Who would know anything about anyone wandering around this place?

She has only to be sure to avoid the two local policemen who drop off any animals they've found in the pound section. Never cross paths with them.

After one, when everyone's left, and she hears the last car leaving the car park, Nina emerges, goes from kennel to kennel, stroking, talking. Now that they know her, the animals are pleased to see her, not wary anymore: she's one of their own. They don't differentiate between her and them.

This month, December 2000, there are thirty-two dogs and forty-nine cats. Once she has greeted them all, she has a sandwich with Lili in the office, at the reception desk. At lunchtime, the gates are closed. They are both at ease, chat about everything and nothing like two old friends. Share the latest news in their world.

"Why are you doing this for me, Lili?"

"And why not?"

## 74

*27 December 2017*

"I know some of *Blanc d'Espagne* by heart," Nina tells us.

Lying side by side on the big bed, we've just watched two episodes of *Breaking Bad*. I loved it, Nina was less keen.

I've gone back to my single bed now. Really, since childhood, I should have always slept in a double bed.

This is the moment Nina chooses to say it, that she knows my novel by heart. She starts to recite a passage from it. In the half-light, her voice pierces me.

*Her. When I ask her: "What would you like to be called in my novel?" she says: "Angélique." He mocks her: "Angélique, how corny." When I ask him: "And you, what would you like to be called?" he says: "Kurt, like Cobain." She makes no comment, is content merely to smile. That's how Angélique lives. Being content. And I feed on that, on her permanent contentment.*

Nina pauses for a few moments. As if she had the book in front of her, was turning a few pages and then continuing with her reading.

*I love to watch them dancing, walking, moving. There are some people one could spend one's life observing. It's not down to them, they do nothing to attract attention. That's why they are different from other people. Even today, I still can't fathom why they so much as looked at me. On the day the register is called at school, our surnames begin with the same letter, follow each other. It's thanks to, or because of, this alphabetical coincidence that Angélique takes hold of our hands. A boy on either side. Like three pieces of a puzzle slotting together, as they should. We cling to Angélique. She smells good. I know her smell by heart. A mix of almond soap and baby lotion. She leaves it on clothing that I steal from her and, finally, return to her: "Here, you forget this at mine." At eleven, she covers herself in vanilla. I could eat her. Her shape changes, her figure softens slightly, gradually. I would like to be her. Every time she draws my portrait, I hope to discover the girl that I am. I dream that Angélique will see me. That her pencils will guide her to me. When I play with Angélique, I am the sister without her knowing it. But I never dress like a girl. I'm not an effeminate boy. I'm a girl who should have been. Failed to be. Was unlucky.*

Nina stops again. I'm incapable of uttering a word. It's been a long time since I wrote *Blanc d'Espagne*, and I've never reread it. Rediscovering it through her lips overwhelms me. Étienne says nothing. I can hear him breathing. Does he fear that Nina will recite a passage that will make him feel uncomfortable, put him in an awkward position?

*He, Kurt, is magnificent. He has that distinctive look in his eyes, a faraway look, that signals his freedom, like a beacon. A nonchalance that can't be shifted. He never begs life for anything. He is at ease everywhere . . .*

"Any wine left?" asks Étienne.

I get up and empty the dregs into a glass that I hand to him.

"Thanks."

Nina grabs my hand as I pass.

"When I first read *Blanc d'Espagne*, I thought I'd die from grief at having been unable to make the real you out. Later, I understood that, essentially, you have but one soul. Whether it's Adrien's or Virginie's, you're the same person, your soul has no gender. We're not drawn to people because they are girls or boys, we're drawn to people because of what they radiate."

I kiss her hand and return to lie in the little bed without a word. Nothing to add.

*

It must be three in the morning, and I can't sleep. I keep replaying memories to myself, over and over again, I can't stop myself. I listen to them breathing, I haven't slept beside them since the burial of Nina's life as a young girl. On that night, we also buried our childhood. Even though Nina isn't reciting extracts from my novel anymore, I feel as if I can still hear her, like an imaginary echo.

I thought they were asleep, but then Étienne gets up and says to me: "I'm missing my kid already." I can't see his features, can just make out his giant form crossing the room.

"Do you want to return?" I whisper, so as not to wake Nina.

"Where?"

"To Lyon. Do you want us to turn back?"

"There's no possible return."

"According to Louise, there is."

"Don't you start on that, too."

". . ."

I hear him opening the small window in the bathroom and lighting a cigarette.

"And also, imagine if it's Clotilde's remains that they've found," he continues, quietly, "I'll be in trouble. I don't want to hear another word about all that. You can't imagine how relieved I was when they fished out that car from the bottom of the lake."

"I'd have thought it would have worried you."

He takes a while to reply.

"On the contrary, it's proof that I wasn't dreaming. I'm not mad, I really did see it going under, that damned car. How often did I wonder whether it had really existed."

"D'you think it was Clotilde who was inside it, for all these years?"

"She was capable of anything . . . Anyhow, I'll never know."

"Why d'you say that? DNA will surely tell, in the end."

"I'll be dead before that."

". . ."

"You'll take care of Louise?"

"Yes."

"You swear to me?"

"I swear to you."

"Do you still hate me?"

"To death . . . I detest you. For using me, blackmailing me."

"I understand. I behaved like a bastard."

"Me, too . . . Toward Nina."

"Why did you leave it all? Paris, your plays, all that? Things were going really well for you."

"I went through hell. Returning to La Comelle saved me."

He closes the window and comes to sit on my bed. I freeze.

"Why didn't you ever get your prick cut off?"

"For god's sake, Étienne, what tact . . . What class."

"Shush . . . Keep it down, you'll wake Nina up."

". . ."

"I'm sorry. You know how uncomfortable that stuff makes me. My IQ is zero for everything to do with . . . with . . ."

"Fags? Is that the word you're looking for? I'm not homosexual, Étienne, I'm a woman."

"You're a bird who loves my sister. So you're a homo."

"I don't want to talk about that with you."

"Why not? I'm going to die, you might as well tell me everything. Are you afraid, is that it?"

"That's exactly it, I'm afraid."

"You're afraid of what?"

"Of happiness, of liberation, of becoming who I am. I don't know who I am."

# 75

*May 2001*

Five Molière nominations for *Des enfants en commun*, but it's Richard Kalinoski's *Une bête sur la lune* that scoops all the awards. Directed by Irina Brook. Phenomenal, masterly. Adrien has never watched anything so deeply moving. He'll remember the performances of Simon Abkarian and Corinne Jaber until the day he dies. As he left the Théâtre de l'Oeuvre, his hands were still shaking.

But he's angry with the voters all the same. It's as if the profession had rejected his play. He broods over it, feels bitter. *It's so much easier to honor the Armenian genocide than a family behind closed doors.*

After the ceremony, he doesn't attend the dinner in honor of the nominees. He'd rather go home, on foot, leaving his whole team in the lurch. He doesn't even feign a headache, just says that it all exhausts him, and he'd prefer to leave. He doesn't feel like congratulating the award-winners.

He walks alone through Paris, the air is sweet. Another summer creeping up on him. And what will he do with it?

For a few weeks now, he's longed for Louise, and no one else. Why does he think that's so? He's never longed only for Louise.

*How dismal your existence is, my poor old boy, oh, sorry, my poor old girl . . . my poor old dears . . . You make a right pair.*

Adrien phones Louise often. This evening, she wanted to accompany him, be close to him, put on a pretty dress. He explained to her that he'd rather "keep up the mystery."

"I won't allow anyone to know that there's someone in my life. You must understand me, Louise, imagine if I receive a Molière, no one must know that you exist."

"That I exist . . . myself? Or that you don't exist, yourself?"
And she hung up.
*Serves me right.*
She sent him a message before the ceremony, all the same:

Good luck, proud of you.

He replied:

I love you.

Adrien has had no news at all from Nina. And neither has Louise. She has well and truly disappeared. But not like Clotilde. With her it's different. Nina left seven months ago without leaving an address, but she did send a farewell letter. Whenever his thoughts turn to Nina, Adrien dismisses them.

After seeing Étienne at the Brasserie La Lorraine in October, Adrien didn't have to think about it, or wait a day, to phone the police station in La Comelle. He asked to speak to Sébastien Larand, as Étienne had told him to, "an old school friend who's a warrant officer over there."

"Adrien Bobin? Yes, of course, hey, you've become famous . . . Me and my wife watched you on Poivre d'Arvor's show. Honestly, you spoke really well."

". . ."

"To what do I owe your call?"

"I wanted to tell you that, on the evening that Clotilde Marais left, I was with Étienne Beaulieu."

"Yeah, he told me about that."

"In fact, I didn't leave Étienne's side all day . . . or all night. After Pierre Beau's funeral, we went to the Lac de la Forêt together, and we waited for Clotilde. I was supposed to leave them when she arrived, but she never came. So we went back to Nina Beau's house together, and—"

"Excuse me, Adrien, but why are telling me all this today?"

"So Étienne isn't questioned. In case he was a suspect. And—"

"You don't know?"

"Know what?"

"Apparently, someone has seen Clotilde Marais."

". . ."

"A woman from Chalon, on vacation in Salvador de Bahia. She's sure it was her."

"How can she be sure? Does she know her?"

"She watched the Pradel program on TV. A girl looking exactly like Clotilde Marais was having a drink, and when this woman approached to talk to her, to ask her if she really was the girl who had disappeared whose photo she'd seen on TV, she left without answering. As if caught out. This kind of sighting can only be taken at face value, but why not. We can't launch an investigation in any case. It isn't an abduction, it's a voluntary departure. People can do what they want. For us, the matter's closed."

*

The news spread like wildfire in La Comelle: Clotilde Marais had been seen in Brazil. Emmanuel is beyond furious. Now that bastard Étienne Beaulieu will never be questioned.

And yet it's not for want of trying.

The first time Emmanuel shook hands with Étienne, when Nina had presented him as her "other best friend," he detested him. An easygoing way about him that Emmanuel Damamme, the prodigal son, had never had.

When he'd greeted Adrien, he'd felt nothing. But the other one, he'd instantly hated him. That way Nina and he had of looking at each other, their complicity . . . It was the day of Pierre Beau's funeral. Nina hadn't let go of her two friends. But it was Nina's hand gripping Étienne's that had particularly grossed Emmanuel out.

After the service, he didn't go on to the cemetery, he'd only known Nina for a few days, it wasn't his place to be there. He would join her later at the Beaulieus' house.

He left with his parents; his father dropped him off at the office.

Emmanuel just sat there for five minutes, unable to concentrate, staring into space. Then he got into a company car, his own being too recognizable, to follow them. To tail the cortège.

He went back past the church, the hearse was still there.

At the cemetery, he remained at some distance from them. The heat was unbearable. He settled under a tree, watching Nina and her two friends stuck together. Three silhouettes forming just one shadow. He waited for everyone to have left before returning to his car. He stopped off at his place to have a shower and change his clothes, and then went to the Beaulieus' house. As soon as he arrived, he saw Nina sitting on a sofa with a lost look in her eyes, and still with her damned hand in Étienne's. Clotilde Marais was sitting near them. A sad-looking pretty blond girl. She never stopped looking at Étienne, who was ignoring her.

Emmanuel approached Nina, who barely glanced at him. At that moment, he realized that he had lost her. That she was going to leave and he wouldn't be able to do a thing to keep her. Emmanuel talked with Marie-Laure while having a drink. What could he say about the dead man everyone around him was talking about? That "fine mail-man," he never knew him. That it was one of his company's trucks that had knocked him down was terrible. Nina was bound to hold that against him. He approached her, kissed her on her hair, she smelt of sweat and coconut shampoo. He felt like tipping her back on the sofa, right there, in front of everyone, and making love to her.

He was done for. Madly in love. He whispered:

"See you this evening, maybe, just call me."

"Yes."

A "yes" released into the air, as if she were talking to the wind.

Emmanuel left the house shattered.

He couldn't bring himself to drive off, so he waited. Waited for what?

First he saw Nina going home, alone, taking small roads, bowed with grief. She was walking fast, as if trying to escape from her own existence.

He followed her cautiously in his car, she mustn't see him, above all. Near the Beau house, he parked in a parallel road, switched off the engine.

Bobin and Beaulieu arrived around an hour after her.

Emmanuel stayed in his car all afternoon, windows wide open, not having enough willpower to drive off and go home.

At around six or seven o'clock, Étienne Beaulieu emerged from the grandfather's house, on his own. Emmanuel, like a man who has taken leave of his senses, followed him from a distance. Unlike Nina, Beaulieu walked slowly back to his house. He disappeared inside for five minutes, before coming back out and getting on a motorbike.

Emmanuel told himself that it was time he went home and dived straight into the pool. That he was behaving absurdly. That his shirt was drenched and he felt nauseous. And all that for a little tart of eighteen. A weed that had grown on a working-class estate.

Just as he was about to drive off in the direction of the Château, he did a U-turn and followed the motorbike. Thinking, for one moment, that he could knock it over. A burst of accelerator and the pretty boy would be forced off the road. And Emmanuel wasn't even at the wheel of his own car, but that of a salesman, and a dent in the bodywork would go unnoticed.

Strangely, Beaulieu had set off in the opposite direction to Nina's grandfather's house, toward the Lac de la Forêt.

*

Seven months, now, that Nina has been hiding at the shelter in La Comelle. Yet the days go by quickly. And Nina is almost happy living this reclusive existence. Until the staff go, at around one o'clock, she stays within her four walls. She makes all kinds of objects that are then sold at the shelter's open days, one Saturday a month: little collages that she frames, candleholders, bracelets, mosaics, hand-painted earthenware items.

Lili is dazzled by her paintings. Nina is evasive, says she had drawing lessons as a child. She no longer touches charcoal or oil sticks. If Emmanuel fell on one of her sketches, he could recognize it and trace it back to her.

During these open days, visitors can leave pet food, financial donations, blankets, detergent, garbage bags. They have a coffee with the staff, meet the animals with a view to adopting. Nina's creations are exhibited at the entrance, and most are bought. People are amazed at the beauty of the various decorative objects on sale. They attract an increasingly large crowd, and are starting to bring in quite an income. And when Lili is asked where the items come from, she invariably answers: "From art schools the shelter partners with."

The days have gotten longer and the countryside Nina sees from her studio, now more a workshop, has changed. The trees have their leaves back and the dandelions have turned the meadow yellow. At around three in the afternoon, she sometimes puts out a chair beside the kennels and just sits there for half an hour in the sun, or then settles on a bench in the cattery. She helps Lili with the caring, treating, bandaging, brushing, cleaning.

Occasionally, once it's dark, Lili takes her for a drive around the center of La Comelle, once the storekeepers have pulled down the shutters, just for her to get out a little. While she's driving around in the car, Nina feels as though she's a corpse returning to the world of the living.

# 76

*27 December 2017*

Romain closes his book. He can't seem to concentrate. He's thinking of her.

Of the different *hers*, more exactly.

The good and the bad are all jumbled up in his mind.

Nina was almost cold yesterday evening, on the phone. Why do some people you've only just met seem to think that you've instantly worked them out?

She told him she was in a *pensione* in Italy, with her two friends, all three in the same room like when they were kids, and that she was sharing her bed with Étienne.

Nina's voice was drowned by the sound of a TV. He had to make her repeat some things several times, which seemed to irritate her. The way his younger pupils can get annoyed with an elderly teacher who's a little hard of hearing.

Selfishly, Romain hopes that Nina will come back soon. That this trip won't drag on.

Just before hanging up, she whispered: "Actually, you never told me why you were transferred from Marnes-la-Coquette to La Comelle."

Once again, Romain didn't understand, or want to hear. He made her say it again. Nina spoke louder: "Why were you transferred to La Comelle? Why did you leave Marnes?"

This time, he understood the question perfectly. In fact, was it a question, or an insinuation? Her words surprised him so much, he didn't know how to answer. There was a long silence. A desire to slam the phone down on her. He felt clammy. Nothing is worse for a man than being condemned before even being judged. Feeling that others will never see you again as they used to. A paranoia he drags around like a chimera, that he's stuck with.

After some time, he replied: "I didn't mention it to you because I really don't want to talk about it." He, in turn, became distant with her. They exchanged small talk about the weather and the car's low gas consumption, and then Nina hung up. Romain felt instant regret. He should have reassured her. Not responded to stupidity with stupidity. Because, for the first time, Nina had been idiotic. How could she be one of those *others*?

No, of course she wasn't one of them.

He rang her straight back.

And she hadn't moved. Was just staring at her untied sneakers on this hideous faded carpet. Wondering how she could have been so dumb with Romain. When the phone rang, she knew it was him. Knew, or hoped. She picked up at the first ring.

Romain will never forget how he left Marnes, but he thinks of it less often. Yesterday, Nina's question plunged him right back into what, for him, had been a devastating episode. Still today, he doesn't know how he picked himself back up from it.

Her name was Rebecca, like the character in Daphne Du Maurier's novel. Was that an omen?

Rebecca Lalo. Her friends called her Becca.

Romain knew her just as he did all the pupils at the school he was in charge of. He discussed the future, choices, and results of each one of them with their teachers, at the staff meeting every term. When a pupil entered middle school, it took Romain a few months to identify them. By the end of the year, he knew all of them, and called them by their first name. Romain wasn't a strict headmaster, but he had to ensure that he was respected. Being relatively young, it wouldn't have done to let anyone think that he was a friend. During his career, he had sometimes lost his temper with a pupil, let anger get the better of him over behavior he deemed out of order. It was known that he could get annoyed, raise his voice and bang his fist on the table to make himself heard.

Rebecca Lalo was in eighth grade. In the third term, on 8 April 2014 to be precise, she burst into his office. Pupils rarely came to see him of their own accord. They only came when summoned, along with their parents, or a teacher. For regular requests, they approached the grade heads, but never the headmaster. Barely inside the office, Rebecca let him have it:

"You slept with my mother last weekend. The pretty, curvy blonde you picked up at the Dickens, that's my mom. I saw you both. She spent the night at yours."

It was the first time Romain was thrown off balance by a pupil. Incapable of saying a word back to her.

"If you don't give me 1,000 euros, I'm going to tell everyone about it."

This last statement left him even more dumbfounded. Then he burst out laughing, a mocking laugh:

"Please tell me I'm dreaming!"

"No, more like a total nightmare. My mother is married. If I tell my father about it, as well as losing your reputation, you're a dead man."

Romain had never allowed himself to be manipulated or intimidated. These last words had fired him up.

"Whether you like it or not, Mademoiselle Lalo, I do what I want in my private life. And I will forget this conversation, forget that you've just tried to blackmail me. You are going to leave my office, we've never spoken, never seen each other, nothing happened, understood? And you'd be well advised to obey me."

"Meaning?" she asked him, brazenly, not even trying to hide a provocative smile.

"To be clear. What has just occurred between these walls never happened. And that's for your own good. Or else—"

"Or else?"

"I will do what's necessary to make you shut up, once and for all."

Rebecca started to snivel. Crocodile tears that more than annoyed Romain Grimaldi. In his entire career, it was the first time he felt like slapping a pupil.

"And if I do talk?" she said, sniffling. "What will happen then?"

"It will be your word against mine . . . And I'll have you expelled from this school for insubordination and blackmail."

Her tears increased.

"No, Monsieur Grimaldi," she groaned, "I beg you."

"Give it a rest, Mademoiselle Lalo, or I'm really going to get angry. This is going too far. I want you to leave my office at once."

She stared at him, beseechingly.

"And if I say nothing to nobody, you'll leave me alone? I'll be able to finish my year?"

"Yes . . . Obviously."

"You promise me?"

"Yes. Now, disappear."

"You'll never tell what happened?"

"Get out of here!"

At that moment, she threw herself at him and kissed him on the mouth. Romain gripped her by the shoulders and pushed her away, Rebecca let herself fall and her head knocked the desk. She got up immediately, a mix of snot and blood running from her nose.

"What the hell—" he exclaimed.

"Goodbye, sir, I won't say a thing."

Romain wanted to follow her, to take her to the infirmary. But then thought the better of it and sat back down, reeling.

Next, the deputy head arrived, in a panic, to ask him what had happened. He had just seen a pupil leaving the office in tears and bleeding. "I'd rather not talk about it," Romain replied, curtly. The other guy didn't persist, but still gave him a suspicious look. The first of many.

Rebecca Lalo's mother . . . Romain remembered her perfectly well. She was called Sylvie. "But everyone calls me Syl." The encounter in the Dickens, the night that had followed the boozy evening. How could he have known that she was the mother of a pupil? He found her phone number on his mobile: "First name: Syl. Surname: beer."

He phoned her to tell her everything. Horrified, Sylvie Lalo made him promise never to say that they had spent the night together. Romain promised.

The following day, he was summoned by the cops and the descent into hell began.

RECORDING SUBMITTED TO AUTHORITIES

REBECCA LALO'S VOICE: If I tell my father about it, as well as losing your reputation, you're a dead man.

ROMAIN GRIMALDI'S VOICE: Whether you like it or not, Mademoiselle Lalo, I do what I want in my private life. And I will forget this conversation, forget that you've just tried to blackmail me. You are going to leave my office, we've never spoken, never seen each other, nothing happened, understood? And you'd be well advised to obey me.

REBECCA LALO'S VOICE: Meaning?

ROMAIN GRIMALDI'S VOICE: To be clear. What has just occurred between these walls never happened. And that's for your own good. Or else . . .

REBECCA LALO'S VOICE: Or else?

ROMAIN GRIMALDI'S VOICE: I will do what's necessary to make you shut up, once and for all.

*Rebecca Lalo sobbing.*

REBECCA LALO'S VOICE: And if I do talk? What will happen then?

ROMAIN GRIMALDI'S VOICE: It will be your word against mine . . . And I'll have you expelled from this school for insubordination and blackmail.

*Rebecca Lalo sobbing.*

REBECCA LALO'S VOICE: No, Monsieur Grimaldi, I beg you.

ROMAIN GRIMALDI'S VOICE: Give it a rest, Mademoiselle Lalo, or I'm really going to get angry . . . All this is going too far. I want you to leave my office at once.

REBECCA LALO'S VOICE: And if I say nothing to nobody, you'll leave me alone? I'll be able to finish my year?

ROMAIN GRIMALDI'S VOICE: Yes . . . Obviously.

REBECCA LALO'S VOICE: You promise me?

ROMAIN GRIMALDI'S VOICE: Yes. Now, disappear.
REBECCA LALO'S VOICE: You'll never tell what happened?
ROMAIN GRIMALDI'S VOICE: Get out of here!

*Sounds of a struggle.*

ROMAIN GRIMALDI'S VOICE: What the hell . . .
REBECCA LALO'S VOICE: Goodbye, sir, I won't say a thing.

The teenager had recorded it all with her smartphone, except for the beginning of their conversation. Showing a head injury, she had told the police that her headmaster had come on to her and made inappropriate gestures toward her. That she had threatened to reveal everything and that he assaulted her and hit her. That she was so scared of him that she had recorded him in case their meeting went wrong.

Romain allowed himself to be accused without denying a thing.

It was all his fault. He should have remained calm. He should have taken her to the infirmary, should have remembered that she was fourteen, should have known that she was fragile, should have.

He didn't wait to be suspended to send his resignation letter to the commissioner of education. He stayed locked away at home, with the shutters closed, for weeks on end. Having meals delivered to him. Not answering the phone to anyone.

Until the day, at the beginning of June, when his parents turned up at his place. They started by opening the windows. "You didn't have to fly for twenty hours just to air my apartment," he told them, in tears.

He learnt that Rebecca Lalo had retracted her statements. Meaning that he had been cleared. But it was too late. His reputation in Marnes-la-Coquette was ruined. He could never set foot in the school again. As it was, he couldn't even buy a baguette anymore without going red and shaking.

He felt as if everyone was looking at him, was wary of him.

Despite the case being dismissed, and thus clearing him, he felt shame eating away at him. A scourge leaving only a yearning to die and disappear.

Instead of soothing him, the teenager's retraction tormented him. Clearly, she was far stronger than him. And was teaching him a good lesson. He sank even lower, falling into an alarming torpor. Only leaving his bed to go to the bathroom. When urged by some former colleagues, he finally accepted to be hospitalized, to be treated with antidepressants. A professor saved his life, a psychiatrist, she made him talk. Why did he blame himself to the extent of wanting to die?

Still today, Romain is convinced that it was all his fault. That he should never have reacted that way when dealing with a child of fourteen.

Despite everything, he did regain a taste for life. Relearned to feed himself, to walk, to love the smell of tea and coffee, to enjoy a pastry, cycling, shopping, listening to music, gobbling popcorn at the movies, browsing in a bookshop. He hesitated for a long time about ever returning to a school. Facing the daily demands of being a headmaster once again. Looking into pupils' eyes without thinking of Rebecca's looking at him as she got up with blood on her face.

He'd been a bad headmaster, a cocky young thing who thought he was guiding and helping youngsters with his grand humanist theories. And when he'd found himself in a tricky position, he'd fallen flat on his face.

A new school was opening its doors in Burgundy, a team was being recruited. A friend and former colleague pushed him to apply: "You're made for this profession, Romain, go on, accept it, stop being afraid."

Romain told Nina everything on the phone. Before hanging up, she said to him: "Thank you for your trust, thank you for telling me the truth, thank you for coming to get Bob."

## 77

*If I were me*
*Neither the pages to be written*
*Nor finding the words to say it*
*Would scare me . . .*
*But I let go of my hand*
*Move away from myself*
*Find myself in the morning*
*On the wrong track*
*When we lose our way*
*How can we get through*
*These inhuman efforts*
*That lead us to us?*
*If I were me*
*Neither the woman I am*
*Nor even the man who sleeps in my bed*
*Would scare me*
*If I were me*
*Nothing that weighs on my mind*
*That I do worst and best*
*Would scare me . . .*

*November 2001*

There are eight of them at dinner, around an elegant table. Fillet of cod with asparagus. They're discussing Tony Blair's speech on the future of Europe. As background music, this song, which Adrien hears for the first time. Lyrics that cut through the conversation, despite the volume being at its lowest. That's all he listens to now, these lyrics. And the more he concentrates on what he's hearing, the slower his movements become. Until they stop. He's transfixed. Someone ends up asking:

"Are you O.K., Adrien?"

He stands up and replies:

"I am not Adrien."

Astonishment around the table.

"My name is Virginie."

No one understands. No one speaks. Or dares to laugh. Adrien asks the hostess:

"This song, what is it?"

"Which song?"

"The one I've just heard."

"I didn't notice."

When he realizes what he's just said, all those eyes on him, the ones he's avoided since childhood, Adrien faints.

He comes to, lying on a stretcher, with someone speaking to him:

"Sir, you're at the Hôpital Saint-Louis, you fainted. The people who called us said you were incoherent before losing consciousness. We're going to do some neurological tests. O.K.?"

"Yes."

"First we're going to check a few things . . . What year is it?"

"2001."

"What month?"

"November."

"What's your name?"

"Adrien Bobin."

"Your date of birth?"

"20 April 1976."

"Perfect."

*

"When I left the Hôpital Saint-Louis, I caught a train and left Paris for good. Without seeing anyone again. I only kept in touch with my editor and friend, Fabien Désérable. It was he who looked after selling my apartment."

Nina and Étienne are staring at me. I find them beautiful in the pale light of morning. I'm telling them about my life in segments, the one they never knew about. The one after we three.

My life after them.

We're sitting behind a plate-glass window at a service station between Genoa and Florence. Nina is dunking a *pain au chocolat* in her coffee, Étienne isn't hungry and is forcing an espresso down. It's a strange place to tell one's story.

Nina's lovely brown eyes widen.

"You left everything because of a song?"

"Thanks to a song. I was fed up with lying to everyone. Starting with myself . . . In the end, *Blanc d'Espagne* was no help to me. I thought that, by setting words down on paper, I would heal . . . But heal from what? I'm not sick, I was born in the wrong body."

"And what have you been doing all this time?" Étienne asks.

"Traveling. I returned to France at Christmas, to meet up with Louise at the Hôtel des Voyageurs. And then I'd had enough. Going away, it's still avoidance. I ended up buying a house in La Comelle."

"But why La Comelle?" Étienne asks, baffled, as if I'd chosen to be buried alive.

"Nina, Louise, my linden tree."

"Why me?" Nina asks. "We'd not spoken for years."

"One can not speak to someone and still know that they're there, close by."

"Why didn't you tell us the truth about yourself?" Nina dares to ask.

"What is true about me?"

"Don't be coy. Admit it, you didn't trust us, did you?"

"Above all, I didn't trust myself."

Nina buries her nose in her mug.

Étienne pulls a face.

"This coffee's the pits . . . Why Virginie? Why not Simone or Julia?" he asks me.

"There's a resonance between that name and the woman I am. Virginie is my identity. I can change Virginie's physical aspect, but not her identity. When I arrived in Paris, I wrote that in *Blanc d'Espagne*. I can change my appearance every day, every hour, every minute, like those kids' games where bodies and faces are interchangeable. And it's become such a habit with me, a bad habit, that I'm appalled by the very idea of transitioning. Today, such as I am, at forty-one, I'm tall, brunette, and wear bangs."

Étienne stares at me the way people stare at lunatics. He tries to keep his face expressionless. But in his eyes I can see the madness he sees in me. The unhinged woman. I realize, yet again, why I never said anything to anyone. As a child, I would have found such incomprehension unbearable. I wasn't armed then.

"D'you make love with my sister?"

"The joker! I'll never answer that question, Étienne. Particularly coming from you."

Nina smiles. A sweet smile. How beautiful she is when she lets the light in.

"For others, I'm Adrien. For myself, I'm Virginie."

She takes my hand. I don't think I've held hers in mine since my mother's funeral. Thinking of her makes me crack. I burst into tears. Nina hugs me.

"I suffer because of myself. Because of my fear of changing my body."

"Why are you afraid?"

"I'm not afraid, I'm terrified at the thought of discovering the *real* me in the mirror. Louise has tried everything, introduced me to the top specialists . . . But I know that some people regret their transition. Sex-change surgery isn't reversible. The hormones, the penis removal, the patching up, the breast implants, all so many mountains to climb. And there's something else."

"What's that?"

"I don't really like feminine clothes, dresses, makeup, heels . . ."

"Neither do I," says Nina. "That doesn't stop me from being a woman."

"I grew up with this scenario, I was born a girl in a boy's body, and I've survived like that for forty-one years. Maybe killing Adrien would be the same as killing Virginie. Like Siamese twins. If one dies, the other follows."

"You're a woman who doesn't identify with the gender clichés," Nina tells me. "Dresses, heels, makeup. But who does fit in with them? Today, they mean nothing anymore. Putting people in boxes makes no sense."

A long silence follows, broken again by Nina:

"In *Blanc d'Espagne*, your character has the operation, he goes all the way. It's a story of liberation. Don't you want to escape from Adrien? I so loved the moment when your character walks in the street in her new body . . . 'Everything has changed, nothing has changed, I have the same perception of everything around me, but others are talking to me for the first time, I've just been born and I'm twenty years old.' It's so beautiful, and it offers so much hope. When you returned to La Comelle, and I'd pass you in the car, I couldn't understand why you were still Adrien."

"*Blanc d'Espagne* is a novel. Novels are for writing what one is incapable of doing in real life."

"But not only for that," Nina insists.

"And my sister?" Étienne jumps in. "What does she think about it?"

"That it's normal to have doubts, uncertainty. But that my being scared doesn't mean I'm not wrong. Louise thinks I've been a caged bird since birth. And that bird must be freed."

"When you think of yourself, do you think of a man, or of a woman?" Nina asks.

"A woman."

"It's the first time you're talking to us about yourself. Truly, I mean. When we've known each other for thirty-one years. That's something."

"Yes, that is something."

We leave the service station to return to the car park outside. Nina in the middle, Étienne on the left, me on the right. She holds our hands. The sky is clear, light blue.

"Shall we stop in Florence?"

"I'd rather sleep in Naples this evening," Etienne says. "But if Nina's at the wheel, we won't get there before tomorrow morning. You'll have to let me drive. That was the original deal."

"We're six hundred kilometers from Naples," I say.

"Étienne, you can drive, but we stop every two hours, like we said."

"Yes, mom."

"How are you feeling?" I ask him.

"Frankly, for a guy who's about to kick the bucket, pretty good."

# 78

*1 January 2003*

Yesterday evening, his Lyon friends came to celebrate New Year's at his house. They have never abandoned him, unlike that other one, that trash, that slut, that bitch.

They are all still asleep, upstairs and in the outhouses. A few empty champagne bottles remain here and there, although Nathalie cleared away the remains of dinner before going home. But they'd carried on celebrating all night.

It's only 8 A.M. Emmanuel hasn't slept a wink. Sitting on his sofa and clutching a mug of coffee, he's mulling things over.

Twenty-six months, now, since Nina vanished. He's lost all hope of finding her.

He went so far as to consult fortune-tellers and clairvoyants. Pendulums, cards, crystal balls, he's tried it all, heard it all. That she was dead and buried in the Puy-de-Dôme, that she was lying low in Ireland, in Cork, to be precise, at an address that Emmanuel went to: no one had ever seen her there. As for the last one, a supposedly reputable astrologer, she claimed that Nina was so close to La Comelle, "within a radius of three to four kilometers at most," that she could smell her perfume. All charlatans, ready to extort as much money as possible from him for preposterous suggestions.

No hope left.

She will never come back. And why would she come back here? To this rat hole?

Unless . . .

Unless she thinks the coast is clear.

Nina is attached to Marie-Laure Beaulieu. If she hears that Emmanuel has left, she might tiptoe back to visit Étienne's mother.

And then he'll nab her. This thought makes him smile.

Emmanuel dials his parents' phone number, in Morocco. After five rings, it's Gé who answers:

"Hello?"

"Happy New Year, Mom."

His mother seems to have just woken up. *Her voice sounds strange*, Emmanuel instantly thinks.

"Happy New Year, darling," she finally replies.

"Has Nina called you?"

"No . . . Of course not."

"Do you swear to me?"

"I swear to you."

"On my head?"

"On your head."

"Say it: 'I swear it on your head.'"

"I swear it on your head."

"Say it in full. 'I swear on your head that I've not heard from Nina.'"

"I swear on your head that Nina hasn't called. And I've not heard from her."

"Is Dad near you?"

"Yes."

"Can he hear me?"

"Wait, I'll pass him to you."

"I've made a decision. I'm leaving France. I'm going to sell Damamme."

*

A few minutes later, Gé is walking alone in the garden surrounding her riad. She's thinking that, by moving to Morocco, she and her husband had been cowards.

The weather's always lovely here, and the scents she's breathing in, this morning, are undeniably intoxicating. And there's that permanent, particular, simply exquisite light. But she knows that the true sun shines where our loved ones are. Those we are viscerally close to.

When Emmanuel was a child, she used to think: "I could hide a body if my son asked me to." She has never loved anyone as much as Emmanuel. He has always been the apple of her eye, whatever he did.

And then Nina arrived. And Gé saw her son change. Saw Nina gradually fading away, and madness stirring in Emmanuel's eyes. First stirring, then taking hold, dangerously. His attitude toward Nina, that obsession with her, following her, tracking her, almost hounding her.

Once, just once, Gé dared to make a remark: "You should leave Nina in peace." Emmanuel rebuffed her, arguing that his wife was very young, that she "needed a daddy."

That response chilled her. *What have I done? How have I raised him? Who, or what, have I missed? Did I put such nonsense into his head? Do our children resemble us?*

Yes, Gé had been cowardly in moving to Morocco.

A year after Emmanuel and Nina had got married, once their son had taken control of the company, Gé had started talking about Morocco, and a new life for her and her husband. They would return to France often, if they missed friends and family. Nothing was irreversible, they could always come back. Henri-Georges, surprised by this proposal, was cool at first, then increasingly enthusiastic.

*How often do we end up closing our eyes?* Gé thinks. *A child crying too often, a violent neighbor, a lonely old lady one knows by sight, or a pet treated cruelly . . . and instead of doing something, getting involved, we pack our bags. So as not to see anymore. Or feel anymore.*

That morning, when the phone rang, Gé didn't think: *It's Emmanuel.* She didn't think: *It's my son ringing me for New Year*, but: *Someone's ringing to tell me that something's happened to Emmanuel.*

She had almost been surprised to hear his voice. "Happy New Year, Mom."

Since Nina's departure, she's aware that her son's madness has spread like an incurable disease, like cancer. She had come back to visit him twice, but had cut her stays short. What was the point of trying to reason with him? He's going round in circles, like a lion in a cage, talks to himself, spends hours on the phone with detectives, witch doctors, and quacks of all kinds. And if Gé tries to get involved, he becomes tense, aggressive, almost threatening. Always throwing back the same thing: "I will find *her*, in the end." While Gé, deep inside, is praying: *Please God, make sure he never finds her.*

Even Henri-Georges had tried to speak to his son, but he'd come up against a brick wall.

During the morning phone conversation between father and son about the sale of the company, Henri-Georges suggested appointing a manager. Emmanuel would hear none of it:

"Appointing a manager means keeping it. Selling means kissing it goodbye. In fact, I've already received several offers from buyers."

"You can't just throw away three generations of hard work from one day to the next. And I'd remind you that I still have shares in the company."

"I don't give a damn about the money. I leave it all to you, Dad."

Things became more heated between them, Gé calmed things down by giving her husband a beseeching look.

"If you're a father one day, you'll be happy to pass something on, like I did to you."

"I will never be a father."

When Emmanuel finally hung up, Gé explained to her husband, again, that, since Nina's departure, their son had lost the plot. So they must let him sell, it was a question of life and death. Leaving must have seemed to him like the only way of surviving. And their son's life was more important than the company.

With a heavy heart, Henri-Georges called Emmanuel back to tell him that he was O.K. with it. That he'd sell his shares so as not to hinder his son's plans.

*

This morning, Nina is wandering freely around the shelter. On New Year's Day, no risk of coming across anyone, apart from Lili. Who has just been called out for an emergency, a large hound, of the Cane Corso type, found tied up beside a railroad line in the Allier *département*. Not fancying going on her own, Lili had set off with a local policeman. Lili is scared of nothing, but in this case, "mustn't throw granny out of the window," she had shouted, jumping into her car.

Yesterday evening, for New Year's Eve, a costume ball had been organized at La Comelle's community center. Couldn't have been further from a Venetian masked ball. Everyone had bought their outfits at the discount store, or found old nightshirts, dresses, and suits, once belonging to their forebears, at the back of wardrobes. There were plastic masks representing President Chirac and his wife Bernadette, feather boas, makeup jobs done at home. All just for a good laugh. There was a local orchestra. A giant *raclette*, plastic cups, and as many kirs with Burgundy sparkling wine as you could drink. Lily dragged Nina along by force. "Believe me, no one's going to recognize you." She dressed her up in an old hippie dress—"A relic of my mother"—put a multicolored mask over her eyes, and a blond wig on her head.

"A relic of my old life."

"You wore blond wigs, Lili?"

"Sure did."

"You've never told me about yourself before the shelter."

"I come from Nogent, I do."

"Where's Nogent?"

"Not far from Paris."

As usual, Lili didn't elaborate. She pulled on a green outfit and, over her head, a Shrek hood, which made Nina laugh like she hadn't for a very long time. She would have liked Lili to tell her more, but Nina senses that her past is off-limits. One day, between sandwiches, when they were lunching together, Lili had said to her: "I won't talk to you about before, my dear Nina, because it's disgusting, and not even funny. The day I quit my old life, I threw it all away. Making a change means moving on. And the present must be kept bright as a new pin. If you knew how much I appreciate every second of my wretched existence."

Lili lives alone. Occasionally, a man spends the night at hers. Nina doesn't know who he is, has never crossed paths with him. When Lili refers to him, she just says: "This evening, I've got my fish stick coming, to spend the night here."

"What do you mean by 'fish stick'?" Nina asked her the first time.

"An old lover. We don't promise each other anything, don't whisper sweet nothings, but we do respect each other and have a good time together."

End of discussion. And Nina isn't the sort to intrude.

It's been twenty-six months, now, that she has been hiding at the shelter. Sometimes, she asks Lili:

"Until when, do you think?"

"Until you feel ready."

"But I—"

"Don't get worked up about it, when you feel ready, you'll go."

Last October, Nina had been horrified, and terrified, by the story of a young woman burned alive in Vitry-sur-Seine. *If Emmanuel finds me, he'll do the same thing to me.* Following this tragic event, Nina had once again sensed his presence in the middle of the night, as if he were leaning over her to finish her off. In the end, she told herself, when she chose to disappear from the surface of the earth, it was to fulfill her husband's darkest desire.

So, yesterday evening, dancing to the accordion version of "Macarena" and "Freed from Desire," decked in a long, yellow and green-flowered dress and a synthetic blond wig, gave her a much-needed break. A breather. She and Lili-Shrek boogied until four in the morning, doing the most unlikely routines, one after the next, on the laminated floor of the community center. Some two hundred people surrounded them, each one drunker than the other. No one paid any attention to anyone. All the same, Nina didn't take off her mask. Freed for a few hours, but not free, always a voice inside her, screaming at her to remain on her guard.

It's noon when Lili returns from her trip, with the mastiff at the end of a leash. She's just dropped the policeman off, at his home. The Cane Corso is impressive. Nina approaches them.

"Is he gentle?"

"Seems to be. Generally, these big dogs are the easiest," says Lili. "He's tagged, but neither phone number nor address is current."

"Where d'you come from, you?" Nina asks the hound.

The dog growls, and before Lili has time to yank its lead and Nina to move back, he goes for her calf and locks his jaw on it.

Despite Nina's pleading, Lili takes her to hospital. She'd applied a tourniquet at knee-level. The closest hospital is in Autun.

"Speak to me!" Lili screams to her. "Don't fall asleep!"

Nina can't stop laughing, while at the same time wiping away tears of pain.

"No chance of falling asleep, it hurts like . . . a dog bite."

An hour later, an intern gives Nina two vaccinations, one against tetanus, the other rabies, because she has no idea where her health record is. Then he stitches up the wound, which is deep. At first, a nurse will have to change her dressings daily.

Nina can't hide anymore; she has had to give her details. And Lili has had to explain about the origins of the dog she knows nothing about.

They haven't even left the hospital before the news is out: Nina Beau was at the emergency department of Autun hospital.

## 79

*28 December 2017*

Étienne can't get to sleep. He's in pain. He senses that his dark thoughts are harming his body, his resilience.

He keeps going over Adrien's confession at the service station. "Virginie is my identity. I can change Virginie's physical aspect, but not her identity."

Étienne had behaved badly. Unacceptably, but it had been so easy to take advantage of the situation. On 17 August 1994, the first time they slept together alone, without Nina. That had never occurred since the Three had met. Nina was always between the two of them. Since they were kids, Étienne had sensed Adrien's difference, that he was seeking, and silencing, something. He had often caught Adrien looking at him, and then immediately looking away. Was Adrien gay, despite his attraction for Étienne's sister?

On that dreadful night, he went back to Nina's, drunk. He needed to cling to someone again, some hope. He found Adrien in the garden, pale and just as lost as him. Étienne drew him up to Nina's room, and Adrien lay down near him without a word, going along with it. It was Étienne who ruled the Three. The one to whom nothing was refused. He had drawn Adrien in, knowingly. He knows it now, in his soul and conscience. He hadn't done it out of despair, or loneliness, but out of desire. They had caressed and kissed each other in the dark. "There's but one step between friendship and love," a stupid thing Marie-Laure used to repeat to them, solemnly, making them feel uncomfortable. "Leave off, Mom," he would snap, gulping down his hot chocolate.

Had he sensed that girl hidden inside Adrien? Had he loved her without knowing it?

After that night, they never spoke of it again. Carried on with their lives as if it had never happened. Étienne played down what he had done: kids messing around, two little jerks of seventeen trying to find themselves.

But how had Adrien felt about it?

When Étienne had read *Blanc d'Espagne*, he had felt both betrayed and ashamed. The same feeling as Nina, the same words used, but with a completely different meaning.

Étienne also knows some parts of that damned novel by heart. The narrator's name is Sasha. He's a few days away from his "gender reassignment" surgery. A barbaric expression, like some scientific formula, to signify "becoming what he is since his birth." Sasha spends a night with a man, a stranger, a single night of love. An accidental night.

*We're lying against each other. I've never touched a boy's body, and neither has he. He sleeps with girls, and I sleep with Louise. We're young, with no experience. It's reciprocal. It's him who makes the first move, is first to place a hand on me, I'd never have dared to touch him. I'm the grain of sand, he's the ocean. We might be in the same room, but we don't live in the same world. He's sovereign, while I'm just one subject among others. He begins by putting his fingers on my neck, I think he's going to strangle me. Why did I think he wanted to be rid of me? We're not gentle, but abrupt and awkward. We don't penetrate each other all night, remain just on the edge of each other. When he places his lips on mine, I realize that this is really happening to us. Still today, I can taste his tongue in my mouth, his salty alcoholic saliva. Our clinch lasts a long time, a very long time, we're both masters of the hours afforded us, like a couple making love for one last time, two condemned people who know that the dawn will end this story that never began.*

*Ultimately*, thinks Étienne, *I betrayed Clotilde, Adrien, and Louise on the same day, that of Pierre Beau's funeral. His burial also marked the burial of my honor and my integrity.*

When Étienne had read that passage, he'd felt like killing Adrien.

How could he have spoken about them, about him? Someone might recognize him, identify him.

When Étienne had blackmailed Adrien, had told him that if he didn't testify he would reveal the identity of the author of *Blanc d'Espagne* to everyone, he was bluffing.

*Thank goodness there's Valentin*, he thinks.

He phoned him earlier, from a kiosk, when they arrived in Naples. Valentin was already in bed, mobile phone in hand.

"Dad . . ." he whispered, with relief.

The only person in the world who sees Étienne as someone decent. The only person in the world who has made Étienne someone decent.

The year he left to study in Paris, Nina was always listening to a song that was too sentimental for his taste, "*Juste quelqu'un de bien.*"

Étienne grabs hold of the sleeping Nina's hand and squeezes it hard. He stifles tears into his pillow. *A man doesn't cry.*

*

*Un homme, ça ne pleure pas.* Nina thinks of the title of that novel by Faïza Guène that she'd so loved. Had read several times. Nina is pretending to sleep while Étienne's hand is gripping hers. Above all, he mustn't sense or guess that she's awake, that she hears him stifling his tears. She plays dead, yet it's him who's probably going to die.

Probably, because she refuses to believe it. There'll be a miracle, a sudden burst of life, a try at treatment, a reprieve. In real life, Étienne cannot die.

She's playing dead when, in fact, it's her own life that's starting. The beginnings of a revival at forty-one. *It's never too late*, as the song would say.

Which song? The one they'd written with Adrien. They must have been around thirteen, fourteen. She can't really remember the lyrics anymore. Something really pathetic along the lines of: "It's never too late to look at yourself in a mirror, it's never too late even when you think everything's black" . . . Since Emmanuel, Nina has learnt that nothing can be built with someone, or for someone. That a life is crafted alone, and if, by some miracle, you run across a soul mate, even part of one, that's a gift. Since Romain, for the first time in her adult life, Nina doesn't feel uninhabited anymore. She'd felt that with Lili, too. But with Romain, it's different. He's her lover. Maybe they won't separate. Maybe they'll stay together. Nina knows for certain that we're made of "maybes."

Nina can feel Étienne going, sinking into sleep. His hand releases hers. His breathing eases. She listens attentively to his every breath, he's sleeping.

*

I hear Étienne breathing. He's sobbing. I dare not move. He couldn't bear me trying to console him, he's too proud. With him, you always had to pretend not to notice how he was really feeling. He's like those guys who show off, who are great to look at, but whose feelings you can never know. Who do everything they can to hide behind a façade.

Same setup as last night, at the *pensione*: I'm in the single bed, the child's one, the third person's one; Étienne and Nina are sleeping in the parental bed.

We found a hotel close to the Mappatella beach.

We ate linguine with clams and drank a bottle of delicious white wine. As if we weren't accompanying Étienne on his final journey, but simply on vacation beside the sea.

No sooner had he left the car than he stripped off and hurled himself into the water, yelping. I couldn't tell whether they were yelps of joy or despair. Doubtless a bit of both. Nina shouted: "The water's freezing! You're crazy!" She tried to talk him out of it, to pull him by the hand to the shore. Étienne begged her: "Let me be crazy, please."

While he swam, Nina didn't take her eyes off him, and I left to buy some beach towels at a general store. When he came out of the sea, chilled to the bone, we gave him a long rubdown, with a towel each. He was shivering but seemed happy. He was smiling, his body ruddy with cold, but his face still pallid. It was the first time I was seeing him stripped to the waist since the burial of Nina's life as a young girl. His skin tone, his shoulders, his stomach, his hairiness, all those of an adult.

*Today we are forty-one, our generation wanted to change the world and we have failed*, I thought.

As soon as we were back at the hotel, Étienne sank into a hot bath, after swallowing a load of pills. Nina and I raided the minibar and downed whatever miniatures we came upon, without looking at the labels. She jumped on the bed. I put on some music, a random playlist.

From the bathroom, Étienne shouted: "You both still have the same crap taste!"

We're just like those brothers and sisters who meet up after being apart and have lost none of their repartee. As soon as you let loose adults who were kids together, childhood resurfaces.

Despite Étienne's instructions, I quickly switch on my mobile to check my emails, and especially to know how Nicola is doing.

"Nina?"

"Yes," she says, in a whisper.

"I've just received a confidential email from the newspaper. The remains in the car, they're those of a woman . . . Just a single person."

"Clotilde?" Nina murmurs, as though scared of saying that name.

"Too soon to tell."

"D'you think, if it is her, they'll find any remains of . . . of the baby?"

"Not after all these years. An embryo, that's cartilage, not bone."

"It's too awful."

"I can hear you," whispers Étienne, "I'm not dead yet. If it is her, they'll find the skull, pelvis, and femurs of the fetus. Freshwater is less corrosive than seawater. And the body must have been protected by the silt. I've thought of nothing else for the past twenty-three years."

## 80

*Saturday 13 August 1994*

A dull pain. Clotilde is trapped in a nightmare she wants to get out of, she counts: *One, two, three, and I wake up.*

And still that Francis Cabrel song, forever on the radio at the moment, driving her mad even in her sleep.

*No point being more precise*
*This affair is already over*
*We'd act just the same*
*If we had our time again*
*It's just simply, simply*
*A Saturday night on Earth . . .*

*One, two, three, I wake up and I'm ten years old. I'm my parents' princess, their only daughter, Mommy has laid breakfast on the veranda, the sky is blue, our life is like an ad in which everyone is perfect, starting with me. I'm blond and the fur on my sparkly mauve slippers warms my feet. I'm in fifth grade. I'm in love with the boy over there, sitting in the second row beside Nina Beau. He's called Étienne Beaulieu. I dab a little blusher on my cheeks and gloss on my lips, so he notices me. But he only looks at his two friends, one an earthworm, the other a brat. He's forever stuck to them. I'll wait. One day, he'll look at me.*

*One, two, three, I wake up. My feet. I'm really cold. They're frozen. A layer of snow on my bed.*

Now, the pain is so acute that she stifles a cry.

Clotilde opens her eyes. She managed it. *One, two, three, and I wake up. The song's finished.*

In life, real life, it's still dark. She can go back to sleep before doing her shift at the pizzeria. Only fifteen days left. She's had her fill of weaving between tables.

Yesterday, while she was serving a quattro-formaggi, a regina, and some lasagnas, the Beaulieus' skivvy must have found her letter in the mailbox, picked it up, and placed it on the desk in Étienne's bedroom. While the holy family sunbathes in the Midi, a time bomb sits in the son's room. One that will blow up in their faces in ten days' time, when they come home.

Clotilde laughs to herself, sweats, is increasingly in pain. It's that blasted nightmare wringing her insides again.

She thought she was awake, but she's a prisoner of her sleep.

*One, two, three, and I wake up.*

And yet, she thinks out loud: "The letter on Étienne's desk . . ."

How often had she and Étienne gotten together in that room, that bed? How often had she put her clothes back on there? Picking up her scattered clothes, thrown off in haste before love? Looking for them like Tom Thumb looks for his white pebbles on the way home? Unlike the child in the Perrault fairy tale, Clotilde would have liked to lose herself in the arms of the wicked wolf and never go home.

Lifting Étienne's jeans off her sweater or socks, how often would she have loved him to say to her: "Stay."

Her, body still tingling with pleasure, leaning over to find her bra, watching him through her curtain of blond hair. Him, stretched out, naked, skin golden, relighting his joint in a way that's both elegant and cool. The vacant look in his beautiful eyes, an enigmatic smile on his lips. What was he thinking about? Who?

He finally did look at her, at high school, having gone through middle school without taking her into consideration. Barely a "hi" between his teeth when he passed her. And then, when they move into twelfth grade, two months go by, and she realizes that, at last, he sees her. Lingers on her. The birthday party of a friend, on 3 November. "Étienne will be there."

*Étienne will be there.*

He doesn't take the time to seduce Clotilde. Chatting up girls, not his thing. He doesn't know how to say charming things, doesn't care, goes up to her and kisses her full on the lips. "Zombie," by the

Cranberries, through the speakers, and everyone around them singing at the top of their voices: "In your head! In your heeaadd!"

And that's it. Her dream as a little girl comes true. They sleep together that first night in Étienne's bedroom. Why wait? Who said, "never on the first night"? Life's far too short. The prince's breath stank of alcohol, but such is life.

Those sparkly mauve slippers, Clotilde had flogged them at a yard sale ages ago. Memories are like wardrobes; one ends up getting rid of what's inside them.

Clotilde is seventeen, but she's already understood that. She's an old young girl. Under no illusions. The only thing that obsesses her is Étienne Beaulieu. Even if, deep down, she knows that one day, she'll end up losing interest even in him.

"It's the first time I really got off."

Étienne is forever repeating this phrase to Clotilde, like a refrain. For Clotilde, that first time has the flavor of love.

Another cramp, Clotilde doubles up with pain. *No, no, no. This isn't the time or the place. This isn't possible. It's too soon.*

Clotilde tries to renegotiate some sleep. *One, two, three, I wake up.*

She presses on the switch. Blood everywhere. She would like to scream: "Daddy! Mommy! Help!" But not a sound comes out of her mouth.

She gets up, goes to the bathroom. It's over. Got to go right back to square one. The fuse of the time bomb has fizzled out. Clotilde pulls off the bottom and top sheets, crosses the corridor, detergent, bleach, washing machine on hot, goes back to her room.

She takes a shower. Isn't in pain anymore. An urge to push that she suppresses. *Not here.* She sobs. Not because she's losing the fetus and Étienne Beaulieu, but because her dreams are disappearing down the drain.

*She's gone under.*

She throws on an ugly, old black dress, bought a couple of years ago because she thought it looked like something a dancer would wear, but never worn. She walks out into the breaking dawn, not a soul in this godforsaken town, her shoes are soaked by the morning dew. She's moving like an automaton, like the living dead in the

Michael Jackson video, or those ghastly films she never liked in which pale and delicate girls, in cotton bonnets, long dresses, and clogs, cry over their fate while their men drink strong liquor and split their sides laughing.

She sees Étienne again on the beach in Saint-Raphaël, the blond girl lying on top of him.

She has no more cramps.

Clotilde crouches down, delivers in a ditch, no pain, she doesn't look, it's not breathing, it's dead. Because it decided to be dead, to come out on its own, to let go of her, not to want her.

She never wanted to be a mother. At eighteen, who would? She just wanted to hold on to Étienne, put him in stocks. Turn him into a doting daddy. For the "happy event" to change him, radically. For him to become docile and considerate. A sweet little puppy dog she'd have ended up loathing. Hating, even.

Clotilde blows her nose on her dancer's dress. *What nonsense, you pathetic girl. Thank goodness this has happened to you. What would you have done with a brat? On the other hand, you'll have to get your revenge, and in no small way. Ruin his life. Otherwise, it would just be too easy.*

She goes home, it's 7 A.M. She lies on her bare mattress, wrapped in a blanket.

She dozes until 9 A.M. She can hear her parents' voices and the clatter of crockery from downstairs.

*Must go to work. Must go to work. Must go to work.*

She's exhausted. She's bleeding again, the return of her period. The return to normal life.

She hadn't seen a doctor. No ultrasound or monitoring. No one ever knew. She'd read a book on pregnancy the way one reads a history book. Things that happen to other people but didn't concern her. "In the fourth month, the fetus weighs about two hundred grams and measures fifteen centimeters." She'd calculated that she'd fallen pregnant around mid-April. A Wednesday afternoon. The day for kids. Not at all an accident, as she'd made out. She'd planned it all. Pierced the end of the condom with her fingernail, sharp as the blade of a penknife.

She remembers the day she did a pregnancy test: two bars yes, one bar no. She'd been thrilled, sitting there on the toilet and discovering the result. *Étienne is mine.*

Clotilde has another shower, puts on another dress, buttons it up at the front, then realizes that she's forgotten to strap down her belly, something she's been doing for about a month. She still has the rounded belly of a pregnant woman. Why? For how long?

Her thoughts are interrupted by her mother knocking on her bedroom door.

"Darling, your friend's grandfather has died."

*I don't have a friend*, Clotilde thinks. *Certainly, no friends who are girls. I hate girls. My fantasy is to be a pimp and put them on the streets, so they earn me loads of cash. The truth is, I'd like to play cards with the guys while my hookers hustle. The truth is, I don't like being a girl.*

"What grandfather? What friend, Mom?"

"The little dark-haired one . . . The mailman . . . Pierre Beau, he got run over. By a truck. The poor man."

Clotilde stays at the door. *That means Étienne will come home sooner than planned. Tomorrow, he'll be here. Tomorrow he'll read my letter. Maybe even . . . today!*

"When did it happen?"

"Yesterday afternoon."

An hour later, just like every morning since 1 July, Clotilde is laying the tables, straightening the tablecloths, checking the china is spotless. The first clients turn up at twelve on the dot, and by 2:30 P.M., everyone has had their fill. During lunch, some clients talk about the accident, the mailman mangled, the truck he hadn't seen coming.

Clotilde gets a break in the afternoon, then starts again at six to prepare for the evening sitting. During her break, she often stretches out on the lawns at the municipal swimming pool, but today she goes to the library and discreetly consults the books on pregnancy. She finally finds what she's looking for: "The uterus needs time to return to its original size after a miscarriage or birth, the abdominal girdle has changed shape and the skin on the belly is stretched. Allow for several weeks to get your figure back." Clotilde has no intention of getting her figure back. Outside the library, she polishes off two pastries, without tasting them at all.

She realizes she still has two hours left, goes back into the library's garden and lies down on a bench under a large fir tree. There's no one around, the swings are empty, the air is warm, she's thirsty. She closes her eyes.

*No point being more precise*
*This affair is already over . . .*

Shut up, song.

Clotilde sees Étienne and the girl on the beach at Saint-Raphaël once more. When was that, again? She counts back in her mind. Three days ago.

She recalls the day when Nina Beau's grandfather had burst into the schoolyard to hit her. She would have died of shame if her parents had pulled a stunt like that on her. She'd have preferred to disappear than go back to school.

Nina, her grandfather run over, Étienne, inevitably devastated. Anything that affects his "best friend" makes him ill. You just had to see the look on his face when the old man had sent his granddaughter's head spinning. Étienne, white as a sheet, could have been knocked down with a feather.

Clotilde looks up at the sky, feels like an empty bag, a bag stripped of its contents by a thief. As her tears come, she closes her eyes, remembers his expression when, last May, just after making love, she told him that she was pregnant. Étienne had groaned: "Oh shit . . . That's shit."

During that evening's shift, she keeps looking out into the street to see if he's there. If he's walking past, if he's watching her. She hopes he'll come to collect her, surprise her. She can't stop looking out of the three large windows facing the street. The boss ends up asking her if she's expecting someone, Clotilde tells him where to go.

On her way home, she takes a detour along the road the Beaulieus live on. She gets a sharp pain in her chest when she sees the family car parked outside their house.

*They're back.*

No light on in Étienne's room. Has he gone out after finding her letter? Is he waiting for her outside her house? She turns around and walks home, not feeling that reassured. *What if he wants to get rid of me?*

Clotilde passes Nina's house and lowers her head, walks faster. Not a soul around. Neither indoors, nor out.

Where on earth can the Three be? Where are they hiding? Where are they consoling Nina?

It's almost midnight when she gets home, worn out. And still no one to be seen. Has Étienne read her letter? Unless he recognized her handwriting on the envelope, and, like a coward, put off opening it? Maybe he even threw it away, tore it up without knowing what was inside it?

Clotilde goes up to her room with a heavy heart. Stands at the window for a long time, watching out for a sign, a movement, a presence in the street. Nothing.

She doesn't bother to go to the bathroom or get undressed, just lies on her bed and instantly falls asleep.

*

Sunday 14 and Monday 15 August. A public holiday, two days of rest. Total dread. La Comelle is empty, oppressively hot. All the stores are closed, shutters down.

Only the municipal pool is open. She won't go near it. With her big empty belly, she'd give herself away. She refuses to go out. Stays at home, waiting for a phone call or a visit . . .

Her mother is concerned, finds her preoccupied. Tries to make her talk, in vain. Suggests going away to spend these two days off wherever she fancies.

"What if we book a room in a little hotel near Valence? Your father has found a nice place with a pool that offers massages. It's a two-hour drive away."

"No, but you go, both of you."

"We're not going to leave you all on your own, darling."

"Yes, do. That's what I want and need. I'm going to start sorting my things out before going away."

She's got a place at Dijon University, for sports management. With top marks in her bac, she'll be the best in her year.

*The best in rank stupidity, sure.*

She won't go to Dijon, not there or anywhere else. She'll go far away. Just as she'd planned if Étienne rejected them, her and the child. Now there's no child anymore. So, even if he thinks she's pregnant, what else can she do? Her belly will soon melt away, like snow in the sun, and Étienne will leave her for good.

She's going round in circles in the house. No more plans, no more future, no more Étienne Beaulieu.

She stuffs herself so as not to lose weight. Keeps eating slices of bread covered in sauces or spreads.

The phone rings. Étienne, at last! It's just a schoolmate.

"Nina Beau's grandfather's funeral, it's on Wednesday, are you going?"

"Yes," she hears herself saying.

"How are you going to dress?"

*What an idiot. We're not going to Club 4 or competing to be Miss France. I'm right in thinking that girls should all be done away with.*

"Dunno."

"It'll be hot."

"Bound to be."

"It's going to be so sad."

The girl keeps waffling on, Clotilde isn't listening to her anymore. Now she can be sure: in three days' time, she's going to see him . . . The idiot's right, actually, how is she going to dress, do her makeup, her hair? She must do all she can to look natural. Clotilde returns to the conversation when the girl asks:

"Any news from Étienne?"

"Yes," Clotilde lies. "He calls me every day. He's back earlier than planned to console Nina. It's tough for her."

"Poor you, you must feel bad for them."

"So bad. Gotta go, someone's knocking downstairs, must be Étienne."

Clotilde hangs up.

On Tuesday 16 August, she goes back to work with a sinking heart. The boss tells her she's looking really pale.

"Should have made the most of your break to get a bit of sun."

Clotilde doesn't respond, folds the table napkins while gazing out of the window, just in case he comes. He's been back for three days, and she's heard nothing from him.

*What a jerk. Apparently, there's just one step between love and hatred. You don't say. A tiny step.*

The day drags on, the clients are a pain, she feels like throwing it all in. Before leaving, Clotilde warns:

"I won't be able to come in tomorrow, I have a funeral to go to."

"Ah, the poor mailman . . . but it won't last all day, that funeral."

"For me, it will."

Her boss grimaces, as if to say: "And how am I supposed to manage?" But he lets it go, he's never had such an efficient waitress. Good at serving, good at the till, good with clients. If he had to rate her, despite her weird mood swings, Clotilde Marais would get top marks. If it was up to him, he'd keep her on all year, but he's under no illusion, the kid won't be staying with him. Even with above-minimum-wage pay, meal tickets, and an end-of-year bonus, she's got better things to do than serve pizzas all blessed day.

After her shift, Clotilde goes straight home, still hoping to bump into *him*.

She's not bleeding anymore. She removes her strapping and looks at herself, in profile, in the mirror, her belly hasn't changed. Since Clotilde is slender, it sticks out all the more.

Three days ago, now, that she lost it. A girl or a boy? What does it matter now?

She puts a clay mask on her face and then moisturizes her skin. Lines her eyes with black kohl. That way, tomorrow morning, the blue will stand out without her seeming made-up.

She goes to bed, and runs through, over and over, what she has to do when she wakes up. Wash her hair with her egg shampoo, dry it a little, putting softener on the ends. Curl eyelashes, dab on concealer, a touch of blush, some lightly shimmery lip gloss, blot it on a tissue.

Apply body lotion all over, spray a subtle perfume on temples and wrists. Slip on a gray cotton T-shirt, the pants that go with it, casual, chic, and discreet, and then her strappy black sandals. Remember to check that her pedicure is perfect. Nothing's more of a passion killer than hard skin on the feet.

*Passion killer.*

She repeats it out loud, for herself: "Passion killer."

What's Étienne doing? Where is he? What's he thinking about? Has he finally opened that damned letter? When did he receive it?

Get her revenge. And find how to. Fast, very fast. Before he knows she isn't pregnant.

*

When Clotilde arrives at the forecourt, outside the church, on 17 August, there's already a crowd. She's relieved to get inside the church, into the cool. She tidies her hair discreetly, tries to find a seat along the central aisle to see them arriving. She almost pushes a fat lady to fit herself in. She's been waiting for fifteen minutes, watching or greeting people, when everyone stands up. The organ music, the coffin, Nina, Étienne, and Adrien behind it. Hand in hand. Like three orphans following a parent. Right then, Clotilde feels her heart break as she realizes how much they love each other. She'd never had such a place in Étienne's heart. Even the earthworm is more important to him.

Nina seems to have shrunk, shriveled with grief. Adrien is as dull as ever. As for Étienne, sun-bleached hair, the perfect tan, and sorrow giving him a solemnity that makes him even more handsome than should be allowed. In contrast to Nina, he seems to have grown even taller.

Étienne doesn't see her, moves forward with head held high. The three are followed by the Beaulieu and Damamme families, and also Adrien's mother, at whose flat everyone had celebrated their bac results just over a month ago. When they were all still carefree. Apart from her, Clotilde. Because she was pregnant, and the only one to know it.

All through the service, Étienne doesn't move. Turns his sorrowful eyes to Nina from time to time. Clotilde can see three-quarters of him. She'd like to touch him and say: "Come, let's get out of here."

On the forecourt after the Mass, while strangers are going up to kiss Nina, Clotilde feels someone grab her arm. It feels like a dream. She can't believe it.

"Hi, are you coming to mine after the cemetery? My mother's doing drinks for nearest and dearest."

Clotilde nods to tell him she'll come. Étienne is already back at Nina's side.

Hope returns. If he's asking her to come to his place, it means nothing's over. Maybe he intends to pick up their relationship where they'd left it, before the vacation? Maybe, in the end, that blonde lying on him in Saint-Raphaël meant nothing at all? He's like that, Étienne, rooted in the present.

Bursting with hope, she stops herself from laughing out loud in front of everyone. She just has time to see the Three getting into the back of the Beaulieus' car, which sets off to follow the hearse.

She turns around, doesn't feel like talking to those not going to the cemetery, who, instead, stand bereft in front of the condolences book, pen in hand. She glances at the words written, line by line, and it's as she reads: "We share your grief, our sincere condolences, we'll never forget our colleague's smile," that it dawns on Clotilde that she must get her letter back. Étienne may not have opened it yet. She has some time in front of her.

She walks to the Beaulieus' house. If drinks have been laid on for after the burial, there's bound to be someone getting things ready. *The skivvy, what's she called again? Madame . . . Madame . . .? Yes, come on, make an effort, you bumped into her every time you arrived at or left Étienne's house . . . A weird name. To do with a feeling. Resentment. Madame Rancoeur! Yes, that's it, of course.*

Clotilde knocks on the door; it feels strange being back. She hasn't set foot there since the start of the vacation. After the supposed abortion, they had both gotten started on their studying, and their afternoon lovemaking had become less frequent, finally stopping altogether. On the night after they'd celebrated their bacs at Adrien's mother's, and then at the Lac de la Forêt, she'd slept at Étienne's. He'd taken her quickly, too drunk to linger and notice that her tummy and breasts had got even bigger.

She waits a few minutes and, since no one opens to her, goes in. She hears some noise in the distance, the door from sitting room to garden is open. Clotilde takes her chance to go up the stairs in front of her, without encountering a soul, and then shuts herself in the bedroom. If anyone asks her what she's doing there, she'll say that Étienne told her to come and wait for him "as usual."

She starts to look for her letter. Nothing lying around. She opens the drawers of the desk, flicks through some *Rock & Folk* magazines, a Larousse dictionary, searches on his shelves, not an envelope to be seen. She looks in the wastepaper bin: just some cigarette butts and an old TV schedule. In the wardrobe, clothes on hangers and folded linen.

She sits on the bed to think. Her attention is then drawn to Étienne's backpack, hanging from the window latch, just behind the curtain. It's covered in graffiti. From tenth grade to twelfth, pupils from successive classes have scrawled any old thing in ballpoint pen on the fabric. Two badges, a Nirvana one and a Pearl Jam one. She recognizes one quote, among others, that she'd written in black felt pen under one of the straps: MORE THAN YESTERDAY AND LESS THAN TOMORROW.

She opens the bag and finds lessons hurriedly copied out onto double pages, messy handwriting, a lab textbook, a compilation with Velvet on the cover. But no letter. She finally pulls out his 1993–1994 diary, on which Étienne has drawn all kinds of little figures, when bored in class, rather than filling in his timetable or his homework due dates. He couldn't care less about his schedule, all he had to do was closely follow Nina Beau or Adrien-the-maggot to get from one class to the next.

Clotilde goes through the diary, page by page, finds a ticket for an Indochine concert dated 29 April 1994. She remembers that Étienne wanted to go with the other two, without her.

Where is that damned letter? And why did she send it? She could slap herself. What if he hadn't received it? What if the mailman's death had sent the post office into chaos?

"Good riddance!"

Clotilde's eyes stop on these two words, scribbled by Étienne on 25 May 1994. It takes her a few seconds to understand. She's not sure whether she's more shocked by the words "good riddance," or by the exclamation mark.

No, what really shatters her is the date on which he's written that: 25 May is the day Étienne left her outside the reception of the hospital in Autun.

How did he dare?

And with no spelling mistakes, at that. When he makes so many.

*That giant shit of a jerk definitely is a bastard.*

So what if he got her letter, she couldn't give a shit either way. She sees red. Throws the diary in the bin, charges out of the room, and comes face to face with Madame Rancoeur.

"Oh, Clotilde, how are you?

"Fine."

"Waiting for Étienne?"

"Yes."

"Didn't hear you arrive . . . Saw you the other day at the pizzeria . . . Is that going well?"

"Yes."

"Dreadful, isn't it, about that poor mailman . . . And his granddaughter, what will become of her? Thank goodness Madame Beaulieu is looking after everything. And just as well Étienne is taking Nina to Paris with him. She'll move on to other things."

". . ."

"It's too hot outside, could you help me bring the garden table inside?"

"Sure."

"It's lucky you're here, I'm running late. You can give me a hand before everyone arrives."

While helping with the final preparations, Clotilde sees that "Good riddance!", written on 25 May, once again. The words won't leave her. She's dying to go up to the bathroom, steal drugs from the family cabinet, and concoct a deadly cocktail to pour into Étienne's drink. She's only just finished putting out bowls of fruit and other snacks when he arrives. She detects his cologne before even hearing his voice. That's what it is, having someone under your skin, it's anticipating their presence.

"Meet up this evening?" he whispers in her ear.

*Good riddance*, thinks Clotilde.

"Where?" she asks.

"Dunno, a quiet spot."

"O.K."

Clotilde goes over to Nina. Quietly says to her: "I'm so sorry for your loss." Nina says: "Thank you, that's kind."

Clotilde doesn't mean a word of it. As for Nina, she's not thinking anymore, she's speaking like a robot.

Clotilde sits on the sofa beside Étienne and his "best friend." She doesn't know what to do with her hands when Étienne is holding Nina's. She tries to meet his eye, but he's staring at the wall opposite him.

An hour goes by, Clotilde finally stands up. She suggests to Étienne meeting by the lake at nine, at the usual place, under their tree. He replies: "O.K., see you later."

And that's it.

The road outside the Beaulieus' house. The scorching pavements. She goes home, alone.

In a fortnight, Étienne and Nina will be living in Paris. And her? What will become of her?

Does she feel like living or dying?

Why had Étienne suggested meeting her this evening? Probably wants to leave her properly.

*Good riddance.*

*

She comes back out at around 7:30 P.M. She's changed, is now wearing a shirtdress that's easy to take off, black with white spots, with ladybug buttons down the front.

*Ladybug, ladybug*

*Fly away home*
*Your house is on fire*
*And your children all gone . . .*

She has an hour's walk to reach the lake. Her driving license can't come soon enough. She was never allowed to have a moped or scooter, too dangerous, according to her parents.

Not as dangerous as loving Étienne.

She crosses La Comelle, passes the church, walks through the last subdivision, which leads to a country road. A car coming in the opposite direction slows down and stops alongside her. She doesn't immediately recognize the driver, who winds down his window.

"Can I drop you somewhere?"

It's the Damamme son. He was at the funeral that morning and at the Beaulieus' that afternoon. It's obvious he's mad about Nina Beau. Clotilde is surprised not to see him at the wheel of his sports car, and to find him here, on this godforsaken road. Not the type to hang out with La Comelle's deadbeats.

He doesn't wait for her to answer, just does a U-turn. Clotilde hesitates, then gets into the passenger seat.

"Going to the lake?" he asks her.

"Yes."

"It's not really a lake, more like a dump, don't you think?" he asks, jokingly.

"It depends."

"Depends on what?"

"Some parts are clean."

"What are you going to do over there?"

"I'm meeting someone. Étienne."

"Ah. Been going out with him for long?"

"Nine months. And you? Are you going out with Nina?"

"More or less."

"More? Or less?"

"With her grandfather's death, less. And they're going to leave. Your guy's taking her off to Paris."

"You seem sad."

"You do, too. We're even."

"There's no room for us around them. They're a threesome. They'll always be a threesome. If you don't like the lake, where are you coming from, then?" Clotilde asks.

"I followed Étienne on his motorbike."

"Why d'you follow him?"

"Wanted to kill him."

"You're talking nonsense now."

"Yes. And no. Wouldn't you like to kill him?"

"Yes. Sometimes," she admits.

"You see, he's harming everyone."

"How's he harming you?"

"Nina."

"But there's nothing between Nina and Étienne!" Clotilde exclaims.

"How naïve you are. Shall I drop you here?"

Emmanuel Damamme leaves Clotilde at the edge of the path, right beside Étienne's motorbike, and drives straight off.

Étienne is stretched out on his back, under their tree. A well-known tree with initials and hearts carved into its bark. Not theirs. Too tacky. High grasses almost hide him. She can make out his hair and T-shirt. He doesn't move. Suddenly, she wonders if Damamme has harmed him. That guy's so weird. He'd told her, after all, that he'd followed Étienne to kill him.

Clotilde approaches Étienne cautiously, feeling very apprehensive, but not the apprehension she'd imagined when coming here. Étienne is totally still, eyes closed, beside him a packet of aperitif snacks and a bottle of whiskey, both started. When he opens his eyes, she pauses for a moment. She lies on top of him to kiss him, can't help thinking of the blonde in Saint-Raphael, feels like ripping his tongue out, but that will be for later. First, she must play, not have fun, but play.

She asks the question she's been dying to ask:

"You didn't get my letter?"

"What letter?"

She sees straight away that he's not lying.

Étienne stares at her, what she reads in his eyes irks her. He hasn't the look of a boy in love, but of one that's embarrassed.

*Good riddance.*

She tells him she wants to have a swim, with this heat. She returns to the subject of Nina's grandfather. And the more she talks, the more sternly Étienne looks at her. She senses he's going to leave, escape from her. So she pulls out all the stops, caresses him in all the right places, the ones she knows. He responds immediately. A victory with very little glory. Étienne's an easy boy. Hard to keep but easy to please.

They get on his motorbike, drive deep into the forest, away from prying eyes.

They get undressed at the same time, him quickly, her slowly, she wants her surprise to have maximum impact.

He dives in, moves away from the edge, swims far off, swivels around occasionally to observe her. She turns her back on him, undoes her strapping, thinks: *What if we drowned, here, both of us? Like in a Greek tragedy. Dying with him, that would be the finest way to go, ever . . .* She can already see the headlines: "Tragic accident, two lovers lose their lives."

They would be buried together. Their two names would be engraved side by side, for eternity, like Romeo and Juliet. "Here lie Étienne Beaulieu and Clotilde Marais. 1976–1995."

But how to get Étienne under the water? He's much stronger than her. He'd have to be drugged or blind drunk.

She watches him from a distance and waits until his head is under the water to jump in herself. She swims toward him, laughing too loudly, she's aware of it, but can't stop her nervous hiccups as she pictures the look on his face when he sees her belly.

She joins him in the middle of the lake, thinking that he might make her disappear, drown her to say *good riddance* to her—once and for all, this time. Apart from Nina and the Damamme son, no one knows they're together this evening.

*All the better, let's be done with this.*

"I have a surprise," she whispers to him.

Clotilde dives under the water, swims a few strokes, and then resurfaces to lie on her back. *The effect must be spectacular*, she thinks, pushing her belly out as much as she can.

She sees Étienne changing color as he stares at her abdomen. She sees him replaying, at speed, that day, 25 May, and realizing that he'd been taken in, that he's a complete fool, that he should have suspected as much.

He is totally dumbfounded, while she pretends to be jubilant, looking defiantly at him, with a mocking smile. She hopes he's going to throw himself on her, push her head down, do her in. She envisages a second possible scenario, the worst one: *He kills me and ends his life in prison. The finest revenge.*

But nothing ever happens the way we imagine it. He disappears under the water. She's scared. Calls out to him. Screams his name, and when he reappears, he's already close to the bank.

*The coward, once again he just runs away.*

She summons all her strength to catch him up, doing the crawl—top marks in the sports bac, majoring in swimming.

In a matter of seconds, she grabs his ankles so he can't get out. She thinks of Damamme's words: "Wouldn't you like to kill him?"

But Étienne is far too strong for her. He fights back and leaps out of the water as if the devil were on his tail.

She grabs onto a root and pulls herself out. There's only disdain, now, in Étienne's eyes. In fact, he's not staring at her belly anymore, but at her, in the eye, with a hatred that makes him ugly.

Clotilde has lost.

She bursts into tears:

"Don't worry, I'll ask nothing of you. No one knows, not even my parents."

She grabs her bag and shows him the cash from her savings account.

"Look, I've got plenty of dough, I'm going to go away."

"Go where?" he asks.

"Don't know yet . . . This evening, this meeting between us, it was to dump me, wasn't it?"

She's losing control, doing his head in. He can't take any more of her. He hates her. If she keeps whining, he'll leave, and she'll never see him again. She must calm down, find a way to hold on to him. Even if it means knocking him out with a rock. She's very close to admitting the truth to him, that she lost the fetus, that nature had done his work for him.

"Fuck's sake, I'm not even eighteen . . . Why did you do that?" Étienne moans, after gulping down more whiskey.

"I wasn't brave enough to have the abortion."

"I don't believe you, Clotilde. Say that you wanted to trap me. But don't try to make me swallow your bravery crap."

She gets dressed as fast as she can. Her belly worked in the water, but now she's scared, she feels empty.

Sitting on the grass, he rolls himself a joint. His hands are shaking.

She sits near him.

"When our parents find out, they'll flip their lids. Yours as much as mine," he says, moistening the paper with the tip of his tongue.

"I'll leave before they know," she reassures him.

"But where can you go, for Christ's sake?"

She smiles.

"I've always sorted things out myself."

"I don't want a kid. I've never wanted one. I never will want one. You cheated me. That's disgusting."

"And you, aren't you disgusting in wanting to dump me?"

He closes his eyes. She senses, knows she's exasperating him. She'd like to make love one last time. Gain some time. Right now, she doesn't care whether she lives or dies. All that matters to her is to touch him. Watch him come. She has that gift that the others don't. With her, he gets off. She knows how to make him crazy. He's stretched out now, she applies nimble fingers to his body, he pushes them away, once, twice, then finally gives in. She fondles him for a long time, watches his erect penis, manipulates it, he groans louder and louder, his breathing quickens, he comes in Clotilde's hands. His eyelids stay closed, he says nothing more, his joint, which has gone out, lies beside the almost empty bottle.

*It's the end of the end of the world*, she thinks. He didn't even look at her. She disgusts him. Her body, deformed by the pregnancy, revolts him. He's seventeen years old, he wants cute girls, not some bloated biddy.

She watches Étienne dozing. His breath stinks of alcohol. Crumbs around his lips. He disgusts her, too.

It's still warm, but she suddenly feels cold. She wants to go home, get back to her room. *No, not my room. Not the shower. Not the drain.* She never wants to see her parents, or anyone else, ever again.

She finishes getting dressed, has got dried mud on her feet and down her legs. *I'm filthy.*

She walks through the forest to reach the dirt road leading to La Comelle. She finds her way thanks to the lights on the horizon. Around ten minutes of walking under the trees, the crunch of her steps on the leaves. From some distance, on another embankment, the sound of voices and techno music.

Once she's back on the road, she'll have two kilometers left to walk before the first houses.

*Two more kilometers to go, two more kilometers of sorrow, two more kilometers to go . . . No point being more precise, this affair is already over . . .*

She won't see Étienne again. In a few years' time, maybe they'll bump into each other in a supermarket aisle, or outside La Comelle's *bar-tabac*, and they'll say to each other: "Hi. —Oh, hi. This is my husband. —Hello, nice to meet you, my wife . . . Are you well? What are you up to? . . . See you around."

*It's over. Over*, she thinks, arriving at the dirt road.

She jumps over the ditch separating road from forest. Hears a car behind her. A car coming from the lake. The Damamme son? Probably followed them. Saw them in the water, perhaps, and afterwards, when she . . . Everything goes dark in her mind.

Third scenario. She's found dead, run over by a car: a banal road accident or suicide? She ruins Étienne Beaulieu's life, he blames himself. *No chance, he'll get over it in no time.*

Clotilde feels an overwhelming fatigue.

*We'd act just the same*
*If we had our time again*

*It's just simply, simply*
*A Saturday night on Earth . . .*
*He arrives, she sees him, she wants him*
*And her eyes do the rest*
*She manages to put fire into*
*Every move she makes . . .*

*Damned song . . . What day is it again? Wednesday. Ah yes, the day for kids. Like when I fell pregnant . . .*

The car, sending up a cloud of dust, will soon be level with her, Clotilde turns around, while still walking fast, judges the distance, can't make out the driver, who suddenly accelerates.

Five meters, four meters, three meters, two meters, she takes a running jump.

# 81

*2 January 2003*

There's knocking on the door of her studio. Two dogs bark. Three sharp knocks. Lili never does that. She knows that Nina lives in fear, if something's urgent or there's news to pass on, she announces herself by yelling: "It's Lili!"

Who has just entered the shelter? At nine in the morning, it's closed to the public. As for the staff, they still don't seem to suspect that someone's hiding in this hut.

Nina daren't move. She's still lying in bed, groggy from the painkillers she'd been prescribed the previous day, at the hospital. She pulls the sheet up to her chin. More knocking. And again.

She clenches her fists and calls out, warily:

"Who is it?"

"It's me."

Nina recognizes the voice, calms down, breathes easier.

She gets up, pulls on a long sweater, winces with pain from the bite. The dog had been scared when she'd approached it, Nina knows better than anyone what fear can provoke.

She runs a hand through her hair and opens the door.

Étienne's huge form in the doorway. His cologne. Nina feels like throwing herself into his arms but does nothing. The last time she saw him, he was furious and had just abandoned her, in the middle of a brasserie in Lyons.

They don't embrace. He comes inside. Looks around the room, lingering on the workbench, with all its brushes, glue, papers, tubes of paint, wire, beads, mosaics . . . A bedside lamp, its base recently repainted, left to dry in the middle.

"It's my contribution," Nina says, as if to justify this odd clutter. "I make items for the refuge . . . How did you find me?"

"An informer."

"As in?"

"The hospital."

Étienne gazes at the bandage around Nina's ankle. She's wearing a long sweater; her legs are bare. He finds her once more as he knew her before, slim, slender arms and wrists. Her body and face have got their grace back. But she's living in a hovel, surrounded by dogs. This place, it's almost destitution. He daren't say that to her. Without that bandage around her ankle, she could almost be just back from vacation. She seems so much more serene than last time he saw her. When she was living in her semi-fortress with that lunatic.

"So, you never actually left La Comelle," he finally says, as if to himself. "You've been living in here for . . . two years?"

"Two years and two months."

"That's crazy."

"I'm scared he'll find me," Nina admits.

"Damamme?"

"Yes."

"I'll sort him out."

Nina's face changes, she becomes tense, panics.

"No one can sort out mad people. Not even the police. Don't ever go to see him. He'll force you to reveal where I am. D'you swear to me?"

"Yup," Étienne replies, reluctantly.

"Thank you," she says, pressing her hands together.

She goes over to her kettle, grabs two cups and teabags. Étienne can't say he doesn't want any tea.

"Have you heard from Adrien?" she asks.

She sees a flicker of jealousy in Étienne's eyes. He's only just arrived, and already she's on about the *other one*.

"Apparently, he quit everything on a whim. Paris, his plays, the high life. According to Louise, he's traveling. She sometimes flies off to see him. You know, they've always been underhand . . . can't they just get married and make babies like everyone else?"

"Why did you come here, Étienne?"

"To see you. The last time, I lost it because of Clotilde's letter. I was angry with myself. Because, after that, you left . . . and I'd let you down when things were hard for you . . . How do you earn a living?"

"I don't."

Étienne stares at Nina in disbelief.

"I don't cost that much. I wanted to sell my family jewelry, but Lili wouldn't hear of it. Lili is the director of the shelter. She's my friend. She saved me. She buys me two or three things to wear in the sales, toothpaste and soap, aspirin if I get a headache. I wash my clothes at her place. She has a vegetable garden; I can help myself whenever I like. She cans some vegetables and makes cakes. In exchange, I help her to look after this place and make lots of things that get sold on the open days."

"But are you planning on staying here a long time?"

"I don't know."

"But Nina, this is no life!"

"It's mine."

"You're living like an outlaw! But you've done nothing wrong!"

"Yes, I did something wrong in marrying Emmanuel Damamme."

"You were eighteen years old! You'd just lost your grandfather."

Nina hands a cup of tea to Étienne and gazes outside, lost in thought.

"Could you ask Marie-Laure to go up to the cemetery, please? I can't go to visit Grandpa anymore, and I'd like her to check everything's okay, take some flowers from time to time. But you've not seen me, okay. You don't know where I am."

"Nina, you can't stay like this."

"This suits me. I'm content here. Étienne, I know you well enough to know what you think about this place, the disgust in your eyes when you contemplate the walls, the joints, the rotten window frame, but if you knew how content I feel. Sure, I'd love to stroll freely through town and have a coffee at the terrace of a café, but I don't feel ready yet. I know that Emmanuel is looking for me, I sense it. It's irrational, you must think I'm crazy, but as long as Lili is close to me, I'll feel safe."

"Your Lili, she's called Éliane Folon. You know she was a hooker?"

". . ."

"She's even done time in prison and—"

"I'd like you to go, Étienne."

"Don't take it badly, Nina, but admit it, you do have a knack for surrounding yourself with weird people."

"Yes, I do take it badly. Did you come here to soothe your conscience? As you can see, I'm just fine, you can go back to Lyon. Don't disparage the only person in my life to offer me a helping hand without expecting a thing in return."

"Until the day she puts you out on the street?"

"Get lost, Étienne"

"As you wish."

"I do wish. Thanks for your visit."

"You're still the same pain in the ass."

"I do my best."

Nina regrets all this. She'd like to keep him here. For him to sit back down. For this conversation to start again. Étienne must have come to suggest some solution to her. He must have meant well by coming here. She must convince him, gently, that she's not leaving this place.

"I've met someone," he tells her, on the doorstep.

"I'm happy for you."

"You can call me whenever you like. My phone number hasn't changed."

"I don't switch my phone on anymore."

They stare at each other one last time. Nina places her hand on Étienne's cheek, he grasps it and kisses her fingers.

*

Étienne walks beside the kennels. Two youngsters are hosing down the floors, a walker puts a leash on a collie-type mongrel and sets off, Étienne reads the dog's label attached to the gate: DEBBY: BREED X SHEEPDOG, FEMALE, STERILIZED. BORN 1999, AT SHELTER SINCE 2001. Two other dogs bark while wagging their tails.

When he passes outside the office, just before the exit, Lili calls out to him:

"Did you see Nina?"
"Yes."
"Did she tell you she's scared?"
"Yes."
"Are you her friend Étienne?"
"Yes."
"You're the cop?"
"Yup."
"Are you going to do something to stop that madman?"
"No."
"What are you waiting for? Him to come and kill her?"
"I'm not taking any orders from you. I know who you are. What you did."
"What I did is my business, young man."
Étienne immediately regrets saying something so inappropriate. It's himself he's angry with, not this poor woman.
"Forgive me."
"Forgiven."
". . ."
"She's a fine girl. When I met her, she looked like a miserable creature. Don't just stand there, come inside and have a coffee before you go."
Étienne follows her. Takes a seat in a rickety armchair opposite Lili. She clears away some papers and places two steaming cups on her desk. Éliane Folon is wearing green-nylon pants and a long sweater with yellow and pink bobbles on it. She's gathered her hair into an improbable topknot, caught in a big black clip.
"You've seen my file?" she asks.
"Yup. Attempted homicide."
"A total bastard."
"I'm not a judge."
"Well, yes you are, young man. You just told me, to my face, that you knew what I'd done, sounding more like a public prosecutor."
". . ."
"But that's forgiven, as I told you."
"How did you end up here?" Étienne asks.

"I was released ten years ago. My prison counselor found me some work in La Comelle. As a cleaner at the Magellan factory. A case of animal cruelty brought me into contact with the former director of the shelter, whom I replaced. Broadly speaking, dogs saved my life. So now it's me who saves them."

"Why are you helping Nina?"

"She reminds me of a girl I knew in my former life. She was really knocked about. When I tried to intervene, her pimp disappeared her. You know, I have an instinct for reading fear in girls' eyes, and Nina was one of them."

Étienne clenches his fists. He realizes how short he'd fallen. A mere semblance of a friend.

"Who was it, this guy you wanted to bump off?"

"My lover."

Étienne is surprised by Lili's answer. He thought she'd say, "my pimp," or "my ponce." She bursts out laughing.

"The look on your face! I'm joking. A nasty piece of work, I can tell you. One morning, after a vicious remark and one slap too many, I made him bleed. He got over it. I left him a fine scar. Later, time caught up with him, he got hit by a stray bullet. Wrong place, wrong time, you might say, but I think the good Lord chose the right place and the right time to push him toward the exit."

# 82

*29 December 2017*

Knees tucked under chins, the three of us are sitting, side by side, in the sunshine, on the deck of a ferry taking us to Palermo. Étienne on the left, Nina in the middle, and me on the right. Leaning against the railing, we let ourselves be lulled by the gentle breeze. The sea seems to be watching us.

"A hundred years ago, it was the First World War."

"That's insane, Nina . . . What makes you come out with that? You haven't changed, and I think that's 'wicked,' as my son would say. Why are you thinking about the First World War?"

Nina smiles, letting the light in.

"Dunno, the trenches, time passing . . . For me, time dragged when we didn't wish each other happy birthday anymore, we three. The first time, it was like a huge silence in my head. All those events that mark a year, and then nothing anymore. Whereas before, we did a running commentary on everything."

"I've never had a memory for dates," Étienne reminds us.

He lights a cigarette. I can tell that Nina is dying to stop him, to blow out the flame of the lighter, but doesn't dare.

As for me, I say nothing, as usual. This silence does me good. And I know that neither Étienne nor Nina will ask me why I'm staying quiet. That's what knowing each other forever is about, too.

"Why are you accompanying me? Why are you doing this for me?" Étienne asks us. "When, basically, I've always been disloyal to the two of you."

"Disloyal?" Nina exclaims. "What about 2 January 2003, the day you visited the shelter? I don't know what you did, or what happened, but it did happen."

"What are you talking about?"

"About that day I phoned you," Étienne says to me. "You were in Cagliari with my sister. Not far from here. Do you remember?"

"How could I forget? That was the last time I spoke to you until four days ago."

"You spoke to each other on that day?" Nina asks me, covering her mouth with both hands, like a little girl caught doing something naughty.

By way of reply, I just smile at her and return to my silence.

Étienne closes his eyes, stretches out his legs.

He remembers Éliane Folon, or Lili, as Nina called her, in the shelter office, her eyes like two green marbles, scrutinizing him. Making him understand that it was high time for Emmanuel Damamme to be "taken care of," so Nina could regain some kind of life.

Upon leaving the shelter, Étienne had called Adrien, without much conviction. He answered immediately.

"I thought you'd have changed phone number," were Étienne's first words.

The two of them hadn't seen each other since their fiery confrontation at the Brasserie La Lorraine.

"What for? No one's trying to contact me anymore, except Louise and my former editor."

"I mainly thought you wouldn't answer my call."

"If you call me, it's to talk to me about Nina. Otherwise, you wouldn't be calling me. You've heard something, is that it?"

"Yup. I just saw her. In the flesh."

"Where is she?"

"You're not going to believe me."

The last time Étienne had set foot in the Damamme residence was the evening of the football World Cup final, in 1998. Why hadn't he rescued Nina from her life that very day? What had stopped him? She already looked so unhappy.

On 2 January 2003, Étienne found Emmanuel at home, at ten in the morning, unkempt, thinner, and alone. He had several days' stubble and was in T-shirt and shorts. A pitiful sight.

"Have you come to wish me a happy new year?" he asked, sarcastically, upon seeing Étienne.

"Why have you got yourself into such a state?"

"Love," he sniggered. "Do you know where Nina is?"

"Forget her."

"Never."

"Why? She wants you to forget her, that's why she left."

"Maybe, but I, myself, want to see her."

"You should just drop it, once and for all."

"Is it to tell me that kind of bullshit that you've come here?"

"You could have problems. Big problems."

"What kind?"

"The terminal kind."

"Are you threatening me?"

Emmanuel started gesticulating, grotesquely, while chanting, louder and louder:

"Étienne Beaulieu is threatening me! Étienne Beaulieu is threatening me!"

"I can understand why she left, you're the worst."

Emmanuel stopped his antics. A long silence set in. Then:

"So . . . do you know where Nina is? Go on, say it. Say it! Say it! Say it!" Emmanuel screamed, while jumping up and down like a hysterical kid.

Étienne sat down on the sofa. Everything was going to plan.

"Why today? Why have you shown up here? Have you seen her? Do you know where she is? Yes, of course, that's it, fuck it! Admit that you know!" Emmanuel bellowed, before slamming his fist into the wall.

"Fucking psychopath . . ." Étienne muttered, between his teeth.

Emmanuel suddenly became serious again.

"To hell with you, Beaulieu, you and your preaching. In any case, I'm selling my company and I'm going away."

"Where?"

"Haven't decided yet. Far. Very far. You're right, I must forget that slut."

Hearing him insult Nina like that, Étienne had to stop himself from smashing his head in.

"Do you know it's me who brought Clotilde Marais to the lake the night she disappeared? You went round saying she'd never shown up, but me, I know that you lied. I dropped her off beside your motorbike . . ."

Étienne acted as if he didn't believe him. But the guy had hit him straight in the heart. He was probably lying to get the truth. How could this lunatic have come across Clotilde on the night of 17 August? Emmanuel had identified what tormented Étienne, who had been prepared for everything but that.

"What the hell did you do to that poor kid?" Emmanuel spat out.

"I haven't come to talk about Clotilde, but about Nina."

"You don't believe me, huh? And yet I can describe to you the dress she was wearing that night, black with white spots. Buttons down the front, red ones in the shape of ladybugs. And on her feet, white sneakers. I remember because I thought to myself that white wasn't a great choice for walking around that place."

"You're a compulsive liar," Étienne hit back. "Everyone knows what she was wearing. It was on the 'missing' posters. And anyhow, what the hell would you have been doing around there? There's an Olympic-sized pool in the middle of your garden. You've never hung out at the lake."

Emmanuel Damamme's smile was both evil and sad at the same time. Étienne was caught between pity and loathing. The snappy dresser, who wasn't so stylish now, was clearly tormented and in control of nothing. He was looking at Étienne without seeing him, lost in his own thoughts.

"It's the first time I've noticed that there's the word '*beau*' in your name."

". . ."

"On the day of the funeral, I saw you arriving at Nina's grandfather's house in the afternoon, you and the fag. I waited, and then you left on your own. I don't know why, but I followed you, saw you entering and leaving your house, getting on your motorbike. I had just one desire: to send you flying into the ditch. I was behind you, not in the Alpine, in a company car. I almost rammed you several times. Adieu Beaulieu. The reason I didn't was Nina's grandfather. Too many deaths in one go. I feared she wouldn't be able to take it. Next, I saw you lying in the grass beside the lake—that is, the public dump, and swigging whiskey like some drunkard. And then I had a moment of lucidity, wondered what the hell I was doing there. Driving back to La Comelle, I came across Clotilde Marais, walking alongside the road. I did a U-turn and drove her to the lake. She told me she was meeting you there. It was obvious as hell that she was madly in love."

"Is it you who harmed Clotilde?" Étienne heard himself asking.

"The only harm I did her was dropping her off beside your bike. You're far from in the clear. So don't start moralizing to me!"

"Did you stay near us? Did you spy on us?"

"No. I came back here."

"Liar."

"I didn't give a damn about you two, the only thing that interested me right then was Nina. I had to be at home in case she needed me. At the time, as you know, there were no mobile phones. One would wait hours beside a landline. And the miracle happened. When I thought I'd never see her again, she called me, asked me to come and fetch her from her place. She was on her own with the fag—"

"Stop calling Adrien that."

"Why? Have you got the hots for him? Nina isn't enough for you?"

Emmanuel cracked up laughing. A painful laugh that deformed his face.

"Talking about Clotilde Marais, you know it's me who regularly phones the cops to tell them that she was with you that evening?"

Étienne stopped himself from lunging at him. This man wasn't mad, he was perverse, manipulative. But this admission almost came as a relief to him. He'd often thought that the anonymous person informing against him was his own father. That father who didn't love him, maybe to the point of accusing him of the worst.

"It's even me who called that TV show, when the case came up again," Damamme ranted on. "I've always dreamt of seeing you end up behind bars. To think that you became a cop. You're a sham, Beaulieu. Go on, admit that you killed Clotilde Marais."

Forgetting his plan, Étienne couldn't help but retort:

"I'm not mad, I don't terrorize girls. In fact, no girl has ever left me. Unlike you."

Emmanuel grabbed a frying pan from the cooker and hit Étienne so hard he blacked out. Étienne hadn't seen that coming.

When he came round, in a pool of blood, his eyebrow had a two-centimeter gash across it. Emmanuel was no longer there. Étienne stemmed the bleeding. He was furious with himself, why had he provoked that half-wit? Étienne searched for him in every room of the house. He even opened the wardrobes in the bedroom, noticing that all trace of Nina having lived there had been removed.

At the same time, he was thinking, so what if he's run off, that assault is fortunate: assaulting a law-enforcement officer, Étienne could have him locked up. If he could just lay hands on him.

Damamme was there, in the kitchen, standing beside the sideboard, white as a sheet, vacant, clutching a glass of water.

It was a good time to come out with it:

"I know where Nina is."

Emmanuel looked at Étienne as if he were the devil. What he'd been waiting for, for more than two years, searching for like an obsessed hunter, he didn't seem to want to hear it anymore. As if finally getting somewhere made his whole quest fall apart.

He sat down, still clutching his glass of water, like a convict awaiting his sentence. And Étienne spoke quietly and condescendingly. Choosing his words.

"I've just traced Nina thanks to an informer. She lives some three hundred kilometers from here. And . . . I believe she's happy. She lives with a man who is ten years her senior. They have a child. A little boy of nine months old called Lino. They're expecting a second child in the spring. Nina met her partner at work."

Emmanuel wanted to scream: "But I'm her husband!" Before realizing that, no, he was nothing anymore.

Étienne continued, as if he were plunging a knife deeper and deeper.

"She works in a painting-restoration studio. That was her dream. You know, she's always loved to paint . . . I'm sorry . . . I've never liked you, Damamme, but you deserve the truth, I can see that you're suffering . . . over someone who no longer exists. Nina has put you, us, Adrien, my parents, me, La Comelle behind her. We'll never see her again."

"Where is she living?" Emmanuel managed to ask.

"In Annecy, a sweet house beside the lake. I went to check. It came as a shock to me. I saw her from a distance, pregnant, beautiful. She was walking with her son in a stroller, a dog on a leash. She's turned the page. Do the same. It's over."

Emmanuel lay down on the floor, in the fetal position, knees against chest, and began to sob. He had imagined his wife lost, alone, repentant, and quaking with fear. That other scenario, he'd never envisaged it. Another man, two children, a dog . . . She'd settled into a new life. Finding her, killing her, killing himself, it all suddenly seemed totally incongruous. Nina, *his* Nina, submissive and terrified, sterile and alcoholic, was dead and buried. The girl in Annecy with two kids, that wasn't her anymore.

Back in his car, Étienne rang Adrien to tell him how successful his plan had been. Adrien didn't answer.

When Étienne had left the shelter, before visiting Emmanuel Damamme, he and Adrien had put their heads together over the phone.

A solution had to be found to free Nina from her husband. Have him killed, impossible. Kill him, no way. Push him to suicide by making him think Nina was dead, wouldn't work. Give him a false address in Polynesia in the hope that he wouldn't return, too far-fetched.

Then Adrien had found it: simply make him believe that Nina had rebuilt a happy life for herself, with husband and children as a shield. Adrien had dictated the words to Étienne: the Lac d'Annecy, the lover, the children, the dog, the stroller, the spring, the restoring of paintings, all that Damamme hadn't been able to offer his wife. He'd never dare confront that reality, and would, perhaps, give up all thoughts of finding her again.

"Clearly, you're the writer here," Etienne had said, with elation. "That's a damn great idea."

After that, Adrien and Étienne had neither seen nor talked to each other again.

## 83

*29 December 2017*

Bernard Roi has always been ordinary. At elementary school, he was generally graded at around five out of ten, and at middle school, ten out of twenty. Nothing to draw attention to himself. If Bernard Roi had done an IQ test, his intelligence would have been described as "normal to average."

In middle school, he went as far as eighth grade, changed path before entering ninth grade, and just scraped through with a qualification as a car mechanic.

But the year he was sixteen, his boss, a garage owner in La Comelle, sacked him for his frequent lateness. Bernard smoked too many joints, hence his difficulty waking up.

At the end of 1994, Bernard started at the Magellan factory, where car parts were manufactured. He worked in quality control, at the end of the production line. As a temporary employee at first, then on a permanent contract. Twenty-three years without rocking the boat. Bernard sailed through staff cuts and other voluntary redundancies. He put money aside, opened a savings account, bought a small house and a car on credit.

During middle school, he listened to The Clash and wore T-shirts with the Sex Pistols on them, but he can no longer remember why exactly. When his children ask him: "Dad, what were you like when you were young?" Bernard says to them: "Tiresome, everyone said I thought I was the king."

When he was a teenager, an old Gypsy at La Comelle's fun fair, to whom he hadn't dared say no when she'd grabbed his hand, had predicted a generally happy marriage and two kids for him, but said that a clamorous event would turn his seventeenth year upside down. "It's hazy, but it is devastating," she told him, asking for ten francs while staring wide-eyed at his lifelines.

Bernard thought nothing more of it. Until the day that "event" took place. Then he remembered the final words of the old woman: "Tell the truth, lad, or you'll be done for."

Bernard never had told the truth.

A kind father, a good husband, Bernard Roi leads a perfectly ordered life: in the morning he drinks his mug of coffee after dunking a factory-baked *madeleine* in it, gets on his bike to go to the factory, one kilometer from his home, eats his packed lunch at five past twelve on *his* bench, and returns home at five-thirty to help his wife with the daily chores.

This year, he took his Christmas break from 22 December. But this year, unlike others, he watched TV programs with his big children without really seeing them, randomly answered yes or no to questions he was asked without really listening to them.

And last night, he decided to come clean.

It's nine in the morning, this 29 December, when Bernard gets on his bike. Not to show up at the factory, but at the police station.

Amidst all his misery, there's a stroke of luck: he comes face to face with Sébastien Larand, just passing through reception, an old schoolmate who wasn't really his friend, but the fact he knows him reassures Bernard. He would have hated to fall on a stranger in uniform or, worse, to have to deal with a woman.

The officer favors him with a smile.

"Hi, what brings you here so early in the morning?"

"Clotilde Marais," says Bernard, staring at his shoes, polished by his wife, Céline, every first Saturday of the month.

Sébastien Larand's smile instantly vanishes—he'd only meant to stay five minutes. For several days now, the people of La Comelle have talked of nothing else: was the body found at the bottom of the lake the young girl who disappeared? Dramas like that aren't very common around here.

Sébastien and Bernard have known each other since they were kids, Bernard Roi must be one or two years older than him, not the kind of guy to mess around, so if he's here this morning, it's serious, the police officer thinks to himself.

"Follow me. We'll be more comfortable in my office."

"You're not putting me into custody?" Bernard asks, amazed.

"Until proved otherwise . . . it isn't *Law & Order: SVU* here."

As soon as he sits down, Bernard Roi regrets coming. What's the point? What's it going to change?

"I'm listening," Sébastien Larand says, encouragingly, while handing him a glass of water.

After a moment's silence, Bernard finally takes the plunge:

"That day, when she supposedly disappeared . . . Clotilde Marais . . . I wasn't in a great state. Six months earlier, I'd been sacked at the garage. I was slipping into bad ways. Smoked lots of grass. Quite a bit of skunk, too. But I never touched any other stuff. I swear on the heads of my kids. It was hot that day. Sad, too. In the morning, we'd buried our mailman, a nice guy. I felt rough. Bored, everyone away on vacation except me, as usual, like every year . . . At our place, we only saw the sea on TV. So we messed around . . . killed time. I'm not looking for excuses, like . . . See how I'm built? At the time, a bag of bones . . . Didn't dare go to the swimming pool. Because of the jibes: 'Hey, Roi, the "king," not very strong, are you, wouldn't give much for your kingdom,' you know the kind of thing. But there was still the lake. Over there, you could smoke and drink in peace. I couldn't be bothered to do anything, had no driving license, and my bro had taken the bike. I decided to grab the Twingo belonging to a neighbor, old Desnos. Couldn't stand him, that one, because he'd poisoned our dog the year before. We had no proof, but we knew it was him. The doors of his banger were always unlocked, easy to start with a Neiman key, I headed straight for the lake, shitting myself: no license, stolen car, skunk and booze in the glove box . . . I knew that I'd never bring Desnos his old wreck back, but that I was going to make the most of it, do some joyriding, and then dump it somewhere. I swam all afternoon, safe from anyone staring at me, smoked, slept, bummed around. When it started to get dark, I got back in the Twingo, and on the radio there was that song, '*Foule sentimentale*,' some soppy story. Never been able to listen to it since.

Because when I got to the end of the track, I saw a girl on the side. She turned around once, I recognized her. A girl from La Comelle I'd come across at school, one who'd never hang out with a bad boy like me. But I got scared. Dope paranoia. I panicked, accelerated so she wouldn't see me in a stolen car. As I speeded up, I thought: *Go fast past her and keep your head down*. I didn't get time to keep my head down. She threw herself from the side, like some diver or gymnast trying to beat a record at the Olympics. She threw herself under my wheels as if flying. She aimed well. No time to slam the brakes on. I screamed. Scared shitless. It was such an impact, the headlamps exploded. I stayed behind the wheel for several minutes, not daring to get out. My hands were shaking. After all I'd smoked that afternoon, I no longer knew if what I was experiencing was real or a hallucination. And that damned '*Foule sentimentale*' on the radio. I switched it off. The engine was still running. Then I cried. Then I reversed. With my sidelights, I saw her, stretched out on the road. A dead animal. I thought again of my big dog that the shit had poisoned, his cold body in the garden when I'd come home. I finally got out of the car. At first, I didn't touch her. In the end, I looked for a pulse. Dead. Why did it have to happen to me? Why had she done that? Committed suicide in front of me? Why was it with a loser like me that a princess had done herself in? I was stoned, I told myself that I must make the car and the girl disappear, and then forget it. Forget it all. In any case, who would believe me? Who? No one. With all the alcohol and weed I had in my blood . . . the stolen car, no license, my father would kill me before the cops came to arrest me. I took her in my arms, blubbing, asking her why she'd done that. I kept asking her the same question: 'Why'd you do that?' Dead people are heavy. She looked light, but I struggled to lift her. She was still warm, sweat on her arms. I laid her down on the back seat as gently as I could, as if scared to hurt her. I hit the lake road in the opposite direction, praying that I wouldn't come across anyone. I spotted an area that led straight to the water, a clearing in the middle of ferns, I accelerated for about a hundred meters, the car roared, I sped up even more, then did what James Dean did in *Rebel Without a Cause*: I opened the door and threw myself out. I broke my wrist. The car flew, like Clotilde when she'd thrown herself under my wheels, and then it went under . . .

"Didn't budge for twenty-three years. I thought it would never be found. Until I read that article in the paper. Don't waste time searching for DNA, or whatever else. It's Clotilde Marais. The worst thing is, that kid, by throwing herself under my wheels, she kind of saved my life. After that I straightened myself out. Never touched drugs or alcohol again. She got me back onto the straight and narrow. I've often thought about her parents. But I preferred them to think that she was alive somewhere, as people all over were saying. There was even someone who said they'd seen her in Brazil. I didn't want to be the one to tell a mother and father that their daughter had committed suicide. I almost talked when I saw them on TV, on Jacques Pradel's show. But at the time, my oldest boy was a year old and my wife expecting our second. They're all very nice, these people in Paris, but they don't know how tough it is to feed and protect one's family. Sometimes, it's better not to tell the truth. It does too much harm."

## 84

*30 December 2017*

Marie-Castille hangs up.

She absorbs the information.

Marie-Laure has just read her the article. Clotilde Marais had apparently thrown herself under the wheels of a car. The guy who was driving has no police record, a good father who chose to say nothing because, at the time, he wasn't thinking straight. That remains to be proved. He might have knocked her down because he'd drunk, and then got rid of her.

The old case solved. The story dug up again. And all because of a very ordinary municipality deciding to smarten up part of their lake.

Marie-Castille was near Étienne three weeks ago when he learnt that a car had been found at the bottom of the lake. He'd turned white as a sheet. Repeated several times:

"I did see it, I really did see it, I'm not mad."

"What, my love? What did you see?"

"The car."

How often had Étienne woken up calling out to Clotilde, she wonders. That's what killed him. Ravaged him. Clotilde Marais is the creature who gnawed at Étienne from inside. In dying, she took him with her, ensured he had one foot in the grave.

Étienne *must* be told. Marie-Castille senses it. It's vital. If he knows he had nothing to do with that disappearance, maybe everything will change. Can rivers be turned back? Sometimes, yes, surely. Countercurrents do exist.

She must get home, the only person who could relay the information is Valentin. Marie-Castille suspects that his father calls him. Their son is the only one connecting Étienne to their world, the world of the living. If her husband went off with Nina and that other one, it's because they represent the past, not the present. They're ghosts.

She gets into her car and repeats out loud exactly what she's going to say to her son: "My darling, when Dad phones you, yes, I know he phones you, say these words, precisely, to him: a man has confessed to the car in the lake. You just say that to him, a man has confessed to the car in the lake. Your father will understand."

*Valentin will ask me questions*, realizes Marie-Castille. *Ask me for details about this business. Shit. What am I going to say? Shit! Shit! Shit!*

She brakes abruptly and pulls over onto the shoulder. She slumps over the steering wheel, racked by violent, uncontrollable sobbing. She really can't say to her fourteen-year-old son: "When Dad was young, he got a girl pregnant, the girl then disappeared on the evening he met up with her. It's haunted him all his life . . . and he's gone to die far away from us."

Her phone vibrates in her pocket, Marie-Castille looks at the screen, unknown number, blows her nose, finally answers. She hears: "It's Nina."

*

Palermo, 65 degrees, out of the wind. Étienne and I are stretched out on the Spiaggia dell'Arenella, just a stone's throw from our *pensione*. I'm drawing in the sand, strange houses with sloping walls, while Étienne gazes at the sea. Far away from us, I can make out the figure of Nina, walking in the water. Winter's beautiful, in Italy.

"You have what you want?" I ask Étienne.

"Yes," he replies, staring at the horizon.

"Are you hungry?"

"No."

"Are you in pain?"

"No."

"Would you like me to phone someone? Give news to your parents?"

"No. My father doesn't love me."

"Why do you say that?"

"Because I know it. He must not like the look of me. Maybe if I'd had other children, there'd be one that I'd love less than the others. There's no arguing with love."

"I've not seen my father at all since I wrote *Des enfants en commun*. Which is ages ago."

"You don't miss him?"

"Strangers can't be missed."

"Does he know that, really, you're a girl?"

I have found a compromise between my two existences to such an extent that Étienne's question catches me unawares. Whenever it's just the two of us, he only ever talks to me about me.

"Not even my mother knew. It's my greatest regret . . . Having let her go without telling her."

"Louise . . . does she know we're here, in Palermo?"

"Louise knows everything. Would you like me to ask her to join us?"

"No. Absolutely not. When I'm dead . . . I would like you to have the operation. Because I know I'm the reason you never had it. You're afraid of how I might look at you. It's me who stopped you."

"You're not to blame, Étienne. It's far more complicated than that."

"Promise me you'll get it done?"

"I can't promise."

"Will Louise be with you? I mean, if you decide to do it one day, will she accompany you?"

"Yes. That's what she's been waiting for, for me. Louise has been waiting for Virginie for thirty years."

"So do it. Swear to me."

"I swear to you."

"On my head?"

"There's no point swearing on your head since you're about to die. One swears on the head of healthy people."

We burst out laughing together.

Nina comes running back toward us, as if she'd seen the devil. When she reaches us, she's too breathless to get a word out. There's just her raucous panting, which we know so well.

Étienne bawls her out:

"Why on earth did you run like that? Are you crazy or what?"

"I ran because . . . because . . . Étienne . . . because . . . Clotilde . . . it's over . . ."

*

Clotilde Marais's mother is sitting on her sofa. She hasn't changed it since her daughter went away, she thinks.

Twenty-three years.

She'd touched up some paintwork, re-wallpapered the dining room, laid a new carpet in the bedroom, but she'd hung on to the old sofa.

She can hear her husband pacing up and down upstairs. He must be thinking about the court case, the attorneys. Probably his way of getting through, of seeking what remains alive inside him. He will want to prove that Clotilde didn't commit suicide but was knocked down by an inebriated man. And possibly worse.

But me, I know perfectly well that my daughter was in a bad way. I will say so. I will say that this Bernard Roi is a collateral victim.

Like us.

We're all victims of "the departed" . . .

For twenty-three years now, to other people, I've been the mother of Clotilde Marais. The mother of the girl who vanished on 17 August 1994. The mother of the girl who disowned her family. The mother who appeared on TV, with dark shadows under her eyes. Who put her life on display.

No one knows what my name is. Just like all parents of missing children. We're now just "the parents of . . ." We're downgraded because our children have disappeared. Gone without leaving an address. I lost my first name twenty-three years ago and I'm old now. Retired.

"That's it, it's over." There's a song that says that. I've never liked it. Far too sad.

The idea that Clotilde lived in Salvador de Bahia, that suited others best. That she drank coconut water for breakfast, her beautiful blond hair gathered in a bun. That she was growing up elsewhere.

We went to Brazil in 2001. We showed people a picture of her that had been slightly aged using software. Me, I knew perfectly well that no one had seen her. I pretended to search to please my husband.

I always thought that she had hidden to die. Not hidden to live.

She didn't tell me a thing anymore, by the end, my daughter. She was nothing but a mystery. She trailed clouds of sadness behind her. She pretended about everything. I felt like I was living under the same roof as a bad actress. A stranger who had smothered my little girl.

When I let others think that Clotilde was forty-one, deep down, I always knew she was eighteen.

A mother senses those things.

17 August 1994. A date that is not that of a birth, or a death, or an anniversary. It's just the date of a disappearance.

And when that woman, the one from Chalon, stubbornly maintained to us that she'd come across Clotilde in Salvador de Bahia, I pretended to believe her. Same thing for the old bag who had supposedly seen her at the station on the night when.

Pretending to believe them allowed us to carry on living without her.

I even ended up desecrating her room, putting her belongings into plastic bags that I left in a charity tub. I removed her bed and put a desk in its place, with a computer on it. A desk with lots of empty files that serve no purpose. My husband was angry with me.

I wonder why we didn't move house. In case she came back? How would she find her way?

Even our neighbors left. The old were replaced by the young, new families, little kids.

We alone remained. Our daughter condemned us to remain. To wait for her. And that's it now, it's over.

We're not waiting for her anymore.

The phone. It won't stop ringing. Condolences, friends, busybodies, journalists. Étienne Beaulieu at the end of the line. How often had her daughter hoped to hear that voice when she answered the phone? How often had she come in asking: "Did anyone call me?"

And now that call comes, twenty-three years too late.

"I'm so sorry, Annie," he manages to say.

"I'm touched you remember my first name."

". . ."

"Your mother came to see me this morning. She told me about your cancer, that you didn't want to have any treatment."

"Stage 3 . . . It's too late."

"It's never too late, Étienne. Apart from when the police turn up at your house to tell you that your daughter is dead . . . Did you know that Clo was pregnant?"

Étienne takes a long time before answering.

"Yes."

"Did you know she had a miscarriage?"

". . ."

"I've never told anyone. Four days before her disappearance, I found sheets in the washing machine. Covered in blood. She never could get it to work. She'd emptied a bottle of bleach into the right compartment before pressing the wrong button. I understood immediately. And later, I found a book on pregnancy in the drawer of her bedside table . . . On the morning I'm talking to you about, I went into Clo's room to tell her that the mailman had died. I knew he was the grandfather of your best friend. It was a pretext, that intrusion into her room. I wanted to see her. I'll never forget her face, she was pale, pallid even. She'd just come out of the shower; I saw her figure. Her shape. I said nothing. I should have talked to her. I respected her silence out of cowardice. I threw the sheets into the garbage and pretended not to notice her sanitary napkins in the bathroom."

A lengthy silence. Étienne thinks the line has been cut off.

"Are you still there?"

"Yes," she whispers.

"There's something I must tell you, Annie—"

She interrupts him, as if not wanting to hear anything else.

"You'll come to her funeral?" she asks.

"I'm going to die."

"What are you talking about? You're still breathing, you are."

"Not for much longer."

"How do you know that?"

"I sense it."

"Fight, for god's sake."

She hangs up.

## 85

*2 January 2003*

Étienne Beaulieu has just left the house.

Emmanuel is still lying on his sofa.

For more than two years, he's been searching everywhere for her, and all the while she's been settled, a mother, elsewhere. All that energy expended just to end up here. The last scenario he could ever have imagined.

What was he doing before he met her? One should always question what one's life was like before encountering the person who ruined that life. And maybe begin again, from where one was before taking a wrong turn.

*What's the point of clinging to someone who won't shed a tear the day you die? Who'll never bother to leave a flower on your grave? Who just upped and went, abandoning you like a piece of shit? Who has made a brand new life for herself in a matter of months, as if your relationship had never existed*, thinks Emmanuel.

He feels like having a wash, a shave, getting dressed. Hasn't felt like doing that for a long time. An impulse.

He stands up and climbs the stairs to reach the bathroom. His reflection in the mirror: dismal. Just skin and bone.

He's going to leave this house, go to Lyon, be closer to his friends, meet someone, not a misfit, a real woman. Too long since he made love. Just that, a hard-on, feeling another body against his own. Sullying *her* by touching new skin, forgetting her, erasing her by flattening her ghost, again and again.

Recently, the Lyon gang signed him up on a dating site. "You need to meet someone." They created a profile for him with a different name. "Emmanuel Mésange, 1m 87, green eyes, brown hair. Interests: golf, classic literature, film, motor racing."

"Why golf?"

"Because it looks good," they told him.

"But I've almost never held a golf club in my life."

"Doesn't matter."

"I don't feel like being on your site thing."

"Well, you're going to be, all the same, go out, have a drink, change your thinking. It doesn't commit you to anything."

"I haven't set foot in a movie theater since *Itinéraire d'un enfant gâté* came out. That's about . . . fourteen years ago."

"Well anyway, on a first date, that's not what one talks about."

"Oh really? What does one talk about?"

"You'll see."

They picked a photo, taken in Mauritius, with Emmanuel in profile, tanned, smiling.

Hundreds of women sent him messages. Girls offering themselves.

Emmanuel reviewed each woman's portrait, as though in a catalogue, nothing of interest. Apart from one that did draw his attention.

Isabelle, thirty-five, living in Chalon-sur-Saône, keen horse-rider. 1m 70, blond hair, blue eyes: physically, the opposite of Nina.

Her first message began like this:

What are you doing on this site, Monsieur Mésange? And *mésange*, that's a bird, what's that about? Who's hiding behind your profile? And don't tell me it's your friends who signed you up against your will, I won't believe you.

Emmanuel replied to her because her message made him smile, and that hadn't happened for ages.

Yes, it really was my friends who signed me up to this supermarket.

Why would they have done that?

They're fed up with me dragging my feet. I'm not a fun man.

I'm sorry.

Sorry because I'm not fun?

They exchanged more emails, then phoned. Their chats continued, and Isabelle finally suggested they get together:

What if we met at the Hexagone bar for a coffee? If it's enjoyable, I'll take you for dinner somewhere, if not, we'll part ways good, or bad, friends.

Emmanuel took a week to accept.

Then left her in the lurch.

The first time, terrible flu. The second, a car accident, nothing too serious, just dented bodywork. The third, an unexpected business trip abroad.

On the night of 31 December to 1 January, Emmanuel sent a Happy New Year message to Isabelle, who didn't reply. She'd thrown in the towel.

What if he threw it in himself? If he threw in Nina?

Wasn't now the time to go for it? To meet some Isabelles?

He gets into his car. He'll phone her when he gets to Chalon. "It's me, I'm here, I'm ready, sorry for the delay."

He drives to Beaune to pick up the freeway. He's halfway there when his phone rings. He doesn't immediately recognize the caller's voice.

"I've found Nina Beau—"

"Yes, I know, she's living in Annecy. I don't care. Just drop it. Send me your invoice and never mention that slut to me again."

"But no, not at all."

The call is cut off. Emmanuel chucks his mobile onto the passenger seat. *Instead of Nina*, he thinks. *Forget her*, *for god's sake*, *forget her*. The detective calls him back.

"She's not in Annecy. She didn't go away. She's living at the shelter in La Comelle."

Emmanuel suddenly feels dizzy.

"What shelter?"

"The Society for the Protection of Animals, if you prefer, she works there."

"Maybe it's someone who looks like her . . ."

"No, it's her. Nina Beau, social-security number 276087139312607. She was at Autun hospital yesterday."

Emmanuel hangs up without a word, spins the car around, and ends up on the hard shoulder. His heart is pounding like crazy. Beaulieu had taken him for a ride. Of course. How could he have believed such nonsense? Nina married . . . who'd have wanted to marry that bloated alcoholic? So, she's wiping mutts' asses, but of course, a slut will always be a slut. How had he believed that she'd had a child? She's sterile. The shelter . . . so that's where she's been hiding all this time, within arm's reach. Couldn't even be bothered to go more than three kilometers, as the crow flies. And that other one, telling him about Annecy, the stroller, and the dog. And him being stupid enough to listen to him. He should never have opened the door to him, let him in.

Two options are open to him.

He continues on to Chalon, parks in the town center, looks for the Hexagone, sits inside, orders a hot chocolate, calls Isabelle and keeps calling until she answers, asks her to join him. "Please, do come, I'm waiting for you at the back, a table for two, against the mirror, I'm wearing a navy pea coat, I'm not budging, I'll attach myself to my chair if necessary, so no one can turf me out at closing time, come, you've nothing to lose. We meet up, we both move on to somewhere else, wherever you like, wherever you fancy. Your work? Just call in sick."

He's expecting someone.

For how many years has that not happened to him?

She finally appears, smiles at him, is even more beautiful than in the photos. He likes her voice, her hands, her smell. She's wearing Guerlain's *L'Heure bleue* and a silver bracelet on her right wrist. Their complicity is instant, they feel good with each other. Don't have to search for things to talk about, the conversation just flows. Isabelle orders a hot chocolate. "Like you," she says. "Have you met any other women from that site? —No, you're the first.—Liar.—I swear. And you? Other men? —No, you're the first.—Liar.—I swear."

She's refined, and from the way she looks at him, he senses that she likes him. The weight that's been pressing on his chest for more than two years lifts, he sits up, feels desired, listened to. The more they talk, the more Emmanuel can see himself with this stranger. Spending the evening, and then the night, with her. And why not tomorrow, and the week after that?

He makes her talk, asks her questions. "So, you have two sisters?" He loves her voice, her answers, her teeth, her mouth. She's wearing a scarf around her neck that she fingers frequently, a long beige coat that she hasn't taken off, just unbuttoned, her nails are manicured but not varnished, there's nothing sophisticated about her, just a touch of gloss on her red lips, her big blue eyes look straight at him, intelligence. *The candidate is perfect*, he thinks. *If this were an election, she'd win*.

He tells her a little about Damamme, that he's going to sell up, relieve himself of family pressure.

"I want to start from scratch—a strange expression. And yet, personally, it suits me down to the ground. And do you go horse-riding often? —Whenever I can, in the evening after work and every weekend. We could say *tu* rather than *vous*, don't you think? —Sure . . . You're beautiful—You're not bad looking yourself."

He likes her boldness. Well, maybe. He doesn't know what he likes anymore. Have to see.

Two options are open to him.

He doesn't go to Chalon, never meets an Isabelle, doesn't look ahead, remains stuck in the present, now and forever.

He drives to La Comelle, stops off at his place, picks up one of his father's hunting rifles, goes to the shelter, finds her, kills her with two cartridges. Yes, two cartridges should be enough to erase her from the surface of the Earth. He doesn't even let her speak. Not a word. Bang.

In fact, yes, before taking her down, he makes her fall to her knees to plead with him. That's the least he deserves, to hear her say the word "sorry." Then he'll go to Lyon, find Beaulieu, he's got his home address and that of his police station. And bang, two more cartridges for the handsome guy who'd really taken him for a ride this morning. "Happy New Year," he'll say to him. *And good health, dickhead.*

Two choices are open to him. Past, present. Nina has dropped anchor in the present and is stopping him from heading out to sea. It's up to him to cast off. He's got five kilometers to decide whether to continue straight or turn around. Once he's past the tollbooth, he can continue to Chalon, or, after checking the police aren't around, he can drive five hundred meters on the wrong side of the road, take the A6, and return to La Comelle.

*

At first, Nina didn't believe Lili: "Your husband has killed himself on the freeway."

Then she thought of Étienne. What had he done after leaving the shelter? What had he provoked? It couldn't be a coincidence.

Three weeks after Emmanuel's funeral, Lili and Nina had gone up to the cemetery to visit Pierre Beau's grave. Then they had gone to Emmanuel's, some two hundred meters away, in the family vault. Gé and Henri-Georges hadn't added a photograph to the black marble. Just a plaque: "To our dearly beloved son."

Why was Emmanuel driving on the wrong side of the freeway? Suicide or accident? Was he disturbed by what Étienne had told him? Had they seen each other?

No doubt she would never know.

Beside his grave she had shivered. Then, gradually, frozen. She had sensed the presence of the man whose name she still bore. As if her husband were hovering around her, bellowing his rage at her being there, present, simply alive before him.

She would never come back.

Upon leaving the cemetery, Nina had switched her phone back on. Emmanuel's voice, as if from the beyond, from that former, distant life. Countless messages, going from threatening to screaming to sobbing to imploring. "Where are you? Come back, I won't harm you."

She had listened to them, one after the other, hoping, among all this insanity, to hear Adrien's voice. To hear: "Nina, it's me."

Nothing.

She'd deleted the lot.

Then she'd asked Lili to take her to the employment office. She must sign up to find work, a life, an apartment.

## 86

*31 December 2017*

An impromptu New Year's Eve party is being set up on the Spiaggia dell'Arenella. Around a hundred *Palermitani*, mostly from the houses along the sea, have lit a giant campfire. They've put up tables, all joined together and covered in paper tablecloths held down by bowls of fruit, on which everyone deposits food, crockery, bottles.

We join them, our arms loaded with goodies: olive oil, herb and tomato bread, various salads, breadsticks, almonds, Sicilian pastries, champagne, whiskey, and wine.

Two huge steel pans full of simmering water await the linguine, to be served with a tomato and garlic sauce and some parmesan.

Everyone has dressed up for the occasion, elegance prevails.

If separation wasn't hanging over us, and the specters of Valentin and Marie-Castille weren't haunting Étienne, we'd almost feel happy to be there, together, in this idyllic setting, lulled by joyous voices and the legendary Italian good cheer. Here, it's as if people were lit up from within. Like when Nina smiles.

Étienne is dressed in white, has shadows under his eyes, looks gaunt, he's getting thinner every day, the blue of his eyes seems clouded, probably due to the cocktail of medication keeping him in a kind of torpor. Despite his lethargy, the ghost of a smile plays on his lips.

Nina and I are convinced that tomorrow morning, he won't be in our room anymore, that he'll have packed his bag.

He doesn't know it, but we know that he's already thought of everything, paid for the room last night, and for our next one in Palermo. No doubt he'll leave us money for the ferry and for the gas to drive home. Like when we were children and he'd intentionally leave a few coins in our backpacks for buying candies at the pool.

And for once, he'll manage to leave a note for us, written all on his own. A piece of paper on which he'll write something like: "Thank you for accompanying me thus far. I'm off to die in peace."

"'*Mourir.*' Is that one 'r' or two?" he asked us earlier, while getting dressed, just before we left the *pensione*.

Nina looked at him and, without batting an eyelid, answered him:

"Just one 'r,' but two when you conjugate it in the future. Otherwise, '*vivre*' is much simpler, it's one 'r' whatever the tense."

Right now, Étienne is thinking only about a solution to the music, at the party coming up. Italian ballads hollered into a microphone by a brunette accompanied by a sinister-looking guitarist just won't cut it for our final New Year's Eve. We need to find a portable speaker, distance ourselves a little, and make his playlist sing.

"I've got one in my case," I say. "I'll wait for Nina to finish her drawing and go fetch it."

"I'll have no right to a funeral," Étienne says to us, "but you never know, so I want you to promise me that there'll be no crap music. I want rock. Only alternative rock. Promise?"

"Promise," we reply.

We're perched on a rock, in a circle. The air is blissfully mild. No wind, just the starry sky. And the aroma of tomatoes cooking, rosemary, and the wood fire. Nina, sitting cross-legged, holds her sketchbook in her left hand and draws us in charcoal with her right hand. She studies our faces, frowns as if seeing us for the first time, returns to her fingers, rapidly stroking the paper. She's wearing jeans and a white shirt borrowed from Étienne. A black sweater covers her shoulders. She's lost nothing of her youthful silhouette. Her dark eyes shine joyously. She's in love.

I was near her when she phoned Romain Grimaldi from our *pensione*, an hour ago. Nina told him she was calling to give him news of his car. She laughed like a little girl when Romain told her he was going to freeze the New Year's Eve dinner until she got back. "Even if we celebrate the new year on 15 March, I refuse to start it without you."

When Nina hung up, I almost asked her if their relationship wasn't moving a little fast, but immediately swallowed my words. What business was it of mine?

I, in turn, called Louise.

"Everything O.K.?"

"Yes."

"My brother's not suffering?"

"I don't think so."

". . ."

"Louise?"

"Yes."

"You fell in love with Adrien, not Virginie."

"Adrien and Virginie are the same person. She's the one I love," she told me, for the thousandth time. "But I refuse to live with an imprisoned woman . . . When you free her, perhaps we can adopt a child."

"But I have a cat, soon to be two cats!"

I heard her smile.

"The one doesn't prevent the other."

"Are you serious?"

"Yes."

"Do you trust me?"

"Yes. Will you call me at midnight?"

"Yes."

When I hung up, Nina pressed herself into my arms. I breathed in her hair, then her neck, soft and warm, my personal Proust's *madeleine*.

"That's good, that is, a child and two cats . . . Shall we go and party?" she whispered. "But I mean *really* party, get drunk, the works."

"You bet!"

She grabbed my hand and started singing, like a sad teenager, as we walked toward the beach. I'd almost forgotten how singular her voice is, a trifle hoarser after all these years. The voice of a smoker who's never smoked.

*And if one day you doubt me*

*I have a pledge of love, triple proof,*
*I love you so, I love you so,*
*With my blood, I scored my arm*
*To our dying day it will never fade,*
*I love you so, I love you so.*

Nina hands us our two sketches. She has drawn me, Virginie, for the first time.

"Thank you," I say.

"I look rough," says Étienne, pulling a face.

We all stand up together, mustn't let nostalgia and melancholy lurk or we'll ruin the evening, which is unthinkable. I rush off to our room to get the speaker.

"I called Marie-Castille," Nina admits to Étienne.

"You didn't . . ."

"I did. And you should phone her. You know, she's not on our tail at all."

In Étienne's eyes Nina sees all kinds of contradictory feelings—fear, joy, annoyance, relief, shame, renunciation, hope.

He rewards me with a big smile when I return, clutching my speaker. Before hitting his playlist, he says to Nina: "You see what a damned great fool I am."

## 87

*27 April 2003*

BADI. BREED X SPANIEL. ELDERLY. MALE. BORN 1991. AT SHELTER SINCE 1999.

"Badi's our last old dog . . . After me," Lili says, with a chuckle.

This morning, she's in black leggings, green sneakers, and a long yellow T-shirt. She's gathered her hair in a scrunchy, creating a palm-tree effect on the top of her head. Altogether, she looks like a pineapple.

Nina has just arrived. She drops by at the shelter every morning before going to her new job at an insurance company. She's renting a little house in the neighborhood she grew up in, with her grandfather, two roads from what was his garden.

It's been three months since Emmanuel Damamme died, and still, she jumps at the slightest noise, wakes up in a sweat after terrible nightmares in which she discovers that his coffin is empty.

"You'll need some time to process his absence."

"How much, do you think?"

Nina is helping Lili to hang up a sign saying: "For the dogs' well-being, please don't linger outside kennels. We count on your consideration."

"You know it's you who's taking over?"

"Taking over what?"

"From me. I'm tired. I've worked all my life."

"What are you talking about?"

"I'm going to retire."

"To do what?" Nina teases.

"Lie in," Lili replies, without smiling.

"Are you serious?"

"Oh yes. Now you're back on your feet, I can quit."

Nina looks at Lili, in a panic. Why the devil does everyone she loves end up disappearing?

"I'm not over it. I'm still scared of Emmanuel, I dream he's not dead . . . If you leave, I'm coming with you," she says.

"Hey, young lady, are you going to give me a break, or what? It goes without saying that you'll be the shelter's new manager. Working here, you won't have time for nightmares anymore."

". . ."

"Some things are obvious, and you're one of them."

". . ."

"Has the cat got your tongue?"

"Where will you go?" Nina asks, unconvinced.

"Cagnes-sur-Mer."

"That's far away."

"There's a lovely yellow church over there, on the Cros beach."

"Lili, you're an atheist," Nina says, with annoyance.

"Just because I'm an atheist doesn't mean I don't love churches. And anyway, you'll come and visit me."

"That's what people say, 'You'll come and visit me,' then—and I know what I'm talking about—they never come."

## 88

*1 January 2018*

Étienne goes into a church, he's alone. He lights a candle, doesn't know how to communicate with God, never did. It's like with his father, you don't know how to communicate with those you don't believe in.

How disappointed he was the day he'd phoned his parents to announce the great news. It was Marc who had answered, just as Étienne, deep down, without admitting it, was hoping he would.

"Dad, hold on tight, I passed my exam!"

"What exam?"

Stunned silence, Étienne felt like he was free-falling into the void. With difficulty, he managed to get out:

"To be a police lieutenant . . . Not many of us got through . . . Which means I'm among the best."

"Oh, that. Well done, we're proud of you, here's your mother."

Just a polite formula. "We're proud of you" doesn't mean "I am proud of you."

It's because his father never believed in him that he ended up not believing in his father anymore. He detached himself from him as a boat does from its moorings.

When he phoned to announce the birth of his son, Étienne hung up when he heard Marc's voice, and kept redialing until it was Marie-Laure who answered:

"Mom, he's called Valentin, he's beautiful, four kilos, blue eyes."

"It might be too soon to know the color of his eyes, darling."

"Oh no, Mom, I can assure you, my son has blue eyes."

This morning, he just wants to leave a light behind him, here, in Italy, once the heavy door has closed again. Like a trace of his passage.

His left ear is ringing. As a child, Nina used to say that when it's the left ear, on the heart side, it means someone's saying nice things about you. "That's bullshit, that is, Nina."

Who on earth could be talking about him at six in the morning? Marie-Castille and Valentin, back at home?

He phoned his son and his wife yesterday evening:

"Happy New Year, I love you both."

"When are you coming back?" Marie-Castille asked.

"I'm not coming back."

"Did Nina tell you about Clotilde Marais? It's over."

"Yes, I know."

He is three streets away from the sea. He can hear it breathing. Étienne has never felt so sure of himself.

A few stragglers are getting home, calling out: *Buon anno!*

He's just enjoyed, without doubt, one of the finest New Year's Eves of his life. As promised, the Three had withdrawn to a distant corner of the beach with their speaker, some champagne, whiskey, olives, and herb bread. They hadn't noticed when it was midnight—it would always be the same year from now on. They had danced to Étienne's playlist until the sky started to lighten, *his* music, Spacemen 3, Sonic Youth, Radiohead . . .

A taxi stops alongside him. He'd found just one Palermo to Paris flight.

At the airport, all the desks are closed. Just a single attendant registers his luggage and hands him a ticket. He embarks almost immediately and falls asleep against the window. It's the first time he hasn't dreamt of Clotilde. She has quit his sleep.

Once past reception, where he's asked for his ID, he settles into room 21. On the bed, he places the portrait Nina did of him the previous day, a photo of Valentin and Marie-Castille, one of Louise, Paul-Émile, and their mother, and one of the Three at the Indochine concert, in 1994.

"Fight, for god's sake." Since Clotilde's mother had said those words, they've been writhing inside him like some rabid animal.

He opens his toiletries bag, takes out some medication, swallows it, stretches out, and closes his eyes. No pain at all anymore. He's in the yard at the École Pasteur, waiting for the verdict, the name of their new class teacher. The moment is captured in *Blanc d'Espagne*: *That morning, I see only them, as if they've swallowed up all the light, as if the other pupils surrounding us were just extras, and it's me they choose, that she chooses, she takes my hand.*

The three of them give a concert on a sidewalk, it's the *Fête de la Musique*, they're fourteen years old, Nina sings, profound joy, inside, a mix of nerves and complete happiness, nirvana. Never has there been such a crowd, or such applause, in the streets of La Comelle. They ride their bikes, go skateboarding, they record themselves on a cassette player, they swim, film themselves with the camcorder he filched from his father, he makes love, he dances, there's sunshine, the summer memories are always the first, he looks at his sister on the quiet, he mixes tracks, tucks a strand of hair behind his ear while checking that the girls are watching him do so, he knows he's good looking, that he "drinks the light," as is written in *Blanc d'Espagne*.

Just before falling asleep, he places a flower on Clotilde's grave. He is alone and voiceless.

He sleeps.

He dreams that he's swimming with his son, they swim further from the edge, it's fun, and then, gradually, it becomes worrying. Étienne tells Valentin to swim back. "No, Dad, I'm staying with you."

Étienne is woken by a stranger in a white coat. Her hand is placed on his forearm, her voice is gentle, light but assured.

"Good day, Monsieur Beaulieu, I was told you were settled in, how are you feeling? The consultant has received your medical file, we're scheduling the operating room for 3 January. Tomorrow we'll do the final tests, and you'll meet the anesthesiologist. I'm giving you a few administrative forms to fill in. Your sister informed us of your wish not to be resuscitated should a problem arise during surgery; you'll need to sign a discharge form for us. Is there anything you need?"

"No."

"The evening meal is served at 6:30 P.M. Do you have any dietary requirements?"

"No."

"Any allergies to report?"

"No."

"Your sister told us that you wouldn't want any outside visitors. Apart from her, does anyone know that you're at the Gustave-Roussy Institute?"

"No. I wanted to get away from Lyon."

"One last thing, this form is for specifying the names of the people to be informed in an emergency. It's preferable to put down several."

"Nina and Virginie."

"Give me their full details. And if they have both landline and mobile phone numbers, that's best."

# 89

*2011*

Seven years after taking over the management of the shelter, Nina receives a phone call, her mother has just suffered a stroke and is in a Caen hospital, between life and death. If she wishes to see her, she must hurry.

"How did you get my number?"

"It was in her bag."

". . ."

Lili returns from Cagnes-sur-Mer to accompany her. "Don't feel strong enough to go there alone."

Where is this place, "between life and death"?

Nina finds a stranger lying in a bed in the intensive care unit. She no longer looks the same as on that evening Nina saw her in the garden, with Odile's sewing machine in her arms. Marion has put on weight. Nina wonders if it isn't a case of mistaken identity, goes to check with the nurses: "Are you sure this woman is Marion Beau?"

"I'll leave you alone with her," Lili tells her, before leaving the unit.

Nina panics. She's scared of staying on her own with the almost dead woman. To kill the silence, she starts talking, as if in a therapy group.

"It's me, Nina. I apologize when I'm invited somewhere. I hang my head. Not eating meat, it's like an alcoholic having to say no thanks to a glass of wine. Not even a little aperitif? Not even a slice of salami? One seems suspect, abnormal, a misfit. We live in a world where cattle are filmed like movie stars at agricultural shows, they are stroked, admired. And a few days later, they are slaughtered behind closed doors. Personally, that shocks me. It reminds me of my life with Emmanuel, when I was more married than happy. I was living in a world where I pretended. That world where people like to say: 'I'd rather not know.' I often hear: 'Looking after a shelter, that's a vocation.' To find what's rewarding and good about it, you have to look hard. It's about surviving. You do it for the way they look at you. It's about liking animals, but definitely not adoring them, or you'll die of sadness. There are many times, in a year, when I just want to give it all up. Abandon the abandoned. Find myself a cushy job somewhere else, where it's clean, warm, dry, and quiet. Where I'll stop hearing them barking like mad or having them sniff my ass when I take them for a walk. Where my clothes won't be forever accessorized with animal hairs. Where it would actually be worth wearing the perfume I was given last Christmas. Where others wouldn't see me as a naïve, crazy, desperate woman. 'Ah, you look after animals, what's the money like, for doing that? Or: 'But there are so many people who need looking after.' It's difficult, if not impossible, to explain that, basically, it's all the same thing. Whether for a man or an animal, the work is exactly the same. As the years go by, it's hens, rabbits, guinea pigs, or ferrets that I find, left in cardboard boxes. People change their domestic animals, but not their behavior. Not to mention the many anonymous calls to report animals going without food and water. Gun dogs and other creatures that die at the end of a chain, in a packed kennel or on a balcony. 'Hello, the neighbors have forgotten their horse in a garden for three months.' 'Hello, there are two circus tigers in a cage, under the sun, by the supermarket traffic circle' . . . Here, it's like a customer complaints service. We do what we can. We make ourselves laugh, organize drinks, coffee-and-croissant breaks, or we'd never last. The winters are tough, the summers depressing. When others are going on vacation, you're slaving away, picking up new dogs that weren't wanted at the back of the car, and cats that are just skin and bone. Space has to be made. The kennels overflow. We work things out and stretch the walls. Here, we keep everyone. We send no one to death row. And all the while, the dog shows continue to get richer with total impunity. It's those in government who make the laws. And the government is worlds away from the shit that sticks to our boots. Maybe the hardest thing is having to collect the companion pet of an old person who has either died, or been placed in a care home, when no child wants them in their own home. I almost quit several times, looked at the job ads in the paper to find office work, retrain, open a souvenir store, but no. Because one morning, you get up, you go there with a heavy heart, and then someone adopts an animal, it changes the whole day, you breathe easier, at least you've helped that particular life, which is no less important than any other life. Apart from that, I had a happy childhood with your father."

While saying all this, Nina hasn't sat down and hasn't touched Marion. She then leaves just as she arrived, with Lili. It's too late. She'd missed her mother, but it was too long ago.

# 90

*2 January 2018*

It's almost midnight. Nina has just dropped me off, outside my house, after a drive of two-thousand two-hundred and sixty-six kilometers, with a few brief stops at service stations for coffee or a sandwich.

It's Louise I find asleep on my sofa, not the cat-sitter. Under a throw, she's wearing jeans, my favorite ones, and a sweater of mine, an old thing that's ugly but soft. Nicola is curled up in her arms. In seven days, he's doubled in size. He doesn't look like himself anymore. I put my traveling bag down quietly so as not to wake them. Louise never falls asleep when she's with me, as if she had to escape as soon as day breaks. A curse hanging over us that only I can end.

I think back to that lunch with my genitor, at the Hôtel des Voyageurs restaurant, on 18 August 1994, the day after Pierre Beau's funeral.

He wanted us to celebrate my bac, and my having just got distinction, to talk about my future in Paris. For more than a week, I'd been preparing my questions: "Your work, your colleagues, life in Paris, the exhibitions, the concerts, do you go to the theater occasionally?" I myself would talk about music, about recent novels I'd enjoyed, about Nina and Étienne. The three of us in Paris, wanting to live together, the student hostel.

And then Pierre Beau was dead. A terrible blow.

He arrived chewing gum, and then stuck it in a paper napkin, much to my disgust. A bad start. He ordered two glasses of champagne. "We must celebrate your results."

He knew me so little that he didn't know I had just lost the man of my life. My only father figure.

We drank a second glass. By the third, I'd exhausted all my topics of conversation, silences were already creeping in, and I was drunk. It was the first time I was getting smashed with my father. The first time I was thinking of him as my father.

"What would you like to eat?"

"The same as you."

He ordered the starter and the dish of the day.

"We're going to drink to your future."

"My future, in general, is uncertain."

"Why do you say that?"

"Who I am . . . there's a kind of manufacturing fault," I said, bursting out laughing.

"I don't understand."

"Have you seen the movie *Dog Day Afternoon*, with Al Pacino?"

"That's old, that is," he said, mopping up his vinaigrette.

"1975."

"Yes, as I say, hardly recent. I must have seen it, can't remember . . . Aren't you hungry? You're not eating a thing."

"It's the story of a man who robs a bank to pay for a friend's operation. A very particular kind of operation . . . A change of—"

"It's sad, your story."

"Yes, desperately sad."

I stood up, going to the bathroom my excuse. I was struggling to breathe, I went up some stairs, arrived in a long corridor with a bloodred carpet, the door to one of the bedrooms was open, the bed unmade, the window ajar, I leant forward, thought of throwing myself down onto the sidewalk, headfirst. Nina was with Damamme, Étienne was lying in Nina's bed. The sheets must still smell of our bodies.

I saw the telephone, dialed the Beaulieus' number, the landline one that I knew by heart. It was Louise who answered.

"It's me. Are you O.K.?"

"Yes. D'you want to speak to my brother?"

"No, to you."

"Where are you?"

"At the Hôtel des Voyageurs, in a bedroom."

"I thought you were lunching with your father."

"I am lunching with him. He's downstairs, in the restaurant."

"Why are you in a bedroom? Your voice sounds odd. Have you been drinking?"

"Can we both come back to this hotel, together?"

"You're leaving to live in Paris."

"I will come back to La Comelle. For Christmas. People always return home for Christmas. Promise me the two of us will be in this room on 24 December, at midnight."

"I promise you."

I hung up. I think, if she'd said to me: "No, get lost, you and your hotel," I'd have thrown myself out of the window. Louise has always said yes to me, and it's been the luckiest thing in my life. Who can boast of just one friend who always says yes? I went back down, finished lunch with a somewhat lighter heart. I wasn't alone. On that day, I knew I'd never be alone.

Louise opens her eyes, smiles at me.

"I know where Étienne is, but I'm not allowed to say, I swore. Happy New Year, my love . . . Was Italy nice?"

"I've brought you back olive oil, pesto, a Pope Francis rosary, and some dried tomatoes. Étienne asked me if we slept together."

Louise busts into laughter, and then tears. I take her in my arms.

"It's been too long, Louise. Are you still happy to accompany me as I take this step into a girl's skin?"

"Yes."

I look at her and find her beautiful. If only, at this precise moment, I could write her beauty, her gaze, her depth, her solemnity, on a face that's kept something of the child. A sweetness.

"If I change my mind, if, once again, I chicken out at the last moment, will you still stay with me?"

"I think so. Perhaps. I don't know anymore. No. I've been waiting for you for too long."

"That's the first time you've said no to me."

"A few days ago, I read something. Imagine you've been unable to move for years because your fist is clenched inside a container, and to manage to pull your hand out, to free yourself, you just need to let go of what you're clutching in your clenched fist."

She uses her hand to demonstrate:

"You open up your hand, you lose what's inside it, it falls to the bottom of the container, but you are free."

## 91

*2018*

It's April and the weather should be fine. Sitting on the pebbles of the Cros beach, Nina gazes at the yellow church Lili had first told her about fifteen years ago. Since then, she has often gone inside to light candles. *Whoever you are, protect those I love*. In recent months, Romain has joined the list of those she prays for.

This morning, the sea is in retreat. Competing tones of blue and green, the horizon violet, wind drying the lips.

Nina arrived in Cagnes-sur-Mer yesterday with Romain, on a whim, to spend the Easter weekend with Lili.

Romain and Lili have gone off to the market. Nina loves this solitude. Listening to music with headphones, cutting herself off from the world on her imaginary island, while watching the Mediterranean, its languorous, dazzling waltz straining her eyes. She thinks of her grandfather who never saw it.

It starts to rain. She goes back to the house, up the three stories of the old building, with its red-tiled floor and cooking smells in the stairwell. On the balcony, where the two glass doors are half-open and vibrating in the wind, Lili has planted cherry-tomato plants in pots that match her clothes: reds, yellows, and greens.

Nina goes into the bathroom to wipe her face dry, looks at herself in the mirror. Today, Romain told her that she looked like a Sino-Afghan. He invents new origins for her every day. It's his favorite game upon waking: "This morning, you've got a Turco-Russian look about you . . . Arabic-Polynesian . . . Thai-Serbo-Croat . . . Italo-Brazilian . . . Italo-Moroccan . . ."

She runs her hand through her dark, bobbed hair, her almond-shaped eyes are the same color as her hair, a few brown marks have just appeared around her full lips.

Her phone rings, a number starting with 03, the Burgundy code. It's neither the shelter's number, nor Simone's.

"I couldn't wait until Tuesday to speak to you."

It's her doctor's voice, snapping like the wind outside. Mylène Vidal replaced Dr. Lecoq in 2006, when he retired. The first time Nina met her, she felt she could trust her, the consultation lasted more than an hour, Nina told her about her childhood and the day she saw her mother's medical file in Dr. Lecoq's hands, twenty years earlier.

Mylène Vidal searched on her computer and saw that Marion Beau's file had been sent to a health center in Villers-sur-Mer in 1999. She contacted her colleagues in Normandy: "Hello, I'm doing some genetic research for an organ donation, I'd like to contact Marion Beau, a former patient, born 3 July 1958 . . ." A minute later, Nina was holding her mother's address and a phone number.

Nina kept that address and those numbers, scribbled in black felt pen, for years, at the back of a drawer. Several times, she dialed the phone number but hung up before anyone answered.

Then she saw Marion again, "between life and death," in 2011. And discovered that her mother had her phone number, too. How had she got hold of it? Why had they never called each other? Why had they been so afraid of each other?

On the day of Marion's funeral, there were four of them: Nina, Lili, the mortician's assistant, and a small bald man, with bright eyes and a kindly appearance. Nina wasn't expecting to see a stranger at the Auberville cemetery that morning, it was like an intruder turning up at a party she'd organized.

"You knew Marion Beau?"

"Yes, she was a childhood friend."

"Are you my father?"

"No," he said, with a smile. "Marion was simply a friend."

"There are no simple friends."

The man found Nina's words unsettling. They said goodbye and went their separate ways.

A few weeks later, Nina received a letter at the shelter.

"Dear Nina,

I'm Laurent, your mother's friend. We spoke briefly at the cemetery, too briefly.

After thinking about it, I think you're right, there are no simple friends. She was, in a small way, the sister I never had.

I knew your grandparents well, particularly your grandmother. That's partly why I'm writing to you. Because one needs to know where one comes from. And I sensed that you were full of questions.

Your grandmother was a gentle and sensitive woman. I want you to know that Odile Beau is one of my loveliest memories. When she baked a cake, she always made enough to give some away to others. Bowls of soup were handed out to single and elderly people in the neighborhood. I never left her place empty-handed. 'Give this to your parents.' Always a slice of tart, a pot of jam, some apples from the orchard. Sometimes I sneaked out of the house so she wouldn't see me, I was fed up with lugging all those things she always gave me. If you knew how much I regret that.

Life is unfair, but you don't need me to tell you that, Nina. The devil targets angels more than bastards, it's well known, their hearts are so easy to devour. In 1973, Odile fell ill. She spoke of her cancer as if it were a bad case of flu: 'It'll pass.' She didn't want to make a fuss, as I told you, she was sensitive. Probably too much so. Her health deteriorated. Now, I'd leave her house empty-handed, without hiding.

Marion changed. Once so funny and light-hearted, bubbly and carefree, she became solemn and hurtful. She would insult me, insult heaven, God, and anything else she fell on. And mainly, she blamed her father. She was mad at him for minimizing his wife's illness.

'He doesn't want to take her to hospital, wants to keep his old lady to hand! Fuck's sake, Laurent, my mother's going to die!' I tried to explain to Marion that your grandfather wasn't solely responsible. I'd repeat to her: 'Let your dark thoughts fly over your head but never let them make their nest in your hair.' But Marion wasn't listening to me anymore.

When Odile died in hospital, your grandfather phoned my parents to say that it was over. Marion was at my house, she smashed everything in the house, she was uncontrollable.

She didn't attend the funeral. That shocked the whole town, but she didn't care about shocking, she was suffering too much to think about what others thought.

From that day on, she never set foot in school again, she started drinking, going out, running away, whatever she felt like doing. The more she destroyed herself, the more she felt as if she were destroying her father. I don't want to go into sordid details that would tarnish Marion's memory, she was far too young for such a tragedy. To lose a mother is to lose the world.

I continued to see her, we'd meet regularly in La Comelle, at a little café that no longer exists.

I've got to you, now.

You asked me if I was your father.

You're not called Nina by chance. If you'd been a boy, you'd be called Nawal.

One evening, Marion announced to me that she was in love, that her life was going to change, she was seventeen, as was the boy. I knew him by sight, we took the same bus to school. He was called Idras Zenati, and was Kabyle, a shy boy, handsome. Marion calmed down after she met Idras. They only ever parted to go home to their parents in the evening. Marion caught the bus with us but didn't attend classes, she waited for him in a café, all day long.

She fell pregnant. The two lovers had planned this pregnancy. Their plan was to leave their respective families and set up home together. Since they were underage, they had already started looking into how they could gain their freedom.

But it was all scuppered.

As soon as Idras started talking about the young girl he was in love with, a French girl, pregnant by him and whom he wanted to marry, his father shut him up. The following day, he took his entire family to Algeria. They left like thieves in the night, abandoning everything to escape the 'shame.'

Idras managed to alert Marion by phone. 'They're kidnapping me, I'll come back when I've come of age. Wait for me, I will come back.'

Marion was six months pregnant. On top of the emptiness and the absence, there was the loneliness. She only had me. The others had shunned her.

The two of us celebrated her eighteenth birthday a month before your birth, and already Marion had come up with a devilish plan to 'destroy' your grandfather, as she put it.

She gave birth and almost immediately left you in his care, before coming to stay with me near Paris. Because it's at mine that your mother took refuge after your birth. The two of us shared a single maid's room. I continued with my studies, and she worked at a local bakery. She didn't want to hear another word about school, apprenticeships, the future, Idras.

'Actually, it suits me that he left,' she kept saying to me, 'what would I have done with a husband at my age?' She was lying. She still hoped that, when he came of age, Idras would come back to France and they'd both go and fetch you.

But he never came back.

And there's worse, Nina. Marion was so angry with Pierre for having allowed Odile to die that she made up a terrible story. She persuaded him that you were the result of rape. 'If you'd seen his face when I told him that,' she admitted to me, with a sad smile, 'Mom is avenged.'

I begged her to tell your grandfather the truth, that you were a child born of love, that if she didn't, I'd tell him. She said to me: 'Everyone has betrayed me, not you now, Laurent, not you.'

One evening, I got back from university and Marion was gone. She'd left me a note: 'Thanks for everything! Big kiss.'

She had quit waiting for you, Idras and you.

I imagine that Idras's father had convinced him that Marion was a bad girl, that he couldn't be the father of the child. If he'd been able to see you, even for one moment, he would have known that wasn't true.

Marion phoned me, years after her departure. She was living in Brittany, was doing the markets with a guy she'd met over there. 'Honestly, Lolo, I'm good, I've got my life now.'

What did 'I've got my life now' mean?

In the summer of 1980, I went to see your grandfather. You were playing in the garden. Seeing you really moved me. You were so pretty, like a fawn. Yes, that's my memory of you, a slight, gentle little creature. You said to me: 'Hello, sir.' And I dissolved into tears.

That day, I told the truth to Pierre, that you were the child of Idras Zenati, that there wasn't a single doubt about it. He pretended to believe me. He said to me: 'Nina is *mon petit*, no matter where she's from, she's *mon petit*.'

There you are, Nina, you know a little more now.

I've enclosed my phone number and a school photo I found. Your father is the second boy from the left in the front row, the one in a blue-striped sweater. In this photo, he's sixteen.

Yours, with much love,

Laurent"

Nina gazed at that handsome teenager, with his clear, gentle eyes, for a long time. She felt like shouting from every rooftop: "That's my father! I have a father! See how handsome he is!"

And the photo went into the same drawer as Marion's address in Normandy, scribbled by Dr. Vidal on a scrap of paper a few years back.

Her father would always be sixteen years old.

Idras and Marion had loved each other, that was the most important thing.

Her grandfather had raised her, that was the most important thing.

She was born out of young love.

She had waited for this letter her entire life. She'd finally received it.

Nina is still in the bathroom, phone pressed to ear. She hears

Romain's and Lili's laughter in the stairs, like two adolescents in a school corridor. Romain is light as a butterfly and merry as the pupils he looks after.

"Nina, the lab has just sent me your test results."

An abrupt return to earth. Mylène Vidal's tone is almost solemn. Nina immediately thinks of Étienne's and Odile's illnesses. That fatigue she's been dragging around for weeks, that shooting pain in her back . . . Nina is shaking, she sits on the edge of the bathtub. Thinks of the three of them, and of Romain. *And yet we were so good together.*

"Where are you?"

"By the sea," Nina whispers.

"You're not in La Comelle?"

Mylène Vidal seems put out.

"No," Nina replies. "Away for the weekend."

"Alone?"

"*En famille*, with my friend."

*How stupid the word "friend" is*, Nina suddenly thinks, *but less stupid than "companion," I keep that for my dogs. And I'm hardly going to say "guy" or "lover" to my doctor.*

It's April and the weather should be fine.

She locks the bathroom door. Listens to the gleeful cries coming from the kitchen, from Lili and Romain *who don't yet know*, she thinks to herself.

Nina feels like hanging up. *How about waiting until next week for the bad news . . .*

"Have I got something serious?" she finally whispers.

"Not at all, Nina, everything's perfect."

"So what, then?"

"You're pregnant."

# 92

*4 December 2018*

This morning, Nina saw me for the first time. She looked at me for a long while as I deposited the thirty kilos of dry pet food under the signs saying ABANDONING KILLS and PLEASE CLOSE DOOR SECURELY BEHIND YOU.

Her eyes didn't slide away like the raindrops on my raincoat.

She came toward me, smiling, it was raining cats and dogs. She was wearing her rubber boots that were too big and holding a long hose, which she finally let go of, leaving it behind her.

## Acknowledgments

Thank you to my readers. For your fervor that dazzles every day of my life and helps me to carry on. You are my brighter future.

Thank you to my three essentials: Valentin, Tess, Claude.

Thank you to my three guardian angels: Mickaël, David, and Gilles.

Thank you to the whole team at the ADPA Refuge Annie-Claude Miniau: www.refuge-adpa-gueugnon.org.

Thank you to Maud, its director, who helped me to bring Nina out of her shell.

Thank you to Annie, its president, who phoned me so I'd become its sponsor.

As I write these lines, Badi, our "last old dog," is off to a host family, and Boulet rejoined Pascale in heaven last summer.

Thank you to www.fondationbrigittebardot.fr for their unfailing help.

Thank you to all animal shelters, of whatever kind and wherever they are. Every living being should have shelter. Thank you to VOLUNTEERS around the world.

Thank you to my matchless Albin Michel family: without you, I wouldn't be here.

Thank you to my remarkable team at Livre de Poche.

Thank you to the enchanters of Indochine, my heroes of all time. Your talents, victories, celebrations, what a story. Nicola, Olivier: thank you for looking in my direction. A cause of great joy and pride.

Thank you to Philippe Besson for *Arrête avec tes mensonges*. The need for *Three* is thanks to, or because of, you.

Thank you to Vincent, Noa, and Boaz for sharing a little of their adolescence with me.

Thank you to Steph for giving me a great deal.

Thank you to Cécile and Dominique, who have lived a thousand lives, including that of a mailman.

Thank you to my personal reading committee, my friends, my family, my good fortune: Maëlle, maman, papa, Tess, Claude, Angèle, Julien C. (who whispered the final lines to me), Juju, Salomé, Sarah, Shaya, Simon, Caroline, Grégory, Amélie, Charlotte, Émilie, Audrey D., Audrey P., Béatrice, Florence, Elsa, Cath, Laurence, Arlette, Emma, Manon, Paquita, Carol, Paty, William, Michel, and Françoise.

Thank you to Christian Bobin, Baptiste Beaulieu, Virginie Grimaldi, François-Henri Désérable: I borrowed your names, and that isn't at all by chance.

Thank you to those who inspired me and are quoted or referred to in this novel: Indochine, Calogero, Zazie, Joe Dassin, Étienne Daho, Francis Cabrel, Michel Berger, Alain Souchon, William Sheller, Alain Bashung, Kurt Cobain, Nirvana, Bono, U2, Depeche Mode, Pierre Perret, Philippe Chatel, a-ha, Mother Teresa, Soeur Emmanuelle, Princess Diana, Jean-Jacques Goldman, Peter Falk, Richard Kalinoski, Irina Brook, Simon Abkarian, Corinne Jaber, Dario Fo, Victor Hugo, Faïza Guène, Nancy Huston, Patrick Süskind, Isabelle Adjani, Camille Claudel, Danièle Thompson, Claude Lelouch, Henri-Georges Couzot, Jean-Pierre Jeunet, Jean-Loup Hubert, Luc Besson, Patrick Poivre d'Arvor, Jacques Pradel, Patrick Sabatier, Christophe Dechavanne, Jean-Luc Delarue, Bernard Rapp, Marcel Pagnol, KOD, les Inconnus, Lio, Jacno, Larusso, Françoise Hardy, The Cure, Madonna, Mylène Farmer, Enzo, The Cranberries, INXS, The Clash, Oasis, The Pixies, Sonic Youth, Spacemen 3, Bérurier Noir, Matthieu Chedid, Billy Ze Kick et les Gamins en Folie, Madame Bléton, Roger Federer, Marie Trintignant, Nelson Mandela, Cabu, Wolinski, Stromae, Prince, Michael Jackson, David Bowie, Jim Courier, Youri Djorkaeff, Cock Robin, The Christians, 2 Unlimited, Bruce Springsteen, Négresses Vertes, Mano Negra, Jim Morrison, Johnny Hallyday.

Thank you to Vincent Delerm, who brought me such luck that I will thank him forever.

Thank you to Éric Lopez, Sylvaine Colin, Alain Serra, Isabelle Brulier, Patrick Zirmi, Marie-France Chatrier, Stéphane Baudin, Émilie and Benjamin Patou, Vincent Vidal, Yves-Marie Le Camus, Didier Lopes, Michel Bussi, and Agnès Ledig.

Thank you to Laure Manel: it's while you were dedicating *La Délicatesse du homard* to me that Virginie literally fell on me.

Thank you to all my animals, past, present, and to come, you make me bigger.

## About the Author

Valérie Perrin is a photographer, screenwriter, and novelist. Her debut novel won the 2016 Lire Élire and Poulet-Malassis Prizes, among others. *Fresh Water for Flowers*, her first novel to be translated into English and a million-copy international best-seller, was an Indies Introduce title and a National Indie Bestseller.